Praise for

The Story of Forgetting

An Independent (UK), *St. Louis Post-Dispatch,* and
Austin Chronicle best book of the year

Finalist for the John Sargent Sr. Novel Prize

A School Library Journal Best Adult Book for
High School Students

A Best First Novel at the Rome International
Festival of Literature

"[An] emotional roller coaster of a novel . . . *The Story of Forgetting* is as true to the anguish of [its] questions as it is ablaze with love and vitality. . . . A fresh, beguiling novel."
—*The New York Times*

"What *The Curious Incident of the Dog in the Night-Time* did for autism, Block's multi-layered debut—about the importance, and pain, of memory—achieves for early-onset Alzheimer's disease."
—*People*

"Magical and scientific . . . compelling . . . [Block] is a talent to celebrate and remember."
—*USA Today*

"Touching, inventive and intelligent . . . Block writes with the certainty and originality of a Nabokov or a Faulkner. . . . [*The Story of Forgetting*] is one of those rare works of near-genius."
—*The Independent* (UK)

The Story of Forgetting

The Story of Forgetting

A NOVEL

Stefan Merrill Block

RANDOM HOUSE TRADE PAPERBACKS

NEW YORK

2009 Random House Trade Paperback Edition

Published in the United States by Random House Trade Paperbacks, an imprint of The Random House Publishing Group, a division of Random House, Inc., New York.

RANDOM HOUSE TRADE PAPERBACKS and colophon are trademarks of Random House, Inc.
READER'S CIRCLE and colophon are a trademark of Random House, Inc.

Originally published in hardcover in the United States by Random House, an imprint of The Random House Publishing Group, a division of Random House, Inc., in 2008.

LIBRARY OF CONGRESS CATALOGING-IN-PUBLICATION DATA
Block, Stefan Merrill.
The story of forgetting: a novel/Stefan Merrill Block.
p. cm.
  ISBN 978-0-8129-7982-4
  1. Older men—Fiction. 2. Teenagers—Fiction.
  3. Texas—Fiction. [1. Alzheimer's disease—Fiction.] I. Title.
  PS3602.L643S76 2007
  813'.6—dc22   2007012062

Printed in the United States of America

www.randomhousereaderscircle.com

9 8 7 6 5 4 3 2 1

With love for my parents

How I remember myself

The Story of Forgetting

Alongside this world there's another.

There are places where you can cross.

Abel

I never found a way to fill all the silence. In the months that followed the great tragedy of my life, I sprang from my bed every morning, donned my five-pound, cork-soled boots and did a high-step from room to room, colliding with whatever I could. The silence meant absence and absence meant remembering, and so I made a racket. The rotting floorboards crying out when roused, the upholstered chairs thudding when upended, the plaster walls cracking when pummeled: small comforts when everywhere, always, the silence waited.

Over time, I learned to divide it into pieces. If, after breakfast, I found myself straining to hear my daughter's voice in the yard, or my brother's hobbled gait scraping down the hall, or Mae fiddling with the radio, I blamed it on the silence that had just collected before me, in my freshly emptied bowl of porridge, and then I chased it away, rattling the bowl's innards with my spoon. Sometimes, from the room that once belonged to my brother and Mae, a particular kind of silence, more profound than the rest, began to seep out under the door, and I had to charge in, fists and feet swinging, to beat it into submission.

I may never have made peace with it, but over the years I began to recognize the possibilities that the silence afforded me. It was absolute. That was its horror but also its blessing. Into itself, the silence promised to absorb whatever I gave it: my delusions, my regrets, even the truth.

But still. Even if the words go straight from my mouth to oblivion, the fundamental truth of my life is so simple, the saying of it makes me feel so foolish I can hardly bear to say it at all:

I was in love with my brother's wife.

But that is far from the story in its entirety. More accurately, I will say:

I once believed I cared more about my brother than any person still living, but I was wrong. I cared even more about the woman he married, the woman that my brother, at times, seemed hardly to care about at all.

Look at me. Still jealous, after all these years. Why should I have to compare who cared the most? Life isn't a competition, is it, with the one who cares the most getting the most? The lethargic and the cynical can live in mansions. And here I've remained, left to silence in this place with walls that barely stand.

Did my brother love Mae? Perhaps, in his way, he loved her; I can't say. She was his wife, and for him that was a simple enough answer. But did I love her? Yes. I loved things of hers that you would think unlovable. For example. I fell in love not only with her feet but also with her toes, misshapen from birth into two rows of adorable zigzags.

And not just that. I also fell in love with the sounds her feet made when they walked. Separately, I fell in love with the sound of her walking on dirt, and on wood, and in mud. These days, there is a young mailman who must have the same leg span as Mae. I know when my monthly issue of *National Geographic* or the latest offering of the Book-of-the-Month Club is about to drop through the slot because I suddenly find myself deeply, completely in love.

The time came when I knew I had to make a decision, or else I might do something severe. I devoted myself to watching Mae do the things that I thought would be the most repugnant to me. I asked myself, What makes a person most fall out of love? I decided the answer was obviously to see the person you love making love to someone else.

My brother's room, which was once Mama's room, was on the second floor. Outside is still the massive willow tree with long, leafy fingers that creep in and tickle your face if you sleep with the window open. And so, because that night I had fallen in love with something hypothetically impossible, the sound Mae's stomach made when it moaned from too much food, I decided I had to climb that tree and watch the one thing that could make me instantly fall out of love.

Up in that willow, behind the leaves, I sat like a dirty old man, like the man I have perhaps become, waiting for something terrible. But instead, my brother and Mae did not even look at each other. They only crawled into their bed, each as far to either side as possible, and fell asleep. The next night, after I had fallen in love with the way Mae shucks corn, I climbed the tree again. Again, nothing came but sleep. For the next five days I fell in love with so much that I prayed they would finally make love, or else I didn't know what. When Mae would pour my brother's coffee after breakfast, her pouring a thing I had fallen in love with long before, I might suddenly stand from my chair and scream, "I'm in love with the way you pour!"

I had sworn to Mama long ago that I would never lose my mind when it came to love. But losing my mind was precisely what I was doing.

Five days passed, and still my brother and Mae had yet to use the bed for anything but its dullest purpose. On the sixth, I did something I knew to be unforgivable. But I thought that I could accomplish the act stealthily, that the shame of the thing would be mine alone. Or maybe I wasn't really thinking at all. As I watched Mae sleep, her face to the window, me falling in love with the way the arch of her nose pressed into her pillow, I began to rub myself in that tree.

The next day, I walked the three miles into town, through some excuse, and when I came back I brought a dirty magazine, filled with detailed images of men and women wrapped up in each other, for my brother to look at. For inspiration. I claimed it was for me, which seemed natural since it had been so long since anyone had seen me with a woman. I left it in obvious places where I knew he would see it. For a time the fish didn't bite; I knew that I would soon have no choice but to take drastic action. Just before dinner one night, after fifteen nights straight on which they had not made love, I saw that the magazine had disappeared from the little shelf near the door of the barn, which made me hopeful. But then, minutes later, I saw my brother sneak it back when he thought no one was watching. He had taken it with him to the outhouse, and so I knew my plan had backfired.

What else of Mae's could I possibly find repulsive? But I had already tried everything. Once, when she had gone to the outhouse, I had peeked through a knot in the wood, watching her do her business, hoping that the most base things her body could produce would repel me. Instead, I only fell in love with the sounds she made and the way her tiny, elegant hands wiped. I was hopeless. I imagined awful things. I imagined ways to kill my brother that would look like accidents but would not be. I imagined kidnapping Mae in the middle of the night and then explaining why I had to do what I did. I imagined simply asking her if she had also fallen in love with anything of mine, and if so, maybe we could escape together.

But, then I would remember, it was hopeless. Who did I think I was? I wasn't about to become the kind of person who can commit fratricide. And I certainly was no kidnapper. Then I thought, What do I really know Mae thinks of me?

Sitting one afternoon in the expansive stretch of our wheat field, where it seemed possible to convince yourself that all human problems were imaginary, that the whole of the earth was nothing more than a shaggy, endless khaki, I nevertheless found myself attempting to conjure potential evidence of Mae's true feelings.

Years before, Paul had traveled to Dallas for great spans, sometimes entire weeks. Eventually, these trips came to an end when he returned, one evening, with Mae. That first night she sat next to me at supper. Trying to flatter Paul, every time she took a mouthful she would say "Mmmm," her breath rushing from her nose and breezing the hairs of my arm. Three times, our knees touched. Once, for minutes.

I chided myself: What does that even mean? Sure. Perhaps, sometimes, as she rests a plate of food at the table, she leans heavily against my back, lingering. Perhaps, sometimes, she smiles at me in the conspiratorial way of a shared secret. Perhaps, sometimes, when we're reading in the evening, she lies on the couch just so, kneading her toes into my thigh. But, no. To her I am just the pathetic, lonely brother. I am the lonesome, clinging third in what would otherwise be a normal marriage of two. I am the one person too many. And if I simply didn't exist, everything would be easier. I am the person she perhaps has seen rubbing himself while watching her sleep. And, of course, my body still remains as it always has been. Still, I am the deformed hunchback, the way my right shoulder and my spine lock bones. Still, I am only cause for disgust.

Maybe I was exaggerating. Exaggerating in the way that a single, frustrated need can compress a life's complexities and convolutions into a wildly simplified story, written in self-pity, of one's own insufficiencies in a world populated by the sufficient. But I couldn't help myself. I couldn't help but trace the history of my sad lot back to its origin. I began to think of when Paul and I were still boys. We were twins. For a time there was no distinction between that which was the both of us and that which was uniquely me: the purest form of love either of us would perhaps ever know, a form to which my brother would one day return.

Sometime near our fifth birthday, my brother and I stepped together into a bath Mama had drawn. Suddenly, the earth rumbled, a great fissure cracked open, and my brother was separated from me for the rest of time. I had gazed at his body. And as I had done so, I had also begun to scrutinize my own. I had, for the first time, begun to take note of that which marked us as different. Most notably, of course, my hump. At some point, as my brother's scapulae had parted with admirable, unfailing symmetry, mine had grown askew, a bony snarl, snaring my right arm like the dead limb of a trapped wolf, to be chewed away for the sake of freedom. My hump. A part of me was in unfortunate excess, perched there upon my shoulder, an excess that telegraphed my future paucity, the women and jobs and love and family that would be forever withheld from me. It wasn't that I ever resented Paul. In ways, it was just the opposite. As the girls of High Plains flocked to Paul at the end of each school day, as Paul's talents for baseball and sprinting grew into legend, as Paul's sturdy, superior frame accomplished work on the farm with startling efficiency (tilling vast fields in a matter of days, bucking chicken feed by the ton, bearing fifteen gallons of milk, from the barn to the house, all at once), Paul was proof of what I would have been, if not for my shoulder blade's poor sense of direction. A notion both heartening and tragic: all that stood between the seemingly boundless possibilities available to my brother and my own lonely lot was a two-pound obstruction of sinew and bone. A part of me was in excess; I tried to accept it, but secretly never stopped believing it a harbinger of a hidden talent to be revealed to me in the future, of a secret capability to possess at last something Paul could not, something that would be mine alone. Is the truth as dark and covetous as that? Is that why the only love of my life had to be my brother's wife? Is it possible that my love for Mae was, in part, something other than love? Perhaps. But at the time, it was enough to say, I was in love.

I decided I had only two choices. The first was that I would kill myself, but I quickly understood that I couldn't do it. As it turned out, I still wanted to live. I couldn't even come up with a reasonable plan for suicide. The second, which was really the only choice I had, was to leave. To leave for any place but there.

It was the night before I would go. I had packed the things I would take and had explained to my brother and the woman I couldn't bear to love as much as I did that I had to make my own life and stop being an intruder on theirs. This was as good a reason as any because it was also the truth. That night, with my last bit of hope, I climbed the willow one more time and watched my brother and Mae go about their sad, silent routine. Climbing into bed, turning their backs to each other, then falling asleep. As I unbuckled my pants and watched Mae's face, I tried to imagine riding away in trains and buses and cars, being in big cities that looked nothing like where I was then. But instead what I imagined was that the thing that was in my hand was instead inside of Mae.

Eventually, I sighed and let go of myself. The thing slouched away like a miserable, malnourished creature all its own. I closed my eyes. I opened my eyes. I looked into the window. And then. Everything changed.

Mae stood from her bed, my brother still sleeping behind her. She came to the window, and at first I prayed that if I remained incredibly still she would not see me behind all those leaves. But she stared right at me. Would I have done something different if I hadn't been leaving the next day? Perhaps. But I did what I did. I stared back.

Then, through the window, I watched her turn and leave, falling in love with the way she walked on her tiptoes. She crept out to the tree. I scrambled to buckle my pants back together. Then she was climbing, and I was falling in love with the way she climbed. I did not move. I was as still as the branches. And then. She was in front of me. There were so many words to say to her then, about all the things of hers that I loved. I couldn't say anything. But Mae could.

"Abel," Mae said. "Don't leave."

And then. She touched me, and I thought, Maybe I am not the one person too many after all.

SOMETIMES, THE PARALLELS are enough to strike me as the darkest, most poignant joke of my sixty-eight years. Sometimes, it is almost as if the mythos of Original Sin was purposefully recast on our little farm for the modern audience: the willow tree starring as the Tree of Knowledge; the bonds of matrimony as God's command; my own hunchbacked, pilose body poorly cast as the fruit dangling from the branch; that pitiable, flaccid thing slouching in my hand making a cameo as the serpent; Mae's touch playing the part of forbidden desire; the great tragedy of my life aptly filling in the role of all human suffering that would follow.

On little more than rumors and lies, Francisco Vázquez de Coronado traveled up from Mexico in search of Quivira, one of the seven legendary cities of gold. For years, he and his army pushed to the north. Many of his men were killed. Disease, bitter cold, and marauding tribes all conspired against him, but Coronado persisted.

And when, at last, Coronado found Quivira, his disappointment was too profound for words. The towns of Quivira were little more than thatched huts and fire pits. And so, Coronado simply turned about, leading his army back to the south.

What Coronado couldn't have known was that he had been within feet of a hidden underground passageway to the only city of gold there ever truly was, the true genesis of every imagined golden city and every fountain of youth: the kingdom of Isidora.

The Quivira tribe had not told Coronado because they knew that, even if they had led him into Isidora, the gold he had sought would be useless. The truth, known only to the Quivira elders, was that gold was the least of Isidora's treasures.

The real treasure of Isidora was the nature of the land itself. Once a man arrives in Isidora, he will not remember the value of gold. He will not remember the value of anything, for that matter. From the empty streets of its ancient, golden capital spreads the land of Isidora, a land without memory, where every need is met and every sadness is forgotten.

Seth

ABSTRACT

By the spring of 1998, it had become undeniable.

My mom came from her room on a Tuesday morning to find me eating a double serving of maple and brown sugar oatmeal. She wandered slowly down the stairs, widening her mouth, as if she was just discovering each step for the first time. When she moved into the kitchen, she paused. She spun about, on her face an expression that maybe resembled *marveling*, but the more accurate description was *bewildered*. Finally, she spotted me and dragged her feet across the kitchen floor in the shuffle that had only recently become how she stepped, the gait of a woman thirty or forty years older, proof of the hypothesis that, however the mind behaves, so follows the body. She sat in the chair opposite mine and narrowed her eyes, furrowed her brow in the unfocused, focused gaze of a person trying to find the 3-D image in a computer-generated field of dots. After a long moment, she attempted a word.

"Seth?"

Because I was always one to make comments my dad labeled "Too-Smart"—the kinds of comments that, to the relief of everyone, myself not the least, I finally came to suppress—I chimed back, "Mom?"

But she didn't catch the sarcasm. She only lunged forward and held me tightly against her chest, pinning my arms to my sides for so long I finally said, "C'mon. My oatmeal's getting cold."

"Sorry, sorry."

My mom pulled away, gaping down the powder blue of her nightie as if she had just realized that the body beneath her was her own. As I spooned the mush between my lips, she raised her face dumbly, her mind so distracted by the shock of discovering herself in her kitchen on an ordinary weekday morning that it couldn't be bothered to attend to a thin streak of dribble drawn from the corner of her mouth.

"What's up?" I tried to speak normally.

My mom didn't reply. She nibbled the flesh of her lower lip. Her clenched eyebrows creased a deep question mark into her forehead. Finally, she rested her chin on her folded hands and asked, "How long have we known each other?"

Suddenly, I couldn't swallow. I bowed my face into the black bowl and regurgitated.

"What?"

"I feel like I've known you my whole life," she explained.

"Me too," I mumbled and then added what I hoped she would denounce as Too-Smart. "It almost feels like I'm your son."

"I know it!"

I didn't tell my dad. If I had told him, maybe we could have prevented what would happen only weeks later, maybe everything could have been different.

But my dad used to find a million reasons to accuse my mom of what he perceived to be her extraordinary selfishness. Once, when I was nine or maybe ten, my dad tried to maneuver past the stove where my mom was cooking to reach his gin from the freezer, but my mom didn't see him and opened a cabinet door with the kind of timing you would expect in a cartoon. My dad's face crashed right into it. You could make out the design of the woodwork on his forehead, as a rising pattern of blue and red. I laughed because I couldn't help it, but my dad raged at my mom, "Christ! Jamie! When will you learn to watch out for other people!"

Every wrong my mom had ever committed my dad would collect to use against her when the opportunity presented itself.

"Yesterday!" he yelled. "You forgot to mail the letters I left! This morning you forgot to reset the alarm! And now you throw a goddamn door in my face! What a fantastic day you've given me. Really."

Because, under the rules of my dad, forgetful and selfish were synonymous, I didn't say a thing.

TWO WEEKS LATER, at one in the morning, I took a break from studying for my Spanish exam to get a snack. I opened the fridge and dug around for some cold cuts. There weren't any, which was strange because when I had gone to the store with my dad three days before, we had bought armloads of ham and turkey and pastrami, as lunch meat had weirdly become just about the only food my mom showed any interest in at all.

In those weeks, my mom rarely even stood to walk about the house, she was almost never so active as to change out of her billowing flannel nightgown, and she hardly ate a thing. She had lost a frightening number of pounds. Her neck had shriveled, its skin drooping at a level competitive with that of the guests on any one of the countless daytime talk shows dedicated to the subject of eating disorders. She grew weaker and thinner by the day; climbing the stairs became a challenge on par with scaling a cliff. It was as if we were forced to watch my mom lost in some desert, weakening and wilting by the minute, stumbling hopelessly forward with a singular dream of water, but we didn't have a drop to give. And, still, my dad and I basically never talked about it. Once, my dad made reference to "your mother's depression," but then neither of us said anything about it again.

Almost every night, my dad used to come home from work to the same routine. He grabbed a bottle of gin from the freezer, mixed a long, generous pour with some tonic from the fridge, and balanced the glass on an arm of the La-Z-Boy in front of the TV as he watched The History Channel into the wee hours. That night, however, I guess his precious gin and tonics had already caught up with him, and he had gone to bed. The house was silent except for a vague rustling of wind. At first I thought it was just the air conditioner struggling against the heat. I turned on the kitchen lights, the fluorescent tubes flickering manically, then casting their crude, green brightness into the living room. That's when I saw that the back door, the one that leads out to the garage, wasn't completely shut. I went to it and pulled it open the rest of the way. In the garage, where it is typically foul and sweet and stuffy with garbage and mildew and sawdust, a fresh, warm breeze stirred the air. The garage door gaped open, the dingy glow of the neighborhood's streetlamps shining across the roof of my dad's BMW.

I bolted back upstairs, into the guest room where my mom had recently come to spend every night and also the majority of every day. At first, when my dad had banished her from the master bedroom, he had blamed her snoring, though it didn't take too advanced a deductive mind to understand that the real reasons were far more complicated. But the truth was that my mom was better suited for her own room anyhow: there she could carry out the vagueness of her days, endlessly caught between sleep and wakefulness, without bothering my dad or so often drawing his complaints ("I'm sorry, but I've got a meeting at seven in the morning and I just can't afford to share a bed with an insomniac tonight!").

I went from room to room, flipping on the switches, praying (even though I claimed 99 percent atheism) that I'd find her hiding in some corner. When I didn't, I went back out to the garage and into the night, not even pausing to wake my dad.

The heat of the day before, still trapped in the concrete streets, warmed my bare feet as I sprinted up and down the grid of our neighborhood, peering into the alleys between houses, getting a silent-film view of backyards through the spaces between the boards of fences as I ran. Eventually, as odd as it felt, I started calling out for her, shouting her name like you would for a runaway dog.

But my voice only echoed across the wide, blank pavement, with only the tungsten streetlamps bearing witness, hanging their heads, apathetically dim. I almost turned back to get my dad and the car, but for fear of losing even a second, I just kept running, beyond the staring, skeletal eye sockets of a thousand darkened windows, past the endlessly churning motorized waterfall at the entrance of our neighborhood, beyond the gilded wooden sign that said, in the kind of Olde English font that is typically reserved for Renaissance fairs and medieval-themed restaurants, BENT TREE ESTATES, EST. 1991.

A quarter mile down Parkside Drive, I found her. If the street hadn't been empty, if it hadn't been past midnight in a suburb that routinely falls asleep to the opening monologues of late-night talk shows, things could have been much worse. But there she was: a dark figure beneath a streetlamp, her open robe casting swirling shadows, forty or fifty feet long. In her hand was her old suitcase, the shade and texture of a mangy Chihuahua hide, which she hadn't used since the last time we all went on vacation together, which had been to the ugly, oily beaches of Galveston six years before. Trying not to startle her, I sprinted up without saying a word, then started simply to walk beside her as if it were the most normal thing in the world.

"Hello there," I said.

"Hello there," she echoed, her eyes locked on some invisible place in the darkness beyond.

"Where are you off to?"

"I'm going home," she replied, not with panic or desperation or helplessness but with simple, firm resolve.

"Oh, good. Me too."

"You are?" she said, almost incredulously, as she paused in the street to analyze my face.

"I think we're going the wrong way."

"The wrong way?"

I laid my hand on her elbow and nudged her to turn. I wrapped my arm around her shoulder blades and guided her to the sidewalk. I flinched; her bones felt as insubstantial as fish ribs.

"What's in the suitcase?" I asked.

"Some things I need."

My mom didn't hand me the suitcase but also didn't resist when I pried it from her fingers. She opened her mouth, as if making way for the passage of words, which—to her utter stupefaction—never came. The suitcase was unreasonably heavy. It gave off a rancid, sour odor similar to the one that had come off the armadillo corpse I'd found rotting in our front yard when I was eight. Similar, but more peppery. I laid it directly beneath a streetlamp and opened it over a long, grassy crack in the sidewalk. In the weird light, it took me a long, horrified moment to understand what I saw: pounds and pounds of stinking meat, at least two or three weeks' worth of hoarded cold cuts. I gagged, almost retched, then didn't. When I turned back to my mom, she shrugged sadly, then began to snicker. I shook my head, trying to play along, pretending to laugh.

I locked my elbow around hers, its bony tip poking my ribs, then walked home: my ninety-pound mom on one arm, a twenty-pound suitcase of rotting lunch meat on the other.

WHEN I CAME home from school the next afternoon, my mom seemed an entirely different person, almost her old self. A rare occurrence: she had gotten out of her nightgown and put on one of her generic Mom outfits, a white blouse and a pair of overly high-waisted blue jeans, squinting elastic sown into the waist.

"How was school, sweetie?"

"Um, good."

"Can I make you a snack?"

"No thanks."

Reassured by the casual, routine questions, I tried to convince myself: Maybe she was just extraordinarily exhausted. Maybe all she needs is to get some good sleep. She'll talk to the doctor about some sleeping pills. Maybe it's as simple as that.

For these reasons, but mostly out of a desperate, stupid hope, I still didn't tell my dad a thing.

FOR AS LONG AS I COULD REMEMBER, I knew I wanted to be a scientist. When I was younger, my primary interests were in the fields of paleontology and astronomy. Because I was naïve, I thought a scientist simply studied whatever science was the most interesting at the time; by age eight I still hadn't decided what kind of a scientist I wanted to be. When I was nine, I read a book called *The Scientific Method,* which taught me about the arduous, minute aspects of empirical research, and also about how major discoveries can suddenly make you see everything differently, as if a light has been switched on, even if it was more comfortable when the light was still off. Then, as if to prove the point, three weeks later, the brightest, most blinding and terrifying of all lights was suddenly lit, and I saw what a cruel, cold, and careless place the universe can be. It happened as my mom read to me Carl Sagan's *Cosmos* and I began to grasp what it meant when my dad said he was an atheist. For weeks after that, night after night, I paced the house, trying to imagine what it would be like if my dad was correct and—one day—in the place where I had once existed there would be only emptiness. What it would be like to simply stop being. Finally, one night, my mom found me exhausted, clutching my head in a corner of the breakfast nook. She explained, as she already had, many, many times in those weeks, that nobody knows anything for certain, but this time she also gave me the rubber band.

"There's no sense in worrying about something you can't control. So every time you start to think about it, just give yourself a little snap, a little punishment to stop yourself."

It was now six years later, and I had flicked myself with rubber bands more times than I could count, probably to the point of near-permanent mutilation. Especially when I was unable to stop myself from remembering the terrible sound. The sound and what followed. Only because I've sworn myself to full and total honesty will I remember it now on purpose. Just this once, and quickly.

Six weeks after my mom asked how long we'd known each other, I woke to the sound.

In my freshman-year music class there was a boy named Mark Jenkins, who had what the teacher described as "perfect pitch," which meant he could hear the differences between two notes that would sound essentially the same to 99.9 percent of the population. Similarly, in the memory of the deep, echoing thud that woke me that night, I can discern the smallest nuance. The slightest crack.

The house was dark, but I navigated by memory. I scrambled to where the sound had come from: down the hall, down the stairs, to the spot directly beneath the place where the banistered platform at the top of the staircase overlooks the living room, an internal balcony. I heard the shallow, struggling sound of sick breath, but that might have been my own. I reached for the lights, the fat dimmer knob that my dad had installed a year before. I twisted it as far as it would go, the room quickly fading into terrible visibility, like theater lights rising onto the first act of a play that opens with a tragedy.

It was as if I was standing on the edge of a black hole, because suddenly time and space were not what they should have been. It could have been an unforgivably long time or it could have been only seconds. Nothing moved, least of all my mom. Her body was sprawled across the tooth-white marble floor. She had fallen from the platform above, and three wicked cracks had broken across the tiles closest to her body.

At first and for a long while, the sight was impossible and I waited to wake up. I opened my mouth, but whatever it was I might have been trying to say was sucked into the black hole because there was only silence. All I could hear was the sound of my own brain, which sounded like nothing and everything at once, like the inside of a seashell. Finally, I made a noise, maybe just a whimper, but it was enough for the normal rules of physics to begin to take hold. Then I felt my throat scream, and soon my dad's footsteps rose from behind me. He nearly tumbled on top of her but caught himself on my shoulder. He leaned over my mom's face and palpated her throat with two fingers. Her eyelids fluttered apart.

I gasped or maybe couldn't gasp her name.

My mom's eyes narrowed then, not in confusion but as if in deep frustration. For a long moment, her mouth hung agape, and I thought that she had escaped death, but her words had not. That she'd become one of those head trauma cases for whom everything remains exactly as it was, except that the link between words and thoughts is broken forever.

But then, in a shockingly strong voice, without the slightest quiver, my mom said only two words:

She said, "I'm here."

IN THE HOSPITAL the next day, two doctors pushed through the swinging doors to the emergency room and came into the lobby with furrowed, thoughtful faces. One, a massive old man with an archetypal Texas accent, a thick brown mustache, and skin the color of raw steak, the other a lanky girl cursed with a nose geological in both size and formation, they spoke to my dad in medical language, which sounded like English but wasn't anything I recognized.

"Classic cerebral edema, with a rise in intracranial pressure," the fat doctor said.

"She's on the verge of pressure-passive flow, which means a huge risk of ischemia," the girl doctor added.

My dad, who always hates asking too many questions, just nodded as if he understood. And the doctors just continued, in their strange, esoteric language ("cortex" and "cerebrospinal fluid" and "herniation"), and then only looked at each other in the same way my mom basically looked at all of life after that day: with the profound confusion of someone trying to solve an impossible problem. The doctors ignored me until, beyond my control, I clutched the scrubs of the fat one (Dr. Pinquit, according to his pewter name tag) and pulled until they began to give at the shoulder. He finally faced me and spoke like a human.

"We've never seen anything exactly like this before. But we've been on the phone, talking to the experts, and we're doing our best."

In my brain, I screamed, *Talking* to the experts? And what kind of a nincompoop are you? But what I said was nothing.

When they turned to leave, I saw a spot of blood far down Dr. Pinquit's back, and because I knew where it had come from, which was an unbearable thing to consider, I decided that I had to think about something else, that I had to at least try to help. I asked the girl doctor, because she didn't look much older than a teenager herself, to explain the problem to me, as I believed I was an expert at solving difficult problems. Dr. Pinquit just charged back into the emergency room, leaving the doors swinging frantically, but the girl looked at me. Maybe because she was so young and not yet numbed by thousands of dramas like ours, she began to cry.

"I'm afraid you wouldn't really understand." Her voice wobbled. "You would have to be an expert on the human brain."

"Please," I said. "Let me try."

"I'm sorry." She turned and disappeared through the doors.

That's when I finally decided what kind of scientist I wanted to be, because that's when I swore to myself that, no matter what, I would become an expert on the human brain.

Hours later, at 3:00 A.M., Dr. Pinquit told my dad that my mom was stable for now but that she needed some rest and it looked like we did too. As Dr. Pinquit spoke, I pinched the rubber band on my wrist, then gave myself a single, sharp snap.

Incredibly, that night my dad stuck to his routine, settling in front of The History Channel, pint glass of cocktail in hand. And so, by 4:15 A.M., when my dad was spaced out with the gin and tonic and the grimy footage of war, it was easy to sneak by to the fridge. I pulled out the big glass jug of Tanqueray and poured some into a juice cup. I hid the cup under my sweatshirt and snuck back upstairs, into my mom's room. I shut the door behind me and took a huge gulp from the glass. I almost couldn't swallow, it tasted like magma; I instantly understood why my dad was always drinking it.

After a time, it was as if all of my mom's things, her poster of Monet's *Water Lilies,* her shelves and shelves of novels and astronomy books, her widemouthed jar crammed with pens, all were orbiting around my head. Not a geosynchronous orbit but one that came closer and closer. I was so dizzy that I spewed, and when my dad finally found me in the early afternoon on the floor of the bathroom, my mouth crusted in the stuff of my stomach, he said, "We'll figure out a way to manage."

OUR BRAINS ARE SO hopeful.

In the months after my mom's fall, I devised a theory:

I decided that, at some point, evolution, which tries out everything until it comes up with a winner, must have attempted to create a truly pessimistic human mind. That maybe earlier hominids had all been pessimists, and maybe that was why they had gone extinct. Early hominids had expected life to be terrible, had thought that misery was normal, and so why would they have bothered having children? Making a baby is typically an act of hope, isn't it? I theorized that maybe the early hominids were too hopeless to procreate sufficiently for the survival of their kind.

It occurred to me that perhaps the missing link between early hominids and *Homo sapiens*, which anthropologists have been searching for, was a species that was neither pessimistic nor optimistic.

I speculated that the first of these Realists came into being when two hominids, drunk or stoned enough to forget how terrible life would be for a child, were able to copulate successfully. In this single act, hominid genetics shuffled about just enough to make a baby who maybe wasn't so cheery but also wasn't all doom and gloom. From this single Proto-Realist baby, grew an entire species of creatures, whose bodies were half-hairy, whose glasses were half-full.

The Realists had conversations, such as:

A Realist man said to his wife, "Life may not be kind, but if we don't try to give it another shot, what's the point in our being here?"

The Realist woman took off her cavewoman pelts, lay on her back, and asked, "Why not?"

Eventually, with the passing of generations and another shuffling of genes, the first *Homo sapiens* was born.

When he was a young man, his idea of normal was something different from anything that anyone had ever known. His idea of normal was happiness. To all the enduring, expressionless faces of the Realist women, he would ask, "Why can't we just be normal?"

The Realist women would reply, of course, "This is normal."

And the first *Homo sapiens* would say, "No it isn't. Normal is happy. Life is a wonderful thing."

Because I knew optimism and romanticism were attractive

qualities, I decided that the first *Homo sapiens* was probably able to talk a great bevy of Realist women into having sex with him. Because he was such a prolific lover, he was able to make many Optimist children, who were also prolific lovers. It didn't take long before *Homo sapiens,* in all their self-deluded optimism, populated the earth.

It also occurred to me that now, despite aeons of evidence that their basic outlook is fundamentally flawed, the Optimists remain such optimists that the earth's population only grows and grows. They are such optimists, in fact, that in the places with the grimmest standards of living people reproduce the most.

I came upon this theory as my dad tried to make something like an apology in his indirect way.

"I just wish you could have a normal family," he said for the three thousandth time.

"What do you mean?"

"You know, happy."

I didn't say anything else because I was busy deducing what I believed to be a revolutionary theory of the origin of the human mind.

If still, after all the terrible things that happened, I could just go on thinking that normal life was basically happy, I knew that my brain must have been purposefully miswired, skewed to hopefulness. Even though I'd come to learn that misery was basically life's status quo, when I thought about what life was like for our family before my mom's decline, the first word to come to my mind was, still, *normal.* Even though I knew, statistically speaking, that our kind of happiness wasn't normal at all. But we exist as the most powerful species on Earth because of our optimism, and so I would say this:

Once upon a time, we were normal.

Once upon a time, we had something to look forward to and we were able to take for granted that happiness would just go on and on.

Once upon a time, when I was younger, my mom would tell me stories about a land called Isidora, a place she claimed was real. Congenitally a skeptic, I once asked her how she knew about Isidora. I didn't know if she was just trying to lend legitimacy to her stories or if she was simply telling the truth, but she told me that she knew the history of Isidora because her parents had once told it to her, as her parents' parents had told it to them, as the stories had been passed along for potentially hundreds of years.

At any rate, whatever Isidora's true origin, she would tell me the stories every night. My chronic insomnia was just starting to become a problem, and so, to try to lull me to sleep, my mom would describe Isidora for me again and again, would tell me to imagine I was there, would try to nudge me from the lonely, sleepless house into a boundless sleep world called Isidora.

"Alongside this world there's another. There are places where you can cross," she would always begin. "This other world is called Isidora, and it's as big as ours, and in many ways it's exactly the same. The same grass grows in the same dirt. The same birds fly in the same sky. Even the people look the same. But the major difference is that in Isidora no one can remember anything. Nobody has a name, or a house, or a family. Or you could say that everyone has the same name and the same house and the same family, a single word and a single place and a single name called Isidora. At first it might sound scary, but if you don't remember anything, then you don't have anything to be scared about. And, anyway, in Isidora you always have whatever it is you need."

During art class in kindergarten, I'd spend my time busily illustrating my mom's stories, rendering Isidora a thousand times over. Once, for example, I used wax paper to trace a map of Texas out of my copy of *Atlas of America*, and when I brought it home, my mom squealed, "Oh! You clever boy! Look how good you are! You've drawn a map of Texas!"

"It's not Texas."

"It sure looks like Texas."

"That's because it's the Texas part of Isidora."

"Oh!" my mom said. "I should have known."

For a long while, she nibbled her lower lip and nodded as she stared at the map.

"Do you want me to tell you a secret?" she finally asked.

"A secret?"

"You can't tell anyone, not even Daddy. Promise?"

"Promise."

My mom led our way into the kitchen, pulled open the junk drawer, removed a felt pen, put the tip of it to the map of the Texas portion of Isidora, and drew a thick red *X* on the top right corner.

"What is that?" I asked.

She smiled, turned to me, and told me a story.

Typically, great monuments have marked the passageways to Isidora. People say that there's one under the Sphinx, another beneath Stonehenge, another under the Acropolis in Greece, and yet another at the bottom of the basement of the Empire State Building.

But once upon a time, there was also a passageway in Texas. The Quivira tribe, which lived here long before the white settlers ever came, hid the passageway beneath the dirt floor of a hut. If a Quivira man or woman lived a good, helpful life, at a certain age, he or she was allowed to pass through. But then the white men came along with their diseases and their guns and their stupidity. The remaining Quivira who hadn't been killed off were eventually forced to leave their ancestral home. As an act of revenge, the Quivira buried the passage to Isidora deep underground and didn't leave any marker at all. I won't tell you how I know, but I know. Now, I don't want you to go up there and start digging up people's front yards, but the truth is that the passageway to Isidora is right there. X marks the spot.

Abel

The country had gone to war, then gone to war again, and the feeling was that the Big One was still to come. Little more than halfway through the century, global conflict was on its way to becoming an essential part of the human condition, an irreversible stage in the development of civilization, like the invention of agriculture, or of steel, or of the city. The inevitability of war was such that, for the first time in the history of America, new soldiers, my brother included, were involuntarily drafted for no reason other than to maintain an intimidating show of force, to attest to our readiness for the next war that the world was busy imagining. With great armies standing at the ready and the power of the sun aimed and waiting to be let loose, battles were fought among minds. And war, abstracted, was more terrifying than ever.

Was it only then that I was finally happy? Was it only when my brother was away, called off to the duties of the world, that Mae and I were able to betray him so fully? Yes. Completely. Yes. Perhaps that, above all, was my sin. Maybe that is why I deserved to be left, for all those years, hobbling around this place in the way I always suspected I would be left. Alone.

My sin, which at times felt like the opposite of a sin, was to thank everything that should be completely unthankable. I thanked the Cold War, which I still knew was a wretched thing, but look what it did for me. I never, of course, thanked the North Koreans or the Russians or Communism in the abstract. Even when I thanked the imaginary war, I would still end my thanks, which I made in the way that most people pray, with my palms pushing at each other as I knelt at the side of the bed, by offering a deal. That even though I was more grateful for the war than I had ever been grateful for anything, if I could trade having Mae for the sake of world peace, I would. I was not evil. I believe that is the truth.

I also, of course, thanked my private most unthankable: the welding of my shoulder to my spine, which I rarely considered to be anything other than a curse, but which I suddenly found, at last, to be the opposite. I was useless to the military. Paul was gone; I was left with Mae.

It began almost immediately. Perhaps, out of respect, we tried to delay the inevitable. For months we had traded the occasional furtive touch or kiss, like children sharing small, pilfered treasures (a cigarette, say, or a half-drained bottle of beer): business to be conducted only in the dead of night, or within a grove of trees, or behind a boulder next to the pond. But now, a mere three days after Paul left, Mae was mine.

The first time was an experience equally sinister and fulfilling. Afterward, sprawled across the bed, Mae set her hands to work in the wiry tangle of my chest hair, twirling her fingers with simultaneous deliberation and speed, as if looming. Mae's voice slipped into a low register as she told me stories I had never heard before, or at least not as she now described them. She told me of her father's drinking and of her mother's soft, slow agony, of her cheating and then of his. She explained that the only kind of marriage she had ever known was the kind that rotted slowly away. That she had grown to understand that the basic transaction of married life was sabotage, that the basic transaction of life itself was a sad, endless amalgam of public endurance and private indulgence.

Perhaps Mae was being cynical; perhaps she was being cruel. On that night, I believed that I alone had tapped some dark well, hidden to all others, a place dank with despair and compulsion and fear. Now, however, forty years hence, I believe that we both may have been deceiving ourselves. That Mae was not, in fact, so darkly compelled but rather—in that night—expanded what darkness she could locate so that we might both have something to fill the newly opened gulf of our vast, plain guilt. Perhaps we knew we could never forgive ourselves, but at least, as caricatures of our own suffering, we could make excuses.

But, whatever our justifications, we finally had each other. We tried to shut out the reasons why. We wanted to make ourselves deaf and blind to the world. We never bought a television. We canceled our newspaper subscription. We would ride to town only when it became absolutely necessary.

We would, however, think of my brother daily. We even had a routine when we ate together in the mornings. We would hold hands and invent the stories of what Paul might have been eating on the base at Fort Hood to which he had been conscripted.

Mae would say, "This morning he's eating alone, at the edge of camp. Porridge and sausage."

I would say, "He's chewing a stick of pepperoni. And thinking about how lucky he is that there's no one to fight."

Mae would say, "As he eats a bowl of oatmeal, he wonders what we're eating. And if we're all right."

Sometimes when the latest news, such as the installation of Khrushchev or the launching of *Sputnik,* would leak into our lives through a neighbor or a swept away page of a newspaper, we would not even be able to eat breakfast. Instead, we would sit there for hours, speculating and arguing the potential consequences.

But other than the breakfasts and the most occasional of news, the world beyond our house was silence. In the mornings, I would hear only the grumbling of dirt and the crackling of dead wheat as I walked in all directions to see nothing but the jutting headstones of my family's plot, the teetering shanties of the horse barn and the henhouse, and the endless plane of clay and wheat meeting the sky at the horizons with a hazy fade, the color of a lake's water. And in the center of that silence, in that old house of clapboard white, sturdy and singular in its decaying way, like an old man's stubborn, final molar, we had a life. A life so happy and simple that, after one year, I began to let myself believe that this was how life was supposed to be. That unhappiness was a rare mistake, that sadness was abnormal. Once, even, when I lay nude on the downstairs floor with Mae seated on my back, rubbing my hump, I thought, Maybe she will be able to convince my shoulder and my spine to let go. Maybe I am the frog prince, and Mae is kissing me.

Mae was mine.

Perhaps it is inappropriate to mention, but the truth is that we made love everywhere.

Her hair would look like a bird's nest some days, the twigs and splinters of dead wheat and corn sticking from the brown bun at the top of her head. My thighs would be cut and bruised from the gravel path that leads up to our house. Her back would be dented with the patterns of bark from the willow tree. Sometimes, when we were both at work in the barn, Mae finessing milk from the cow, myself changing the hay, our eyes would catch in a certain way, and hours later I would still be peeling sticks of hay from my sweaty rear end. The bed upstairs, which had been Mama's, then my brother's, was now ours.

Though I know it is inexcusable, I began to let myself see Mae and me together in that bed as my rightful inheritance. I took my brother's letters home from Fort Hood as evidence that what Mae and I were doing was natural, even right.

"Dearest Abel and Mae," he would begin each letter, and to see our two names written there together, it was easy to believe that he also thought of the two of us as now being one. When he would write:

Abel, I hope you are taking good care of Mae. Providing for the both of you, and that you are both happy.

I would think:

Isn't it true that Mae and I are the happiest we could possibly be?

Maybe I was only fooling myself. But it was understandable because Mae was finally mine.

Now, everything is so different. Now, when I go to the grocery place down the road, the place that has more varieties of cans and boxes and cartons than you would ever imagine possible, I think, How easy it could have been if only this monstrous, strange place had existed then. Sometimes I push a huge plastic cart down an aisle that says at the top FEMININE HYGIENE / ADULT HYGIENE, and I see things like rubbers and "contraceptive jelly" laid out just like any other product to purchase. Now, it's that simple.

But when I had Mae, contraception was not a primary concern of the Rural Texan Mind. More than that, it was practically a sin. Such things were unbelievably difficult to come by. And so, to keep separate the two halves of a child who would be ours, we resorted to techniques both ancient and inadequate. It is almost laughable now. Or would be laughable if what happened had never happened. Our options were household vinegar, tomato juice, a perfectly sized rock, or good, old-fashioned timing. We did all these things. At least, we planned to do all these things, but with the way Mae wanted so badly to have a child and the way my brother had no interest in the mechanics of baby making, who knows what she might have done? Maybe she said the rock was in when it wasn't. Several times, I did not feel the sting of vinegar but pretended not to notice. And sometimes I would just stay inside of her because that was what my body wanted, even if my mind would try to argue otherwise. What happened is probably obvious, was probably inevitable from that first night in the willow tree.

In November 1958, Paul was given three weeks' leave before being shipped off with the rest of the Second Medium Tank Battalion, thirty-seventh armor, Second Armored Division, to a military base in Bremerhaven, West Germany. In a simple letter, Paul wrote from Fort Hood that he was coming home. Three days later, two days before my brother's return, Mae walked through the back door from the outhouse and told me, "Something isn't right."

"What do you mean, something?"

"I'm late. Twelve days."

So lost was my mind, I said, "Maybe it is right."

Mae said, "No."

"We can do something about it."

"No."

I said that I was sorry.

Mae said, "I'd tell you we have to stop. This madness. But it's already too late."

"You think all of this was wrong?"

"Your brother is a good man, Abel. And here we are, doing everything we can to betray him."

"I know. But still. You know that he could never love you like I can."

"What's more important? There's reason for me marrying him in the first place, you know. His goodness. Never doubted that. Not for one second. 'Love don't matter so much as goodness,' my mama said. Then she dies, and three weeks later there he is, right in front of me. And here I am, just making a mess of it."

"But what are you going to do? You are mine now. I'm yours."

Mae yelled, "Stop it! Stop it right now and listen to me! Don't pretend. You know we've done the worst thing we could've done to him."

"I know."

Tears rising to her eyes, Mae cried, "I only pray he never finds out."

"But if we don't do something . . . I know a doctor."

Mae struck her palm with her fist and said, "No."

"You know about my family. Our—"

"You should've thought about that before."

"But now is now, and we have to deal with this."

Regaining her composure, speaking with an unshakable resolve, cold and hard, Mae declared, "Ain't 'this.' It's my child. No doctor."

"Then what?"

"I've an idea."

It was as simple as that. No lie was ever told, but neither was the truth. My brother came home, happy, effusive even. He told us stories of the army. He told us of the remarkable coincidence that Jamie Whitman, a long-lost friend from when we were children, had been assigned to the very same battalion as he. He excitedly stumbled on his words as he spoke of Elvis Presley, who had arrived at Fort Hood a month before Paul. (Once, Paul had KP with the King himself, and according to my brother, Elvis sang through the shift, a private concert with only my brother and the crusty flatware as audience.) As we devoured a great homecoming feast, as we laughed at my brother's stories, as we were all together again, I began to understand the loneliness for which Mama had so often tried to prepare me.

It was the first night when Mae acted upon her plan. I would never have believed it possible that the soft squeak of such tenderness could crush one so completely.

But such is my story. What is right and good for the world is what ruins me. All places I have found happiness have been in the tentative, temporary, fleeting spaces just beyond life as it is and should be. And that night, I lay awake, alone again in the periphery. Simple reality, my brother with his wife, whining its rhythmic cry on the other side of the wall. I curled myself beneath my hump, excess beneath excess, but still could hear.

I kept count. Perhaps setting a record for a marriage such as theirs, my brother and Mae made love seven times in the three weeks of his return. And in the months after he left again, what had been planted in an impossible place grew into reality, Mae's belly swelling with the impossible truth, the plausible lie. Reality, as ever, insisted upon itself, and Mae was never mine again.

Beyond the golden city lie the endless gardens of Isidora, where simple desire controls everything. In the gardens, two Isidorans will meet with no memory of each other, without realizing they have already fallen in love a thousand times over, and will simply fall in love once more. As long as they are near, they will live only to make each other happy.

Eventually, of course, hunger will strike. Because Isidora is a land of plenty, the Isidoran, when hungry, will feast, briefly living only for the pleasure of eating.

Once full, an Isidoran might happen upon a new lover or the same lover as before. Either way, she'll once again fall fully in love. In a single, busy day, an Isidoran woman might fall in love with fifteen Isidoran men or—if chance will have it—the same Isidoran man, fifteen times.

As Isidorans can't hold on to any memory, even the memory of death, they never know that death is a possibility. The moment that an Isidoran dies, she will likely have just fallen in love again, for the one hundred thousandth time.

Seth

Here's what little I knew.

Before they ever met, my parents already had three things in common: they were both from Texas, both had unspeakable, lonely childhoods, both had decided to leave for New York City, since New York City seemed like the one place they would be least likely ever to be alone again.

In New York, my parents tried to invent new stories for their future, freed from the past. But the only stories my mom ever told took place in a fantasy world, and my dad rarely told stories at all; before long they searched the strange, endless maze of New York City's streets for any scrap of the people they had tried to forget that they had been.

They spoke for the first time in a café on MacDougal Street, where my mom served coffee, scraping through NYU on measly tips. My dad had just gotten a new job, his first foray into his career as a prison product supplier. After four miserable years of temp work in the strange city of sneers and dirt and car horns, something in the combination of his recent employment and the comforting dustiness of a suppressed Texan accent in the far corners of my mom's words made my dad feel like he was finally finding himself. He asked my mom where she was from. Though he'd never heard of Bethesda, Texas, though he had never really been anywhere other than the greater Houston area and the streets of the lower half of Manhattan, they both felt the immediate, unreasonable draw of compatriots in a foreign land. My mom neglected her duties with the coffeepot, leaving the café littered with empty mugs and scowls.

Eventually, my dad found the courage to do something he hadn't done since leaving Houston. He asked a woman on a date. The next night, in a café a million miles away from the life they had escaped, they found themselves talking about almost nothing other than Texas.

In their wedding picture, taken in front of City Hall in Manhattan twelve weeks later, my parents look like Hollywood versions of themselves. The beauty my mom continued to possess throughout her married life is amplified by the photographer's romanticizing haze filter. In the picture, her long brown hair shimmers with the flash, her skin is pale, almost to the point of translucence, and her slight body is clenched in a genuine smile, clutching the arm of a man who looks like an actor hired to play the part of my dad. A young man, a smooth, broad-faced man, whose beaming eyes are not yet ringed by his now constant bruise of exhaustion, whose body doesn't yet sag with the middle-age fat that has come to pin him to the La-Z-Boy, whose square, confident jaw doesn't show a trace of the jowls that have come to hang from it.

A few years after they were married, my dad was offered a promotion to the company headquarters here in Westrock, and he agreed without consulting my mom. In her sixth year of NYU classes (though, because she couldn't afford much, technically she was only a sophomore), my mom (according to my dad) felt conflicted about dropping out and returning to Texas and (according to the obvious) felt like she was betraying herself. But, as my dad loves to inform me, he was persuasive. He shared his vision of the life they could make together, freed from the cage of New York City.

"At any rate," he told her. "New York would be no place to make a family."

Though the only stories my dad recounts without prodding are of his supposedly legendary skills of persuasion, it doesn't take too advanced a deductive mind to understand that the real reason she finally gave in has everything to do with the fact that, six months after they arrived in Westrock, I was born.

MORE THAN ANYTHING, my parents never wanted to think about what was behind them. Because of this, they told me almost nothing about the time before they moved to New York. All I really knew was that they had both been only children and also poor, my mom rural poor, my dad urban poor, and that all of my grandparents were dead. Their motto, with which they answered nearly all questions relating to the topic, was this: "It's better to try to never think about certain things."

Remarkable as it might seem, there is documented proof that my dad had parents. Though almost all the pictures we have from his childhood are of him alone, as if my dad grew up in an air-brushed land of gray backdrops, hidden in the back of one of the drawers of my desk I have a picture of the three-year-old version of myself balancing on his mother's knee in the living room of our old house. Her husband, one of the two grandfathers I never met, had died ten years before the halves of me brewing in my dad's seminiferous tubules and my mom's ovarian follicles would conjoin. My grandmother died from a heart attack the year after the picture was taken, and I don't remember a thing about her, except maybe a smell like gardenias (but that could just be my mind inventing things). In the picture, my miniature hands are clutching my grandmother's two index fingers and my whole body is leaning slightly to the left. My grandmother is laughing, her eyes as white and round as plastic coffee cup lids. At first, you wouldn't notice it, but from the side of the image, two arms reach toward my body, ready to catch me should my grandmother let me fall. And hovering at the edge of the frame is a set of tightened lips, a single eye, half a nose, the rest of the face sliced away. That's my dad.

The only times my mom ever talked about her life before New York City was to remind me that she never wanted to talk about it. All I really knew was that she had grown up in a town called Bethesda, a nowhere place, without a single traffic light. Her family had lived on an old farm, ten miles from the nearest neighbor. When she did tell me anything at all, she would talk almost solely about the gravel path that went up to the house. Down this path she would sometimes walk, sometimes run, sometimes with a runaway's backpack, sometimes empty-handed, but always believing that somewhere down the path, down the road, beyond the rusted, worn sheds and the slouching, frowsy houses, past the school where she was one of eight members of her graduating class, she would find her way to a place like the New York City in novels by Jack Kerouac, where loneliness like hers could never exist.

Many times, I asked her to take me to Bethesda, since it couldn't have been more than four or five hours away. Every time I asked, my mom wouldn't say no or offer any explanation. She would only scoff, then sigh.

Many times, I also asked for more details. Such as: What kinds of people were my grandparents? Were they tall or short? Strict or lenient? Did they talk a lot about everything, or were they quiet and secretive just like her? What I really wanted to ask, but never could find a way to ask, were questions like How, exactly, did they die? How often did she think about them? How much time had she spent crying for them? An hour? A day? A year? Did she still cry?

Whenever I would ask anything except the vaguest of questions, my mom would kiss my forehead and say, "My life started when you were born."

WHEN I WAS LITTLE, I would ask and ask so many times that it turned into a game.

"Smith?" I would guess.

"Patterson?"

"Or how about Silverman?"

My mom would only laugh.

"Give me a hint," I would plead.

"You'd never guess."

"Can I ask you yes or no questions?"

"Well, you just asked one."

"One syllable?"

"Maybe."

"Two syllables?"

"Could be."

"Three syllables?"

"Perhaps."

"Rumpelstiltskin?"

I would narrow my eyes, but my mom would only snicker. If my dad was in the room, he would chortle, half-cruelly, then offer even fewer clues than she. A thousand times, I almost asked the question that I knew was against the unwritten rules of the game but that I could barely keep myself from asking:

"What are you trying to hide?"

Instead I would say:

"Why don't you just tell me your maiden name?"

Then my mom would invariably signal the game's end by casting her hands into the space before her face in a theatrical, magician's way, declaring, "If I told you, there wouldn't be anything for you to discover."

Once, after the conclusion of a particularly long, particularly persistent bout of guessing, I overheard my parents whispering in their bedroom.

"Of course," my dad reassured her. "I'd never say anything you didn't want me to."

AS I GREW UP, my mom grew down.

When I was little, I thought *forgetful* and *impulsive* were the ways my mom had always been. Always carrying herself at an airy, spacey remove, never mindful of things like the location of her keys in the house, or her car in the parking lot, or the fact that the stove was still on. Always depending on others, specifically my dad, to take care of the day's thousand little needs.

In my earliest memories, my dad constantly attends to her, constantly asks my mom what he can do for her.

"Can I get you a glass of water?" he shouts from the kitchen.

"You're so sweet to me," my mom replies.

"You're looking weak," my dad declares. "Can I make you something to eat?"

"That'd be great," she says. "Why are you so good to me?"

"Anything I can get for you on the way home?" He calls from the office, almost every day before leaving.

"Could you pick up my dry cleaning? Love you."

At my mom's command, my dad would nod, smile once, kiss the crown of her head, and then barrel into the task required like a soldier into battle. Just watching him happily scurry about was enough to exhaust me, and my skin would start to itch with annoyance to the point that many times I almost yelled, "She can get her own cup of water!"

But then I would think that maybe that was just what love was like, or at least that was just what love was like for my parents. It was as if that cliché about two people becoming one was true, but of the one that my parents formed, they had each been assigned specific anatomical regions: my mom to the majority of the brain, especially those portions relating to aesthetic appreciation, child rearing, and bodily need. My dad to the lower extremities: the arms, the hands, the legs, the feet, the limbs of burden.

Sometimes, I would think that their marriage was little more than an agreement that my mom would be allowed to issue forth any need and that my dad would be allowed to fill it.

Maybe my mom's commands gave my dad the structure he craved, and maybe that was why he had once performed a seemingly endless procession of unreturned favors, but at the line between *taking care* and becoming *caretaker* he balked. As my dad had been all movement and action, and my mom had been the structuring consciousness, the fundamental order of my family had been unfortunately wired into my mom's doomed neurology.

ONE TIME, when I was eleven, the three of us went to Khan's Kitchen, a Mongolian grill where you pick out your own ingredients, then hand the bowl of raw materials to two sweating men, dressed like ninjas, who cook it up on a wide circular grill, their long steel spatulas flying, fast and unforgiving, like a sword fight.

My dad and I stood transfixed as long, bloody strips of steak and chicken were transformed into delicious stir-fry. When we sat down at our table, we found my mom already eating.

"I don't know if I like this place," she sighed. "It tastes funny."

We looked into her bowl to discover, to our shared horror, that my mom had skipped the last, crucial step. Slumped at the far end of her fork was nothing more than a mess of raw, tangled flesh, stippled with a scattering of hard, ripe peas. But before we could say anything, my mom extracted a long, flopping finger of uncooked beef and slurped it into her mouth like spaghetti.

My dad's voice suddenly rose with the strictness he typically reserved for my Too-Smartness. "Spit that out."

But my mom didn't obey, the slimy tissue slithering down her throat with a gulp.

"What in the hell are you doing?"

"What?" my mom asked innocently.

"Do you see those two nice men over there? They are here for a reason, Jamie. You're going to make yourself sick!"

My mom gaped down at her bowl, instantly repulsed. She looked at my dad, then at me, with all the terror and wonder of a child separated from her parents at the zoo, glimpsing her future under the care of a family of caged bonobos.

"God," she said. "What am I doing?"

My dad sighed a long, slow sigh, and when he finally spoke again, it was as a patronizing, syrupy jingle, two octaves above his normal tone. "No, no. It's okay. I know it's a little confusing."

He palmed the back of my mom's head in a pathetic, demeaning way that made every vessel in my face open its mouth, releasing a bloody blush across the skin of my cheeks.

My mom, surprisingly, did not smile as she always had to every one of my dad's million favors. She did not say, "You're so good to me" or "Why do you love me so much?" or even "What a sweetheart you are!" Instead, she sneered, swatted his hands, briefly held aloft her bowl of raw meat, only to slam it back down, striking the copper table with the deep reverb of a Chinese gong.

She yelled, "Hey! Go to hell! I made a mistake, all right? Don't treat me like a child!"

My dad said my mom's name once. He said, "Jamie." Then he stood before the turned faces of the surrounding three tables and flummoxed expressions of the Mongolian chefs, and explained, "I'm sorry. My wife doesn't quite seem to be in her right mind today."

Then, to prove himself above the moment, to prove himself bigger than his plain and simple embarrassment, my dad extended one arm in a weird, courtly way, folding the other into his waist, simultaneously sitting and taking a bow. As if he had just concluded a performance of *King Lear*.

In the three years that followed, incidents like this became increasingly common. And my dad, who had once found a way to help my mom do everything, could not so much as help hide the embarrassment. Instead, as more and more faces began to turn, as more and more store clerks began to squint their dumbfounded eyes, as more and more of my parents' married friends began to watch in dismay, silently rehearsing the horrified conversation that would commence as soon as they were safely in the privacy of their cars, my dad would only slouch and cower, trying to shrink to nothingness, wanting nothing more than to become a spoon on the table or a panel on the wall.

After my mom's fall, when I would watch my dad jingle his tall glass of gin and tonic, clanking around the ice cubes in a futile effort to free a last, hidden drop, I would think that maybe all it would take for him to instantly resume his vanished, helpful ways, for him to get out of the chair and charge, headlong, back into the world, would be to ask him a single favor, to ask for his help with anything. But I knew we were already far beyond anyone's help.

WITHOUT THE CONTEXT OF SIBLINGS, or even of a single classmate who wouldn't cringe, swear, or knee me in the nether region at my use of the word *friend,* I sometimes had to wonder if it was really my parents who were changing, or if it was just me. I had to wonder if there was an inevitable stage in cognitive development, around seven or eight, when you begin to understand what normal grown-ups are like and thus start to know why your own parents aren't normal, until eventually the idea of normal—once applicable to vast swaths of the earth—erodes to the tiniest tidal sea stack, half in ruins, half-submerged. But by the time I turned fourteen, it was easy to tell that it wasn't just a shift in my perception. That as I got older, learned more, became more like an adult, my mom only got worse, forgot, acted more and more like a child. If it hadn't been for that terrible sound from under the balcony, who knows how long it might have been until I would have known that all of her strange behaviors were not just eccentricities but the symptoms of a devastating, genetic, neurological condition?

At first, because we told no one, the doctors thought that her problems remembering (for example, her constant vows from the hospital bed that she would "never stay in this hotel again!") were purely the consequences of her fall. But as her stay wore on, she only got worse, fingering the bandages at the back of her skull, demanding to know who had tried to murder her. Matthew Pinquit, the neurologist I had concluded to be a perfect example of the type to which I would one day be far superior, only scratched his mustache when he called my dad and me in for meetings. As Dr. Pinquit's whiskers wriggled behind his forefinger like the legs of a pinned insect, he explained that he had never seen anything quite like this before. That sometimes people with head traumas lost memories, but never in the way she did, a gradual way that only got slightly worse and worse. When he asked if she had ever shown any "symptoms" before the fall, my dad and I looked at each other.

A week later, Dr. Pinquit stopped fiddling with his face.

After visiting my mom, who begged to know when her mother would be coming for her, Dr. Pinquit sat us in his office and rested both hands neatly on his desk's dull pane of frosted glass.

"I know this might seem unlikely," he said in his practiced way. "But I want you to keep an open mind."

"We're wide open," my dad said, though I can't say that I agreed. "Tell us."

"We've been running test after test. At first it was the least of the possibilities, but now we think it's the most likely."

"What is?" I piped, nearly lifting myself from the chair.

"People usually think it's only a problem of the elderly, but in fact the first diagnosed case was a fifty-one-year-old." Dr. Pinquit paused, his eyes lingering on my dad. "It's even been seen in people as young as thirty, thirty-five."

"What's been seen?" my dad demanded.

Dr. Pinquit inhaled theatrically, as if he had been rehearsing this moment for hours.

"There are two kinds of Alzheimer's disease."

"Alzheimer's?" I said.

"Yes, there are two kinds. There is the normal, late-onset kind that no one knows the exact reasons for. And there is the other kind, called 'early-onset' or 'familial Alzheimer's.' There are a few variants of it. But there's this one kind. It's variant EOA-23. It seems to be caused by a single gene. On the fourteenth chromosome."

"The fourteenth chromosome?" was the moronic thing my dad managed.

"We've run the test for it, and I don't know exactly how to say this except to just say it. Your wife tests positive for the gene."

"You're saying she has *Alzheimer's?*" My dad was leaning against the impossibility of the word.

"Well, there's never any way to be certain. Before autopsy, at least. But in my report, I'm suggesting a diagnosis of probable early-onset familial Alzheimer's."

After I gagged on the word *autopsy*, I thought, in a million ways, *Impossible*. But when I turned to my dad, expecting him to rail against the stupidity of the doctor, since he was such an accomplished railer against all forms of the idiotic, he only bowed his head and watched his fingers press against one another.

"Tell me, Mr. Waller," Dr. Pinquit continued. "Is there any history of this sort of thing in her family?"

Almost indiscernibly, my dad shrugged.

BEFORE WE LEFT THE HOSPITAL, I tried to kiss my mom's forehead without crying and nearly succeeded. But then three nasal tears,

...sors of their orbital counterparts, plunked down from my nostril, staining Mom's paper pillowcase. I had to turn away.

Though many things my mom said after her fall could have been taken in a hundred ways, what she said next was clear.

"I think I might be terribly sick."

For a while, my parents only watched each other watching each other. My dad's face wasn't sad, more like *alert*, more like prey spotted in the wild, waiting for the predator to make the first move. Finally, my mom spoke.

"How did I let myself be so selfish?"

ONE OF MY SECRET LAIRS was a spot behind three huge boulders next to the creek that runs through the park in front of our house. Maybe I was already too old for secret lairs, but that was what my mom had called the places no one else knew about or would ever come across, and so I was not about to call them anything else. The creek, over millions of years, had cut a ravine into the earth, twelve feet deep, sedimentarily striped with the colors of great geological epochs. One afternoon, a couple days later, I sat in this lair as I read the first book about Alzheimer's I could find. I had stolen my dad's MasterCard, walked to the bookstore, and purchased sixteen neuroscience books, anything that looked like it might contain information about memory loss, early-onset Alzheimer's, or head trauma. In my lair, I read a book called *Common Descent: An Introduction to Alzheimer's Disease*. After settling myself into a smooth hollow in the creek bed, I flipped through the opening pages, which described the first diagnosed case of Alzheimer's, the one Dr. Pinquit mentioned. She was a German woman, named Auguste D., who came into the office of Dr. Alois Alzheimer and explained to the doctor, "I have lost myself."

Halfway through the first chapter I became impatient, gave up on a page-after-page reading, and instead searched for a reference to my mom's particular variant of the disease. Four times over, I read the book's one short paragraph on the topic. According to *Common Descent*, scientists believe that the EOA-23 variant is one of the most recent, having begun only somewhere between 200 and 250 years ago. "Remarkably," the author comments, "if one considers this small figure along with the assumption that all sufferers of the EOA-23 variant share a common genetic origin, one can extrapolate that any one sufferer of EOA-23 *Morbus Alzheimer* is at most the twelfth or thirteenth cousin of any other."

I then quickly flipped to a section called "Prognosis" and tried to force my eyes across the pages. Though Dr. Pinquit had already explained what to expect, I wasn't about to just take his word for it.

When I started to read "Prognosis," I took a breath after each paragraph, in which I thought, or said out loud, *Impossible*. But the more I read, the more accurately the description of the disease's pathology applied to my mom. Yes, she had begun to lose track of social obligations. Yes, she did become disoriented in new settings. Yes, she did get unusually, unreasonably emotional. Yes, of course, she did forget the nature of long-maintained relationships. Eventually, my hands began to shake with the paranoid sensation that some complete stranger had written my mom's biography in intimate detail, which was followed by a feeling far worse: the sickening, dehumanizing realization that the same descriptions must be applicable to millions.

And so, when I got to the part about what the disease was like in its late stages, I knew I was reading her future.

Though I might have thought that Dr. Pinquit was extraordinarily subpar, this once I knew he was right.

What both *Common Descent* and Dr. Pinquit said was this: it's not just memories that people with my mom's disease forget but increasingly basic things. How to write, how to speak, how to walk, how to sit up, how to swallow, how to breathe, and—eventually, after five to seven years—how to stay alive.

I flung the book from my hands, as if the cover had suddenly turned red hot. I snapped the rubber band on my wrist eight times, rapid-fire. I began to climb up the rope that I had tethered to a tree at the top of the ravine, but when I made it a little more than halfway, my hands gave up and I landed with a sharp thud that emptied my lungs. For minutes, I wondered how much time it would take me to die without oxygen. I hoped it wouldn't be long. But, eventually, my throat started to wheeze, and air that felt cold and painful, like winter air, filled my chest. When I sat up, I knew it was hopeless.

In his recently published meta-analysis of North American cases of familial early-onset Alzheimer's, Dr. Marvin Shellard, with impressive and exhaustive diligence, through a combination of narrative and genetic data, successfully traces the EOA-23 variant to a single point of origin in late-eighteenth-century England. However, as he has yet to be able to discover the name of the Georgian-era Englishman in whom this particular variant began, Dr. Shellard has assigned him the scientific handle of A-496.

Reflecting on A-496, Dr. Shellard writes, "Though we have been unable to locate the actual name or any biographical information for A-496, given both the pervasiveness of this particular variant and the extraordinary number of offspring produced by A-496, it follows that A-496 could only have been male." Continuing in a way that detours slightly from cold, hard empiricism and reveals something of the frustrated curiosity of one who has spent years retracing history to locate a single, nameless phantom, Dr. Shellard speculates, "Given his prolific genetic output, it seems likely that A-496 was either some sort of British nobility or perhaps an extremely popular male prostitute."

In fact, A-496 was the former. His actual name was Lord Alban Mapplethorpe, a scion of the Mapplethorpe family of Iddylwahl, England (now long since wiped from map and memory alike), a clan of high-level gentry that had long held rule over a modest dukedom.

Alban Mapplethorpe's particular variant of early-onset Alzheimer's came into spontaneous being in the soft fallopian tissue of his mother, the latest Duchess of Iddylwahl, as the nascent duke emerged from dual haploid cells to multicellular zygote. Soon after the spermatozoon of Lord Alexander Mapplethorpe and the ovum of the duchess were united, the double strands of the future duke's DNA pulled apart for the first time, baring the nucleic teeth of his genetic code. In less than a second, a small band of polymerase enzymes, more creative than their countless, tireless peers, did not fulfill their endless charge, did not simply order the replication of the section of the fourteenth chromosome to which they were assigned. Instead, they improvised, jotted down their own ideas, and thus—in a single moment—invented the EOA-23 variant of familial early-onset Alzheimer's.

As with most imaginative bouts of improvisation, it's impossible to know exactly the source of the enzymes' inspiration. Maybe it was somehow related to the three cups of wine the duchess always had to consume before approaching the swollen, gouty mass of her husband's body. Maybe it was somehow related to the interconnecting limbs of British nobility's family tree, gentility's notions of its own superiority leading straight to genetic inferiority. Or maybe it was simple Life, burdened with its endless typing and retyping, making its small innovations as it perpetually will. A typo here, an omission there, a rearrangement of genetic text for the sake of diversity itself, an endless process of trial and error, making new offerings that may or may not prove helpful to its living creations. Whatever the reasons, the EOA-23 variant of familial early-onset Alzheimer's had begun. In a single instant it sealed itself into the genome of the duke (and all of those to follow), like a jacket's zipper pulled up too quickly in a frigid gust, which is only one or two teeth away from its original, intended configuration but which—from that instant onward—may never be unzipped again.

For the first decades of the young duke's life, no one would have guessed that a neurological time bomb was rigged into his genes. The duke was everything his parents could have hoped for: a remarkably handsome young man, touched with just enough of a slight, endearing shyness to make him a moderate and humble ruler. In his youth, the duke had one or two dalliances with the women in town, never bearing any living, illegitimate result. As the young duke neared his thirtieth birthday, his father's health began to decline. His father's final wish was for the duke to find a suitable wife, a wish the young duke happily fulfilled. This was easily enough accomplished; for landed gentry of the time, it was hardly more than an act of proper correspondence. Though Alban Mapplethorpe may have married Catherine Wellington of Bath without real romantic motivation, he was nevertheless an affectionate (if distant) husband, and his wife came to love him with the kind of passion that is typically reserved only for love of the unrequited variety. Soon they had a child, a son, Phillip Mapplethorpe, or—as referred to in Shellard's report—familial early-onset Alzheimer's Sufferer A-495.

The first symptoms of the newly invented EOA-23 variant began in the duke's thirty-fifth year, as the trillions of cells in his body began to fulfill the orders made by that renegade posse of enzymes thirty-six years before. As new polymerase ran its awkward thumbs over the DNA of the duke's fourteenth chromosomes, reading them like ticker tape, the duke's mutation began to call upon his loose phosphates to clog the microtubule tracks that held the neurons of his brain in place, causing them to fray and recoil like hair over a flame. To make matters worse, the mutation also began to use the abundant energy that the duke's lavish meals provided to produce a particularly tenacious, insoluble protein—eventually to be called "amyloid"—with which it began to smother the duke's hippocampus, an effect similar to pouring corn syrup over a computer's motherboard. And soon, the duke began to forget. At first, in subtle ways: the castle of Iddylwahl had countless wings and passages in which the duke had always gotten lost, but now it might take an extra minute or two to find his way from the third parlor to the second dining room. When, however, the duke's symptoms became more pronounced, when he began to lose track of social obligations (once, in his nightgown, entering the grand parlor where the Prince of Wales himself was waiting to greet him), the duchess became infuriated and demanded to know why her husband no longer bothered to make even the slightest of efforts.

But it wasn't until the duke's thirty-seventh year that the real trouble began. Trouble that would result, by the fortieth birthday of Alban Mapplethorpe, in the creation of familial early-onset Alzheimer's Sufferers A-456 through A-494.

THE FIRST encounter was with a woman the duke had always secretly admired, to whom he had sometimes taken an opportunity to whisper a flirtatious word or two, with whom he had—in his youth—occasionally imagined himself defying his parents' strict social mores and marrying. Her name, coincidentally, was also Catherine, and she was married now, unhappily and without children. The duke, taking his morning walk through town, happened upon her alone at the well. Watching her hoist the splintering bucket from the watery depths, the duke offered his assistance, offered to carry the bucket home for her. Catherine blushed at the notion. She politely and humbly refused, but the duke persisted.

When they arrived at her house, a clay-and-straw bungalow, he found it empty, her husband, the surly blacksmith, still pounding away at his forge in town. The duke, resting the bucket on the bungalow's single table, noticed a dark smudge at the nape of Catherine's neck, and so he dipped his fingers into the water and pressed them against her, thumbing the darkness from her skin. From that single touch, the rest happened with the logic of a chemical reaction: a single sour taste of acid in the mouth of a base, and suddenly every atom of both loses its mind and it won't be over until the system has burned itself to neutral. The duke's finger on Catherine's cheek became his hand on her cheek, became the other hand against her back, became their bodies pressed together, became lips pressed to lips, and so on and so on.

Research (Tafarodi et al., 2001) has shown that line between what one remembers of the past and what one feels in the present is all but nonexistent. We remember what we want to remember, and the duke, in the early stages of the disease, had particularly keen powers of selective memory. As they fell to the hay of the floor, the duke forgot his wife, his age, his position, everything but the unrequited affection he had always carried for Catherine. And so, forgetting themselves, the duke almost completely, Catherine just enough, they did not stop touching until they touched everywhere.

The next day in town, the duke, again on his walk, again happened by Catherine. She, to his surprise, pulled the duke by the lapels of his coat into an alley not far from her husband's workshop.

"Forgive me, my lord," she implored. "It was a mistake. A grave mistake. I know that now. We must act as if it never happened."

The duke, assuming the poor woman had lost her mind, placed one hand on her shoulder and said, "All right, all right, my dear. Compose yourself and tell me. Precisely what is it that we must act as if never happened?"

Catherine, assuming the duke was making a sly joke, assuming this was his way of assuring her he would never say a thing, kissed him once on the cheek, said, "Thank you, my lord," and scurried away.

The duke was perplexed, but he happily returned to the castle with the gift of a single kiss from a woman he had always secretly admired.

Catherine told only her closest friends of the affair, and also of the duke's sly secrecy. And so, when the duke—weeks later—happened upon one of Catherine's friends and began a flirtatious banter, the friend knew she could return his advances with impunity. Before long, the friend, who like many of the women of Iddylwahl, often imagined elaborate romantic scenarios with the duke (especially as she endured her husband's sloppy, unsparing thrusts), found herself behind the locked door of her bedroom, the duke surpassing every one of her erotic inventions.

The legend of the duke's sexual prowess and discretion spread among the dissatisfied wives of Iddylwahl, and soon the affairs were daily occurrences.

The only danger posed to the duke's liaisons was that of being discovered in the act itself. This happened twice at the castle, when the duchess came into the grand parlor to find her husband and some peasant woman spread shamelessly across the divan. Both times the duke was unrepentant, could not remember what he had done, and so could not understand the reasons for his wife's hysteria. Both times, however, the duchess was able to get the duke to sign papers calling for the women's permanent expulsion from Iddylwahl. The duke's lovers soon realized that complete discretion could be had only in their own homes. And so, by carefully exploiting their husbands' daily schedules, they accomplished the feat with near-perfect secrecy (other than, of course, sharing the story with a select number of lady friends). Only once did a husband catch his wife in the act. In a fit of rage, he did not bother to see the face of the man who was pelvicly bludgeoning his wife. Instead, he charged into the bedroom, ceramic chamber pot raised in the air, and shattered it over the duke's skull. The next morning, when the duke awoke with a splitting headache, he asked his wife how badly he had been drunk the night before, but she only sighed (as she was now accustomed to sighing) and said, coldly, "We had a light supper and retired early."

As the duke's madness worsened, his lovers came to the realization that his unwavering discretion was something other than slyness: that he truly, simply, incredibly did not remember. When the duke would make love to a woman for the fourth time, he would explain how he had imagined that moment, the two of them together, for years. And then, days later, the fifth time they made love, he would say precisely the same. For his lovers, the duke's declining memory solved more problems than it caused. Though they might have felt a pang of unworthiness or of anger that the duke carried no memory of the earlier affair, they knew they were assured, completely and exquisitely, of secrecy. Also, the tiffs that sometimes flared among Mapplethorpe's lovers, sparked by postcoital bouts of possessiveness, were settled with relative ease. The duke declared his undying affection for each and every one of his lovers, swore he loved each as he had never loved before, and at the moment he said it, he meant it. When the women began to argue about whom the duke cared for the most, they would soon remind one another that the answer was obviously whoever was before him at that moment.

As the women came to understand that the duke's madness was their bliss, they projected into that madness, as people sometimes will, the hand of the divine. Naked in their beds, their hands caressing the duke's face or grazing the hairs of his chest, or cupping his manhood, they would hang on every senseless word he spoke. Listening to his vows that, with them, he would abandon everything; or that he could persuade his parents (both long since dead) and they would be married soon; or that he had never made love to a woman before, but what a wonderful initiation it had been. Straining their ears, the women could hear the voice of God.

The men of Iddylwahl, not knowing any better, for the most part clueless about the duke's liaisons with their dissatisfied wives, were easily influenced by the reverence and awe with which the women now spoke of the duke. The divine origin of his madness was soon accepted as universal fact. In the duke's final years, the men of Iddylwahl, many of whose wives the duke had shared, would sit at the duke's bedside, transcribing whatever illogical utterances came to his lips, knowing a precious conduit had been briefly opened before them, from God's mouth to his. After his death, they would meet to pore over their notes and would argue furiously about the meaning of the obtuse, divine words.

As perceptions of the duke's beatitude inflamed, so did the women's passions. Women who normally would never have considered such a thing became overwhelmed by the possibility: that not only the most handsome man they had ever known, not only a duke, but a messenger of God himself was willing and ready to be theirs. And without apparent repercussions. At the height of the duke's sexual powers, he would make love to three, sometimes four women a day.

Making predictions, one would probably assume that a disease like Mapplethorpe's was destined for eradication by the natural processes of mate selection. After all, how many women would choose to have a madman's child? But Life isn't interested in predictions. Life, a behaviorist in the tradition of B. F. Skinner, is interested only in measurable, consequential action. Regardless of the reasons, regardless of its unforeseeable Darwinian success, the fact is that the gene that had been invented in the first moments of Lord Alban Mapplethorpe's creation was successfully slung into the bodies of nearly one hundred of Iddylwahl's women, sixty of whom would carry his offspring, thirty-eight of whom would carry, in turn, the disease. The afflicted of Iddylwahl, and their cellular constituents with them, reproducing and reproducing. A single genetic phrase recapitulating itself through the generations with more exactitude than even the most cherished of stories.

Isidorans have a language, but they don't talk like we do. The Isidoran language is based not on words but on touch. In three specific places on their bodies, Isidorans touch one another and conduct their feelings. If one Isidoran eats something bad and wants to keep another from also eating it, he will place one hand on the person's stomach, which conducts the feeling of pain, and one on the person's forehead, which conducts the feeling of danger. When Isidorans touch one another on the chest, an untranslatable sensation, something akin to pure bliss, overtakes them both.

Abel

Even if it was in an antiquated, simple way, when my family was with me, we were a part of the world, selling what we raised and buying what we needed. But then years passed, I lost everything, and I became more alone than I would have thought a person could bear. However, what it turned out I could not bear was not how alone I was but every place where I might not be alone. What I could not bear was the world outside this place.

And so the farm, with me, regressed.

If Alexander Hartdegen, the hero of H. G. Wells's *The Time Machine*, had gotten into his contraption, pushed the lever, watched the world twirl and blur, then ended up in the middle of my little farm, he would have thought that his machine was broken, that instead of traveling forward in time, he had traveled backward. After my family was gone, I adopted the same ancient ways that people had once lived for thousands of years. Nearly everything necessary for survival I made for myself. Through letters and only two meetings in person, I sold most of what was left of the farm that had been my family's. It was now just me and little more than ten acres.

And still, I cultivated so much, so well. For breakfast I would eat eggs that came from the henhouse, sometimes with a side of potatoes I had nourished from seedlings. For lunch, I would occasionally mash the corn and the wheat I had grown and perhaps make myself a sort of primitive quesadilla with the cheese I got from my milk cow. On special occasions, perhaps my birthday, I would perform the darkest act of animal husbandry, opening a bloody throat, then would enjoy a bit of a heifer that I had fed and watched grow from a newborn calf. At night, before mounting the bed, I would brush my teeth with a homemade paste of baking soda and salt.

When no one saw me, I could sometimes pretend not to believe in the idea of others. Somedays, even, I wouldn't think of Paul or Mae at all. However. Though she seemed further and further from real, I could never stop thinking of my daughter.

SO MUCH HAS CHANGED. Sometimes, in my imagination, I would tell Mae, "You wouldn't believe what's happened. What the world has done to this place, our little town of High Plains. The world now builds houses in a matter of days. Mansions like you wouldn't believe could ever exist in a place like this now line up, one after the next, all the way from Dallas to here, and our little farm is surrounded. I can't even go outside to pick corn or pluck berries without the mansions, and the faces within, staring. Our house, once the most silent place I knew, now roars and wheezes with car traffic."

For so many years, I could live so simply without being reminded of the world. But now I need only open my eyes or hear through my ears, and I have no choice but to remember everything. So much has changed.

Suffice it to say that, after sixty-eight years on this planet, my body wasn't what it once was, whatever little that had been.

To the question of whether I could continue to survive in my primitive ways, I never answered myself in the definitive affirmative. For decades, I watched the sagging flesh of my belly neither wax nor wane, but I knew how things could suddenly change. A thousand things could fail me: the weather, my body, my animals, the well, my mind, et cetera. I knew not to take the state of my survival for granted; I would only let myself think, For now, at least, I'm managing.

If I'd been asked to guess, I'd have guessed that my mind would have been the first to go. In a way, you might say the fact that it was my body that finally failed me came as a kind of pleasant surprise.

Regardless, the final, inevitable answer to the question of my survival arrived: the fatal, inescapable *no*. Everywhere, the answer pronounced itself.

In the feathery old henhouse, I would crouch to lift eggs from the collection tray, and my knees would lock with a firm *no*, the jutting bones of my rear end crashing pitifully to the old hay, the eggs' gelatinous goo exploding in my fists.

When I would bend to uproot my newly tumescent potatoes, my arms would heave for a moment with a slow yet determined *maybe*, but my spine would soon pop with a harsh *not on your life*. As a right angle, I would hobble home.

Trying simply to slaughter a chicken, I would pin down the poor bird, French Revolution style, its eyes gazing into the head-catching basket, but my executioner's blow would falter, my wrist and shoulder and elbow each cracking with a timid *I don't think so*. The blade would bounce, listlessly, off the neck of the condemned. Hence the still-tender four-inch scar just beneath my left thumb.

If I was ever so foolish as to attempt the hoisting of a bag of grain or seed, every bone, and joint, and muscle, and tendon, and nerve in my body would scream in unison, *Most certainly not!*

Things were getting complicated; even the line separating earth and sky had grown convoluted. A geometric jumble: the irregular triangular rooftops, the lonely cylindrical water towers, the repetitive, oddly sacrosanct steel pyramids that carry the city's humming power.

· · ·

FOR YEARS, real estate offices had sent me the occasional letter, the occasional offer for what little land I had left. I quickly became skilled at spotting these without the need of opening. I would simply rip them to pieces, then dump the pieces onto my heap of compost.

Years and years before, when I sold the majority of my family's farm (nearly one hundred acres) to fund my agrarian enterprises, as well as to pay the annual tax the United States government tolls upon a person for simply existing, the check I received contained so many zeros, I was certain someone had made a mistake. Of course, I wasn't about to set things straight. It was not as if I suddenly became wealthy, certainly not what you could call "prosperous," but—by a margin—it was enough. Assuming a clerk at the real estate office would someday check his records and recognize his error, I kept the money in an ancient tin box beneath my bed, just to be safe. When he would come to ask for it back, I would simply lie that I had already gambled away every last penny.

Years passed; I never opened the occasional letter. Ten acres, I would think. To the world it would be nothing, but to me it's everything. If for no other reason, I couldn't bear to look at the letters for fear that I would be shamed by the meager value at which the world appraised the poverty of my existence.

But my body had become ragged and useless. The food I had stockpiled and preserved was beginning to dwindle. Already, I had little more to eat than strawberry jam and pickled cabbage. Perhaps this was the death I deserved. A fading, not of will or effort but simply of means. For years, I would have believed that, if I stood before two doors, behind one of which was the world as it had become, behind the other of which was death, I would choose the latter without a breath of hesitation. But, when push came to shove, it turned out that I was still a human being. Or had at least that most human of qualities: in a panic, I clung fearfully to life, regardless of what sort of a life that might be. When the pangs of my stomach began, they rose as bubbles of dread through my esophagus and popped with a fearful muttering at the back of my throat.

"What will happen to me?"

There was only one way to survive, and I plucked it from where it had fallen through the mail slot. I sat for a long while at the kitchen table at which I had sat once, years before, falling in love with the way Mae ate beans. I stared at the sealed envelope and read the address of a corporation named Morningside Realties.

For minutes, I played Guess That Number. I thought, $8,000? $12,000? $3,000? I tried to calculate how long each of those figures might sustain me. For a time, I considered disposing of this letter as I had done with the rest. I even tried, in a brief fit, to rip the envelope in half, but again the decrepitude of my body had its own resolve.

I don't think so! my fingers snapped, hardly bending the rigid paper.

And so, instead, with the help of a rusted steak knife, I opened the thing.

Forced for years to bear undue burden, my body parts instantly rebelled. My liver puckered, my heart rose, my colon constricted, my elbows locked, all of my hairs wriggled in their follicles. My eyes, however, functioned. When they found the number printed within the letter, it seemed as if the page held so many zeros that they might roll off and go skidding across the floor.

I signed a paper and sent it back. More were sent. I signed more papers and sent them back. More were sent. I signed and signed. But I'm no sucker. I read each word, often consulting my 1954 edition of *Webster's* for the precise definitions of the terms.

The language was convoluted, but the gist was simple. In exchange for an amount of wealth I would never have imagined possible, I would forfeit everything, except my house and the land immediately surrounding it. Offers were made for that too, but I could only think, Impossible. Life in the world outside would be terminally unbearable. Going out into it will be bad enough, all those faces, everyone looking, staring, gaping. But at least when I come home I will return to an alternate universe that is mine alone.

But the true reason I would not part with the sagging, peeling remnants of my family's farm was simple: still, I was waiting for my daughter's return.

A LIFETIME AGO, in the weeks before my daughter's birth, my brother came home early, a month before the end of his three-year service, honorably discharged with a limp, a crooked nose, and the loss of one of his front teeth.

After his return, even the simplest tasks seemed to require more than he could muster. If Mae prepared something delicious, his favorite meal, a foot-size fillet of beef, Paul could not so much as lift a fork. Some days, after quickly plucking tomato after tomato, I would stand in the garden to find Paul gazing into an empty basket. Even with his daughter's birth imminent, even with Mae's head resting on his shoulder, Paul looked at the entirety of the world as if it had been blown from glass and he could see straight through. He rarely spoke of anything at all; for a long while, he told us nothing of his injuries or the true reason he left the service early. This is not, however, to say we didn't know the truth. Two weeks before his return, Gregor Dempsey, who lived in the derelict trailer just beyond the southern border of our property, stood in our doorway. In his tight, white fists, he displayed the headline, rendered in a font of heart-stopping boldness on the cover of *The Dallas Morning News:*

LOCAL SOLDIER KILLED IN W. GERMANY EXPLOSIVES ACCIDENT

My eyes sprinted across the first paragraph. When I saw the name of the deceased, my heart dropped to my liver, yet resumed beating. The dead soldier was Jamie Whitman. It had started out as a game, the article said. They had been teasing Jamie, flicking the pin of a hand grenade strapped to his belt, and when the joke went too far, they had only five and a half seconds to react.

Mae and I ran to the car, drove into town to the nearest pay phone. After an hour of transfers and eight dollars in nickels, Paul's voice crackled from across the ocean.

"I'm coming home," he said.

But after he returned, a word rarely slipped from my brother's lips. For months we never said a thing about it. We hardly ever spoke about anything, in fact. Mae and I had to assume his state indirectly, based on schedules and patterns, the way one predicts the coming of seasons. In this way, we tried to offer him food when it seemed he should be hungry, or tried to distract him with an evening at the cinema in town when a gloomy cloud of particular opacity seemed to descend upon the hidden atmosphere of his mind. Paul would neither resist nor comply with all of our efforts. He grew more obscure to us by the day.

I thought, What could it possibly be? I could watch cities burn, I could watch people boiled alive, but if I were Paul, if I were with Mae, I could find happiness.

Now that I know the truth, it is so obvious. The answers to the biggest mysteries of Paul, once so bewildering, are now so apparent that I can feel like nothing but an old fool.

As Mae prepared herself for delivery, for the insane possibilities and practicalities that come with the opening of new life, Paul appeared to brace for the opposite. Week after week passed before him like the inscrutable moments just before sleep. He would watch from a chair in the passive way of a dreamer, as if he had no bearing on the life before him or, rather, would knit his brow and squint his eyes at that life as if it were an internal experience arranged around the whimsy of his own wandering mind.

Only at night did Paul become lucid. Hours after Mae and I went to bed, the newly acquired scrape of his wounded shuffle would startle me from sleep. Before Paul's insomnia would become routine, before I would simply sigh, throw a pillow over my head, and attempt to return to sleep, I would creep halfway down the stairs, covertly peering at my brother through the ornamentation of the banister's spindling ribs.

In the place of what was now lost to him, the place just beyond his closed eyelids to which he forgot the way, Paul replaced sleep with a few solitary, frantic hours. Sometimes, he would climb from bed and take up a random task, perhaps digging a new trough near the barn, or painting the walls of the living room, or rearranging furniture in a thousand ways, before returning it all to the initial arrangement.

Most surprising, however, was my brother's primary nocturnal occupation. Though he was never much of a reader (at twenty-nine years of age, he still would fumble and pause when reading out loud), Paul would now spend the majority of his sleepless nights poring over the pages of our old books. For these hours, his eyes would widen and his head would tilt, like that of the RCA puppy before the gramophone. Paul would move his fingers down the pages hurriedly, would flip pages with such feverishness that sometimes, as he dozed late into the morning, I would lift a book resting on his knees to find dozens of loose pages, madly plucked from the binding. It was as if, each night, Paul just discovered what a book was. Or it was as if every page of every book held a piece of an equation that, once solved, would return him to life.

I cannot say why or when it was that Paul opened the long dormant pages of the hefty leather journal in which Mama had once written. Since Mama had died, the book had lain on its side on the top shelf in the living room, like a miniaturized tomb. Somehow, at some point, the memory of Mama and the book became entirely entwined, as if to rustle through its pages was somehow to disturb her final rest. Perhaps that was why Paul had to begin with all the books on the shelves below, serving a studious penitence, earning his way up to Mama's book, the reading of which was the point all along. At any rate, in the weeks before our daughter was born, Paul read only Mama's stories. I would come downstairs in the morning to find the book spread open on his lap, pages flapping in the breeze, or to find it dropped from his slumbering hands onto the balding planks of the floor, or to find it still under Paul's restless eyes, scanning its sable, blotchy lines next to a lamp whose flickering light had been recently overwhelmed by the dawning sun.

Somehow, eventually, Paul must have found some measure of peace. Or if not peace, a way to restfulness. Days before our daughter was born, Paul finally retired from his nocturnal enterprises. He went to bed and woke with the rest of us. At breakfast, he spoke with vehemence and certainty, his old familiar voice. A shock to discover it had not yet evaporated entirely.

"I have a name for our baby," Paul declared, clutching Mae's fingers in his fist.

"You remember Jamie, don't you?" The startling resolve suggested something more significant than the moment, more significant, even, than the naming of his child. As if he were explaining every vague, disengaged moment since his return, as if naming the impossibility of happiness.

"He died in the army. The same day as——" Paul gestured to his mouth, his leg, then opened wide both of his hands, signifying everything. "I want our baby to have his name. Boy or girl."

Carefully, exactingly, we nodded.

And so, my daughter was named by what was already lost. Appropriate, perhaps, because as my daughter grew inside Mae, so too had grown the impregnable barrier: between Mae and myself, between Paul and what he had lost in Bremerhaven, between the sad poverty of what actually occurred and the boundlessness of what might have been.

However. In the years that would come, in the manner of so many before us, Paul would find a way to remove that wall, stone by stone. That wall into which the stain of impossible love can seep, on which the stories of our family are written, through which the unbearable groan of faithless tenderness can creak. And eighteen years later, in the rubble of what would remain, I would find Paul's face, content, nearly beatific. And though the people from town would offer their condolences, and though the police officers would lower their heads and sigh, "Tragic, tragic," and though the shock of it all would be too much for my daughter, I would understand how he, unlike me, had simply found a way to walk through walls.

SOON AFTER I SIGNED AND SENT the final papers to Morningside Realties, a white truck, wires and ladders dangling from its flanks, parked right in front of the house. Skinny men in collared shirts emerged bearing strange instruments on tripods. For hours, they spoke to one another in loud, careless voices.

"Someone really still lives there?" I heard one say.

"Yeah, some hermit."

For a moment, I considered taking what was left of the grits I had for breakfast, spreading them over my face so that it looked like I had a horrific skin disease, perhaps leprosy, and charging out of the house, exaggerating my hump in the way that I have practiced, the way that makes me look monstrous.

"Some hermit!" I would scream. "Try hermit king, peons!"

Mae would have loved it.

But, instead, I did nothing. After all, the land no longer belonged to me. Within a month, they built a fence. On the other side of the fence, they began to lay the foundations for yet more of those mansions. (How could so many people live in mansions? Had the world become extremely wealthy as I lived in ancient history?)

As the henhouse and the pasture were scheduled for demolition, I sent my hens and my goat in for slaughter. It was now just my horse, Iona, that poor, skinny old beast, and myself. Her dilapidated barn and my sad old house. Little more than one acre.

When the news of my newly acquired wealth reached my bank account, I suddenly became the most popular man on Earth. Popular, at least, when it comes to bankers. Daily, a heap of offers would gather beneath the slot of my front door. Some letters proposed indecipherable schemes, written in language that might as well have been Cantonese. Words like *annuity*, and *liquidity*, in letters that I received so regularly I gave up on consulting *Webster's*.

Most of the envelopes, however, simply contained credit cards. Soon, in every color and design imaginable, countless credit cards arrived. I received so many credit cards that, if I had been planning ahead, I probably could have used them to shingle the roof. Instead, I destroyed all but one, chosen at random. I called the phone number affixed to this card, then slipped it into my pocket.

When I finally left home, the situation was already far beyond absurd. I was now spooning wheat germ from the bottom of a rapidly dwindling jar. Daily, my teeth dreamt of meat, my tongue of cheese. My anatomy threatened to crumple.

Many times I told myself I was being ridiculous. All that it would take to allow a vast improvement upon my condition would be a simple trip to the grocery. But now that I had the money to be a regular man of the world, all I needed was to summon the courage to match. I looked at the silver rectangle of my credit card. With my thumb, I felt my name embossed into the plastic. It was my passport to the world in the year 1998. As is the story of my life, my mind never consciously made the decision, my body simply began to take action on its behalf.

In the past, any trip away had been something I had to prepare for, sometimes by drinking a bit of the scotch I had made myself in a massive barrel in the cellar, but this time I emerged from my house in state of placid acceptance. Iona neighed and wheezed as I saddled her. It wouldn't be exaggeration to say that it had been more than twenty years since I had driven a car. I didn't have anyplace to go anyway, and even if I did, a horse saved on gas. Not untrue. But still, sometimes when I think of all the ways that I have rejected the whole of the Industrial Revolution as if it were only one man's opinion, of how I have dreamt of the nineteenth century like an old man reminiscing about a boyhood lover, I'm mortified.

And so, with a slight but pronounced pang of shame, I climbed on top of Iona and said, "I'm sorry. But it's either this or death. I, for one, always seem to want life."

Where there had been nothing but emptiness not long ago, there were now endless rows of mansions, nearly identical, differing only in shade, all capped in sloping black, all recessed from the street in fecund swaths. The houses themselves each appeared to wear a single, shared expression: the tirelessly recurring arched glass windows creating in each facade a wide-eyed, expectant face, each cheery and pretty in the same dull way.

As Iona's hooves began to clunk on the fresh, smooth cement, I got ready to see, among the new faces of the world, those I had spent years and years trying to stop seeing. The faces of Mae and Paul and Jamie everywhere.

Isidorans bury their dead in a great field far from where they live. They do this for a good reason: similar to the ways that Isidorans conduct one another's feelings through their hands, the earth that holds the dead Isidorans' bodies conducts the unique sensation of each death. This, in fact, is the only kind of memory the Isidorans know, each step across the cemetery filling them with the startling sensations of their ancestors' final moments, the corpses conducting their own epitaphs.

And so, you will know that you are almost to Isidora when you come to a sprawling field and you are suddenly seized by the sense that you're standing upon the threshold of eternity.

Even when Isidorans' bodies have dissolved into nothing, the earth remembers every death. Each step you take will reveal another. When you put down your right foot, you will be taken by the memory of a young Isidoran face, smiling down at you in your final moments, conducting your love with her hands. An instant later, as your left foot touches the ground, you will feel as if you're falling from a great cliff, wishing there was some word for "Noooo!" With another step, you'll suddenly realize that the white, spiky berries you just ate were terribly poisonous. Another still and you feel yourself gnashed in the jaws of an Isidoran beast that looks vaguely like an oversize warthog.

When a gust fills the meadow, flowers exhale their pollen, dead leaves go airborne, dandelions lose their heads, and for a moment the true history of Isidora is written in the wind.

Seth

My room had become a case study on the principles of entropy. Because I had trouble parting with just about anything, the floor had become impassable. If, say, an empty foam bowl from Raja's House of Curry struck me the right way, I would find a prominent place for it among my things. Everywhere was a collection of the evidence that I had continued to live as my mom's memory had continued to fail. Stacked in piles that reached nearly from floor to ceiling, resting in long rows beneath the desk, on the tops of shelves, clumped together in tremendous heaps, were all the books I had read, nearly every homework assignment I had completed, all my back issues of *Discover* and *Science News*, discarded tissues, socks that were torn, T-shirts that were stained the foul shades of sweat, receipts for almost every product I had purchased, taped to the original packaging, et cetera, et cetera. At night, when the lights were off, the darkened city of refuse towered above me. Though I might have feared that one night a chain reaction would begin, prompting all my worthless shit to come crashing down, suffocating me in my sleep, when I thought of throwing away a single thing, it seemed like an impossibly daunting task. As if an empty hamburger box weighed a thousand pounds and moving it to the trash would be enormously exhausting.

Sometimes, in the mornings, walking/climbing/army-rolling over my piles of crap, I would make my way to the bathroom mirror and stand naked before it. Or, maybe, if I'm being honest, *sometimes* is inaccurate. *Often* is more accurate. Often, and with bizarre contortions. Sometimes I would lurch forward so that the chub of my stomach folded in on itself and I would shake it about with an angry growl on my lips, wondering how far I would let my gut grow, how long it would be until even girls who might be attracted to me for my mind could no longer be attracted to me.

Other times, in a rapid, manic bob, I would hop up and down, watching the knobby dongle at the nexus of my legs wobble and vibrate like a miniaturized, tightly wound Slinky, and I would think that maybe, just once, I should have clicked through one of the thousands of e-mails I received on a daily basis for the creams and devices that spam mailers promised would help people with problems like mine. Puberty had been a while ago, but I was still hopeful that it hadn't run its course completely down below.

And also: I watched myself squint and pinch my face in a demented twist better suited to a comic book supervillain, which had the effect of making the ever-widening patch of acne between my eyebrows protrude even farther, redden even more deeply. I had once been able to conceal the flourish with two fingers, to try to make myself hopeful for the face that might remain when the craggy topography of my brow finally eroded, a square, angular face that could even be described as "attractive." But then it took all four fingers, and I started to wonder if maybe, like the Himalayas, my acne, in all its eye-catching drama, was still only growing. If only a hormone realignment device had existed that would have allowed me to rechannel the growth of my acne to a more beneficial kind of growth down you know where.

AT SCHOOL, I had become a Master of Nothingness.

By *Nothingness*, I mean this: I could find a place in a classroom that was perhaps not the farthest to the back but was simply the place where I was least likely to be noticed.

And also this: between classes, I memorized the way from room to room, and so, as the others passed me by, I only stared at my feet.

And also this: I was an expert in the delicate balance of maintaining/avoiding just the right amounts of eye contact with teachers to basically never get called on.

By the end of my freshman year, the other kids were mostly past calling me names, which was at least some sort of an improvement. In disappearing, as in the course work, I was a success.

But I learned that such success could also be a burden. So much had I become Nothing that, no matter how long I looked at Cara Crawford (with whom I'm still helplessly in love), no matter if I tried to speak to her, my Nothingness was complete and she looked right through me.

Though I might have mastered my own particular kind of Nothingness—subtle, slight, and mute among the masses, like an anyone or else like a no one—when it came to the power to disappear, I was far from alone. There were others, many others, who all attempted to pull off the feat in their own unique ways. There was Jenny Campo, who tried to camouflage her orange, freckled, pimpled face in a mass of overlong, unbrushed hair as red and frayed as stripped electrical wire. There was Ben Hoberman, who managed to escape extraordinary stretches of the school day in the toilet stall of the boys' room, where he would even eat his lunch. There were the Goths, who disappeared by becoming more visible, their purple eyelids and albino white face paint like flashing neon signs to look, to insult, to abuse in an oxymoronic effort to deflect, so that the faces behind might be spared. But when it came to disappearing, there was no one whose strategy was as radical or as insane as the Sloth.

The Sloth was the school's official name for Victoria Bennett, the moniker having been used, shamelessly and for years, right to her face, having been accidentally slipped from the lips of more than one teacher, having been long since immortalized in playground couplets ("Fatter than the refrigerator, dirtier than a moth / Look out, here comes Victoria Bennett, the gross and stinking Sloth!").

The name was fitting. Like those of a sloth, Victoria Bennett's movements were slouching and sluggish; one could measure them by the millimeter. Her hair was a long brown tangle that she appeared not so much to wash as to delouse with her fingernails. And her most remarkable slothlike trait, which was also her own particular means of disappearance: whenever possible, she avoided predators by disappearing into the trees. The trees were the Sloth's domain, her only companions. Before school, after school, during lunch, you could always find the Sloth straddling the limb of an elm or a juniper, eating a sandwich, or bobbing her head awkwardly to her Discman, or reading one of her weird novels with the purple and black dragons on the covers. Though kids would try to yell their insults up into the branches, would occasionally fling chewed gum, would invent crude guns from rubber bands and textbook spines, trying to hunt her like wild game, it took until the end of my freshman year for anyone actually to shake her from the trees.

Three weeks after my mom's fall, the Sloth had a fall of her own. That afternoon, Suzy Perkins hooted as three boys in muscle T-shirts, displaying varying insignia of the Abercrombie & Fitch corporation, spotted the Sloth, her legs dangling from a high branch of the massive live oak tree just behind the school. The boys began to throw everything they could get their hands on: pine cones, sticks, pencils, rocks. The Sloth hissed and howled, hypothetically to drive them away, but the fact that her squeals had a particularly apelike quality only delighted the boys, who escalated the onslaught of debris. To protect herself from the rising storm of stone and wood, the Sloth first crossed her arms over her face un-helpfully, pebbles striking her stomach, bruising her arms, and soon she began to wobble on her branch. The Sloth tried to resort to the natural defense of her kind, dexterity among the trees, bal-ancing upright on her branch, then leaping for a grasp on a higher limb that was protected behind a veil of leaves. But as she leapt, an acorn missile fired from below struck her right in her forehead and she stumbled. Despite all of her efforts, the Sloth was still a human, and in a frenzy her human instincts took over, her agility in the branches abandoned her, and with a gruesome landing that shat-tered her left femur, the Sloth learned that she was not made for the trees but, sadly, like the rest of us, was made only for the earth.

THE HUMAN MIND knows itself the least. The human mind may be able to trace the origin of life through billions of years to hy-drothermal vents in the ocean's floor, it may be able to compre-hend and replicate the means by which the sun produces energy, it may even be able to describe events that took place at the beginning of the universe, 13.7 billion years ago, but when it comes to exactly how we have made these discoveries, exactly how our thoughts are thought, we know a minuscule amount. And much of what little we do know we've learned indirectly and for the saddest of reasons, by the ways the mind malfunctions.

There are so many forms of neurological malfunction, each of them tragic and fascinating. There's the man known as H.M., the famous psychological case study who had his hippocampus re-moved in a surgery in 1953, losing all ability to make new memo-ries, yet keeping all of his memories before the surgery perfectly intact, his mind frozen in an endless present, now more than fifty years in the past. There's the turn-of-the-century Russian man known as S., who seemingly could never forget a thing. S. remem-bered every detail of every day he had lived. Researchers gave S.

hundreds of pages of random numbers, and S.—months later— could replicate these tables perfectly. But, oddly, S. couldn't find patterns in anything. If scientists gave him a document listing all the numbers from 1 to 100, S. could memorize it but had no idea of how one number related to the next. Life was endless random clutter, all falling toward S., never falling away. Later in life, drowning in data, S. could be found writing down endless pages of numbers and then setting them on fire, with the futile hope he could burn them from his mind. Listless and desperate, S. remembered everything. Theorists use S. as a datum to support the hypothesis that our success as a species is based as much, if not more, on our ability to forget than on our ability to remember.

But H.M. and S. are only two case studies; there are also neurological disorders, strange and illuminating, that have claimed thousands. There's Cotard's syndrome, which René Descartes could have mulled over for years, in which sufferers become convinced they don't exist. There's Fregoli delusion, in which sufferers are certain that all the people they see are actually the same person, wearing ingenious disguises. There are forms of coma in which sufferers are conscious and receptive yet totally unable to respond externally, their thoughts, desperate and unspeakable, thumping endlessly against the walls of their skulls, like being buried alive. There's adrenoleukodystrophy, which isn't entirely unlike early-onset Alzheimer's (except at an even younger age, five to ten), a genetic neurodegenerative disorder in which sufferers cannot form myelin sheathing around their brain cells, quickly resulting in the loss of the ability of one neuron to communicate with the next, all thoughts and gestures soon stopped dead in their tracks. Adrenoleukodystrophy was made famous by the movie *Lorenzo's Oil*, which tells the story of the parents of a boy diagnosed with the disease who dedicate themselves to challenging the medical and scientific establishments until they find a treatment, and eventually they do.

After my mom's diagnosis, in my own modest or immodest way, I was determined to do the same. I knew that my age, inexperience, and total lack of research knowledge might be against me, but I told myself that sometimes a fresh, uncynical perspective was exactly what was needed. And so, for weeks, I spent every free hour I had sitting in my secret lairs, reading every book of neuropathology I could find at the bookstore or at the library, casting webs of notes into the margins, waiting for that moment when, in a single blaze of awareness, all would be connected and I would go marching on the University of Texas Department of Neurology with my revolutionary discovery. Or, at any rate, I had to distract myself by thinking about *something*, so why not at least try?

Meanwhile, in the weeks after my mom's skull reossified, we put her in a place she never belonged.

"It's not an 'old people's home,' " Dr. Pinquit tried to correct me. "It's an assisted care facility. It only happens to be the case that the majority of patients who require such care are elderly."

By "majority," Dr. Pinquit actually meant everyone but my mom.

I tried to argue with my dad a million times for my mom's emancipation.

"I'll take a break from school and take care of her full-time," I would suggest.

With his voice always straining to the same grating falsetto, my dad would say, "This is hard for me too. You don't think this is hard? It's the worst thing in the world. But what else can we do? You know that Mother wants you to keep living your life. It's the only way."

Even though I would sometimes try to argue, and I never technically agreed, the shameful truth is that I didn't fight his decision as much as I could have. It was as if some part of me, terrified and shamed and unspeakably depressed by the mere sight of her in the weeks after her diagnosis, unconsciously agreed that it might, in fact, be easier just to put my mother away.

The place was technically called Willow Acres Assisted Care Facility, but I dubbed it "The Waiting Room."

Only once my dad asked, "The waiting room for what?" and I said, "You know what," and he never asked again.

There were countless things about The Waiting Room that are too terrible to name, but the worst was the policy that I'll never understand. Though our house was only minutes from that place, though I could practically have yelled my mom's name from our front yard and she could practically have heard me, they let me visit only in the middle of the day, from ten to three, which meant that, if I went to school every day, I could see her only on the weekends.

Nurse Jenny, a plump woman with cheeks the color of rash, explained to me too many times to count that any additional visitation would only confuse the patients. Or worse, could threaten the process of their acclimatization to life in The Waiting Room. "They need routine."

"Maybe what they need," I would counter, "is a life."

Over the course of the first two months after Mom's fall, all of my trips to The Waiting Room blurred together. Always the same smells of ammonia, urine, and the strong detergent used to cover the odors more awful and true, those of old men and women crapping themselves. Always the same blank linoleum hallways, as sunny and empty as the dementia-ridden, Haldol-pumped brains of the residents. Always their mindless gaping. Gaping at the enormous television screens everywhere. Gaping out windows. Gaping at the lime and ivory synthetic tiles of the floor. Always the loose skin of the old, skin hanging in ways skin was never meant to hang. Hanging in wobbling lobes from oversize ears. Hanging in sagging ridges from resting arms. Or hanging in jowls from the snarled, upturned faces of stroke victims.

And, of course, always my mom in her sad, small room, the one empty of nearly all traces of life. A sterile box with a single table, a single chair, a single bed, and the few mementos that I placed about, hopefully:

Pictures of her holding the baby version of me. Her wedding picture. The only picture we had of the child version of her, eight years old, and leaning against the trunk of a tree. My ninth-grade school picture, which was the only current image of me devoid of my acne-speckled forehead, because you could pay for the airbrush. Her favorite pen. Her favorite novel, *Jane Eyre*. Every A I had gotten on a test since she had been put in there, which had come to over seventy.

For her, however, *mementos* would not have been exactly the right word. For her, the right word would have been *objects*.

Six weeks after the fall, when I would sit in the chair of her room, watching her count cars out the window, I could no longer get her attention by calling her "Mom." As awkwardly as the word emerged from my mouth, I had to say, "Jamie."

In the beginning, I would waste my three hours trying to gauge how much worse she had gotten from the previous week. I even had a checklist, with questions such as

1. Does she remember my name?
2. Does she remember her fall?
3. Does she remember the diagnosis?
4. Does she realize she is in The Waiting Room and not a hotel?
5. Does she remember my dad is her husband?

For a while, I even made a graph, adding up her score, plotting a point for each visit and connecting it with a line to the last. Before she was put in The Waiting Room, the generated curve would have spiked in both directions: bad days, when her mind was as placid and murky as swamp water; good days, when I could have convinced myself that the only delusions were my own.

Soon, however, the curve adopted a strictly linear function, negative rise over positive run, and by the time summer started, the line never deviated significantly from the x-axis, the rubber band had begun to inflict grave harm upon my wrist, and I threw away the graph.

And so, during my visits, my mom was nearly incoherent. Her voice had a point to make, but the words were useless to the task.

She would say, "Out in the garden there's a thing that needs my approval. That woman might come soon and without me it's all blue. I think Daddy knows the secret about why it is that the woman might come. But I can't say anything. It's all just so insanely bloody this time of year isn't it? I'm afraid it might be broken before I can make it all the way downstairs."

Or sometimes she would simply say, again and again, "I need, I need, I need, I need."

Occasionally, I would try to clarify. I would ask a hundred questions to try to understand what fragment of a thought or memory she was trying to describe, but it only got worse, and so I would soon only nod my head and laugh when she laughed, sigh when she sighed, tear up when she started to cry.

ONCE, IN A STATE OF PANIC, I asked Dr. Pinquit to test me to see if I had the gene for the disease.

It's a simple test, a vial of blood, a few procedures of machines, and its results can change everything.

My dad asked, "Are you sure? Maybe you should wait till you're older to decide if you really want to know."

Maybe just to spite him, I insisted.

The nurse tried not to look me in the eyes as my vein dribbled into the little vial.

The blood was drawn, but when the nurse turned to take it to the lab, I grabbed it from her hand, the glass still warm from my body. I chucked it in the trash.

"Maybe later. Not now," I said.

"You don't want to know?"

"I don't know."

"Are you sure?" she asked.

I said, "No."

IF I HAD BEEN BORN TWENTY YEARS LATER, none of this would have been a problem. In 2002, four years after my mom's fall, four years after any of this, a team of scientists from the Reproductive Genetics Institute in Chicago, using a technique called preimplantation genetic diagnosis, drew two dozen unfertilized eggs from a woman with a variant of familial early-onset Alzheimer's disease and tested each for the gene. There was a 50 percent chance of the woman passing on the disease, and so the researchers located the eggs bearing the gene and simply threw them away. In a petri dish, the scientists fertilized one of the remaining eggs with the husband's sperm and reimplanted the embryo in the woman's uterus: a designer baby, the end of hundreds of years of a family curse.

While this may be good news for the future generations—the devastating gene simply selected against—it's probably terrible news for those still suffering from the disease. After all, why would scientists bother to waste time and money finding cures for a disease that won't even exist in fifty years? And so, for those who still have it, it could become like one of those disaster movies in which everyone knows the world is about to be destroyed but there's not a thing anyone can do about it. All order breaks down, desperation seeps in everywhere. The common wisdom would be just to accept what you can't change and enjoy what time is left. But, of course, easier said than done.

In the future, this is how more and more will be, the burdens of the past selected against, disease and ugliness and disabilities not actually cured but simply removed from the gene pool. Maybe in the future, when a child asks his mother where babies come from, she'll explain, "When a man and a woman fall in love and get married, they decide they want to have a baby. And so they go to a doctor who harvests the mommy's ovaries. Meanwhile, the daddy masturbates into a cup. The doctors could make lots of little babies, but the mommy and daddy throw them all away except for the one they want."

If I had been conceived twenty years later, I would have known there was absolutely no chance that I had inherited the disease. The dread wouldn't be the same, and I could stop living my life as if I might start losing my mind by the age of thirty-five. But how would I live then? I would still have had to watch my mom slide into oblivion, one memory at a time, but then I would have known that I would never follow in kind, losing my mind as she had lost hers, as those before her had lost theirs. As a part of a new breed of human, unstained by history, would there not be an odd if irrational kind of sadness to it: a parent's death as the end of her kind, the mother one thing, her descendants forever another?

AT LUNCH, as a benefit of being in the tenth grade, they let us go outside to eat. If I was careful and got the timing just right, just when Mrs. King, the lunch supervisor, was looking the other way, I could sneak off to the best Nothing spot at school, the four-foot trench carved by the little creek out back. And so, during lunch one day near the end of the school year, when I thought no one was looking, I grabbed my backpack, clutched it to my stomach, and made a break for it.

Once in the trench, I took off my shoes and let my toes dangle in the creek while I made notes in the margins of the "Memory" section of *The Human Brain: A Portrait*. After five minutes, I almost forgot that I was still at school, that I was still in hiding. But then I heard the sound of footsteps approaching, and since I assumed I had been found out, I clenched my eyes and tried to invent an excuse. But when I turned, I discovered it was only the Sloth, hobbling toward me on her crutches with remarkable, wholly unslothlike speed, her thigh-high neon pink cast swinging as dumb and dead as a mannequin's leg. Her crutches landed with a loud clang as she tossed them to the edge of the creek and lowered herself next to me.

Before she was hunted from the trees, the Sloth had almost invariably worn baggy denim overalls, but now the girth of her cast made all pants unwearable, and she resorted to skirts of incredible shortness, revealing the surprising shapeliness of her one good leg and the entirety of her cast's naked pinkness on the other. That day her skirt was a pleated purple, like the closed head of a pansy, constantly threatening to blossom.

"You big sneak," she scolded. "Did you really think no one would see you?"

"I just wanted to read," I said.

"Right." She laughed, the mess of her hair swaying, spreading the sweet and sour smell of her oils. "You probably needed to jerk off, huh?"

"Fuck you," I said, because that was what you were supposed to say.

I tried to read again, or at least pretended to read, as the Sloth settled herself, producing a black box of Minute Maid from her backpack. Her fluorescent limb lay like deadweight on the rocks. It was grayed with dirt but otherwise bare except for a single signature, her own, "Victoria Bennett," which she underlined twice, as if a silent reply to every pair of eyes that spotted her in a classroom, or glumly shuffling down the hall, and could only think, Sloth!

"What are you looking at?" the Sloth said.

"Oh nothing," I mumbled, fixing my eyes back on a crosscut diagram of the temporal lobe.

"You were trying to sneak a peek up my skirt, weren't you?"

"No," I said, my eyes stuck straight ahead. "I mean, your cast. I was looking at your cast, I guess."

"Oh," she said. "Do you want to sign it?"

The Sloth wedged her Minute Maid between her thighs, revealing three inches of skin above her cast, leaving little else to be revealed. She waved a Sharpie in front of my nose with a methodical flourish, like a magic wand from one of her fantasy novels.

I said, "Um."

The Sloth clutched my right hand in hers, pressing the marker's shaft into my palm. Surprisingly, her hands weren't like an animal's at all, not hard and calloused but soft and sweating.

I paused for a second, the marker's felt poised over the pink expanse. I knew that I shouldn't sign, that doing so was like putting my name on a petition to attest to the actual existence of an actual girl actually named Victoria Bennett. Maybe it was because I desperately avoid conflict with all people other than my dad, or maybe it was because the emptiness of her stupid cast made me sadder than it would seem like it could have; before I knew it I was spelling my name.

I capped the pen, handed it back to her without looking, tracing my left index finger across sentences in my book, again pretending to read.

"What are you reading about?" the Sloth asked.

"Nothing."

"C'mon. What is it? A novel?"

"No," I said.

"Then what?"

I sighed, then lifted my eyes, incredibly slowly and strenuously, as if I weren't so much raising them to her but being forced to pull her down to them.

"Brains," I said.

"Brains?"

"It is a book about brains."

"Well, what about them?"

"I'm trying to read."

"C'mon," she whined, grabbing my knee and shaking it in a way that made me jolt upright.

"Fine. I'm reading about the temporal region of the human brain. People think it is where God comes from. When scientists zap it with electricity, people see angels, God, dead relatives, all sorts of things." I turned back to the book, but her eyes prickled at my cheek, rendering me illiterate.

"What?" I said.

"Nothing."

"Then why are you staring at me?"

"Let me ask you a question," she said. "Have you ever even seen a vagina before?"

"What?"

"A vagina, heard of it?"

"God. You're a freak."

"I'm not a freak, you ass-munch."

"Right," I said.

"You want to see mine, don't you?"

"Huh?"

"Huh?" she imitated, dumbly.

"Um, no—" I started, but it was already too late.

It was so simple. She pulled the purple pleats of her miniskirt over her hips, revealing the thing. The thing gaping up at me like an open wound, mottled with miniaturized tangles of black. I pushed myself up with my palms, half standing, my head darting every which way, as if I were the one who had inflicted the wound, a fatal blow, as if I were a murderer searching for witnesses.

"Don't worry," she said with a laugh. "No one can see us."

"What the fuck are you doing?"

"Do you want to touch it?"

"What?"

"Do I have to say everything twice?"

"Please, just—"

The Sloth grabbed my hand. I swatted her away, started to stand, but then, for fear of being found out, didn't stand. She grabbed me again, this time firmly by the wrist.

"Don't think you're the first," she said and laughed again.

DISCLAIMER: Before I go any further, it is important to say something more about human sexual arousal. Specifically, a study conducted by Chivers et al. (2004), which involved heterosexual women watching lesbian pornography while devices attached to their genitals measured arousal, found that heterosexual women are basically just as aroused by watching lesbian sex as are lesbian women. The point being that the fact that you aren't normally attracted to a thing, the fact that you would normally choose to have nothing to do with it at all, doesn't mean you aren't helplessly aroused by it. Hence:

The Sloth guided the tips of my fingers into the wound, a damp, smooth place, viscous with fluid. The smell was like nothing else, or like everything else: dirt, fish, spit, sweat, yeast, roses, blood, to name a few. I started to shake uncontrollably and also, for some reason, to cry. I turned my face away but did not—I admit—pull my hand free. Everywhere, my blood pushed at my skin, vasodilating, engorging. Everything swelled. My tear ducts, my skin, the vas deferential plumbing of my cock. I only wanted everything to stop, I only wanted to escape, the Sloth to disappear back into the trees, the world to leave me alone, but it was already too late. Soon, my penis cried its cum, and a mushroom-scented splotch spread over the fly of my jeans.

"Gross," the Sloth hissed, curiously cocking her head in her animal way. "Did you jiz yourself?"

I didn't say anything.

"Can I see it?"

When I turned my face to hers, I had to bite my bottom lip to control its tremble. Tears dropped from my cheeks and plopped in the dirt.

"What is wrong with you?" I said.

"Sorry." The Sloth fumbled, pulling the bottom of her skirt back over her cast, looking genuinely sorry, genuinely human, genuinely *Homo sapiens,* in a way I would never have imagined possible.

"Sorry, sorry. Most boys like it. I'm sorry. I'm sorry."

"Just leave me alone," I cried.

For the rest of the semester, I went to great efforts to avoid the Sloth at all costs. Fortunately, her pink cast made her easy to spot. When I would catch a glimpse of it hobbling down the other side of the hall, I'd duck into the crowd. When I'd see it laid across a bench outside the school's front doors, I'd make a quick about-face and go out the back. When I would hear it scraping toward me as we settled into Mrs. Patterson's geometry class, I'd look sharply away and, if necessary, scowl. Thus, I earned the unique, pathetic distinction of being the Sloth's largest natural prey in the animal kingdom.

THAT WEEKEND, under the enormous trapezoidal skylights of the Westrock Public Library periodical room, I read the article on the EOA-23 variant cited in *Common Descent.* Written by Dr. Marvin Shellard et al. (Dr. Shellard, it turned out, lived in Austin; he was a professor at the University of Texas main campus), the article appeared in *Neuropathology Quarterly*, a thick blue volume with an image on the cover of an antique phrenology bust side by side with an fMRI printout.

For the most part, the study ("The Family Tree Is Sick: Genetic History of the EOA-23 Variant of Familial Early-Onset Alzheimer's") seemed to be a complex, statistical, jargonistic explanation of how the authors arrived at the central argument (that all living EOA-23 sufferers are descended from a single, remarkably recent source, twelve or thirteen generations back). The detail and esotericism of Shellard et al.'s article was sickening and awesome. It was like the first time my mom and I read Carl Sagan's *Cosmos*, or the time I was struck by my first undeniable pang of sexual desire (for *Full House*'s Jodie Sweetin), or the time Mrs. Greer, my old science teacher, had us look at a drop of rainwater under a microscope: the discovery that my daily world, fairly predictable and maybe even boring, turned out to take place on the skin of other worlds, a million times more complex, even incomprehensibly so.

I couldn't have hoped to decode fully the precise meaning of each sentence, but Shellard et al. seemed to describe how they drew their conclusions by constructing an extensive database from the "genetic histories" of EOA-23 sufferers in America and Canada. Though Shellard et al. never clearly defined the term, a genetic history appeared to be a combination of a person's DNA and his or her family's history of the disease. Apparently, by running all of these histories through their convoluted statistical equations, the authors could create a kind of backward chronology of the EOA-23 variant.

But the process was still incomplete. In the "Future Directions" section, Shellard et al. write: "The current study is ongoing and expanding. The authors continue to seek out and construct the genetic histories of newly diagnosed sufferers of EOA-23 variant. Hopefully, with sufficient data, an even fuller and more precise story will emerge of this particularly instructive variant's origin, dissemination, as well as its genotypic and phenotypic variety."

And the goal of this endless, meticulous exertion? According to Shellard et al., a vague but hopeful one, affixed as a single sentence to the final paragraph: "It is the authors' belief that an intimate and complete understanding of the EOA-23 variant's pathology and history will prove an integral part of the body of research that could someday lead to a cure."

I rested the journal on the table. Deep in thought, I soon began, as I sometimes do, to stare inadvertently at the person sitting closest to me. This person happened to be a woman, in her sixties or maybe even seventy, wearing a pink knit sweater vest, enthusiastically transcribing recipes from one of the library's cookbooks. Eventually, turning pages, she glanced at me and our eyes met; she smiled and winked. If a face can stutter, that's what mine did, ticking and jerking for an awkward second. I turned back to the dense text of *Neuropathology Quarterly* and had to let a minute pass before my mind could relax enough to return to the tasks of higher-level cognition.

Being honest with myself, which I knew was one of the central tenets of the scientific process, I had to admit that my research supposedly to come up with a cure for the disease could take years and years of work, maybe an entire career. Maybe I was only trying to justify my failure, but I told myself that oftentimes intensive studies of the smallest parts can inadvertently lead to the biggest discoveries. Alexander Fleming stumbled upon the curative powers of antibiotics accidentally as he was probing the minutiae of how staphylococcus bacteria function. The German physicist Wilhelm Röntgen was investigating different forms of radiation in his primitive cathode-ray tube when he noticed that it produced a slight glowing emission on his wall, despite having been obstructed by the various books and instruments in his office: the world's first documented X-ray. Scientists in a British laboratory of the Pfizer corporation labored for months to create a compound called sildenafil, supposedly to help with angina and high blood pressure, but when they tested it on a group of aging men, it ended up giving them the kinds of boners they hadn't known since their youth, and thus, the world had Viagra. I told myself that, if Shellard et al. needed my help, then I should do what I could. My first official research project would be to construct my mom's genetic history. I only needed to figure out where to begin.

In his final report, the furthest Marvin Shellard is able retrospectively to trace the genetic history of the EOA-23 variant of familial early-onset Alzheimer's is the variant's invention in eighteenth-century England. However, by making certain reasonable assumptions, one can speculate about EOA-23's origins in history far more distant. For example, one can assume, from fossil record and recent astronomical findings (Benítez, Maíz-Apellániz, and Cañelles, 2002), that the sufferers of EOA-23, like the rest of us, are descended from a great ($\times$ 10^5)-grandmother who likely lived somewhere in Africa, one of the world's first *Homo erectus*, born to prehuman, apelike parents. For it was precisely then, two million years ago, just as everything seemed to be going well, just as our primate predecessors had gained mastery over their niches and were steadily reproducing in dependable if predictable ways, that two stars, dangerously close to our solar system, happened to explode, turning into supernovae and spewing radiation. A single supernova would have been bad enough, would have produced a toxic shock wave from the heavens like a plume of industrial waste lapping to the shores of a great city, and a short but devastating age of cancer would have commenced. But the unlikely, almost statistically unthinkable concurrence of two stars spontaneously combusting at that precise moment ensured that hominid life on planet Earth would never be the same.

Life, the bored transcriber, had been plodding along on its insane, endless project, recapitulating the same old language through the generations, with only the occasional substitution, rearrangement, or error, as if just to make things interesting. For example, within the primates' DNA, a piece of code that used to read

CAGTACTGTACATGGGATACTTTA

might become

CAGTACTGTACATGGGATACTTTT

And a primate might grow a third nipple, or develop extraordinarily acute hearing, or lose the spaces between his toes. And that was about that.

But the supernovae, a pair of critical, unsparing editors, revised the primates' subcellular narrative with their own demands, bursts of radiation like red felt pens through the genetic code.

"To begin with," the supernovae decided, "the posture of these creatures is wholly unappealing. Make them stand up straight, for God's sake! And their hands are always just hanging around awkwardly. What if we gave them some tools to use?? I like the sex scenes, but I think they could be more involving. What about the idea of sex for pleasure??? Also, they seem to lack any real motivation. How about some higher-level reasoning? It might be more intriguing. Just an idea. While we're on the topic, all their stories are just one thing, then the next. They lack coherent narrative arc. Sophisticated memory is a must."

And, in a stroke of cruel genius: "No one seems to be trying hard enough to do anything. . . . What if we made them all chronically dissatisfied?"

As a final touch, perhaps with a dry, mordant wit, the supernovae made the first *Homo erectus* (and thus all of us who would follow) as denuded as an orangutan's butt.

ONE MILLION, nine hundred ninety-nine thousand, eight hundred twenty-six years later—in the year 1826—an entire town somewhere two or three hundred kilometers north of London seemed to have adopted a relatively significant revision to the relatively new invention of the human.

As the numerous progeny of Lord Alban Mapplethorpe reached middle age, a collective madness seized the town of Iddylwahl.

First, there was the madness of Mapplethorpe's children: twenty-six of the sixty showing the first symptoms of their father's genetic legacy by their mid-thirties, forgetting names, forgetting responsibilities, forgetting children, forgetting husbands and wives, forgetting to put on a stitch of clothing before leaving home. Then there was greater madness, the madness of the nonafflicted, left to remember everything and so to assume anything. Though the theories of the great naturalist Charles Darwin had yet to be written, Iddylwahlians certainly knew that specific traits—a father's hazel eyes, a mother's awkward nose—were passed from parent to child. It's likely that even as mass hysteria escalated in Iddylwahl, many of Mapplethorpe's now aged lovers guessed the simple truth, that their children had simply become heir to their father's strange disease of memory. But in the closing years of their lives, confronted with the specter of their sullied legacies, not a single one of Mapplethorpe's lovers said a thing. And so, in the absence of any obvious explanation, insane theories abounded.

As has often been the case in the history of madness, the madness of one had been thought to be the work of God, a cerebral Pentecost, but the madness of many could only have been the work of Satan himself. The minister, a strong proponent of the demonia-cal thesis, attempted both to comfort and to provide tangible legiti-macy to his sermons when he stood before his jittery flock and explained, in his calm, low voice, that Iddylwahl's cursed were cursed for a reason. That each had heard Satan's whispering voice in one form or another—perhaps tempting with a sin of the flesh, or offering a false idol—and when they had capitulated, they had opened a passage to their souls through which they let Satan enter. It was the minister's belief that the afflicted were now Satan's minions, carrying out his insidious work on Earth, and that others should avoid them at all cost or else invite the affliction upon themselves.

While the minister's explanation was the most widely accepted, two additional, less popular explanations were also discussed. One had been concocted by Marjorie Davenport, the obese spinster who devoted extraordinary amounts of time to her study of Pagan traditions. Marjorie held that certain wicked spirits, malevolent for no reason other than to offer themselves a diversion from bore-dom, had leapt into the minds of the afflicted for the sheer fun of it. The other theory, the one that most resembled a scientific explana-tion, was devised by the young Dr. Bennington, who ran the town surgery and prided himself on being a practitioner of the very most modern variety, a firm believer in the insane practices then associated therewith: burning gunpowder in the rooms of the sick; extreme, abusive douching to cure any number of feminine trou-bles; and, above all, bloodletting. Walking Iddylwahl's streets with a protective respiratory filter made of ground cloves and herbs, Dr. Bennington chided the superstitious, expounding his own the-ory that Iddylwahl's curse was not, in fact, a curse at all but a dis-ease. As their great nation had entered a new age, that of the mind, so too had come into being a new plague, that of the intellect.

Regardless of which explanation Iddylwahlians accepted, the means by which all theories speculated Iddylwahl's curse could be conquered was one and the same: the eradication of its human hosts. And so, plans were soon made for mass execution. Though there was hardly a family left unhaunted by the specter of tragedy, though many secretly prayed that their children or brothers or fathers or wives might be spared through some miracle, most Iddylwahlians tried to convince themselves of the truth of what the minister told them: that the Devil had the ears of the afflicted and that this bloody work was also that of the Lord. In the town square, a great platform was built in a circular shape so that as the cursed Iddylwahlians prepared themselves for eternity they might find comfort in one another's faces.

Mapplethorpe's one proper son, the new Duke of Iddylwahl, himself only two or three years from the first symptoms, was in charge of determining the names of the condemned. In the beginning it was easy, there were twenty or twenty-five of his illegitimate half brothers and sisters who could hardly recall their own names. But in subtler, less developed cases, the line between satanically possessed and nonsatanically possessed was vague. How much could one forget before you knew it was Satan's work? The duke, in an ironic fit of empiricism, resolved to determine the answer statistically, creating a memory test to be administered to all citizens of Iddylwahl, with the most poorly performing 20 percent to be excised from the population by way of the noose. In the weeks before the examination, families stayed awake for days on end, quizzing one another on every factual detail they could think of, knowing they could not allow themselves to forget a single name or date or place.

"How many varieties of cheese are available at Billington's Cheesery?" a man would ask his wife.

"Nineteen."

"Good. What was the name of your great-grandmother's sister on your father's father's side?"

"Edith."

"Good. In what year was the Iddylwahl library built?"

"Sixteen forty-five. No, 'forty-three. No! 'twenty-two."

"Fifteen ninety-four," the man would say, choking on the number. "You're dead."

When a woman's son or brother or sister could hardly recall what was served for dinner, she knew the best she could hope for was to spread factual lies around town, loudly, falsely practicing for the examination, reciting wrong answers, hoping the misinformation could fool others into the failing 20 percent.

Suffice it to say: the execution happened as planned. In the final moments, as the nooses were lowered around the hundred heads like one hundred upside-down, oversize ties, one of Mapplethorpe's lovers finally shouted out the truth. Watching her son's feet tremble on the stool that held him over eternity, she cried out, "He got it from his father! The Duke Mapplethorpe was my lover!" But the men of Iddylwahl knew she was just lying to save her son's life, and she was hanged a week later under charges of slander.

The execution, of course, failed in its purpose. Even as the surviving citizens of Iddylwahl watched their relatives hanged, the mutation repeated itself, countless times over, as the onlookers' cells cleaved and split. In the months after the hanging, it still seemed as if every day someone new would forget the name of his child or would wander Iddylwahl's few crooked streets, utterly lost.

Abandoning the theory of demonic possession, the town fell into a deep, depressive state of remorse and helplessness, knowing that the curse had come not to the weak, tempted few but to Iddylwahl in its entirety.

It didn't take long for the story of Iddylwahl's curse to spread through the British countryside, giving rise to yet more ridiculous superstitions and theories. Soon, for example, it was generally believed that to enter the walls of Iddylwahl was to submit yourself to its affliction. And then, in some frenzied leap of irrationality, it was believed that to speak Iddylwahl's name, or to look directly upon the town, or even to think of it at all was to invite Iddylwahl's pernicious curse into your own memories, where it would carry out its depredations.

As one traveled the road to Iddylwahl's south, which led from the Irish Sea to London, the town's rooftops could just be discerned out in the distance. When a child who knew nothing of Iddylwahl or its curse would point out the carriage and ask his father the name of the town, his father would panic as the word *Iddylwahl* leapt up, uncontrollably, from long suppressed memory. He would soon push thumb and forefinger into his clenched eyes as he would say, "There is no town."

"But—" the child would begin.

"You're seeing things."

"But it's right there."

"Maybe," the father would say, feigning a sigh, "we should look into getting you some spectacles."

Eventually, the people of the towns closest to Iddylwahl, terrified by Iddylwahl's persistence in both place and memory, petitioned King William IV to do something about it. The conversations that the king had regarding the town's fate often bordered on ridiculous.

"When are you finally going to take some action, sire?" an earl from a nearby manor would beg the king.

"Take action on what?" the king would ask.

"Beg your pardon, sire?" the earl would say, pretending to look quizzical.

"But you—" the king would begin. "Oh. Right."

King William IV, growing tired of the absurdity, eventually did take action. But as he could hardly find a single British soldier willing to enact the deportation orders that he signed, could hardly find a Brit willing even to discuss the matter, he was forced to contract a renegade militia of mercenaries, too cynical for superstitions.

It happened on an afternoon in June. By the time that night descended upon Iddylwahl, its buildings and streets were empty, the architecture of life still in place yet devoid of life itself: an immaculate metaphor for those still suffering Mapplethorpe's disease.

The mercenaries, unsurprisingly, were not experts at crowd control. They simply went from house to house, drawing bodies by the arm or the leg or the hair. If one put up too much fight, he or she was cut down, dead. The people of Iddylwahl were shoved into sealed carts, bound for the port of London, for a nameless ship, itself bound for a nameless place on the western coast of Australia.

At the port of London, however, all was chaos. The nameless ship's captain had heard of Iddylwahl, knew all about its curse, but would never have assumed that his new consignment of prisoners was, in fact, its citizens. However, in an insurrectionary fit, just as the mercenaries backed the carriages up to the loading plank, Dr. Bennington, outraged by the astonishing reach of human ignorance, was suddenly struck with an idea. Transforming his powerlessness to strength, jujitsu-style, the doctor began to scream, "I am from Iddylwahl! I am from Iddylwahl!"

His fellow Iddylwahlians, catching on, joined in a rousing chant of "Iddylwahl! Iddylwahl! Iddylwahl!"

The ship's captain, horror-struck by the discovery of his ship's true charge, ordered the helmsman to pull away. The Iddylwahlians, seizing the moment, leapt from the back of the open carts into the water below. While the mercenaries opened fire and managed to kill five or six Iddylwahlians before they swam out of range, most were able, amid the chaos, to secure their own freedom, scrambling back to shore and blending into London's masses or else climbing aboard neighboring vessels, bound for all corners of the earth. In this way, in a single afternoon, the EOA-23 variant of familial early-onset Alzheimer's was scattered across the civilized world like pollen in a strong breeze.

ONE OF THE PORT'S SHIPS, bearing the name *America Vestpoochy* (sloppily painted to its side by its semiliterate captain), took pity on two of the former citizens of Iddylwahl. The *America Vestpoochy* was filled with a third-class cargo of Europe's outcast ragamuffins, all fleeing one thing or the other, packed into the hold like sardines. Though some aboard the *America Vestpoochy* had witnessed Iddylwahl's insurrection, they either knew nothing of Iddylwahl or had seen enough misery to make them fearless of anything as intangible as curses and superstitions. With the camaraderie that is sometimes born of suffering, the men of the *America Vestpoochy* lowered ropes for the two escapees to grab hold of. The two were saved this way, pulled by the hands of poor Irish and Germans and Jews and Gypsies onto the deck of the creaking ship, bound for New York Harbor. These two, two of the first vectors of the disease's dissemination in North America, are referred to in Dr. Shellard's report only as A-474 and A-453, a young, strikingly beautiful widow and her five-year-old son. Their actual names: Millicent and Charles Haggard.

The first night aboard the *America Vestpoochy*, Millicent Haggard climbed down into the cabin, where human bodies slept like puppies, nestling into one another's folds. She found her son murmuring in his sleep, his face pressed between the wide, flopping breasts of a woman who smelled of olive oil and—also, like everyone else—rancid sweat. As Millicent settled herself next to him, the boy awoke.

"Shh," she said. "Try to sleep."

"I don't feel very good," the boy said, his skin a diaphanous white, revealing frightening blue undertones.

"It's just seasickness. Nothing to worry about. Now go back to sleep."

"I'm too scared to sleep," Charles whispered.

"But why would you be scared, my darling? You know I would never let anything bad happen to you."

"I want to go home," Charles said.

"But we're going to a place better than home."

"Where?"

"Well, we're going to America."

"What's better about America?"

"There is a place in America waiting for us," Millicent said, improvising a story for her son, as she occasionally did. "It is a city of gold, like El Dorado. When we arrive, we will have everything we need and there will never be any reason to be scared."

"Everything is gold?"

"Everything. Churches are made of gold. Houses are made of gold. Even the trees, the leaves. Every blade of grass is a little golden shaving."

"And that's where we're going?"

"That's where we're going."

Charles thumbed his chin, his eyes squinting with rational consideration, like a grown man twenty years older, surveying a prospective purchase of land.

After a time, he asked, "What is it called?"

A story Millicent hadn't thought of in years suddenly came back to her. It was the story her father would tell about why her mother had left when Millicent was still only a baby. Before Millicent knew better, before she learned that her mother was banished in disgrace, was one of Mapplethorpe's two lovers to be discovered by the duchess, Millicent had believed her father. Millicent's father, who wasn't actually her father, told her the story of a saint in the fourth century named Isidora, who banished herself to the desert rather than be honored by her family for her piety and virtue.

"She left out of humbleness," he told her. "Just like your mother."

"She left because she was *good*?" Millicent asked, struggling to comprehend.

"She left because the world could never be a place as good as she was."

And now, somewhere eight or nine hundred kilometers to the southeast of Iceland, the pitch and heave of waves dully tumbling the resigned human cargo back and forth, Millicent smiled at her son and told him, "It's called Isidora."

In the months that would follow, Charles would watch, through barely parted fingers, the maniacal electric insanity of three storms at sea. Despite every vow he would make to start acting as grown-up as his mother needed, he would begin to cry in the deafening crush of city crowds. On horseback and on train and in wagon and on foot, he would travel endless grass plains, as stupid and boring and lonesome as the surface of the ocean. All the while, Charles would imagine his future home, could practically see the tips of golden cupolas and church steeples at the perpetual edge of the horizon. When desperate or lonely or scared out of his skin, Charles would say the name out loud. He would say, "Isidora," again and again and again. Just as every cell of his body, dividing and dividing and dividing, would replicate the truth of Charles's genetic legacy, and also his destiny, in the strange lexicon of nucleic acid:

```
CAGATACAGATCTATATGTGAGTTGAGATGAGGACCGTTAT
CGTAGGCGAACGAGAGTCCAGATACAGATCTATATGTGAG
TTGAGATGAGGACCGTTATCCGTAGGCGAACGAGAGTCCA
GATACAGATCTATATGTGAGTTGAGATGAGGACCGTTATCC
GTAGGCGAACGAGAGTCCAGATACAGATCTATATGTGAGTT
GAGATGAGGACCGTTATCCGTAGGCGAACGAGAGTCCAGAT
```

ACAGATCTATATGTGAGTTGAGATGAGGACCGTTATCCGTA
GGCGAACGAGAGTCCAGATACAGATCTATATGTGAGTTGAGAT
GAGGACCGTTATCCGTAGGCGAACGAGAGTCCAGATACAGAT
CTATATGTGAGTTGAGATGAGGACCGTTATCCGTAGGCGAAC
GAGAGTCCAGATACAGATCTATATGTGAGTTGAGATGAGGAC
CGTTATCCGTAGGCGAACGAGAGTCCAGATACAGATCTATA
TGTGAGTTGAGATGAGGACCGTTATCCGTAGGCGAACGAGAG
TCCAGATACAGATCTATATGTGAGTTGAGATGAGGACCGTTAT
CCGTAGGCGAACGAGAGTCCAGATACAGATCTATATGTGAGT
TGAGATGAGGACCGTTATCCGTAGGCGAACGAGAGTCCAGA
TACAGATCTATATGTGAGTTGAGATGAGGACCGTTATCCGTAG
GCGAACGAGAGTCCAGATACAGATCTATATGTGAGTTGAGAT
GAGGACCGTTATCCGTAGGCGAACGAGAGTCCAGATACAGAT
CTATATGTGAGTTGAGATGAGGACCGTTATCCGTAGGCGAA
CGAGAGTCCAGATACAGATCTATATGTGAGTTGAGATGAGGAC
CGTTATCCGTAGGCGAACGAGAGTCCAGATACAGATCTATAT
GTGAGTTGAGATGAGGACCGTTATCCGTAGGCGAACGAGAGT
CCAGATACAGATCTATATGTGAGTTGAGATGAGGACCGTTATC
CGTAGGCGAACGAGAGTCCAGATACAGATCTATATGTGAGTT
GAGATGAGGACCGTTATCCGTAGGCGAACGAGAGTCCAGAT
ACAGATCTATATGTGAGTTGAGATGAGGACCGTTATCCGTAG
GCGAACGAGAGTCCAGATACAGATCTATATGTGAGTTGAGAT
GAGGACCGTTATCCGTAGGCGAACGAGAGTCCAGATACAGAT
CTATATGTGAGTTGAGATGAGGACCGTTATCCGTAGGCGAAC
GAGAGTCCAGATACAGATCTATATGTGAGTTGAGATGAGGAC
CGTTATCCGTAGGCGAACGAGAGTCCAGATACAGATCTATAT
GTGAGTTGAGATGAGGACCGTTATCCGTAGGCGAACGAGAG
TCCAGATACAGATCTATATGTGAGTTGAGATGAGGACCGTTAT
CCGTAGGCGAACGAGAGTCCAGATACAGATCTATATGTGAGT
TGAGATGAGGACCGTTATCGATACAGATCTATATGTGAGTTGA
GATGAGGACCGTTATCCGTAGGCGAACGAGAGTCCAGATACG
ATCTATATGTGAGAGAGTCCAGATACAGATCTATAT

Isidora has gone by many names. The Muslims called it Al-Khidr, the Christians called it Bethesda, the Jews called it Shehaqim, the Arawak tribe called it Bimini.

Isidora, the most popular and enduring of its names, was coined by the Italian explorer Pietro Martire Vadini. The story goes that, soon after the Italians landed upon the Caribbean Islands, a leader of the native Arawak tribe, named Sequene, fell in love with Vadini's wife, Isidora. Isidora returned Sequene's affections. Vadini, who chose to spend the great majority of his life in the company of men, was happy for Sequene and his wife, was happy to be freed from the bonds of marriage when the Arawak left camp all at once in the night, taking Isidora with them. Vadini's men, however, were enraged, stirred with ridiculous romantic visions of rescuing Helen of Troy. It wasn't like Vadini could just tell them to forget it.

When the Italians came upon the Arawak, they attacked. Sequene tried to hide Isidora beyond the battlefield, in a cave carved from a bluff. But Vadini's men were thorough and quickly found her. It still isn't known whether the Arawak or the Italians fired the arrow that passed straight through both of Isidora's temples, though each claimed it was the other.

Desperate and miserable, Sequene took what was left of his tribe and set north on an expedition, in the way that the feet can sometimes attempt to compensate for the heart.

When Sequene was never heard from again, many believed that he and his men had found "The Fountain of Youth," a legend that would grow, bringing countless explorers, of the likes of Ponce de León, to the Caribbean in search of it.

But the truth, as Vadini suspected, was that no such fountain existed. The truth was that Sequene and his men had vanished, instead, to another place, a place unhaunted by memory, a place where Isidora had been no one, or could be anyone.

And so, to this day, on this side of the passageways, Isidora is still called Isidora, if for no other reason than to have something to call it.

But still. Some say that Isidorans, in their primitive ways, have a name for their land, untranslatable into words. That each time two Isidorans touch each other on the chest, the true name of Isidora fills them both.

Abel

Spanning the rusted steel archway that stands tenuously over the entrance to this old place, the name HAGGARD, stenciled in cast iron, now sits in self-definition, rotting with age: the D bent in half along the vertical, forming an awkward v, the horizontal of the H snapped in two, creating a pair of disembodied lowercase T's, one of the G's gone altogether. Maybe that was the handiwork of the pack of boys that I see, from time to time, roving the streets with their fluorescent plastic rifles.

After I sold almost all of what remained of my family's farm, the endless mansions, once held at the periphery, quickly surrounded my house on all sides, the construction occurring all at once, as a single thought. The faceless walls of gray brick and Spanish stucco now cast long shadows across Iona's barn in the evening and eclipse the sunset view once available from my bedroom window.

Just days after the new homes were completed, a battalion of massive moving trucks hissed and rumbled up the street. What followed, for a brief time, was a series of amicable, if odd, visits from my new neighbors.

"This is just fantastic," said a Mrs. Stanasel, poking her head into the ruins of my house. "Neighbors to a real-life cowboy ranch. It's just so, I don't know, just so authentic!"

Perhaps, as the developers were unable to remove me from the last bit of my land, they chose a different tack, attempting to make me the local attraction, ringing the neighborhood with a thick, nostalgic wall of Austin stone, placing two steel-mesh sculptures of longhorns at the entranceway, labeling this particular partition of tar-roofed endlessness that has colonized High Plains "Mockingbird Ranch."

But authenticity, I suppose, is only so desirable. Not so desirable, for example, is the authenticity of the droppings Iona would leave on the immaculate concrete streets, or the authenticity of the smell interred by hundreds of years of animals that wafts off this place in the heat. Soon, the same neighbors who at first had enthused they were like "real-life pioneers" living alongside me, who at first had tried to lure me as a prime conversation piece for their Texas-themed parties (it was suggested I wear overalls), now stood before the old place, miniaturized dogs tethered to their hands, shaking their heads. Sometimes, when passing Iona's barn, some would emit a "Pee-yew!" loud enough to ensure it reached my ears. If I happened to be outside, tending to my last garden (a few modest rows of tomatoes and carrots and corn and rhubarb), and a small child would walk past with his mother, he would catch a glimpse of my varicose hump bulging at the confines of a tattered undershirt, then would dart behind her legs, sometimes in tears. Once, a posse of boys loitered beyond my gate for hours, cursing at competitive volumes, until I finally emerged from my front door. Suddenly, one of the boys leapt over the tangle of my ancient fence and made a break for me. For some reason, like a creature more primitive, I stood there immobilized, bracing myself, covering my face with my hands, waiting for the first blow. The boy, however, only tapped me lightly, once on the hump. Then, quickly pivoting, slipping a bit, he darted away as if I had just passed him a baton. The other boys cackled and swore. Through my living room window, I watched as the boy who had charged me was paid his dare money.

And then, one day, my immediate neighbors on both sides convened on my doorstep to inform me that, should I ever want to sell, they would be eager buyers. When I told them that I was an old man and that once I was gone they could do what they liked, one of them (the husband in the house to my right) attempted to inquire, in the nicest possible way, as to my best guess of when that might be. Incidentally, I find a perverse pleasure in the fact that, when the time comes, the expression "bought the farm" will be wholly inapplicable to me.

THINGS WEREN'T ALWAYS LIKE THIS. Sometimes, in the twilight dreams that fray both edges of sleep, I can turn to the window of the mansion beside me, with its bespectacled girl caught in perpetual silhouette before the glowing screen of her computer, and the darkness of her head expands, filling the room, blotting out the house, the neighborhood, returning only the moonlight to my window. If I'm able to master just the right balance of concentration and abstraction, I can then walk down the stairs without leaving my bed, the stairs not moaning as they have come to moan, the window transmitting clean, unsullied light, the sofa, the kitchen chairs, the pathways from front door to back not browned, not creaking plaintively from countless years subjected to the burden of my body. A fire sputters in the old Ben Franklin. A radio slurs Glenn Miller through the walls. Then I take my place next to my brother, sitting Indian style at the foot of Mama's rocker. She is lucid; we are just boys. One minute follows the next.

Nine months before Paul and I were born, Mama tells us, she had let herself think, for a single moment, "Why do I always got to question *everything*?"

Mama bends her elbows to her knees, stoops down, and declares, "But that thought, that wasn't me. I'm always one to question a thing over and over again, especially a thing of such repercussions. And that's all I got to say. That's it. Make sure your thoughts are your own."

Mama falls silent then, speaking again only with a clenching of fist, such a clenching required for Mama to conjure the memory of that man, Phillip Brooker, our huckster father, the hobo salesman to whose charm Mama offered a night's stay at our house and, by midnight, herself.

"That man." Mama shakes the tight knot of her fist over our faces. "That man had a way, didn't he? Simple as that, he had a way."

Once, when we were nine and Mama told us the story yet again, I asked, "But would you do it different if you could?" A gentler way of asking, "Do you wish we never existed?"

Mama only snorted. A terse, ironic half laugh, the kind of angry chortle that powered Mama through her daily drudgery, as if it were the exhaust from an internal engine that ran on pure sass.

"Course not," she sniggered. "That's the whole thing, ain't it? That such things as you boys could come out of the worst of regrets."

Beyond her admonitions, Mama would also tell us stories. Every night she would tell them. So often did she tell these stories that still—to my sixty-eighth year—each word has remained, interred within me. On certain warm nights, with the assistance of my home-brewed scotch and the drowsy limbs of the willow grazing the windowpanes, the memory is pellucid: Mama's lips parting, her mouth opening and then issuing forth story after story after story of an imagined land, the land of the golden kingdom, where not a thought can be found.

Isidora.

Her father, the grandfather I never met (who died in precisely the way that she too, like so many others, would one day die), told her the same stories she told me, as his father had told him, as had his father before him, as I would one day tell my daughter.

Who can say when it began? With a family such as mine, even conjecture is impossible.

What is known is that, over an untold number of generations since it was begun, the history of Isidora has deepened, filled out with tales of heroes and quests, of historical epochs, of wars, of love that was lost and love that was found, the endless story of Isidora running alongside ours.

When we were seven, Paul and I would plead with Mama to tell us the stories again and again, to the point that we had nearly memorized each syllable. Mama, in a fit, purchased a cushiony leather journal from Chapman's Pharmaceuticals in town. In a single week, she filled it with every story of Isidora she could remember. Sometimes thereafter she would still tell us the stories, but more often than not, when we asked she would only point to the book.

THE HAPPINESS OF OUR CHILDHOOD was a total ignorance to the millions of ways life could be different. We were only what we were. Twin brothers. One a handsome, exuberant dreamer. The other a taciturn, brooding cripple. When we were old enough, the days meant work on the farm. Tough, limb-numbing work: for years, Mama had eked out an existence by renting the fields to sharecroppers and filling the gaps with seamstress work, but as soon as our bodies grew into the ability to till, and seed, and pluck, and milk, we began to bring the farm of her childhood back to life. In modest ways at first, only enough vegetables and cows and hens as were needed to feed ourselves. But as our bodies grew, so did the acreage of our agricultural ambitions. If not for my hump and the arm it claimed, there would have been no stopping us. At night, when Paul and I were exhausted from our efforts, prostrate after meals of thick creams and meat, Mama would perch at the corners of our beds and tell us stories in the bedroom that my brother and I once shared. Our situation was as unique and unlikely as a single fingerprint; maybe I sensed the truth, but how could I have truly known that life beyond would complicate ours with a billion alternatives?

"Thing's gonna be different for you," Mama would try to warn me, her long, soft fingers stroking the place where my shoulder and spine meet with a crest. "I only wish you'd never have to find out what a cruel place the world can be."

"At least Paul and I have each other," I would try to comfort her.

But Mama wouldn't say anything, and all I could feel were her fingers rising and falling on my hump as she sighed.

IT TOOK ONLY MINUTES on my first day of school to grasp what Mama had tried to explain to me for over a year.

"What's wrong with you?" asked Marla Neuberger, whose head, incidentally, bore a shocking resemblance to a circumcised male organ.

"Nothing's wrong. It's just a birth defect," I said, trying to mimic the technical authority of Dr. Haywood, who came by the house for the occasional checkup or to offer a new correctional brace for my spine, all of which proved ineffective. "Congenital kyphosis."

"You look like a regular caveman," Marla said and laughed, and thus the sobriquet of my first three years of school, Ugh, the Caveman, was born.

When I would try to speak on the playground or in Mrs. Chastain's classroom, the other children would only grunt, would only scratch themselves in dumb, troglodytic gesticulations. And so, instead of attempting to speak or even to be a part of the class, soon I would rest a copy of *Great Expectations* or *Adventures of Huckleberry Finn* under my desk and read, flipping its pages with my feet as the other students sounded out sentences from the chalkboard. During recess, I would lower myself between the thin, red-brick belfries of that old schoolhouse, reading my way through all eight shelves of the school library. Thus, the only subject that school really had to teach me was the fine art of silence.

I may not have mastered much in all the years that followed. But silence, of that I am something of an artist, able to plumb its depths, to bend it, to project into its place whatever it is that I require. For example. Sixty-two years later, in the silent reprieves between my forays into the strange place that the world has become, I would often conjure Mae out of the silence, mold the silence into her form, and there she would be with me again.

To my delusion, I would mutter, "You should see this place now. The world. You should see what a person can now buy, just blocks away. Years ago, if you had a headache you would have thought aspirin the best you could hope for, wouldn't you? Now, you would be wrong. Endless shelves of medicine are now common, specific medicines for specific headaches. Is it a sinus headache or a migraine headache? Now, it makes a difference. Yesterday, I bought a product called Advil Cold and Sinus. You know how mutinous my sinuses can be? No longer. And the magazines. You would not believe what's on the covers. Not inside for men to contemplate in private, but right there on the cover. Last week, on the front of a *Cosmopolitan,* for even children to see, was a woman whose nipples peeked out from behind a wet T-shirt. Her fingers were sliding down her belly to you know where. And everywhere, Mae, there are computers. An average person, even a cashier at the grocery, now does little more than push buttons that make computers do the labor. Mae. You wouldn't believe it."

But how quickly even all of this became routine. Twice a week, I would climb onto Iona, who began to know the route to the grocery by heart.

By degrees, I became like anyone else. For no reasons in particular, there were specific types of products I would buy, such as Cracker Barrel Vermont Cheddar cheese and Cool Ranch Doritos. I would hand the metallic credit card to the people behind their computers, and I would ride back home.

I have come to believe that you could put me anywhere, into any place unlike anything I have known, and I could make monotony of it. You could place me in the Elysian fields, surround me with nothing but ambrosia, wine, and virgins who wanted to make love to me, and in not long I would wake in the morning, eat the same four ambrosia fruits, drink the same two skins of wine, make love to three virgins, and then spend the rest of my day thinking how things can never change, how vapid and how miserable life can be.

But the faces. Now, just going through my routines, the faces were there, in front of me, everywhere. And, as expected, they stared. I thought, Makes sense. After all, just look at me. Before the endless rows of modern cars, sleek and curvaceous contraptions that appear aerodynamically engineered for spaceflight, here I am, riding a tired old horse who can barely keep hair on her body. While people walk by with their clean faces, upright posture, and fresh clothing, here I am, a bearded, white-haired old Neanderthal, hobbling about with my hump in overalls that are as ancient as the world from which I come.

Though they only stared and stared, I did not consider altering my appearance. Because every time I glimpsed a person asking with her eyes, How could you be so inadequate? I would also glimpse Jamie, whose eyes, before she had left, had asked precisely that. And so, in a manner of speaking, I got to see Jamie everywhere.

When all the faces looked, I looked back. With a suck of my top lip, a squint of my eyes, and a cock of my head, I tried to make an expression that said, I know. I know. I'm sorry.

Typically, the people of Earth would return the look in sad, pitying ways that said, I'm sorry too.

Sometimes, when a child would point from the seat of a grocery cart and ask his mother why I looked so weird, I would tell myself, This is what I deserve. For the world to see how unfit I am.

But still, after months of this, I began to feel as if I was losing my sanity. Not in the total, consummate manner of others before me, but a considerable loss nonetheless. I had imagined my daughter's face everywhere, but the more time I spent in the world beyond the farm, the more I was starting to learn what *everywhere* actually meant. Jamie had left for New York City years and years before; I had no reason to believe that she was anywhere but there. And still, here in High Plains, her face only multiplied. Riding Iona, I would tread on the sides of busy streets, and great phalanxes of Jamies would rush past. I would close my eyes at night and every one of the characters in my dreams would be Jamie in a different form. Out of the corners of my eyes, I would catch a glimpse of a parking meter or a sapling tree and swear for a brief instant that it had Jamie's face. I wondered if someday soon going to the grocery would become impossible because all the people there, even children and old men like myself, would also be her. If I would become so insane that when I looked down into a bowl of soup and saw the face reflected back, it too would be hers.

RETURNED TO ACTIVE DUTY after all these years, Iona, valiant in her efforts, was nevertheless no longer the beast of burden she once had been. Now, she wheezed and bucked and more than occasionally defecated wildly under the strain. Once, on the ride home, Iona paused in the center of a nameless street in the land of endless mansions that stretches between the grocery and my house. At first I tried to coax her gently, whispering into the broken triangles of her ears, "Come, come, my friend." Still, Iona stood motionless, and so I squeezed my legs, even slapped her on the backside, even yawped a "hee-yaw." Iona, however, only gazed longingly to the endless pastures of startling green that unfurl before the rows of mansions. Disregarding my commands, Iona mounted the curb, trotted up to the faceless windows of a faceless house, and lay down in a bed of daisies. To get her to budge would take nearly half an hour and countless threats, I threatening Iona, the homeowners (a young couple, their faces pinched, as with constipation) threatening me.

And so, one afternoon, I found myself riding Iona to a place that I had spotted on a particularly adventurous expedition weeks before, a single shabby ranch house (at least thirty years old, practically antediluvian for the new High Plains), in front of which were parked four vehicles, three cars and a truck, their prices scrawled in soap across the windshields. Wadded into my sagging shirt pocket was most of what remained of the stash I had kept for years and years under my bed.

Months before, happily cultivating my own private antiquity, pretending as if the world beyond simply didn't exist, I would have gone to great efforts not only to ignore the idea of car ownership but to deny its overwhelming prevalence altogether. Set against my archaic ways, cars such as those parked in that balding yard would have been impossible. But now, as a hunchbacked caveman straddling a wheezing horse, I was the impossible one. If my mission had not been absolutely imperative, I would have been ashamed of myself.

Instead, I dismounted and walked to the gray front door, which still bore a desiccated Christmas wreath that April afternoon. Distorted through the stippled glass window came a man's short round form (vertical and horizontal measurements nearly identical). As the door swung open with a grunt, I was confronted with his face: a thick mustache (made of hair so black and curly as to be vaguely obscene) that failed to hide his wide, mocking smile. He asked if I needed help. I thought, Well, obviously.

"I need to buy a car."

"Well, well," the man said. "Sounds like you've got yourself a plan."

"I suppose you could call it that."

"What kind of car are you looking to buy?" he cooed, as if speaking to a lunatic.

"I'm not insane." And then to prove that I was at least a guest member of planet Earth, I produced my wad.

"I guess I will need something big enough to drive my horse home. The truck," I said, gesturing to the glistening mass of red paint and chrome.

"Your horse?"

I pointed. And just as I did, Iona took the opportunity to let loose a small but intense geyser of hot, steaming piss, blasting the gravel drive. The man clutched his knees to keep the laughter from toppling him.

"This . . . this . . . this is a first," he stammered.

To cover my shame, I narrowed my eyes and told him I meant business. With a second glance at my wad, he led the way.

Though it was a great strain to lungs, heart, joints, and muscle, I climbed into the truck's bed. I hopped about for a moment, as if testing the shocks. The man did not even try to conceal his grin.

Standing at that height, I could see down the enormous highway that hedged the western edge of the man's property. On the sides of the road, as far as I could see, were the pristine cubes and rectangles of new buildings. Everywhere were signs.

Because my heart started to pump too quickly, and I knew that at my age that was something you had to watch out for, I spoke to try to calm myself.

"I wish to buy this truck," I said.

I squinted. In the distance, the highway met with other roads in a chaotic jumble that looped and veered across great bridges suspended hundreds of feet into the air, one way leading to the next and also doubling back onto itself. Standing there, at that moment, I was struck by a memory, the image materializing before me. Or, rather, within me. My mother's eyes, her mouth, the sheets drawn across my body. She speaks:

If you want to look for Isidora, the best way to begin is to try asking around. Most will probably smile and nod when you say Isidora's name, and then they'll tell you all about it. A kingdom of gold, complete with golden steeples, golden bricks, golden soil sprouting golden trees. Some of the proud or the stubborn or the deluded will suggest a route. But, truth is, no one's really got the slightest clue of how to find Isidora.

If you want to look for Isidora, my advice won't be much of a help either, I'm afraid. You can go east or west or north or south, one way is just as likely as the other. Even if some have lived happy lives looking for Isidora, most have gone mad. If you can find a way never to look, to content yourself with life in this world, count yourself among the blessed.

But still, truth is, whether or not you look for Isidora, the idea of Isidora is unshakable. It's often been said that even the cynic, laying his practical old head on his pillow, can't help but see Isidora in his sleep, can't help but dream of Isidora beyond all reason.

Seth

School was out for the summer. It was June already, and everything started to sweat.

Just before the end of the semester, I heard that the Sloth's dad, a relentlessly successful software developer, semifamous for his eccentricity, had gotten a new job in Seattle. I was relieved and also jealous, as moving away is the single shared fantasy of Masters of Nothing everywhere. Also, when I thought about the endless redwood forests of the Pacific Northwest, with branches that form a canopy a hundred feet above the earth, out of range of even the most expertly thrown rock, I was happy for her.

In the first weeks of summer, when I left my house in the mornings, my backpack would be heavy with books about the human brain and enough food to last the day. I would go to any one of my secret lairs and read until it was dark. When I would return home, no matter how late, my dad would never ask where I had been. He would invariably ask only, "You eaten?"

Shamefully, though I now could have visited my mom seven days a week, I stuck to my routine, showing up only on Saturdays and Sundays. Whatever the reasons, when I considered visiting her, a certain dread (nearly identical to the paralysis that ensues following intensive contemplations of death) would fill me, and I would have to release a rubber band snap upon my wrist so severe that I would cry out.

BECAUSE IT QUICKLY BECAME EVIDENT that my dad would be use-less as an empirical resource in the construction of my mom's ge-netic history, I decided that my first step was to follow one of the few leads I had about my mom's past and find out more about Bethesda, TX, the tiny town in which she had spent her childhood. I thought that maybe I would look up the names of all the people who still live in Bethesda, find their phone numbers and addresses, and start asking around about my mom or my grandparents or even my great-grandparents. I read in *The Scientific Method* that often you have to open yourself to the possibility of a thousand dead ends, to the potential of tremendous wastes of time, in order to put yourself into a position to stumble upon a major discovery. And so, I was ready to call every resident of Bethesda, TX, on the off chance that one of them might know something.

I went online and did a general search for "Bethesda, TX." I found a few webpages of people named Bethesda who lived in Texas, but nothing relating to the town of Bethesda. Since my mom had only told me the name of the place and never spelled it for me, I tried every variation I could think of. Bethisda, Bethesdu, Bethesdah, et cetera. Still nothing. Eventually, I downloaded a de-tailed map of Texas and combed it for a name that rang a bell.

"There's no such place as Bethesda, Texas," I told my dad as I burst through the double doors of the den to find him sitting in the La-Z-Boy.

"Excuse me?"

"The place Mom said she's from. I don't think it exists."

"What?"

"I've done research. No such place as Bethesda," I explained.

"What do you mean 'no such place'?"

"As in it doesn't exist."

My dad sighed, then returned his attention to a ridiculous reenactment of Lewis shaking hands with Sacagawea on The History Channel.

I stood up straight, like a soldier called to formation. "Did she make it up?"

"What on earth? Come on."

"Explain it to me then. I searched online. I looked all over a map. Nothing."

My dad waved his hand in front of his nose, as if fanning away an offending fart. "You must have the spelling wrong or something. Why are you wasting your time on this anyway?"

"Spell it then."

"I don't know. B-E-T-H-E-S-D-A?"

"Nope. Not real."

"It is real. What do you think, your mom's a liar?"

"Explain it then."

"Christ," my dad said. "Who knows? She said it was a tiny place. A couple hundred people. Maybe they all just left. Or maybe it was so small that a bigger town incorporated it. Happens all the time with places like that."

I blushed at my own stupidity that this hadn't occurred to me before, at my shame at assuming right away that my mom had lied. Nevertheless, I tried to keep my combative tone.

"Well, have you ever seen it?" I asked.

"Of course not. Of course she never wanted to go back. It's like me with Houston. Please. Just give it a rest."

I parted my feet to the width of my shoulders, lowered my head, and braced myself, as if I were about to face a tsunami head-on.

"It's for the sake of science that I have to find out more," I declared, coldly, indignantly, dramatically, Too-Smartly, without explaining anything more about Shellard et al. and the construction of my mom's genetic history.

My dad made balloons out of his cheeks and exhaled for what could have been a minute. He gazed at the TV screen, on which a white man and a Native American man traded blankets and dead chickens.

Then, with surprising calm, he said, "The sake of science, huh? Well, for my sake, please. Give it a rest."

I, of course, did not.

WHEN I WAS LITTLE, my mom and I had a game no one else knew about. There weren't any rules, or winners, or necessary playing elements like boards or dice. In fact, all there was to the game were two words.

At night, after my mom would tell me a story, we would say "good night" to each other dozens of times. After each time one of us said it, the other would have to say it in return, because when it got to the point that no one was saying "good night" at all, that meant that day was really over, and as remarkable as it may seem now, that was once something we hated to admit.

My mom and I also had another game. While the first we could play only in my bed at night, this game we could play anywhere, anytime. Sometimes, when I would think my mom was being eccentric (or maybe something worse), I would suddenly realize that she was just playing the game.

The game was simple: one of us would start to pretend to be the other. It might not sound like much, but sometimes it seemed like more than a game, like we actually could almost become each other, sharing thoughts like the Isidorans. Once, as she sat on the corner of my bed, after we played the first game for close to ten minutes, to the point that a book of psychopathology would categorize it as *obsessive behavior,* we were silent. I knew she thought I was asleep, but I was awake, thinking about how I didn't want her to go to bed because then I would know that I was the only one awake in the whole house, maybe the whole neighborhood. Maybe the only one awake in the whole city, who knew?

Suddenly, into the darkness, my mom said, "I can't sleep because I'm worried about not being able to sleep."

I said, "Me too."

"The thing I hate the most is to be the only person awake when the whole world is asleep," she continued.

"Me too!" I said.

I was little and not yet good at the game, so she made it more obvious.

"When I grow up I want to be a famous scientist," she said.

!!!, I thought.

"You're me!" I said, so loud it could have woken my dad.

"Bingo," she said.

"Ohhh," I said.

And then, after a long time, my mom said, "Good night."

"Good night."

My mom said, "Good night."

I said, "Good night."

And because my mom didn't say anything for a long time, I said, "Good night."

And then I said, "Good night."

THE LAST TIME I visited my mom for a long while was the first Saturday in June. I went to see her alone, as was increasingly the case. Months before, after going to The Waiting Room for the first time, my dad promised that he and I would go together every Saturday and Sunday, for every second we were allowed. But, as was always the case with my dad, the promise faded. On that Saturday my dad was still off on a trip to a prison somewhere near Gary, Indiana, trying to peddle thousands of bagels whose major selling point was a shelf life of over nine years. Though I had learned from him how to store up such obvious failings to use in later fights, the truth was I liked going alone more. When my dad came with me, he would only lean against the window, obsessively consulting his watch. If he ever spoke, it was only to correct my mom's unending succession of inaccurate, fragmentary, and contradictory sentences. If, God forbid, I laughed at all with my mom, he would glare at me in the same way Mrs. Meeks, our fifth-grade teacher, used to glare when the boys would tease Thomas Dookin, who has Down syndrome.

Once, my dad did something so unforgivable I would never have wanted to bring it up again, even to use against him. The Waiting Room has no mirrors for a reason. But, once, my dad clutched his scalp when my mom settled into one of the most well-worn verbal grooves of her madness, prattling on, with undeterred insistence, about how her mother would be coming soon to take her home. In a fit, my dad pulled out the mini-mirror he carries in his wallet to groom himself before meetings with wardens and tossed it onto my mom's blanket.

He screeched, "Christ, Jamie, take a look at yourself! You're nearly forty years old. You're my wife, for Chrissake!"

I don't think I could ever imagine fully the horror: my mom looking into a mirror, expecting to see the teenage version of herself and instead finding the reflection of a woman more than twice that age.

THE SQUAT WHITE BUILDING shone like plastic. I was thirty minutes early for visitation time, but I wasn't about to let anyone stop me. I charged up to the front door, with its frosted windows and red enamel, a door obviously intended to be hinged to a structure far less industrial. I shoved it open, and the desk where I usually signed in was empty. I held my breath and practiced my mastery of Nothingness, watching my feet chase the reflections of the fluorescent tubes on the linoleum. Just as I reached my mom's room, I heard Nurse Jenny's voice call after me, but I pretended not to hear. For obvious reasons, the doors of those rooms have no locks, and so before I even said hi to my mom, I dragged the chair in front of the door and sat. Fortunately, Nurse Jenny did something extremely rare: she let the transgression slide. I was relieved not to have to put up a fight.

"Hello, dear!" my mom chimed so clearly it stirred a brief and helpless hope, of the kind that I would spend every minute leading up to the visits trying to reason away. "I hope you can stay awhile."

"Of course."

"This hotel can be so drab when I'm alone."

"I'll bet."

"I keep telling the woman that if we leave it out in the rain, everything might be lost."

"Uh-huh."

"They don't listen to a word I say, naturally, because you have to believe."

"I know, I know it."

"Right, well, at any rate. It's too late now. That's for sure. I only hope Mama isn't worried."

"Mama?" I asked.

The people from her childhood, who I knew next to nothing about, would often reappear this way, as unexplained characters from the pieces of a past life that increasingly made up the whole of her present. Soon after she was put in The Waiting Room, I had a perversely optimistic thought: that maybe if my mom forgot all the ways she had tried to make herself forget, she would be left with no choice but to remember.

I asked and asked, but it was like being an archaeologist of ancient civilizations, trying to piece together how people lived from a few stacks of broken rocks.

I would ask, "Who's Mama?"

But she would only say, "My mom."

"But tell me about her."

"She is my mother."

"But what is she like?"

"She's Mama."

"Yeah, but—"

"Shave and a haircut!" my mom would suddenly begin to sing, simultaneously rapping the tune with her knuckles on the beige drywall.

It occurred to me that maybe the past for my mom was like random data for S. But whereas S. failed to remove a single datum from his memories, my mom was on her way to succeeding beyond reason.

IN THE FIRST HOURS OF THAT AFTERNOON, nothing remarkable happened. My mom only babbled with the logic of a dream, one thing linked with the next by some unknowable, unconscious association. I only reacted as she expected me to; the content was impossible to decipher. It was what symphonies must be like for the deaf.

My mom's room, like the rest of The Waiting Room, felt warmer than could sustain mammalian life. I tried to open a window, but its latch was broken, slamming shut as soon as I let go, as if the building itself refused to let in a single breath of actual, unregulated, unfiltered oxygen.

Finally, Nurse Jenny knocked at the door in an aggressive, unforgiving rap. She threw it open, slapping it hard against the back of my chair.

"I'm sorry," she declared triumphantly. "Visiting hours are over."

My mom looked at Nurse Jenny with a furrowed brow and asked, "Is my dad here to pick me up?"

Nurse Jenny, without missing a beat, said, "I'm sure he'll be here soon."

She tapped her keys against the frame of the door, producing a noise as urgent and annoying as that of an antique stock ticker as she waited for me to stand. Before I did, I pressed my mom's hands between mine. "Your dad?"

My mom squinted, then craned her head out the window as if watching for her father to drive up.

"Oh, well," she sighed. "He's never on time."

I stood, her hands falling from mine. For just a fraction of a second, barely observable, my mom's face flinched with something resembling terror.

"What's wrong?" I asked.

She squinted again, her mouth slightly open, as if she were about to tell me something unspeakably important. Or maybe there was something, in the place severed away by the disease, that she was trying to say.

"Visiting hours are over," Jenny barked again.

I rose to follow her out of the room, but—suddenly—I was frozen by a sound I had not heard for at least ten weeks.

"Seth?" my mom said.

For a minute, I thought my amygdala, the part of my brain that processes emotions, had gotten overexcited and started making things up, but when I turned, she was gesturing for me.

"What is it?" I asked, stooping so close that the slightness of her breath whistled in my ears. My arms shook under the weight of my body as my palms pressed into the sheets.

"Can you find out when I can go home?"

"I'll try," I promised.

AND YET, it was already weeks into the summer, and even though I had sworn myself to the construction of my mom's genetic history, to the discovery of at least a fragment of the truth of where she had come from, or who her parents had been, I had let my investigation be thwarted at a single dead end. I didn't know anything: I couldn't even locate the name of her town, or her maiden name, or even the simplest facts about who she had been. For all I knew, my mom had been created out of the ether, which is the term astronomers use to describe the vast places of nothingness in the universe, which seemed fitting because right then it felt like Nothingness was the only thing I could ever master, and was exactly where my mom was going, and like there was no way that I could help her or understand her or save her or hold on to a single thing. Even to hold on to the most basic facts about who she had been or why she couldn't stay with us or why she had thrown herself off a balcony and almost died when I still needed her, and would have done anything and taken care of her and been with her for every second until the end, if only she had told me why, whatever the truth was, she couldn't trust me with it.

THE NEXT AFTERNOON, after I had been lying in bed for hours, the paint splatters of my ceiling exploded orange and red with the sunset, then melted to blue, then to gray, then to nothing. For hours, I had slowly plucked at the rubber band on my wrist, Chinese water torture style. When it was dark, I stood, left my room, and—drumroll please—walked all the way downstairs to the fridge. I picked at some General Tso's chicken that had possibly lingered at the back of the bottom shelf since the time of Tso's Qing Dynasty. I thought about the scalding lava burn of my dad's gin and pulled it from the freezer.

As per my dad's religious observance, I settled in the leather folds of the La-Z-Boy and balanced the gin on an armrest, sipping it medicinally. I didn't worry about him coming home from work and discovering me. It was still early for that, eight, and even if he did, he would probably be mad at me only for taking his chair. I flipped through the channels. I wanted to watch something explode. I settled, finally, on The History Channel, with a documentary about World War I that I had heard my dad watching approximately nine hundred times.

At first, I thought about nothing other than getting myself to swallow more gin. Each time a grenade landed or a man in a biplane, dressed as the Red Baron, dropped a missile from his leather-clad fist, I felt the pleasure of the explosion just behind my eyes. I turned up the volume, and the applause of a machine gun echoed all around the house. I saw lines of men, holding their faces with one hand and one another's shoulders with the other, wade through the murk of mustard-gassed air. Before long, my brain caught a whiff of drunkenness as my ear canals rang and trembled with the sounds of war. When they showed an aerial shot of Belgium, which looked like the apocalypse, I exhaled.

But then.

I saw a young man, in a helmet like an upside-down salad bowl, watch the horizon explode as he sucked on a cigarette. The documentary then cut to a shot of the same man who was, incredibly, still alive today. His face looked like it was made of oatmeal held in plastic Baggies. I don't remember his name. But I do remember what he said. Through the worn strings of his throat, with a voice little more than breath slightly shaped into words, he said, "All of us, what fought in the war, carried it with us the rest of our lives. It don't matter what kind of men we've become or what we've done with ourselves. Some part of all of us will always be standing there in the trenches, shoulder to shoulder. Faulkner says, 'The past ain't ever dead. Ain't even past.' I'm telling you, son, that's the truth."

I thought, Of course. What kind of an empirical investigator are you? You idiot. Of course.

I thought, The database!

It was so obvious that I actually slapped myself on the forehead.

The thought was this: if all people with my mom's strain of the disease were part of my enormous extended family, at most my twelfth or thirteenth cousins, then didn't that mean that at least some of them must be cousins of a much closer degree? And if Shellard et al. had a massive database of all North American cases, then wasn't it possible that the database could contain people as close as my mom's third or second or even first cousins? And wouldn't that mean that some of them could know something more about my mom's family, since they were part of that family too?

I charged into the study with such ferocity that each window of the French doors rang out a high, sharp note. The swivel chair, absorbing my velocity, skidded from the plastic mat onto the carpeting.

Online, I searched for " 'Marvin Shellard' AND Alzheimer's." Within a minute, the University of Texas Neurodegenerative Studies' astoundingly ugly website (rendered in the colors of bodily functions, pee yellow text atop puke green background) glowed before me. For a laboratory that I would later learn receives an annual endowment of over $750,000 to spend on technology alone, the website was astonishingly useless. Other than links to course descriptions, a vague, dull "statement of purpose," a bibliography of Dr. Shellard's work that spanned tens of pages, and a few fMRI images, there was only a single, intriguing link. Hidden at the page's bottom corner, in white, eight-point Arial font, was the single abbreviation "admin." I clicked.

A prompt window opened, asking for a password. I thought. The answer, of course, could have been anything. But it seemed possible that Dr. Shellard would choose a password that was relevant and therefore memorable. I plumbed the history of psychology and neuropathology for potential answers. I tried, without success: dendrite, Skinner, temporal, hippocampus, James, Freud, cerebrum, Broca, cerebellum, amyloid, memory, Alzheimer, Alzheimer's, ALZ, et cetera.

I'm not certain if any conclusions can be gleaned about the limits of Dr. Shellard's imagination or the extent of my own deductive powers, but I guessed the password within the hour, and I should have thought of it even more quickly. Or maybe I did think of it, but it initially seemed too simple to be possible. The password was "brain."

Within "admin." there were four files: two containing nothing other than smiling photographs of Dr. Shellard and his family on trips to Rome and Hawaii. The third was a time sheet for research assistants. The fourth held a long list of Microsoft Excel files. Most of the files began "Data for," as in "Data for ALZ chrom. study" or "Data for ALZ behav. pattern study." But then, when I scrolled down farther, there it was. The fact of its existence before me, that it was simply a file in a list of files that I could click and open, seemed simultaneously impossible and perfectly reasonable; my hand began to shake. As I guided the cursor to the file name "Database EOA-23 master list," my convulsing fingers traced a broken line across the screen identical to what a seismograph would produce after an earthquake that registered 9.0 on the Richter scale.

The document opened; the names of my distant relatives, forgotten and forgetting, were revealed to me. A list of addresses and phone numbers, a number of which (seventeen, I later counted) were within the Austin area. The title, written at the top in all caps, said:

CONTACT SHEET——EOA-23 VARIANT SUFFERERS——FOR LAB USE ONLY

My sympathetic nervous system suddenly lit up with the same terrifying thrill that it had once before, the time I accidentally walked into the girls' locker room at school; just as then, the con-

tradictory compulsions to look and to run away tugged me in opposite directions, effectively holding me in place, motionless. I almost started to read the database, then I almost closed the window,
and then I just closed my eyes. I tried to convince myself that, even
if I had to obtain it illegally, Shellard's database was crucial to my
investigation. I opened my eyes and let myself hit Print.

Hours later, when I was back in my room, the floor rumbled as
my dad's car pulled into the garage beneath. I counted the hours
until it would be daylight. My head hurt a little. I guessed it was a
hangover, which made me oddly proud in the way that all evidence
of oncoming adulthood then could. But nothing mattered except
for what I might have been just hours from discovering.

I had compared the database with the Capital Metro bus system's map and had decided—on the basis of no criteria other than
accessibility of public transportation—that I would start with
early-onset Alzheimer's Sufferer A-50, Conrad Hamner, who
lived in Pflugerville, just off I-35.

As I didn't want to risk the possibility of anyone checking with
Dr. Shellard for my credentials or my right to have access to the
list, I decided I would have to do what would normally be unthinkable for a Master of Nothing: I would have to simply show up,
unannounced and uninvited, at the doors of the EOA-23 sufferers
and not only speak to them but also persuade them to speak to me.

When the house was blue and gray just before dawn, I gathered
my courage, then tiptoed past my dad's recliner, in which he was
unconscious, his mouth huffing in great gasps, producing a sound
almost identical to that of the ventilator that had been attached to
my mom's mouth for days and days after her fall.

If you promise never to tell a soul, I'll tell you the secret of the gates of Isidora. Do you promise?

All right. To begin with, once you find yourself on the other side, in the land of Isidora, you'll walk and walk across an enormous field and eventually find yourself at the first gate. You probably won't think you've found what you were looking for. This first gate isn't much, only a low-lying tangle of warped iron, with a creaking door that can be opened with the slightest shove.

Beyond the first gate lies a wide meadow. After days of walking this meadow, you'll arrive at Isidora's second gate, a great brick wall, one hundred feet into the sky. If you look long enough, you'll eventually find a place where the wall can be climbed; a series of jutting stones seem to have been placed precisely so, just for this purpose.

Just beyond the second wall is a moat, churning and violent. No matter how long you circle the moat, you won't find a bridge. It's either swim or turn back. The good news is that most survive the swim.

Across the moat there is another meadow, and beyond it there is a cliff so tall you can never see to the top. There's no way to climb it. Instead you have to spelunk its caves and try to find an internal passage. There's no way of knowing just how many caves hold the bones of Isidora's countless pilgrims.

Even if you make it through, your heart will sink once you get to the other side. Still more walls lie before you, each *slightly taller than the last, looking from a distance like a staircase that you could climb, if only you could leap over the wide gap between walls in a single bound. But you can't, and so you'll have to learn the unique secret of each gate. While some can be passed through a simple door, most demand your creativity. To dig tunnels beneath, or to pick away a body-size shaft with a stone, or to master a series of locks that require a thousand tries and unreasonable, precise timing.*

Moving through gate after gate, you might start to despair. But here's the real secret that I'll tell only to you. The extraordinary few, destined for Isidora, will never let themselves feel hopeless, because the only way you can find Isidora is to be content with the gates themselves, to think of nothing beyond the next gate and remember nothing of the last, to live only for the riddle of the gate before you. Only when you've forgotten both your life before the gates and the hope of anything beyond them, only then will you find the walls all golden, and only then will you know you are in Isidora already.

Abel

Of course I had driven a car before, but never anything like the 1993 Dodge Ram six-wheel, V-8, extended-cab pickup truck that I now owned. However. Even with the car that I had once driven, years before, I had, in truth, little experience. It was a 1953 Oldsmobile that Paul drove home from Dallas. A clunky barge of a car: a rattling, wheezing, shining, beautiful blue thing with so much space inside that you could recline to full horizontal in its seats, a feature of which Mae and I made frequent and happy use for the years of Paul's military service.

Operating Paul's Oldsmobile had been a careful act of balance, like juggling. It required just the right movements of the stick, the right pumps of pedal, or else the engine would suddenly cease, with a great, mechanized gasp. I was never anything like an expert with it, but I could usually make the entire drive into town with only the occasional near-catastrophe.

Sitting in my newly purchased 1993 Dodge Ram six-wheel, V-8, extended-cab pickup truck, I discovered that a pedal was missing. I looked for it everywhere. I looked over the wheel, on top of the dashboard, I even felt for it under the seat. The man with the mustache stood outside my window with his stupid, disbelieving smile. I wanted nothing more than to find the pedal and leave that face behind.

"Anything wrong?" the man asked.

"The clutch?" I asked.

"It's—it's an automatic," he managed, through fits of laughter.

"Isn't everything now?" I asked, and then thought, You better hope I don't figure out how to drive this contraption.

Before I could lock the door, the man, biting his lower lip, which wouldn't stop trembling, hopped into the passenger seat.

"You've got two settings to worry about. Reverse and drive." He pointed to the letters *R* and *D* over the wheel. "And that's it."

I turned the keys in the ignition, and the engine sounded nothing like the clanging of Paul's Oldsmobile. This engine only hummed, one might say *ominously.*

"That's all you've got to worry about," the salesman repeated.

"That," I said. "And also how to get you out of my truck."

His cheeks, which had been two tight, red little balls, now drooped. He narrowed his eyes, told me he was just trying to help, and then climbed down from my truck.

I checked in the rearview and saw Iona's nose pushed against the glass that separated cab from bed. Getting her into the thing hadn't been easy. It had required six wooden planks, and the man's less than helpful assistance (his pushing abilities seriously diminished by hysterical laughter). The wide cataract cloud of Iona's eye stared wearily as I gripped the stick that projected from the steering wheel and pushed it into *D* with my fist.

"I know what I'm doing," I lied. "Don't worry."

As I pulled away, the salesman started flapping his arms, calling out to me with the question that I had feared since Iona and I had first trotted up. But, fortunately, this was the kind of man who collects the money first and settles details later. Which meant I was already the owner of my 1993 Dodge Ram six-wheel, V-8, extended-cab pickup truck, which was already in motion.

"Hey! Guy!" the salesman shouted. "You even got a license?"

I pushed the button that operated the window, stuck out my head, and yelled the truth.

"I haven't driven a car in twenty years! Of course not!"

On the drive home, I cursed at the traffic that honked past me. To all of those cars, I yelled at the windshield, "Believe me! This is as fast as you want me to go!"

The truck felt too easy to drive. Turning the wheel of Paul's Oldsmobile had been a muscular feat, getting it to accelerate had meant a great effort of the thigh. But everything about my new 1993 Dodge Ram six-wheel V-8, extended-cab pickup truck worked incredibly easily. With just the slightest motion, I could turn all the way in any direction. With the faintest pressure from my foot, I could gain enormous speed.

I decided that my 1993 Dodge Ram six-wheel, V-8, extended-cab pickup truck needed a name simpler than "My 1993 Dodge Ram six-wheel, V-8, extended-cab pickup truck." At first, I thought I would name it *Iona, The Sequel*. But because I didn't want to disrespect Iona, who was still my preferred means of transportation, and still a living creature and not a machine, I decided a better name would be *The Horseless Iona*.

In no time at all, I turned *The Horseless Iona* onto the balding gravel path that leads up to our old house. With the help of old crates, combined with the original Iona's enthusiastic relief, getting her out of the thing was a cinch.

I don't know what it was. Maybe it was the shining, lustrous newness of my truck set in contrast to the muted, decrepit state of my house. After I'd hurled my weight against the front door (as I must to enter), it was as if a thick, stinging haze of loss suddenly settled over my eyes. I could suddenly see everything in the house differently, for what it was. It was hardly a home at all. More like the shambles of what had once been a home. Some cabinets hung at awkward angles, others simply lay on the floor. The original blue plaid of the couch in the living room was unrecognizable now under years, lifetimes, of clay dirt. On the bookshelves were rows of the tattered things that I had read countless times. Even the beams of the ceiling, the ones for which my great-grandfather had famously sacrificed two massive oak trees out front, now bowed and, in many places, cracked. Each time I stepped, the boards moaned with the same sound. Straining my ears, I understood they were speaking my daughter's name.

JAMIE.

In the hospital, Mae couldn't even look me in the eye. But then I too could look only at the face of our daughter. Her delivery had come late, as if her peerless beauty had taken the extra time to accumulate.

Mae said, "Meet Jamie Haggard."

But, no. There was no word for it. Even to say "Beautiful" would have been to demean the truth.

FOR THE YEARS THAT FOLLOWED, our situation could have easily passed as normal: a father, a mother, a child, and a crippled uncle, kindly allowed to stay for obvious lack of alternatives. A normal family and a hunchback. But to me, the evidence of our lie was everywhere.

When Jamie was a baby in the arms of my brother, I would sit quietly in a corner, peeking from behind a book that I pretended to read as I contemplated the truth growing from her scalp, her hair the same feathery bronze as mine (at least before it had whitened with age). As I pretended to scribble words in the leather journal Paul had brought back for me from West Germany, I would tap my toe in time with the truth, Jamie humming as I too had always hummed. When Jamie cried, my tears—the kind that fall from the nostrils, not the eyes—would spill from her nose, the truth dribbling down her chin.

I would remind myself to show some restraint. I would think,

So much is she my daughter that if I say too much, hold her too much, try to explain to her too much of the world, the wall we have built between the truth and how we live will come tumbling down. If I start to act like a father, there will be no stopping me.

When aggrandizing, I reminded myself that this was my penitence for the unforgivable betrayal of my brother. When angry, I would blame Mae for her demented insistence upon this most colossal of falsehoods. When honest, I knew that both Mae and I were simply so fearful and ashamed of the truth as to agree upon this most fundamental lie, a lie we continually told to our daughter by our silence.

Many times I thought, If not for Mae, I'd tell everything. Often, I would lie in bed, whispering the truth into the void, just to feel the shape of its words in my mouth. I imagined it and imagined it and imagined it. So many times I came so close to simply saying it. The truth that could be said in a single sentence and could change everything. I never said a thing.

And so. For years, Uncle Hunchback waited, as he had waited before: mute, unmoving, observing the life that could not be his take place just beyond the pages of his books. But, as with Mae, watching without acting became a kind of madness.

AT DINNER ONE NIGHT when she was four, after I had spent a long, soggy day laying fence in the rain, Jamie made her little hands inky, fingering the pages of *The Dallas Morning News,* pointing to sentence after sentence, pestering Mae to read them aloud.

I recognized my opportunity and seized it.

"Maybe I should teach her to read," I offered.

"Perfect," Paul agreed. "Better you than us. Books have always been more your thing than ours."

Mae opened her mouth, but the objection would not pass. She only looked at me, the silent space behind her lips imploring.

In my mind, which was already made up, I thought, I'm sorry, but you of all people know that there are certain compulsions that are impossible for me to resist.

And thus began the happiest tradition of my sixty-eight years on this planet. Nearly every night, for years and years, Jamie would climb into my lap, or would pull her little chair next to mine, and together we would read.

On one unremarkable day when Jamie was seven, I decided it was time to tell my daughter the stories that had gone untold for over twenty years, the stories Mama had told us when we were children: the stories of Isidora.

Beneath her quilt, Mae's patchwork of fleurs-de-lis and demented ducklings, I tucked Jamie in in the way she would insist, pushing the blankets beneath her body with my fingertips, giving her the appearance of having been made into the bed, her short form lying embossed before me.

"Do you want to hear a story your grandma used to tell me?"

Jamie asked, "Is it real or make believe?"

"Real. But you have to promise that you'll go right to sleep when it's finished. Do you promise?"

Jamie nodded, and so I began.

"All right. Once upon a time, there was a girl about your age. She had always been a sad little girl. She lived on a farm with her evil parents, who made the girl do all the work while they lounged in rocking chairs, cackling and ordering her about. One morning, after the little girl had been up all night shucking her parents' corn, she came into the house for some breakfast, but her parents were gone. She ran back outside, but they weren't there either. In fact, no one ever saw her parents again. The truth of what happened to her parents is an awful thing, and you have to promise you won't get scared if I tell you. Promise?"

"I don't get scared," Jamie replied.

"Okay. The truth is that her parents had always wanted to take a trip to Hawaii. They had always been penny-pinchers and had more than enough to go, but they decided to save money anyway. Instead of buying plane tickets, they bought two boxes, wrote the address of the hotel in Honolulu on the tops, and tried to have themselves shipped. Only they'd gotten the zip code wrong. The water they had packed with themelves ran out after three days. The boxes just sat in a warehouse, where nobody could hear their screams. Months later, the boxes were marked 'return to sender.' And eventually they were returned, nothing more than two boxes of dust and bones."

Although she was trying not to flinch, a short, startled gasp nevertheless rose from my daughter.

"When the time came for their funeral, the groundskeeper dug two deep graves to bury the bones. The night before the service, the little girl, sad and lonely, walked to the graveyard and looked into the empty graves. She sat down, her legs hanging over the edge, and started to cry. Even though her parents had been cruel, now that she was an orphan, she was the loneliest girl in the world. And so she cried and cried. She cried so hard that she lost control of herself and fell into the grave. Now you might think she would have been scared. But not this little girl. She was so sad she didn't care if anyone found her. She didn't care if they buried her beneath her parents' bones. She lay down in the dirt.

"But then she realized it wasn't just dirt she was lying on. Just beneath the soft, red soil at the bottom of the grave was something hard. The girl stood, then jumped up and down. Whatever was beneath her must have been hollow, because as she jumped, it beat like a drum. The girl knelt down and cleared away the mud and discovered a door."

"A door?"

"A door. It was a tiny wooden door with a tiny crystal knob. And what do you think the girl did then?"

"She opened it?"

"She opened it. She turned the knob and pulled."

THE OLDER JAMIE BECAME, the more like a father I became. In the mornings, I would often walk her to school. Nearly every afternoon, I would wait out front for the bell. After we returned home, I would play along when she would hide in her "secret lair," just beneath the rusted iron doors to the basement outside, claiming to be invisible. I would stand above her and exclaim, "Now where could Jamie be! She's just disappeared!" From beneath the hatch, her stifled giggles echoed. On the weekends, she helped me with my labors around the farm, fascinated by my routine, cheerfully jostling on my lap as I watered the crops with the tank tractor, or helping haul the bucket in which I tossed freshly plucked corn, or emerging from the henhouse, displaying collected eggs like unearthed diamonds. At night, I helped her with her schoolwork, and if she needed no help, I taught her things far more interesting than what she learned in class. I taught her about how life came to exist from the elements of the universe. I taught her all about Darwin and the survival of the fittest. I taught her the true history of how people like us came to live in a place like Texas. I told her countless things, but what I never told her was the truth.

For all the ways that I was simply becoming what I simply was, Mae and I spoke of it only once. Perhaps we both knew that openly discussing our suppression of the truth would only acknowledge it more.

One night, after Jamie and I completed *Charlotte's Web*, Mae waited until Jamie was asleep, then took her place in the little folding chair next to my ancient plaid recliner. When I felt the heat of Mae's breath in my ear as she whispered, my heart sagged with the remembrance of everything that was now impossible. The truth was that, even as she became the primary (or at least the most insistent) author of our intolerable fiction, there was still so much of her with which I was helplessly in love. Even more in love as I witnessed Mae's features find new form in our daughter: the high crescents of her cheekbones, the persistence in her voice, the eyes that constantly, wearily scrutinized the life set before them.

"You've gotta stop acting like her daddy," Mae whispered.

"It is not acting," I said.

"Please."

I did not have to say that there was no way to stop. Mae sighed deeply, and her breath howled at my eardrum. She kissed the long crease the sun had pleated into the side of my cheek and made me swear that I would never tell.

"Of course not," I said.

Yet the truth is that I then thought, But then, lying to a person I love doesn't mean what it used to.

The little girl had discovered a hidden passageway to Isidora, had opened its door and fallen in. At first there was darkness, but soon it became light. For a while, there wasn't anything other than pure brightness, but she wasn't scared. The fall was as gentle as a slide, and so was the landing.

Now in another place, the girl stood. She looked around. In one direction was an endless field, in another was a gigantic city made entirely of gold. Golden castles and houses and roads and churches. But the little girl didn't care about gold anymore. She couldn't remember a single thing, not a single word, which meant that she couldn't even remember her sadness. As she had fallen, her memories hadn't fallen with her. Time in Isidora was immeasurable. It was a simple, endless now. And so the little girl smiled, then walked to the city that marks the center of the place which we call "Isidora," but which Isidorans don't call anything at all.

Seth

PROCEDURE

Before conducting my first deposition, I established the guidelines of my empirical modus operandi, for reasons both scientific and personal. As I understood that direct conversation with strangers (anathema to my daily, Nothing existence) was a necessary part of my procedure, I decided that if I could develop something like a routine, it would let me feel more like a machine reiterating its programming than an actual person, which meant that, even though I was going door to door, talking with complete strangers, I could hide behind my rehearsed pitch and, in that way, still be a Master of Nothing.

I rehearsed a script in my head and thought up the three primary tenets of my modus operandi, which were as follows:

1. All questions I ask will be for the sole purpose of data extraction.
2. As a good empiricist, I will keep all personal influence as removed from the deposition as possible.
3. Even if my digestive system goes nuclear and my skin feels like it will decompose off my face, I will continue the deposition until I have acquired all useful data, no matter how awkward its collection.

I don't know if it says something about my failure as an aspiring scientist or about the fundamentally untenable position of the so-called objective researcher, but despite my efforts, over the course of my investigation, my three tenets were about as reliable as a memory in my mom's head.

EARLY-ONSET ALZHEIMER'S SUFFERER A-50, my (possibly first, possibly thirteenth) cousin Conrad Hamner, came to the door disheveled. His face, his hands, his Texas Rangers T-shirt, and his carpenter jeans were all finely crusted in what looked like a light gray mud. He was a tall man, thin and stooped. His hair was a snarled, charcoal mess, and as he walked, a clump of it occasionally would stand upright for a split second, then fall back down, like a dog trying to keep his balance in the backseat of a moving car. Only his face, taut and red behind the smatterings of gray, gave away his age, which looked like it couldn't possibly have been more than forty or forty-five.

Conrad Hamner lived in one of the endless apartment complexes they built ten years ago, and all at once, alongside I-35. Mr. Hamner's complex was nothing more than two buildings, repeated over and over, all the way to the brick fences, as if the architect had OCD and would have covered the entire earth with his fixation if not for zoning laws. Within the complex (Willow Tree Residences, not to be confused with the nearby Willow Tree Plaza and Weeping Willow Homes), the only differences between one door and the next were the three pewter Lucida Sans digits screwed in just beneath the peepholes. When Mr. Hamner pulled open the door, I saw that, on the back of his hand, in a black felt marker, he had written the number on his door, 705.

"Hello, Mr. Hamner," I began. "My name is Seth Waller, and I got your address from Dr. Marvin Shellard. I don't mean to be a nuisance, but I have—"

"Wait, wait. Sorry to interrupt," Mr. Hamner said. "I know this must be an awkward question, but have we met before?"

At first, I thought that I was already on the precipice of a major breakthrough, that maybe Mr. Hamner was someone my mom had brought me to meet in the time I was too young to remember, that maybe he was some old relative we had visited before she decided never to think about the past again. And that maybe, somehow, he remembered me. And all this on my first try!

"I don't think so . . . ," I trailed.

"No, no, of course not then," he said, flapping his hands. "I'm sorry, I know it's awkward, but I have to ask everyone. I have this. Well . . ."

Mr. Hamner reached for a stack of papers leaning in a black plastic cubby nailed beside the door.

"Here," he said, handing me a single sheet, punctured on its left edge by a three-hole punch. He produced a ballpoint pen from his pocket and clicked it once. "I ask all my visitors to fill out one of these guys. I'm really sorry if this all seems strange to you."

The page that Mr. Hamner put in my hands had a short paragraph at the top, followed by a list of questions.

"Look at me," Mr. Hamner said, biting his lips with obvious embarrassment. "I'm so impolite. Please, please, come on in."

I carried the pen and paper into Mr. Hamner's living room, which wasn't like a living room at all, more like a workshop or an artist's studio. The carpeting was obscured beneath a thick, cloudy plastic, and the only furniture was a single table with two wooden chairs, lopsided and cracked. On the table was a pottery wheel, gray and slimy, holding a half-formed vase, its bottom a crude mass, its mouth puckering open. Everywhere, Mr. Hamner had stacked his completed vases and pots and bowls, and the room shone with their glaze. He gestured to me to sit near the wheel. The table was covered entirely with clay, as if the table itself was Mr. Hamner's most massive and bizarre creation. I found a spot that was smooth and dry enough to rest the page. Mr. Hamner watched carefully, scraping the clay from his hands onto his carpenter jeans as I read.

The page said:

HELLO. MY NAME IS CONRAD HAMNER. THANK YOU FOR VISITING ME. I KNOW THIS ALL SEEMS TERRIBLY RIDICULOUS AND FORMAL, BUT I ASK ALL MY FIRST-TIME VISITORS TO FILL OUT THE FOLLOWING QUESTIONNAIRE. IN JULY 1996, I WAS DIAGNOSED WITH A RARE GENETIC DISORDER. IT'S A NEUROLOGICAL DISORDER CALLED FAMILIAL EARLY-ONSET ALZHEIMER'S. IT AFFECTS MY MEMORY, SO PLEASE FORGIVE MY STRANGE COMMENTS, AND TAKE NO PERSONAL OFFENSE IF I FORGET WHO YOU ARE ALTOGETHER. AS CONVERSATION HAS BECOME INCREASINGLY DIFFICULT FOR ME, I MAKE A HABIT OF KEEPING THE ANSWERS TO THE FOLLOWING QUESTIONS IN FRONT OF ME AS WE TALK, SO THAT I MAY BE ABLE TO CONVERSE TO THE BEST OF MY ABILITIES. ALSO, SHOULD YOU DECIDE TO VISIT ME AGAIN, I WILL KEEP THIS DOCUMENT SO THAT NOT ALL RECORD OF OUR INTERACTION WILL HAVE FADED WITH MY MEMORY. IT'S A PLEASURE TO MEET YOU, AND I THANK YOU FOR YOUR UNDERSTANDING.

And then I answered the following questions:

NAME: *Seth Waller*
AGE: *15*
BRIEF PHYSICAL DESCRIPTION OF YOURSELF:

At first I considered the most obvious descriptors: Gawky, acned, bad posture, mumbler. But instead I wrote: Tall, brown hair, white, small birthmark on right cheek.

RELATIONSHIP TO ME: *Stranger*

JOB: *Student/empirical researcher*

REASON FOR VISITING ME: *To ask you questions about your family that will lead to a better understanding of how familial early-onset Alzheimer's is passed from one person to the next, with the hope of learning more about the disease to eventually find a cure.*

DO I OWE YOU MONEY? IF SO, PLEASE DESCRIBE HOW MUCH AND FOR WHAT: *No/nothing*

I handed Mr. Hamner the form, and he nodded as he read it over.

"So you already knew about my, uh," he said to the page.

"Yeah, I got your address from Dr. Shellard."

"Who?"

"Dr. Marvin Shellard. I think he's spoken with you?"

Mr. Hamner clenched his brow, causing a brief flurry of dried clay particles to snow from his forehead. "Hold on," he said.

From underneath his desk, he hefted a thick green binder, on the front of which he had written the word *Visitors*. The cover opened with a loud *flop*. Though Mr. Hamner's apartment was in sufficient disarray to assuage at least partially my guilt over the state of my own room, the binder's material was immaculately organized. There had to have been at least three hundred pages bound into its rings, neatly alphabetized with plastic tabs in every shade of every color of the rainbow.

Though I had determined that my modus operandi for my empirical depositions would be strictly professional, I couldn't help but say, "Wow. Looks like quite a system you've got."

Mr. Hamner looked up for a moment from the binder and smiled at me in a way that launched my body into the familiar itching frenzy that the direct gaze of a stranger invariably does, instantaneously turning every place where my skin folds into my

skin—my armpits, my elbows, my knees, my crotch—into a bubbling field of rash. Sometimes I wonder if there is a name for that,
an anaphylactic shock triggered by eye contact, or if my body has
invented an entirely new form of allergy. Maybe I'm a genetic
fluke, the first human being to be allergic to social interaction. At
any rate, when Mr. Hamner finally spoke, I started to calm and my
crevices began to cool.

"Yeah, I guess it's really something, huh? Sometimes, I pull it
out and just read through it like a novel. Like a novel, except that
I'm the main character and every day it seems almost entirely new
to me. I guess I'm lucky that way. Most people don't ever get to
read about their own lives with complete objectivity."

"I guess," I murmured.

Mr. Hamner grabbed a thick section of the binder between his
thumb and forefinger and then watched with a sigh as the pages
danced, one after the next, before his eyes.

"Only someday," he said, "I won't be able to read it at all. But
here I go, feeling sorry for myself, and I've completely forgotten
what I was looking for. How do you spell your name again?"

"No, no, not me," I said, pointing to the recently filled-out
page that lay on the table. "You were looking for someone else, but
it really doesn't matter."

Mr. Hamner dropped the pages and shrugged, then looked
back at me with a broken smile.

"Just ignore me," he said. "What can I help you with?"

"I came to ask you some questions about your condition," I
said in my best scientist voice. I produced a little spiral pad of
paper from my pocket and perched Mr. Hamner's pen over the first
blank page.

"Well then, by all means. Ask away."

"Most of the questions I have really concern your family more
than you in particular."

"Ah, well, then you might have the wrong man, I'm afraid. I don't have much of a family. I have a son. We don't talk, but it's my fault. He's a good man. Put me up in this place when I was diagnosed. But we haven't really said a word to each other since then. Or maybe we have. It's true that I might have forgotten. I should keep notes. His mother and I, we were never really more than friends, truthfully. Made mistakes on top of mistakes. Maybe that's one of the blessings of this thing I have. I've always been a silver lining kind of guy, maybe it's stupid. But at least someday, I'll forget what a mess I've made of my life. Anyway, don't really have much more than my pottery these days. Maybe it seems pathetic. A batty old man losing his mind with only the clay for company, but I—"

Beyond the venetian blinds, the sun shifted, and a hundred horizontal rays filled the apartment, wrapping around vases, bending across Mr. Hamner's nose, collecting in the blue and red glazed bowls, radiating their colors. For a moment, Mr. Hamner watched, transfixed. A small smile grew at the corners of his lips. His eyes hung as wide and receptive as a baby's: the immaculate, inviolable pleasure, freed from thought and meaning, of a world of bewildering, glowing surfaces. There was something unsettling but also familiar about it, like a déjà vu with inexplicably ominous undertones. It took me a second or two to realize that what his expression reminded me of was, of course, my mom. I thought about her then, what she must have been doing at that exact moment, making that exact expression, entranced by the infinite ways the life outside her window reflected the sun's light, thinking of nothing. Or, at least, definitely not thinking about me. Trying to distract myself, or maybe to focus, I looked back to my notepad, where I had written only "No immediate family to contact."

I was about to ask another question, about to say that what I was actually interested in was the medical history of his parents and grandparents and great-grandparents, but when he turned back to me, his eyes narrowed with a concentrated enthusiasm, and for some reason, he started to tell me a story.

"Stop me if I've told you about this before. I probably have. But there's this story I love, about Willem de Kooning. I think about it all the time. It goes like this. It starts when de Kooning was a young man, and he's a genius, undisputed. He made art like no one had seen. De Kooning made this art that was— It was fresh, and new, and different, and at the same time it all just seemed like the most natural thing in the world. These endless canvases, filled with abstractions. Beautiful. Just beautiful. You like de Kooning?"

"Um," I said, trying to come up with some sort of comment that wouldn't reveal that, when it came to art, my body of knowledge bordered on moronic.

"Doesn't matter. He wasn't for everyone. To me, the stuff was beautiful. At any rate, de Kooning gets to be a middle-aged man, and his stuff sorta, I don't know. It gets repetitive. He tries to put new things into it. Pictures, newspaper, things he finds around the house, but it all just sort of, well. Anyway. So de Kooning finally becomes an old man. His best work is long behind him, everybody pretty much thinks he's just this washed-up has-been. That he's tried to change with the world but nothing is close to as good as when he started out and was just, for lack of a better term, being himself. But then, a funny thing happens. When he's in his seventies, de Kooning starts forgetting things. His wife takes him to the doctor, and it's Alzheimer's. Well, now. De Kooning despairs, who wouldn't? They always say the same thing. Maybe seven or eight years left, but in five you won't even be able to talk. Desperate, terrible things. I can't tell you the horror of it. To know that you'll still be here but you won't. There aren't words for it. There's really nothing—"

For a moment, I thought that Mr. Hamner had forgotten his

story entirely. His eyes filled; across his cheek, a tear returned a vein of dry clay to life. Spreading from my own eyes, I could feel the flush of pretear warmth. Fortunately for both of us, Mr. Hamner remembered the story and continued.

"So de Kooning thinks it's all over. He and his wife start making the final plans. Painting's the furthest thing from his mind. He gets worse and worse, and for a while he just panics. Flounders. All of his ideas about art, society, life, everything. It's all going. Everything he's learned about art is vanishing, so you'd think he'd never be able to make another thing. But, turns out, it's just the opposite. It gets to a point where. It's hard to say what it is exactly. It's like everything de Kooning had learned, every way he had tried to be something he wasn't, it all just vanishes along with everything else. So de Kooning gets up one morning, walks to his easel, and just starts to paint. It's what his hands want to do. There's nothing more and nothing less to it than the reason he started in the first place. The compulsion to watch these colors and shapes and lines and strokes take shape in front of him. So he paints and paints. The people who see it can't believe it. It's not just that the paintings are as good as they were when he was young. The truth is that they're something else, something new. And the worse his disease gets, the less controlled, more spontaneous and fanciful the stuff becomes. De Kooning makes maybe the best work of his life. And the best part? Each day he gets up and sees his paintings from the day before, and of course, he doesn't remember a one of them. Doesn't really even know he's a painter. He just looks at his canvases and sees what, for him, was the most beautiful art in the world. And every time he looked at each one, it was for the first time."

Mr. Hamner pointed to the single poster on his wall, a swirl of bright red and blue emanating from a yellow disk, vaguely reminiscent of a computer-generated rendition of the Milky Way. Beneath the image, the poster said, "De Kooning: The Late Years."

I, of course, managed the lamest possible response to Mr. Hamner's story.

I said, "Wow."

"Yeah. Wow. Exactly," Mr. Hamner enthused, peering at the print for a satisfied moment, his face appreciative, almost transcendent. But then his expression fell, and he looked back at me.

"But de Kooning had a wife, someone to take care of the day-to-day stuff. Someone who could make his art possible. I'm not so lucky. There's a woman who comes by every now and then to help me out."

Mr. Hamner gazed for a long moment at the plaster ceiling, his eyes two concentrated slits, as he tried to conjure the name out of the oblivion.

"Cheryl. She comes by every now and then, but I know that someday soon they won't let me go on like this, and they'll put me away. I only hope they let me keep my clay and my wheel. I'm still in the early stages. The way I see it, I have my most inspired three, maybe four years ahead of me. I only hope they let me keep my things."

"I'm sure they will," I said, though I actually knew what places like The Waiting Room are like.

Mr. Hamner grinned, then looked again at the form I had filled out.

"So you know about my condition."

"That's why I'm here, to ask you questions."

"Really?" Mr. Hamner said, frowning and shrugging with a look of both skepticism and compliance. "Well then, by all means. Ask away."

"The questions I have left are really about your past."

"Good thing. The past is all I really can talk about these days. It's weird. They say I'm losing my memory. But all I really feel like I'm losing is the present. The past, my childhood, stories I love, my memory of things like that. Never been more clear. If I didn't look at myself in the mirror every day, I could probably convince myself I'm your age."

Something about this made my skin start to itch again, and so I said, "My next question is whether either of your parents had the disease."

"Yeah. Oh yeah. My mother, and her mother too. And my mother's mother's mother. Before that, who knows? That's half of what makes it so terrible. It's the real burden of my family, you know? Knowing what's coming. As my mom got worse, my dad couldn't take it. Not for long, anyway. So by the time I'm nineteen, I'm changing my mom's diapers."

I wrote:

MOTHER—YES
GRANDMOTHER—YES
GREAT-GRANDMOTHER—YES

And then I decided to just ask. To just ask if he knew anything relating to Isidora or Bethesda, the two words that were almost all I knew about my mom's life before New York.

"Huh. Nope. No. Can't say I know of any Bethesda, or what did you say it was? Isidora? Love the name, though. Is it in Texas?"

I wasn't sure how to answer the question, and so I only sat there in silence, watching the sunlight descend and then vanish across the face of my distant cousin.

Mr. Hamner, observing me, cocked his head and creased two parallel lines into the flesh over the bridge of his nose. After a time, his expression smoothed, his face as serene and aloof as if in a deep, dreamless nap. Because of my mom, I recognized this as the expression that accompanied the complete evaporation of everything just thought or said. After a time, Mr. Hamner lifted my question-naire from the table and read it once more.

"Seth Waller . . . so you came to ask me some questions. About my condition?"

Mr. Hamner smiled at me once, then palmed his chin with a quiet laugh as he rested his elbow into the soft clay before him.

"What are you?" he asked. "Some sort of science prodigy or something?"

"I don't know. No. I mean, yeah, I came to ask questions, but I think I have everything I need now."

Mr. Hamner didn't appear to be listening to me any longer; he was devoting himself instead to the observation of my face, which he scrutinized as meticulously and appreciatively as if it were a great work of modern art.

"It says here that we've never met each other, but I feel like I know you."

I smiled, then arched my eyebrows and gestured to the page in his hand. He handed it back to me. I lifted the pen, scratched out "Stranger," and instead wrote, "Long-lost cousin."

I handed the page back to Mr. Hamner and watched the aston-ishment leap into his face. Eyes wide, he said, "Really? That's ex-traordinary. This might be a terribly rude question, please forgive me. But have we met before?"

IN THE FIRST FIFTEEN YEARS OF MY LIFE, I only once attempted to ask a girl on a date. Where we would have gone, me with no car and no money, I can't say. It wasn't rational, I only asked. If she had said yes, who knows what I would have done? But, obviously, I had no reason to worry.

Cara Crawford not only was the most beautiful girl in my grade but also seemed the most sophisticated. Her nose was pierced with a stud the color of Neptune, and her hair was as short as a boy's (indicative, or so it seemed to me, of her membership in a vast, liberated counterculture I could only begin to fathom). Most of the girls from my class had incredibly wobbly, knobby, skinny bodies, as if they got drawn out on a torture rack every morning, but Cara had the body of someone much older, the body of a woman.

Cara and I had first-period English together freshman year. Once, in January, I found myself on a lucky streak, of the kind that I spent the majority of class periods daydreaming about. Three days in a row, Cara and I got to class before anyone else and had the whole room to ourselves. All three times, we talked about the book we were reading, *My Name Is Asher Lev*. Sometimes, it was hard to carry on a decent conversation; my interpretations of the importance of the symbol of the crucifix or of the role of Orthodox Judaism in contemporary culture were interrupted with the persistent realization that, if she was willing, we could simply lock the classroom door and have at it on Mrs. Muirhead's desk.

But. On the third day, just before the first bell of the morning rang, I asked Cara what she was doing that weekend, which wasn't exactly asking her for a date, but she got the gist.

She said, "Busy," then made a break for the water fountain.

That night, knowing how badly I had botched my time alone with her, I decided I had to give Cara something, maybe a note, something to explain myself. But what would I say? And how could it possibly help? I flipped through my collection of astronomy postcards and selected the most beautiful, a Hubble image of a star being born in a glowing, placental shroud of celestial gas. On the back of the card, I wrote my favorite Carl Sagan quote, which is, "We are a way for the Cosmos to know itself." The next day I slipped it into a ventilation slat of her locker.

But whatever the card's intended purpose, it obviously failed.

For the rest of the semester, I still arrived at school thirty, forty-five minutes early, but from then on Cara always came in right when the bell rang, flanked by friends.

Since the beginning of summer, I had thought of Cara many times, especially when I did you know what, but other than the fantasy version of her that invited me to shower with her sometimes several times a day, I hadn't seen her once.

The day after I conducted my first deposition, I decided to go over my notes in my tertiary lair, the one I had made with a plywood platform in the armpit of a live oak. Unnecessary, maybe, especially as Mr. Hamner hadn't told me anything particularly useful. Though doing so might have been needlessly forestalling the cause of empirical progress, with the bulk of the investigation laid out before me, I seemed to want it to last as long as possible.

As I made my way to the lair, I saw Cara walking up the sidewalk, laughing with three of her friends. My heart constricted.

Even I didn't know what I was doing. I only walked to her, and my mouth did all the work. It was like watching myself in a movie about a dweeb, a real loser, who everyone laughs at, except to me it wasn't funny but tragic. I stood directly in her path, and she stopped. Her friends sniggered probably, but I wasn't paying attention. If I hadn't just found the courage to engage Mr. Hamner, a complete stranger, in the longest conversation I had carried on in months, I definitely wouldn't have had the courage to utter a single word in Cara's direction. But right then it almost felt as if when I had spoken with Mr. Hamner I had discovered a different version of myself, a version that wasn't really me, more like a role that I could play of a seminormal person who is able to carry on a seminormal conversation, a role I believed—for a few halcyon hours—I might be able to don at will.

But this time, thirty seconds after I opened my mouth, my

courage vanished and I became only what I was: a twittering, stammering nothing.

"Hi."

"Hi."

"It's been a while," I said, then thought-screamed, *It's been a while?*

"Yeah."

"So how was it?"

"How was what?" Cara was looking everywhere but my face.

"You know, from when school got out until now."

"Oh. Fine."

"Good." I had to tuck my hands into my pockets because they appeared to have suddenly developed some temporary form of Parkinson's disease.

I can't say why, but I did it. I asked in a way that came out of my mouth rehearsed, a way that some part of my brain, the part that was doing the talking now, must have been planning for months and months.

"Listen," I said. "I was wondering if maybe you'd want to hang out sometime."

"Hang out?"

"Yeah, you know."

"Oh." Though I had rarely seen her look awkward, her lips now fumbled, as if she was trying to find a better word for "no."

"I think I'm busy," she finally said.

"Oh," I said, and then I heard her friends giggling, especially that bitch Suzy Perkins, and so I couldn't help saying, "I'm sorry."

"It's okay," Cara said.

"I'm sorry."

"It's fine."

"I'm sorry."

"I know."

And then, I don't know why exactly, I said, "My mom's sick."

Cara twirled the toe of her sneakers against the sidewalk and said, "I know she is."

I remembered then that when I came back to school for the first time after my mom's fall, Lori, the school secretary, had started to cry at the mere sight of me. From her purse, she'd extracted a pamphlet on which the words "Healing with Jesus" radiated like a halo from a particularly foppish-looking Christ. In Westrock, beneath one infrastructure, that of the immaculate asphalt, towering power lines, and strip malls, there is another, equally efficient infrastructure across which gossip moves at the speed of sound. Cara, like everyone else, knew everything.

I used to think the sadness of my life was as invisible as I was. I believed that I had made myself the Master of Nothingness, but it turned out I'd only been the Master of Freakishness all along. I snapped myself so hard that the rubber band broke.

WHEN I FINALLY CLIMBED into my bed that night, there was a smell, a rot really, and I sniffed myself to discover, much to my horror, that it came not just from my collection of useless shit, and not just from my gross sheets, but also from me. I thought, Jeez, I stink. I thought, What a disgusting freak! I karate-chopped my bed as I raged against what kind of a person I was letting myself become, collecting pieces of trash as if they were ancient artifacts, mastering freakishness, rarely showering.

And, worst of all, I had still made zero progress in the construction of my mom's genetic history.

The next day was a Saturday, but when I thought about making the trip to The Waiting Room, it felt as if I would have to walk a thousand miles in shoes of lead. And so, I didn't budge. Not that I did anything so important; I spent all three of the hours I would usually spend seeing my mom, agreeing with her insanity, just sitting around, imagining it. Imagining what she might be thinking at that moment, but of course there wasn't any way to know for sure. But this much I could deduce: she wouldn't even notice I hadn't shown up. It occurred to me we could never play the game of pretending to be each other again.

That night, in a fit of frustration, I found a sheet of paper and wrote in a manic, illegible script:

WHAT I HAVE TO DO WITH MY LIFE

1. Stop looking for answers that won't answer anything.
2. Stop spending all my time waiting around for something to change when nothing will.
3. Stop being in love with girls who are way out of my league.
4. Start acting like a normal human being.

THINGS WERE ONLY GETTING WORSE, and soon I started to behave drastically. My first mistake was to stand between my dad and The History Channel.

"I'm trying to watch this," he whined.

"You've seen this like seventeen times," I said, because even I had practically memorized the voice-overs.

"Still."

I almost didn't say anything more, but somehow I found the courage or the stupidity or whatever it might have been.

"Are you going to start dating other women soon or wait until Mom's actually dead?"

"Jesus Christ. What the hell are you—"

"It's a natural question. She wouldn't know the difference anyways."

"It is *not* natural!"

"Sex isn't natural?" I asked.

"I mean," my dad said, the way he always says "I mean" in arguments as if clarifying a point he has never actually made. "I mean. Show me a little respect."

"Is that a no?"

"Christ, Seth."

"Just curious."

"What are you really trying to ask me here?"

What I could not find the courage to say was what I thought, which was, Why don't you care about us at all?

I turned, my dad cranked up the volume, and a great number of explosions chased me up the stairs. In the muffled booms of war, I wrote a fifth thing that I urgently needed to do with my life:

5. Start getting over the way things aren't.

If everything that happened in the next weeks had never happened, who knows how long that might have taken?

The *America Vestpoochy*, carrying an almost perfectly representative statistical sampling of western Europe's genetic groups and subgroups (carrying also familial early-onset Alzheimer's Sufferers A-474 and A-453, Millicent and Charles Haggard), arrived at New York Harbor at dawn. The ship's captain, a drunkard who was known often to find his vessel coming to land at the wrong port, or at no port at all, heartened at the rare evidence of his competence: an amassing flotilla, then the tips of Lower Manhattan's steeples, then the wide stone face of the Battery, luminous with dawn. With a depth and magnitude that he could usually summon only after the fifth or sixth drink, the captain of the *America Vestpoochy* bellowed, "*Land, ho!*"

The ship's masses swarmed the deck. Charles Haggard, sprinting ahead of his mother, got lost in the crush, and though he tried to leap up for a glimpse, an impenetrable wall of coats and hats and hair and skin stood too far above him. Eventually, a smiling Pole spotted Charles squirming and dodging and pushing his way forward, and kindly hoisted the boy onto his shoulders. In an instant, the promised city of gold rose before Charles. In the dawn light, gold houses clustered together on the waterfront, gold carriages alighted on golden roads, gold plumes billowed from gold chimneys, molten gold lapped at the golden fortifications. Though no one could hear the

THE STORY OF FORGETTING 167

boy amid the clamor of cheers, Charles whispered the only word for the sight that shone before him.

He whispered, "Isidora."

Inevitably, however, the sun rose, and by the time the *America Vestpoochy* docked at the harbor, Charles had watched his city of gold vanish before his eyes. It's hard to imagine that the simple ascent of the sun has ever disappointed anyone more.

Charles was too embarrassed to mention his misperception to anyone, even to his mother. As the two made their way to the immigration office of the city that was not golden, that was made only of dirty grays and pale blues, Charles glumly clutched his mom's hand and watched his feet step over rotten apple cores, dead pigeons, the feces of dogs and also of people.

After waiting in a sweltering, endless line in the Castle Clinton to get the proper papers in order, Charles and his mother waited in yet another interminable line outside the Catholic church for a free meal of thin stew and crusted rolls, which they ate—with the rest—wherever they could find an unclaimed spot on the steps out front. And as they ate, a small regimen of fast-talking men in moth-eaten knickers and shabby top hats canvassed the crowd, passing out inky woodcut prints of idyllic pastoral landscapes with names like "Missouri," and "Indiana," and "Texas" printed at the top. It was unclear exactly where the profit lay for these men, who would talk off your ear about the superiority of eastern Ohio or southern Mississippi or northern Texas above all others. In Iddylwahl, Millicent, the daughter of a hopeless, banished romantic, had prided herself on her own pragmatism. And, indeed, here in New York, Millicent could see through these men as plainly as one could see the hairy specks of their legs through the holes of their trousers. They were nothing more than predatory hucksters, Millicent knew this. These were men who spent idle hours dreaming up ways to exploit even the penniless. But she was in New York

City now, an unimaginable place to stay and try to make a life, and she didn't know a soul. And so, when a weary-eyed Englishman, no more than twenty, who looked perhaps slightly more honest than the rest, handed her a print of a city called St. Louis, shining like the sun (THE JEWEL OF THE WEST! proclaimed the flyer), where—according to the young man—"free land is just waiting for your claim!" Millicent knew that she was letting herself be duped, that she was letting the man take advantage of her natural disadvantage. But sometimes a delusion, a dream of a false place, is exactly what's needed for the sake of momentum, if not for the sake of hope alone.

"How would one get to St. Louis?" Millicent asked.

The man led Millicent and Charles through the grimy snarl of city streets, extolling the virtues of eastern Missouri, telling Millicent again and again of his jealousy, of his plans to go there himself one day.

The train station was a massive, sooty enclosure, the air toxic with gases of coal and steam, like a single, oversize lung of a chain-smoker. The man waited with Millicent and Charles for hours, crowds rushing past, cramming themselves into trains, flinging themselves out of trains, the trains themselves whistling, trembling, galloping into the distance like spooked horses. At some point in the midafternoon, a behemoth of cast iron and rotting wood pulled into the station and the man told Millicent that it was time. With the aggressive impatience of a local, he pushed their way through the crowd to the wooden door of a cab near the caboose, inside of which was a mess of hay and body-size lumber frames, the vaguest acknowledgments of the train's human cargo. A rotund man with a face of protruding brown birthmarks (or were they warts?) stood by the door in a felt cap and flashed a smile at Millicent and Charles's escort. The two men turned to Millicent.

"Now," the young man said, his eyes flickering. "There's the issue of payment."

"But I told you I haven't any—"

The man, who had mentally appraised Millicent's single piece of jewelry (a ring inherited from her father) even before he had approached her, now lifted Millicent's hand to his face, as if he might kiss it, but instead plucked the ring with a pickpocket's dexterity. The man produced two one-dollar bills from his coat pocket, handed them to the clerk, wished Millicent and her son all the luck in the world, and disappeared into the crowd.

In ways, the train was worse than the *America Vestpoochy*. There wasn't the seasickness to worry about, but the car was even more crowded than the ship's cabin. Lying down, one had to struggle to touch the floor's wooden planks. Realistically, one could only try to balance oneself on the arms and legs of a hundred other aspiring pioneers. The train often crawled forward at a slug's pace, or would inexplicably stop altogether, for hours. Also, there were the obvious sanitary concerns, which were alleviated only by the paucity of food and water allowed the passengers. An abiding, unrelenting nausea seized Millicent for the trip's duration, not only from the squalor but also from the shadow of guilt cast by the loss of her father's ring.

Suffering these conditions, Charles and Millicent kept their sanity by taking turns describing a million imagined details of Isidora. "What about the city's walls? Are they made with gold bricks?" Charles would ask. "Of course," his mother would reply. "And the mortar is made of platinum!" "And the food. Is it all sweets, or will they also have breads and meats?" Charles would ask. "They have whatever it is you want," Millicent would say. "You need only think of a thing, and it's yours to be had." Some of the train's other passengers would often smile at Millicent's descriptions and then add one of two of their own, in the way complete strangers are sometimes quick to attest to the existence of Santa Claus in the presence of a dubious child. In this way, an amiable if desperate community developed in Millicent's overstuffed car. But still, all told, it was eight days of pure misery.

And then there was St. Louis. Not shining as THE JEWEL OF THE WEST! but steaming, fuming, smelling in a way hardly better than New York. And in St. Louis, just steps off the train, it seemed as if the jabbering flock of snake oil salesmen had followed them, greeting the weary, sniffling, conjunctivitis-ridden lot with more pamphlets, more of their romanticized, lying woodcuts. Feeling unbearably foolish, every bit the naïve, exploitable immigrant these men seemed to expect her to be, Millicent nevertheless showed the flyer of St. Louis she had carried with her from New York, inquiring as to where, exactly, one might find the promised unclaimed land. Most hardly heard her question. Most would simply throw themselves into their own pitches, extolling the virtues of the Pacific Northwest, or of building a career in St. Louis's booming textile business, or of investing in California gold speculation. One man, a land peddler up from Texas named Benjamin Dempsey, took one look at the flyer and then proceeded, in his thick Irish brogue, to break into hysterics.

"This here should be in a museum, it should!" he hooted. "Same frolickin' paper they gave me in eighteen fifteen!"

Millicent grabbed the flyer from Dempsey's hands. She was not angry exactly—she had known what she was getting herself into—but the expression of anger somehow made her feel less powerless. She sighed and asked Dempsey exactly where then in God's creation might some decent land be had.

Dempsey bared his teeth, nodded, and a single word rolled from his tongue:

"Texas."

"Texas?" Millicent asked.

"Have myself thousands and thousands of acres, I do. Take you to it myself. Hardly cost you a penny."

"But I haven't anything at all," Millicent said, which was plainly true. Dempsey frowned but then nodded. He leaned in, copping a feel of Millicent's breasts on his swollen belly, then told her that he didn't know about England, but here in America there were other forms of currency.

Millicent took a step back to evaluate Dempsey. He wore the same Swiss cheese pants as the other men but without bothering to adorn himself with the gaudy pseudorefinement of his urban counterparts. Millicent took this as a sign: if not of honesty then at least of Dempsey's practicality. She closed her eyes for a moment, considering. She understood that what Dempsey seemed to be suggesting might be only a hairsbreadth from plain and simple whoredom, but unlike the others among the fast-talking lot, baiting and baiting for a chance to make the inevitable, unspeakable switch, at least Dempsey proposed an arrangement with knowable costs and benefits: his land for her body. What else was there to do? Maybe she was allowing her vulnerability to get the best of her, but Millicent sighed and nodded.

The ride to Texas in Dempsey's wagon had its own horrors. The first night, by a campfire, Dempsey began to collect payment, in no way trying to conceal the transaction from Charles's horrified eyes. Charles watched as the man appeared to inflict grave harm on his mother. He even tried, wailing and grabbing with all his five-year-old's strength, to pull the two apart. Dempsey, feeling the boy's hands tugging the hair of his backside, laughed and told him to wait in the wagon.

"Do what the man says," Millicent told him.

When Dempsey was satisfied, Millicent crept away to her son but could not coax him to pull his hands from his eyes. Tears trickled down Charles's wrists.

"Shh," Millicent said. "I'm all right."

"I want to go home," Charles sobbed.

"Shh. Soon, we'll be somewhere better than home."

"Where?"

"Isidora, of course."

"I don't want gold! I want to go home!"

"Ah," said Millicent. "But you forget. Gold is the least of its treasures."

Charles didn't say anything, and so his mother continued.

"The real treasure of Isidora is that, once you enter the kingdom's gates, you never have a thing to concern yourself with ever again. Whatever it is you need is yours. You can eat until you're sick. You can sleep all day, if you like. And no one will ever take a single thing from you again. But do you want to know the best part of Isidora?"

Charles didn't say anything. His hands still clutched his face, but he stopped crying.

"Charles, I won't tell you the best part unless you remove your hands and look at me."

Slowly, cautiously, as if Dempsey might come charging up at any moment and bend his mother beneath him again in that terrible way, Charles withdrew his fingers. Millicent kissed his cheek, which tasted of his tears. Then she said, "The best part of Isidora is that, once you arrive, you forget every bad thing that has ever happened to you."

When the three finally came to Dempsey's land—astonishingly, expansively flat and barren—he showed the two to their faceless, anonymous piece of it. Dempsey helped them set up a tent and swore he would help them build more permanent accommodations soon (which eventually he did, constructing a one-room shack, just shelter enough so he wouldn't have to worry about the elements playing at his bared backside when he came for his fee).

After all the ways Charles had imagined Isidora, after the countless details of streets and corners and buildings he and his mother had invented, the startling nothingness of High Plains, Texas, looked to him like the very opposite of Isidora. The opposite of anywhere, really.

He asked his mother, "But why are we stopping here?"

"It's not our turn to go to Isidora just yet," his mother improvised. "It's not far, but they have a list of names, and you aren't permitted to see it until it is your turn."

And so, over the years, whenever Charles would ask his mother if their time had finally come, Millicent would tell him and tell him again, "Soon, very soon, darling," until he was old enough to know better. As he grew into a man, Charles all but forgot about the land his mother had invented aboard the *America Vestpoochy*, concerning himself instead with the practicalities of building a decent house, a decent farm, a decent life on the little plot of land his mother paid for with her body. Over the years, Mr. Dempsey would come by, almost as regularly as the mailman, to collect his carnal remuneration. And so came into being Charles's three younger brothers, EOA-23 familial early-onset Alzheimer's sufferers A-452, A-451, and A-450. Eventually, in the midst of a particularly stubborn bout of constipation, some crucial passage of Dempsey's heart burst, and the land became the Haggards' to keep.

Eventually too the gene that had been invented on the fourteenth chromosome of Duke Alban Mapplethorpe IV began to conduct its microscopic operations deep within Millicent's brain. As soon as the symptoms were undeniable, as soon as she could never seem to recall the name of her youngest boy, both Millicent and Charles knew, with the dread of certainty, what lay ahead.

One day, years into the disease, Millicent woke in a frenzy just before dawn. She leapt from bed, charged out of the house, and gaped at the endless blankness that stretched in all directions. Her sons, waking to her screams, scrambled after her. When the boys found their mother, fallen to her side, her face pressing against the orange, rusted soil, Charles knelt beside her.

"What's wrong?" he said.

"Where has everyone gone?" she asked.

"We're all right here," Charles said, gesturing to his brothers. "Everything is all right."

Millicent sat up a bit and squinted tearfully at the horizon, as if waiting for the vanished town of her childhood to materialize before her.

"But where are we?" she asked.

"We're here. We're in Texas," Charles said.

"I need to go home," Millicent said.

Though Charles had not thought of it for years, though he would knowingly and adamantly try to suppress the memories of life before Texas that would occasionally grab at his thoughts, he now remembered the story his mother had once told him, the promise she had made, yet to be fulfilled.

"We're just here for a little while," he assured her. "Soon, we'll go to a better place."

"What place?" Millicent asked.

"Isidora, of course."

"Isidora?"

Charles described for his mother the land she had invented all those years before. To the rapt attention of his mother and younger brothers alike, Charles retold her stories to the best of his recollection, describing Isidora as if he had been there himself, as if its golden capital had not vanished before his eyes. A land without memory, where everything one needed was at arm's length, where there was never reason to be afraid, where nothing was ever possessed and so nothing could ever be lost.

In the last months of Millicent's life, the youngest of Charles's brothers would ask Charles again and again what was wrong with her, knowing the answer and seeking its comfort.

"Nothing is wrong with her at all," Charles would tirelessly repeat. "It's just that her body is still here with us, but her soul has already gone to Isidora."

Just as, years and years later, when Charles's own children would ask their uncles what was wrong with their father, they would tell their nephews and nieces precisely the same.

And so the history of Isidora was passed along: sometimes to offer the younger generation comfort, sometimes for the sake of tradition, and sometimes to express what would otherwise be inexpressible in the finite words and spaces of simple reality. Over the generations that would follow, the descendants of Millicent Haggard would expand upon the epic of Isidoran history, adding new adventures, revealing details yet to be described.

In this way, the stories of Isidora were recapitulated, alongside Mapplethorpe's gene, from one generation to the next. Two ideas spontaneously improvised, altering in slight ways with each passage, yet remaining, fundamentally, themselves. The past and the future were the same place, an impossible but inevitable destiny, to which they all, together, were bound.

Once upon a time, the little girl who had slipped through the passageway to Isidora made it to the golden city. For those of us on Earth, the golden city would be a spectacular place, but of course it wouldn't last long here. A rooftop would be worth billions; you could retire off of a single cobblestone. On Earth, the golden city would be sacked and looted. But Isidorans have no need for money, just as they have no need for cities, no need for the things that are produced in cities, no need for the comfort that can be found in crowded, bustling city streets. Isidorans don't know who built the golden city or why, but it doesn't matter anyway.

As the little girl had not a single thought in her head, as there was no reason for her to stay in the golden city, she wandered far beyond its walls, deep into the gardens of Isidora.

Abel

It was dark, and the street was empty. I was sitting across from my daughter's house. I had been waiting for hours. The world, that strange thing, did an old man the respect of disappearing for a time so that it would be just Jamie and me, if she would ever come. Her street, its red-brick houses and sidewalks, vanished. Other than her door (walnut, bearing a wreath of flowers) and my patience, the world beyond was black.

But I was looking in the wrong direction. From behind me came a hand. The hand was no different than I remembered. Soft like a child's, but with long, womanly fingers. Without turning, I pressed it to my face and said, "I thought it was impossible."

Jamie's voice floated from behind. Two words, carried before me, as if on a breeze.

"I'm here," she said.

I said the only thing I could think.

"I'm sorry."

And then:

"Did you know?"

Suddenly, a sharp rapping of knuckles to wood perforated the darkness of Jamie's street with dull afternoon light.

I had been napping on the bed that had once been Mama's, then my brother's, then mine, then my brother's, then no one's. With the back of my hand, I dusted the window (the same window through which I had once, waiting and hoping, watched Mae and my brother climb into bed). I peered out. At the front door stood three of my neighbors, fidgeting with their blazers.

I was wearing no more than an ancient pair of B.V.D.'s, the thin strip that connects front to back as sullied as the floor of Iona's barn. The nearest clothing was Mae's old robe, still hanging in the closet, where she had left it. And so, swaddled in pink satin and doilies, I emerged.

They had a plan for my removal, described by them as both "generous" and "equitable." They presented a document, signed by dozens.

"We had an estimate taken recently, Mr. Haggard," said one of the three. "If you were to leave, the houses immediately surrounding yours could go up in value as much as ten or fifteen percent."

"I don't understand," I said, though that was untrue.

"Mr. Haggard," a woman wearing a suit like a man replied in a scripted way, as if eager for the chance to perform a memorized speech. "It's just that when new families move to a neighborhood, they, well, they like it to be a particular kind of place. They want it to be a single thing, something familiar. And right now, as it is, we have two different worlds existing here at the same time, and I don't think that's really good for anyone, do you?"

For a long while, I didn't say a word. Some part of me had been expecting such an appeal for years, was surprised it had taken so long.

"I was taking a nap," I finally said, producing the stereophonic sound of all three sighing in unison.

"You seem like a reasonable man," the woman told me (a bearded hunchback wrapped in pink satin!). "And we have a reasonable offer. Because of the added value that your leaving would create, your neighbors are prepared to offer you two hundred percent of the estimate."

"I'm afraid you've woken me." I began to shut the door.

"That's twice its value, Mr. Haggard! Twice!"

And now the door was shut. However, for a long moment, none of us budged. We only stood there, staring at one another through the grime of the window.

"Sir," the woman said, dispassionately. "If you aren't agreeable, we have other avenues we can explore."

THERE IS SOME CRUEL IRONY that those to whom this place should rightfully belong have long since vanished, and yet I'm still being crowded out. But the fact that I'm the only Haggard left in this place is only the way it happened. It could just as well have been someone else. When my mother was a child, she had two sisters and a brother. They fled soon after my grandfather's death, and other than the occasional regretful letter, she never heard from them again. Likewise, my grandfather had a brother who left soon after my great-grandfather fell ill. Sometimes, I like to imagine that the offspring of these people might one day return to me, demanding their fair share. I would gladly grant it, if for no other reason than the opportunity it would allow me to look into their faces and perhaps find a trace of my brother or even my daughter. But I know that, with a family like mine, history moves in only one direction: that of dispersion, that of getting as far the hell away as possible.

The disease of my family. Its story, like the unending history of Isidora, is inseparable from ours, its sad arc written in miniature upon on our most fundamental places before we were ever born, its devastation curves all our stories into its own tragic narrative.

Perhaps it was better when it still went unnamed. There was a time when it was only the mysterious affliction of the Haggards, the madness that seized my mother and grandfather and great-grandfather, and undoubtedly countless others before them, but of course, in its unsparing erasure, there's no way to know for certain just how many. Just as there is no way to know how or why it makes its claims. Why my grandfather but not his sister (my great-aunt Betty, who survived into a ripe, old spinsterhood), why my brother but not me. The disease has a twisted logic of its own. Sometimes, I like to think it has spared me for a reason, but what reason could there possibly be to spare a hermetic, hunchbacked life like mine? No, perhaps the reason I have kept my sanity is only another part of the disease's cruelty, taking the valuable, necessary lives, leaving behind the useless, the hunchbacked brother, to allow itself a crippled audience to its horror.

The disease of my family: the disease of the old, the familiar collapse of memory, as ancient as time, simply come too soon. A full, unyielding reversal of life in media res, like a conclusion arrived at too quickly, a book abandoned, thrown into the fire, half-written.

For example:

I was fourteen the first time I met my daughter's namesake, the original Jamie, Jamie Whitman. A slight, whispering orphan who carried with him the chronic, acrid, sweet smell of his aunt and uncle's fruit stand, Jamie moved back to High Plains, under the care of his dead father's sister, when his previous adopters gave up on him. Jamie didn't know for certain if it was money or patience they had run out of, but after twelve attempts at makeshift families, he knew it was always one or the other. That year, before his uncle located another family for him just outside Waco, Jamie came to our house nearly every day, a temporary third brother.

One day, after we had spent months and months with Jamie, Mama spotted the three of us walking home from school. She pushed her way past the screen door, marched right up to Jamie, stuck out her hand, and said, "I'm Miss Haggard. Pleasure to meet your acquaintance."

"Very funny," Jamie said then laughed.

"What is?"

BY THE TIME I WAS SIXTEEN, Mama's only memories still fully alive were of the already dead: her mother, her father, her life as a child. For every one day we grew older, Mama regressed ten. It was as if she were observing a movie of her life, except with the reel of film playing backward. For a brief time, the reversal of her life and the progression of ours came into perfect alignment: as we witnessed Mama's decline, she believed herself to be witnessing again her father's.

"Daddy ain't doing so good today," Mama would say when I tucked her in at night. "Don't even recognize me."

"Let's just try to stay hopeful," I would say.

"Ain't no sense in hope when it's hopeless."

I would have to pinch my nostrils shut, holding the mucous tears at bay, until I was on the other side of the door.

After a time, I became so accustomed to Mama's life in reverse that, as Paul and I would eat dinner, I would watch Mama, half-expecting her to un-eat: to un-digest, to un-chew, then to return food to plate.

Dr. Haywood, who oversaw three generations of the Haggard curse, came by on occasion to place the disk of a stethoscope to her chest, to press Popsicle sticks to her tongue, and then to shake his head and declare in the authoritative voice he could slip into as simply as his long, white jacket, "It just defies description. Never seen anything like it in the literature. Sorry I can't tell you boys anything better. Baffles the mind, truly."

Every reversal, every subtraction of memory, was a little death. The border between the existent and the nonexistent, so certain for most, was a thing Mama would cross carelessly, constantly. By the end of her life, her old soul had not so much vanished as eroded, worn away by a million rubs. I stopped praying.

By the time we turned eighteen, all Mama had left was her name, which she would holler.

"Sarah want!" Mama would hoot, pointing at the jar of cookies.

"Sarah tiiirred!" she would fuss in the afternoons.

We were nineteen when the disease commenced its final, irrevocable, backward march, death finally coming for all that life first brings:

The death of speaking.

The death of walking.

The death of control over the bowels.

The death of standing upright.

The death of self-feeding.

The death of crawling.

The death of sitting up.

The death of sleeping at night.

The death of swallowing.

When the final death came, that of the beating of her heart, so much of her had died so long before that this death was no more than another, was simply the last.

But at the end, modest solace: after countless deaths, after a full reversal of a life, what was left of Mama finally came to rest in the fragile circle of an unborn baby, her emaciated knees drawn snugly to the chest. The only word for her then was not *dead* but *returned*.

When I was still a child, when I still prayed, I would pray once a day that, if the curse of our family had to come to one of us, it be me. Since my teenage years, I have often searched my mind for the first signs. At seventeen, when I forgot for a week where I had put the key to the front door, I thought, It can't be. Not yet. When I was twenty-six and set out to bury seeds in the farthest fields to the south, only to arrive at the fields and the memory that I had already seeded there, just a week before, I thought, So this is how it begins.

However. Despite the endless list of my abnormalities, my mind has remained normal. Or perhaps, more accurate to say, *intact*.

But Paul. At first, for so many slips and substitutions, there was a single, simple excuse. Of course I knew better, but the excuse itself wasn't untrue.

"Since he left the army, he just hasn't been the same," I would say.

He hasn't been the same since the army, I reminded myself when Jamie was ten and Paul attempted to drop her off at a science fair in Dallas, only to return, hours later, with Jamie still in the car.

Paul said, "I think they've changed the roads."

"Just the army," I explained to Gary, the new mailman, after he had knocked at our door with a letter addressed to Mr. Paul Haggard. Gary had looked at the envelope and asked Paul for his last name.

Paul had said, "Um. Paul, I think."

"Just the army, the terrible thing that happened," I thought with such desperation that it must have sprung from my lips when Paul asked Mae when Mama was coming back from town.

Sometimes, Paul's confusion seemed to understand more than he. One night when my daughter was thirteen, Paul came in from the outhouse to find her in my seat, reading *Jane Eyre*.

"Where's your father?"

"Um. Standing in front of me."

"Huh," Paul said, slouching away.

Jamie crept into my room that night and told me the story.

"It's just the army. Something terrible happened to him there. Things like that—they can change people. They can confuse people in ways you wouldn't expect," I explained.

She nodded her understanding, but lightly; we both knew the viability of the excuse had begun to thin.

"I wish all war could just stop forever," she whispered.

I held her, covered her, as if my arms could possibly come between the future and her.

"Me too," I said.

And then, to distract her, I told her a story:

For her first years in the gardens, you wouldn't have been able to tell the little girl apart from any other Isidoran. The girl happily disappeared into the oblivion of Isidoran life. Conducting bliss, eating, conducting bliss, sleeping.

A year or two after she had first come to Isidora, who could say what it was? Maybe it was the smell of fruit and mud in the air that reminded her of her old home. Maybe it was the hand that the boy in front of her placed on her chest, which was as soft and rounded as her mother's. Maybe it was something else entirely. But whatever it was, the girl turned away from the Isidoran boy, and for the first time since she had come to Isidora, the words of the world she had left leapt to her lips.

"I'm just sad, okay?" the little girl said, then turned away.

The boy, startled, leapt back. He put his fingers to her mouth and knitted his brow. This was the first time an Isidoran had ever felt confusion. The boy opened his mouth and, after a few unsuccessful attempts, found that he too could make nearly the same sounds.

"Ahhhhm joos ssad, ahky?" the boy said, and as the girl had turned away from him after she had spoken, the boy now turned away from her.

By the next day, everywhere the little girl went, Isidorans were saying the same thing. "I'm just sad, okay?" they would say, turning their backs on one another. At first,

Isidorans might have had little idea what these words meant, but as they became addicted to the saying of the only words they knew, they kept turning and turning from one another, leaving bliss dangling from the tips of their fingers, unconducted for the first time. Eventually "I'm just sad, okay?" became exactly right for what they felt.

Once the idea of words settled in, the little girl didn't have to say anything else. Now that one thing had a name, Isidorans had to name everything. And as the word sad had led to the discovery of sadness, new words led to new thoughts and new feelings, until the Isidorans became as fearful and jealous and lonely and hopeful as are we.

By the time the little girl grew into a young woman, a full Isidoran language was well on its way. Isidorans just gabbed and gabbed and gabbed, finding tremendous excitement in describing anything—leaves, berries, headaches, constipation—for the first time. The girl was sadder than she had ever been. All the words of the world she had left had returned to her, and so had her memories. She was as sad as before and now lonelier still, burdened with a prophet's curse: could there be anything more sad and more lonely than remembering what terrible things the future will bring?

Seth

Dr. Shellard's database listed an additional 103 sufferers of the EOA-23 variant who lived within Texas but beyond the area covered by the Capital Metro bus system. Maybe, if I had been a more enterprising and persistent researcher, I would have snuck away from home, either taking the Greyhound bus or stealing my dad's BMW, and sought them out. Whatever it might say about the limits of my inquisitiveness, I never traveled beyond the greater Austin area.

But even within that small radius, over the course of my investigation, the majority of potential depositions never happened: my distant, neurodegenerate relations were either unresponsive or already dead, as was the case for Subjects A-64, A-10, and A-45. At the end of lengthy, sweaty bus rides and hikes, the faces of their spouses shook slowly at my shoes, then told me I was too late. Maybe the spouses could have provided useful information, but as soon as they told me, I immediately made my graceless, awkward exits. Subjects A-43 and A-60, by contrast, were both still living and at home but in the final stages of the disease, their families perched among ventilators and IV drips, hunched over gurneys supplied by hospice. With four steps into both of these houses (one in Jollyville, one in Georgetown) and a single glimpse of my mom's shriveled, incontinent, insentient future, my lungs forgot how to find oxygen and I quickly mumbled something about coming back at a better time. The husband of Subject A-34, the husband of Subject A-46, the wife of Subject A-23, and the son of Subject A-8 were all as dubious and cynical as my dad, asking for my credentials, or telling me they'd already told Dr. Shellard to leave them the hell alone, or simply saying, "Not interested," and closing the door in my face.

The day before I was finally able to depose another one of my distant (or possibly not so distant) relatives, I went to three separate houses, all in Round Rock, all with no one home. Into my notepad, I copied their addresses. When I returned home, I sent each a copy of a letter I had written, describing my scientific interest in speaking with them, as well as a separate self-addressed and stamped envelope they could use to provide more information about themselves, or to suggest a time that would be better for me to return. I decided it was better, for the sake of keeping my investigation from my dad, to supply an address instead of my phone number. There were a million daily tasks that my dad had become too lethargic and inert to tend to when he came home from work each night; any time in the last months that the mail had been emptied from its box, I had been the one to do it.

The next morning, I climbed aboard the first Capital Metro bus 145 to depart. It pulled up to the little glass shelter just as the sun inched over the roof of the Tom Thumb grocery store behind me, producing my silhouette portrait on the side of the bus in Halloween colors.

By the time the sun rose high enough that the bus no longer cast an elongated shadow across the interstate, I recognized something familiar, the tower of the University of Texas, from which a madman once sprayed down a locker's worth of bullets, killing fifteen. Eventually, the bus came to a stop exactly where the schedule promised it would, directly in front of the state capitol building: a gigantic marble head with a hundred Corinthian pillars for teeth.

As I walked up Congress Ave., it was as if the entire city existed only as backdrop for my empirical investigation.

According to the list, Barbara, Judith, and Patricia Llywelyn (early-onset Alzheimer's Sufferers A-57, A-58, and A-59) lived together on the north side of downtown Austin, in a suite that was part of Fenton House, an assisted-living facility that went to great extents, both grander and more minute than The Waiting Room, to mask its true purpose. I walked for twenty minutes before I turned onto a winding sidewalk that meandered around a garden of hibiscus and roses. A few steps down the path, I came across two or three of Fenton House's more adventurous residents, shuffling in their geriatric white loafers. By the time I arrived at a clearing in the shrubbery and the massive columns of Fenton House came into view, the sidewalk bent to meet the artificially circular shore of a pond in a spanking-white promenade crowded with the institution's doddering residents, their expressions as meaningless and happy as the roses, their enfeebled bodies relying on all means of external structural support: aluminum walkers, the kinks of volunteers' elbows, the shoulders of visiting sons, wheelchairs both electric and manual.

A camp of cognitive psychologists (e.g., Rosch 1983) has theorized that we categorize all knowledge by comparison against a series of prototypes we carry in our minds. Whether or not that can be empirically supported, Fenton House was an indisputable prototype, an almost dead ringer for the mental projection that would be conjured in 99 percent of people asked to free-associate on the word *mansion*. It was a brick-and-mortar antebellum, like a dream you might have of a plantation's big house. A white colossus, lesser imitations of which have been constructed, a million times over, in cheap plaster on wooden frames, throughout the endless neighborhoods ten miles to the north on I-35.

Though the heat and humidity of the day verged on Venusian,

the thick metal doors of Fenton House hung wide open, and as I entered I passed through an invisible curtain of air-conditioning.

In the lobby, behind a mahogany desk as huge and intricate as an elephant hide, a dark man with a slightly handlebar mustache straightened the lapels of his blazer and smiled toothily as he directed me to the Llywelyn sisters' suite.

As I bounded up the staircase with its green and gold runner, my clown-stiltlike legs taking in two steps at a time, a group of four residents inched down, clinging closely to one another. All had waxy, vaguely translucent skin that ended at the crowns of their balding skulls in wispy puffs of white, giving the four the appearance of having been spun from cotton. If it had been nighttime, and the lighting had been just right, it would have been enough to convince me that the four were the ghosts of the original Fenton family. The only proof that they were, in fact, of this world was their bright cotton clothing, a thoroughly representative sampling of the pastel spectrum.

The living room of Suite 206 was actually two rooms. The first, which ended five paces beyond the door, matched the rest of Fenton House, with intricate molding in baroque patterns on the wall. Beyond that, the rest was a modern addition, made almost entirely of glass, through which lazy sunlight filled the suite. At the far end of the room, near the wall of floor-to-ceiling glass, the Llywelyn sisters reclined on a wide suede sofa and matching armchair, their bodies outlined in glowing light, their hair like three unkempt halos.

All three Llywelyn sisters were astoundingly beautiful, like the series of water lilies by Claude Monet: a study on the variations of beauty, each uniquely beautiful and also beautiful in the same way. But they were also like the neurological equivalent of that famous diagram of the evolution of man (the one where all the *Homo sapiens'* predecessors, from ape to *Homo erectus,* are lined up in profile, usual suspects style), except in reverse. The youngest, Barbara, who looked approximately my mom's age, was sharply coherent; the middle sister, Patricia, would launch into fits of rage; the oldest, Judith, sat in a wide armchair, absentmindedly slurping juice out of a sippy cup while engrossed in a weirdly psychedelic episode of *Teletubbies* that cooed from the television bolted to the wall.

I knocked on the already open door, the first bar of "Shave and a Haircut," which was once my family's secret password in case of emergency but had more recently become my mom's strange obsessive compulsion. The younger sisters, Barbara and Patricia, turned, but Judith's intense focus on the television couldn't be broken. For a few sputtering seconds, the sisters' quizzical faces rendered me temporarily mute, and when I finally spoke, introducing myself and mumbling something vague about the study I was ostensibly conducting, the words came out in a single, breathless rant.

"Mr. Waller, you said?" asked Barbara, folding a dog-eared hardcover edition of *Pride and Prejudice* onto her lap.

"Um, yeah," I said.

"A pleasure to meet you, Mr. Waller," she said, as if I had just stepped into early-nineteenth-century England. "Please, do come in. My name is Barbara Llywelyn, and these are my sisters, Patricia and Judith."

I stepped into the sunlight, which caught on my eyelashes, blinding me like cataracts. Before I knew it, the middle sister, Patricia, ran up to me and slung her arms around my waist.

"Bucky!" she said and kissed my face. "Buck-eee!"

Behind her, Barbara balled her fists into the sofa with a loud *humph* and stood to peel Patricia's arms from my sides.

"You've got the wrong boy, Sis. This is Mr.——" Barbara said, trying to finesse my name from memory with an open palm and twirling finger in a way more than slightly reminiscent of my mom.

"Seth Waller."

Barbara turned to Patricia and said, "Mr. Waller. Bucky's not here, darling."

Patricia glared at Barbara and clenched her face in the ugliest way a face as beautiful as hers could possibly be clenched.

"Not . . . here . . . ," Patricia echoed.

"No, now why don't you sit back down, dear?" Barbara suggested, leading her sister by the elbow back to the sofa. But after three or four steps, Patricia refused to be calmed. She freed her arm and slapped her sister's hand, inexplicably in a sudden rage.

"Fucking bitch! No! Fuck you, you fucking—!"

"Patricia Llywelyn! Sit down!"

"No! *No!*"

Patricia and Barbara fell into a shared, silent glare. Meanwhile, in her armchair, Judith's total concentration was unbroken, a small smile expanding and contracting on her lips in rhythm with the fluctuating colors on the screen. Patricia eventually turned from Barbara to Judith, and the knitting of her indignant expression loosened as she slouched back to the sofa. Barbara turned to me, shrugged, and shook her head.

"I'm really terribly sorry about my sister," she whispered. "You'll have to forgive her, she never had a mouth like that, and then one day. Well . . ."

Barbara gestured me to follow her into the kitchen, where we spoke, seated at a wide walnut table. From my chair, I could see into the living room, and watched as Patricia fixed her gaze on the Teletubbies for a moment, then sneered, flapping her hands, squinting at Judith incredulously.

"These days, my sister seems to believe that every boy she sees about your age is our brother. Sadly, the truth is Bucky passed more than thirty-five years ago."

"Oh."

"At any rate, what may I help you with? Or have you already said?"

"Not really, no. I came to ask you some questions."

"Really? What sorts of questions?"

"I guess," I mumbled. "I guess about your family."

"Well why, may I ask," Barbara said, "have you chosen me?"

"Well, um, I got your name from Dr. Shellard, and I— Well, it's sort of a research project that I'm—" I fumbled.

She smiled sympathetically, then asked, "Oh? Like a census?"

"Yeah. Sort of like that."

"Well, dear. You've come to the right person. On the particular subject of my family, I could tell you volumes. Where to begin?"

Onto the table I dropped my spiral notepad, which was wrenched and squished by my anxiety. I pulled a blue Bic pen from my pocket and pushed it against the page. I told her that I was interested in questions such as whether her parents had the disease, or her grandparents, or even her great-grandparents.

"Well, now. My mom, she's the one," she said. "There's a certain, shall we say, discretion among people like my parents. She died in a place not unlike this. Soon after I was born. Judith knew her the best, and used to tell us stories. But I'm afraid Judith won't be much use to you these days."

For a while, neither of us said anything, and so eventually Barbara continued.

"My father was from Boston, but my mother's family is from Texas. When she was a child, Fenton House was the place to which you entrusted problems like us. Still is, I suppose."

Of course, at the word *Texas*, I perked up, writing it once in my spiral notepad and then underlining it three times. Maybe it was because of that, or maybe it was only the gentle, receptive face of Barbara Llywelyn, but all of a sudden I wanted to tell the truth, the whole story about my mom, and how all I knew about the person she had been were the names Bethesda and Isidora, and how, if I didn't find out soon, there would probably never be a way for me to know the truth. Instead, I reminded myself of the three tenets of my modus operandi, straightened myself, and asked, "Where in Texas?"

"Not far from here, actually. Downtown, I believe."

"This might seem weird, but have you ever heard of a town in Texas called Bethesda, or a place named Isidora?"

"Excuse me?"

"Bethesda and Isidora."

"Should I have?"

I didn't reply.

"Oh please, don't mind me. Perhaps I have. I'm certain I've simply forgotten. Please, remind me."

"No, no," I said. "It's okay. Never mind."

"Oh, Lord, just please don't take me too seriously. These days, I get lost in conversations the way children get lost in the woods. It's as if the path suddenly disappears and then there are only the trees. But I'm making it sound worse than it really is. It's not so bad for me at the present. I wouldn't even be in this place if not for my sisters. Certainly it is true that I cannot hold a phone number or a name in this old head of mine to save my life. That is true. But then, sometimes I start to believe that perhaps my diagnosis was simply a foregone conclusion."

We were both silent again as I shrugged and Barbara's face fell into a close examination of the branches of a juniper tree outside her window.

"There are so many ironies, though," she eventually said. "The greatest being that I hope the doctor is correct. As sad as it may seem, all I want is to forget this horror. My sisters and I, we've always been cut from the same cloth. The three of us have always been like one. Perhaps that is why we've never married.

Perhaps that's also why we've ended up like this. When I look at Patricia and Judith now, there is perhaps a certain kind of comfort, knowing that we're all descending into the same thing. Ah. Maybe I'm romanticizing. I know it might seem awful, perhaps macabre, but that's another irony, maybe the greatest. At a certain point, the worse you get, the worse it is for everyone around you, but the better it is for you. Judith, for one, has never been happier or more agreeable."

In the living room, Patricia stood from the couch and pressed herself, ten-year-old-girl-style, against the wall just beyond the frame of the kitchen doorway to snoop on our conversation. When the conversation turned to Judith, Patricia suddenly shouted.

"She's talking about you!" she yelled at Judith, finally pulling her sister from the Day-Glo Teletubby paradise and returning her to the living room of Suite 206, around which her eyes darted with the startled horror aped by a million actresses in a million scenes in which the heroine wakes up from a drunken stupor in the bed of the worst imaginable man.

Judith turned to me, her mouth falling open, curving into an O, as if trying to shape her silence into a question. I smiled a bit and shrugged. Judith raised her arm in a child's clumsy way, knocking her sippy cup onto its side, dribbling apple juice over the faces of the birds printed on her TV tray.

"Judith! Ach! You dummy!" Patricia yelled, standing with a huff, lifting the cup, and slamming it back to the tray. The corners of Judith's mouth disappeared into her cheeks as she started to cry. She reached her arm toward me, her fingers grabbing the air again and again, the innate universal hand gesture, known to every baby on Earth, for "I need."

"You don't have to mind her." Barbara sighed. "She's probably just hungry."

"No, no. I mean, it's cool," I said, then stood from the kitchen table and walked to Judith. As soon as I was in reach, Judith clutched my arm and pulled me to her.

"I, I, IIIIII—" she stuttered.

"Say something, you old dingbat! It's Bucky!" Patricia shouted. "Do you understand? Bucky! It's Bucky!"

"I, I, I?" Judith asked, pulling my arm against her neck.

I leaned in even closer. I could smell the apple juice on her breath.

"I, I, I, I, I, I, I," Judith said.

Even though I knew it was a futile gesture, even though I knew that, neurologically speaking, Judith was the equivalent of an eighteen-month-old, I couldn't help but think that somewhere deep within her frontal lobe there was one last island of untouched memory, the tip of a single word, tall and sturdy enough to rise just above a sea of plaque and tangles.

"I, I, I, I, I!" Judith grunted.

Beneath my breath, inaudible to Patricia and Barbara, almost inaudible to myself, I whispered it.

"Isidora?"

Judith smiled and touched my face. Typically, an unbroken, shared gaze with a stranger would be enough to make me want to scarf a fistful of Prozac, but when Judith reached for me, pressing her fingers to my jaw, I only smiled. After all, when it came to Nothingness, she was the real master in the most complete, most profound way. In the way that there is a 50 percent chance I will also someday learn.

ALTHOUGH I WAS EXCEEDINGLY HUNGRY and it wasn't the quickest way home, after I got off the bus back from Austin, I walked by Cara Crawford's house. The sun was coming straight through the rear, illuminating the interior. I paused and searched each window for any sign of Cara, but all I could make out was her mom's immaculate, generic home decor: the grandfather clock ticking in the doorway, the gleaming dark wood of the dining room table, the Thomas Kinkade perched over the staircase. For a long while, I stood there, lost in a daydream in which Cara bounded out the front door and took me by the wrist to a hidden spot in her backyard, where I told her all about my investigation. Where I told her everything, all at once, hardly stopping to breathe, as excitedly as I had spoken for those three mythologized mornings of my freshman year.

There was so much to tell Cara, but of course she wasn't interested. I tried to stop myself from deducing the unfair truths, I even tried to snap myself with the rubber band again and again, but it was useless. I thought, A mom in The Waiting Room and terrible acne? Helplessly in love and the girl is embarrassed to breathe the same air as me? I know nothing about my family and I have a practically worthless dad? Tears gathered in my eyes. Cara's house turned into a Monet.

Psychologists say that "belief in a fair world" is one of the most basic and also one of the most fundamentally deluded characteristics of the human brain.

When I got home, I found my dad crouching on the far edge of the living room's expansive faux-Persian rug, excavating our boxes of old family photos from the bottom shelf of the armoire. On the floor surrounding him, distributed radially around the inevitable half-empty gin and tonic, was a glossy, Technicolor spread: hundreds of pictures from my dad's brief but enthusiastic photography period, the sudden decline of which coincided with that of my mom's memory. My dad must not have heard me come in, because when I was within inches of him, he startled violently, sending the remnants of his cocktail across three out-of-focus extreme close-ups of my mom's painted toes. He looked up to me apologetically, his eyes glassy and ringed with flush, a sight so rare I at first assumed it to be some sort of allergic reaction.

"Oh, Jesus. You scared me," he said, rushing to the kitchen for paper towels. When he returned, he hid his face from me as he pressed his weight into the work of soaking up the spill. "You eaten?"

"I'll make something."

"Cold pizza in the fridge."

For a moment, I stood there as my dad nervously cleared his throat, again and again, a sound nearly identical to the attempt to turn a stalled engine. Eventually, I crouched and lifted a photograph of my mom and me, dressed in clunky, knitted clothing, smiling at my dad's camera on the single day of snow from the year I was ten. My dad wadded the dripping towel, then paused, examining the photograph in my hand.

"Remember that day? The spill your mother took on the ice? Epic. Her butt was bruised for a month."

"What is all this?"

My dad plucked the scattered ice cubes from the carpet, dropped them into the jingling glass, and stood. He shrugged, turning his face in to his shoulder as a covert way of wiping his nose.

"I thought maybe if we could show your mother some pictures, you know. Things she can't remember. I don't know, maybe she might. Well, anyway. It might be nice for her to see them."

"Pictures?"

"Yeah, you know," he said. "Right. Well, you're right. Stupid idea."

As my dad stooped to pick up the photos, I bared my teeth, and a rising, teary swell nearly broke through: not of nostalgia or of sadness but of anger. If my dad was so worried about what my mom couldn't remember of the past, why didn't he seem to care at all about what I had never even known? The gaps in my mom's memory were the result of a disease. That was one thing, terrible but beyond our control. But the gaps in my memory, those were deliberate; those were his decisions and hers. What was he trying to keep from me? What did he actually know about my mom's family? Why had both he and my mom told me so little about what their lives were like before I was born? If early-onset Alzheimer's is an inherited disease, then didn't that mean my mom had to have always known about it? Did that mean he also knew? And if they knew all about it and knew anything about genetics, how could either of them possibly have been so irresponsible as to have a kid? Was I the result of their selfishness or just an accident, and isn't that the same thing anyway? And how the hell could he go to work and drink gin and tonics and watch The History Channel when my mom was alone in some godforsaken geriatric prison? How could we ever be anything like normal again?

I HAD TO ADMIT THAT, when it came to constructing my mom's genetic history, I still hadn't made any real progress. I was starting to wonder just what kind of scientist I was. Maybe I wasn't even one one-googolplexth of a deductive mind of the likes of Santiago Ramón y Cajal, widely considered to be the father of neuroscience. Maybe I was a lot more like Richard Herrnstein and Charles Murray, the infamous writers of the great classic of racist pseudoscience *The Bell Curve*, who probably couldn't deduce their way out of a blanket thrown over their heads.

THAT WEDNESDAY, there was a message from Dr. Shellard on our machine. Someone must have ratted; it could have been the subject of any one of the many empirical depositions I had attempted to conduct. As soon as Dr. Shellard introduced himself in his nasal, deliberate singsong, a plague of blush and itch descended upon me. I almost couldn't stand to listen. Fortunately, however, he was kinder than I might have predicted, explaining that he didn't quite understand what I was up to, asking me if it wouldn't be better just to talk to him if I had any questions or curiosities, then pausing for a moment, with something like awe, as he asked how in God's name I had been able to get the list. But then he informed me, bluntly and entirely without sympathy, that I had violated an ethical code, and if I didn't cease my efforts, it could jeopardize the whole program. He begged me, for the sake of his peace of mind, to call him back, to let him know I understood. Though my respect for Dr. Shellard bordered on absolute, I knew from a hundred biographies of famous scientists that sometimes the greatest discoveries demand pushing the boundaries of what is acceptable. Or at least that was the excuse I allowed myself for not returning his call, for pretending that I'd never even gotten his message. Forgive me, Dr. Shellard. But, as you well know, I had to continue my empirical investigation. The Breakthrough still lay before me.

Once upon a time, in the years after the little girl brought the first words to Isidora, Isidorans began to remember, to think, and to speak just as well as we do here on Earth. As Isidorans began to understand more about everything, they also began to understand death, and so they soon started to ask the question *What might follow the end of life?*

Many came to believe that the discovery of memory was no accident, that memory itself was a part of a higher power, and that, when an Isidoran died, he would merge with Total Memory, spending eternity in omniscience.

For certain Isidorans, Total Memory meant a reunion with all they had lost. For others, the reward of death was to shed one's self into something far greater. For still others, the afterlife was identical to life, with the exception that all other Isidorans' motives and desires and needs were known and so there could never be misunderstandings.

Debates between Isidorans grew more and more heated. In fact, some say that all war in Isidora was born of the desire of each group to convince itself of its own rightness and the wrongness of all others.

After a time, there came yet another perspective. A perspective shared by only a small, wise circle of friends, formed years into the War of Isidora. Discussing the loss, sadness, violence, and betrayal that had seized their land since the little girl had spoken the first words, these Isidorans hoped for a different fate. They dreamt, instead of Total Memory, of no memory at all. They dreamt of a return to the blissful amnesia of Isidora's past, dreamt and hoped that, in the moments after death, they would discover simple nothingness.

"To remember nothing," they would say. "What more could one possibly ask of eternity?"

Abel

I believed I knew what to expect, but I was wrong. Instead of nearly precise reverse chronology, in a single generation the disease mutated. Jamie was still, usually, Paul's daughter, Mae was still, usually, Paul's wife, our house still, usually, our house. Even Gary, our mailman, was still, usually, Gary, our mailman. It was the memory of me that died first. I died in my sleep.

In the days and months that followed that night in the willow tree, years before, I often woke to find Mae lying against me in my bed, having stolen away from my brother. Though years had passed, and Mae had not come to me for over fifteen years, one night the familiar weight of a body pulled me from sleep. As in a waking dream, I thought Mae had returned to me. Fingers brushed my eyelids open, and a fog of sleep muddled my eyes. It took a long moment to decipher what I saw: not Mae, but Paul.

For all the years of Jamie's life, I waited for that ax, the truth, to fall. As I woke, my only thought was equal parts horror and relief. I thought, He knows.

In the dark, I tried to search Paul's hands for the instrument with which he would exact his revenge, perhaps a kitchen knife. But his hands were empty, and so I attempted to speak.

"Paul?" I asked. "What's wrong?"

Paul didn't say anything. He only looked into the blurred sleepiness of my eyes.

"I think everyone's asleep," he whispered.

"I think so too."

"We're alone."

"Yes, we are."

"How long have I had to wait?"

"Wait for what?" I asked.

"For you."

Paul stooped over my forehead, and I waited for the first blow, perhaps a fist to the nose. But instead, Paul only kissed my hair at its graying peak.

"You're so beautiful," my brother told me.

"Excuse me?"

"You are beautiful."

"Thanks."

For a long moment, silence. Eventually, Paul's breath began to rattle with tears.

"What's wrong?" I asked again.

"Jamie."

"Jamie? What about Jamie?" I said, panicking upright in bed.

But Paul only snorted with a sad half laugh.

He keyed the bedside lamp; the room reddened with light. As he stood up from the bed Paul's nose cast a void for his eyes.

"Jamie," Paul spoke, managing a smile that bent the lines of his tears. "Jamie. We're together again."

He knelt toward me then, pressed the flaking flesh of his lips against my forehead, then against my cheek in such a way that precisely then, in that instant, the world inverted. Or rather, appeared to invert as my foolish eyes, oblivious for decades, snapped into sudden, vertiginous alignment with the sheer obviousness of the truth all along.

Once the conclusion was made, a million pieces of evidence lined up. As boys, we often hid together by the creek, rubbing our fingers against dirty photos, but Paul's choice of the images on which we lingered always seemed terrible, the ones where a massive male rear end obstructed a clear view of the maneuver itself. And then there was Jamie Whitman. There were always rumors about him. In my condition, I learned deafness to children's name-calling. Perhaps "Ugh, the Caveman" would not be a preferred term for conditions like mine, and yet I won't be the first to deny my distinctly caveman-like, ill-fated construct. Perhaps, in their terrible way, they had also only dreamt up the worst terms for what Jamie Whitman was. What else? The time Paul lingered at the strongman competition at the county fair when we were fifteen. The time he hugged Mr. McGreggor, our high school Latin teacher, until Mr. McGreggor's face began to convulse. The time I watched him in class, his fingers alighting on the hair of Michael Specter, the boy who sat in front of him.

And, not including the most recent, most irrefutable indication, the primary evidence was, of course, Mae. How many times had I wondered how my brother could be married to someone of such beauty and touch her so little? I had even cursed him for it. How could my brother take a woman such as Mae so for granted? Silently, night after night, I had waited in the tree, desperate to be shown otherwise. But now, such an explanation as I had never once truly considered was so simple and so obvious.

A million times I have tried to untangle the motivations of the human species, and concluded such deliberations with complete resignation. We are too complicated to be understood even by ourselves, I have thought. Perhaps. But here was an explanation for so much, so simple.

Another thought came to me. Perhaps, as Mae insisted upon the concealment of the conditions of our daughter's creation, she had also, equally, made other concealments. How many things, simple facts, I wondered, might her simple silence obscure?

My brother smiled, then whispered, "Jamie. Here we are again. Together."

ONE DAY, while convalescing from a trip to the grocery (a trip I took, for old times' sake, on the original Iona), I gazed through the granular smut of my kitchen window, considering the shapes of clouds. In the sky, a massive zeppelin with the rear end of a dog was about to crash into the fallen face of an old woman when I heard Iona neigh wildly from her barn. As fast as the rusty sockets of my hips would allow, I went to her.

The trip to town had been too much. On the way home, saddle-bags heavy with Jif peanut butter and gigantic plastic bottles of Snapple sweet tea, a deep croaking rasp had strained the edges of each huff she produced. When I put her into the barn, she had leaned at a thirty-degree angle, as if gravity had suddenly strayed from its routine. And now Iona lay before me, each of her legs flaying like cut, live wire. Against the hay, however, her face was peaceful, was nearly transcendent. Rarely one to look me in the eye, Iona nevertheless turned to me in such a way that I knew then, beyond a doubt, what was about to happen.

I sat beside her and would not budge until she was gone. I rubbed her mane. Iona, my only companion, was slipping away. She may have been only a horse, but—as ever—I spoke to her as if she were something else, the speaking more for me than for her. I told her what I never had a chance to tell my brother or Mae. I told her that it was all right for her to do whatever it was she needed to do. I tried to tell her not to be scared, but what did I know? I may even have told her I loved her. I was helpless. I wept like Jamie wept at the death of her first pet, a rabbit named Constantinople.

I read once, in a *National Geographic*, that the mind lives for minutes after the heart stops. Time may become malleable, as it does in the moments just before sleep, drawing out like taffy, but the person can still hear. The advice, the magazine seemed to suggest, was to give it a good ten minutes before you go anywhere. After all, could there be anything more horrible than being left for dead when some part of you was still, in fact, alive? Minutes after Iona stopped breathing, she began to convulse, her head bucking from my lap and knocking the wind from my lungs. I tried not to cry. I didn't want Iona's last experience of Earth to be me blubbering. I had a good six minutes to fill, but I didn't know what to say.

A trickle of blood came from Iona's eye and dripped onto my overalls, but I only kissed my horse's forehead and spoke to her. What came to my lips was a story I heard my brother tell my daughter years before, the only story of Isidora he ever, to my knowledge, concocted on his own. And it came back to me exactly, word after word:

No one knows exactly how the War of Isidora began. No one can even remember who attacked whom first, or the reasons why, or even exactly which people were on which side. Somehow war became a state of mind. Being at war simply became a part of what it meant to be.

Once into these terrible years a boy was born. A boy who would become a man, who would become the one soldier to rediscover the idea of peace that had been lost for hundreds of years.

It was so simple, really. He was in a strange battle as he had been in countless battles before. Weapons fired. He fired back. He pointed. He killed. He reloaded. This was what it meant to be alive. Kill or be killed. And then. It was so simple. By some invisible hiss in the air, the torso of the boy in front of him was torn in half. Revealing its gore and also—suddenly—the idea. He dropped his gun. Something opened inside him. Something that, once opened, could never be closed. The idea.

Minutes passed, and the idea blossomed. It was so simple it was ridiculous. Life was one thing. Miserable. Fearful. Primal. The idea was simply the opposite.

He kept running. He ran and ran until he came to another battle. He tried to hide, but it was too late. The commander didn't recognize him but shrugged anyway and handed him a weapon and ordered him to fight. Again he dropped his weapon and again he fled.

And once. It could have been a year later. He had abandoned countless battles and had run countless miles. The soldier found himself in another trench next to another man. As always, the soldier dropped his weapon at the first sounds of shots. To the soldier's surprise, the man next to him made an expression the soldier had never seen before. Something more complicated than simple rage. Something lost and horrified and deeply sorry.

The soldier looked into the man's face and didn't need to say anything. The soldier placed his hand on the man's chest and conducted an instinct even more fundamental than war. The soldier's hand told the man everything he needed to know. How the soldier had become the opposite of all others. And how he would become the same. An insane idea. So simple and impossible. That was peace.

Seth

During that summer, I often had a recurring dream, a psychic conflation of actual memory and the most horrifying story I had ever heard when I was a kid.

The dream always began the same way, with an actual memory: I'm nine and my family is in Galveston for a hazy July week. We are in the ocean. I'm floating on an electric blue foam mat, and my mom is swimming in the water alongside. The sun has evaporated an afternoon of salt water across my bare chest, and my skin feels tough and cured. My mom is laughing at first, and I'm laughing too, but I don't know why. She's telling me a story. Not about Isidora, but the one about the girl with the ribbon tied around her neck who was warned never to allow it to be untied. One day, her lover (in an overt cautionary metaphor) wanted only to undo the ribbon's knot. She capitulated, and as soon as he loosened the ribbon, her head came tumbling off. At this point in the dream, my mom's hand brushes against her neck, and I notice that she too is wearing the ribbon. I'm panicked and curious and astonished. I'm about to ask her if she has the same curse, but before I can say a word, her smile drops, she stares gravely at me, she reaches behind her neck, and then she unties. As in the story, her head instantly comes tumbling off, right into my hands. I'm trying to scream, but my voice is paralyzed. The mat bobs carelessly. I look in all directions and can't see the shore. At this point in the dream, I either wake up or instantly switch to another scene, in the entranceway to our house when I'm even younger. I'm now four, maybe five, and bundled in a down jacket that is bright yellow. I'm about to go outside, but my dad is standing over me, looking annoyed. I ask him what's the matter, and then he tells me that I can't go outside looking like that. "It's embarrassing," he says. I ask him why, and he stoops down and reaches for my neck. I didn't know I was wearing it, but I suddenly realize that a ribbon is now tied around my own neck. "It looks stupid," my dad chides, then grabs for the knot. I clutch my throat with both hands, and I try to get away. But my dad only says, "Stop fussing." Between his thumb and forefinger, he grasps one of the ribbon's loose ends, and just as the knot comes undone, I'm my fifteen-year-old self again, convulsing in my covers, sometimes waking to a bruising pain in my foot as it strikes the frame of my bed.

I LET A WEEK PASS before even attempting another deposition. I told myself that I would wait to see if I heard back from any of the Round Rockers to whom I had sent letters, and that in the meantime I would catch up on my lapsed self-education on the subject of neuropathology. But I think the truth might have been that, as I knew I was already nearing the end of the list of EOA-23 sufferers in the greater Austin area and things weren't looking good, I had subconsciously, almost consciously decided that, as long as there were still names on the list, I could still delude myself into hope. I could still lie in bed at night, for the three or four blue-black hours that I inevitably spend trying to coax myself to sleep, and imagine what it would be like if just one of the EOA-23 sufferers, one of my long-lost cousins, would throw his or her arms around me, having waited for some word from my mother for years. How much would I have to say before he or she understood who I was? Would I have to explain all about my mom having the disease and the stories of

Isidora and the possibly nonexistent town of Bethesda, or would he or she recognize me without a word? Would he or she collapse against me in tears, or just stand there shocked, his or her mouth wide open? And would it be like cutting skin, a single opening and then an uncontrollable rush? Would I find out everything I would ever want to know about my mom's genetic history in an instant? Or would he or she be able to offer only a few small pieces?

When I finally conducted my next deposition (EOA-23 Sufferers A-67 and A-24, Claire and Dave Bennington), it again didn't provide any pertinent information about my mom's genetic history, but it was a fascinating case study worth note.

Mr. and Mrs. Bennington actually lived near me in Westrock, in the Sunny Acres neighborhood, which according to the Internet was exactly 6.4 miles from my house. Though it might seem like this proximity would make the trip more convenient, there wasn't any bus to take, and so I had to walk the entire way. That morning was inordinately hot, and by the time I finally reached the house, my face was burning from my caustic sweat.

In the neighborhoods of Westrock, the developers have a set of fifteen blueprints that they repeat over and over, as needed: enough variation to ensure no two houses on the same street are identical but little enough variation that if you drive around the neighborhoods for ten minutes, you'll come across somewhere between eight and ten exact duplicates of each house. When I was younger, I was fascinated by our house-clones, stalking them for hours, expecting to see families that looked almost exactly like mine emerge from their front doors. Almost exactly like mine, but maybe just slightly different, as if these families might offer a glimpse of what mine might have been if my mom's head weren't always in the upper stratosphere, or if my dad weren't always sucking down gin as if his life depended on it, or if I weren't the most awkward person on the face of the planet. But, to my disappointment, these families never really looked anything like us, which was bad because it gave me a sense of how alone we really were, but was also comforting because it somehow seemed to suggest that we could never be any way but the way we were. At any rate, Mr. and Mrs. Bennington lived in one of the houses with an architectural scheme identical to ours, which meant that after an hour and fifteen minutes of walking, my house stood before me again.

Mr. and Mrs. Bennington came to the door together, walked me into the living room together, got me a glass of water together, did nearly everything at arm's length of each other, tapping each other with their fingertips, pressing their hands against each other's backs, holding hands with their fingers interlocked, maximizing the surface area of contact. As if, like the Isidorans, they could communicate through their skin.

As they spoke, they also narrated together, companionably completing each other's sentences. According to Daniel Wegner et al. (1985), married couples develop "transactive memory," a process by which one spouse fills in the gaps of the other's memory, the two splitting the labor of remembering like any other housework: as they jointly recall stories, their neurological functions glow in complementary patterns, their individual light and dark spaces combining to a single, uniform image. Or at least that's the way it's supposed to work. But in the case of Mr. and Mrs. Bennington, who needed the dyadic boost of transactive memory more than most, each was a wobbly crutch for the other, dark regions staying dark, conversation occasionally dissolving into mystified, blank spaces.

Within one week of each other, Mr. and Mrs. Bennington were diagnosed with the EOA-23 variant of familial early-onset Alzheimer's. They hadn't known each other then—it would be more than a year before they would even meet. They had both been busily maintaining their own lives, at the peak of their adult respon-

THE STORY OF FORGETTING   213

sibilities. Mr. Bennington had been a wealthy website designer who had "gotten in on the ground floor," as my dad would say, and made a modest fortune, something involving credit cards and security. He had also been a father of three teenage boys, as well as the husband of an incredibly beautiful wife (whose picture he dug out for me from a tattered box of old photos that he kept under the couch "for no good reason"). Mrs. Bennington had been Mrs. Charles, a third-grade teacher at Westrock Day School, with a daughter, a son, a husband, a normal life. As with my mom, in the months before their diagnoses, both had become the objects of their families' exasperation and derision, both forgetting crucial responsibilities, leaving their children with unpracticed violins and trombones in hand, leaving the dry cleaning endlessly orbiting about the cleaner's mechanized racks, returning from grocery stores empty-handed, crumpled lists in their pockets. Both had often become livid, flying into rages, accusing their spouses of selfishness, of becoming intolerable burdens, of carelessness and heartlessness, as they too were accused. Eventually, both were divorced several months before their diagnoses, and upon their diagnoses, both—under the advice of their separate doctors—had joined the unfortunately named Alzheimer's Anonymous, a support group downtown.

"We met there," Mr. Bennington said.

"And two months later we were married," Mrs. Bennington added.

Mr. Bennington smiled. "We had so much in common. It was as if we were meant for each other all along, without our knowing it."

"Really, so much. Our families, our divorces, our interests. Even right down to the same variant of the same disease. What are the chances?" Mrs. Bennington chimed.

Later, alone in my room, I calculated the chances of two people with the EOA-23 variant meeting randomly. They were approximately 14,640 to 1. I almost called to tell this to the Benningtons but then decided not to. Explaining it would probably have required me to mention the fact that all the people with our particular variant of early-onset Alzheimer's are at most twelfth or thirteenth cousins.

During my visit, Mr. and Mrs. Bennington, for long and awkward moments, would stare at the same spot of their spotless walls, as if locked in rapt attention to music that was playing for them alone. Eventually, one would lift a face and speak.

"One of the terrible curses of the thing is that you forget the most recent," Mr. Bennington explained, gripping his wife's hand with both of his, as if at any moment she might be forcibly pulled away. "Sure, I'll remember this girl Sheila Marks, the girl who punched me in the groin when I was twelve and tried to kiss her. Long before I'll forget her, I'll have forgotten my wife's name. One day we won't even be able to speak. But at least if we have to lose our minds, we'll do it together. That's not the worst part, not nearly—"

As he said this, Mr. Bennington and I looked directly at each other. Typically, of course, eye contact triggers in me a fever-inducing, skin-grating autoimmune reaction, but this time, as Mr. Bennington spoke, I could watch him as if it wasn't even me doing the watching. When he finally paused, I looked down to my hands to discover they mimicked Mr. and Mrs. Bennington's, tightly locked and squeezing.

"The worst part," Mrs. Bennington continued. "The worst part is our children. None of them have been tested. But they know. A fifty-fifty chance. Can you imagine how anything could be more methodical, and more random, and more cruel all at once? And not just that. They also have to watch us go. The guilt— Well, there aren't words for it. All I can say is that, if it wasn't for Dave, I don't think that I could handle it. I really don't. I'd have to do something, I just—"

Mr. Bennington unraveled his fingers from his wife's, then briefly pressed his hand against Mrs. Bennington's back, then lifted both hands to his face. For some reason, as if being in the duplicate of my house made me replicate every one of the Benningtons' gestures, I also pushed the fingers of both my hands into my hair, could practically feel their words in my own throat.

"Just by having children, trying to have a life that is ours," added Mr. Bennington. "Sometimes, I think I'll lose my mind. It's such a cold, uncaring thing. And the sad truth is that I can never even hold on to my guilt long enough to get a sense of it all. It's like when you have a to-do list in your head but you can't remember what was on it long enough to do it all. There's just no way of understanding it all at once."

"The real curse isn't ours but our family's. It's harder to survive, I think," Mrs. Bennington concluded.

I nodded. For a long while, the three of us gazed vacantly through the Benningtons' glass coffee table, tracing the swoops and curls of the paisley rug with our eyes.

"But one day, at least, we won't even remember—" Mr. Bennington finally said.

"The place is decent. Not where you'd choose to end your days, I suppose. But that won't really matter, because by then . . ." Mrs. Bennington's voice trailed off.

"By then all that will be left will be her face," Mr. Bennington said, lifting his free hand to tuck a strand of hair behind Mrs. Bennington's ear. "Just her face and nothing else."

THE NEXT AFTERNOON, I found one of my self-addressed, stamped envelopes in my mailbox. My heart palpitated. I examined it and found no return address. I tore it open so quickly that its contents fluttered down to the weeds near the sidewalk. I stooped over and grabbed it.

The letter, the only letter that had been returned to me (and, in fact, the only letter that ever would be), was written on a sheet of substantial ivory card stock in a handwriting that, line by line, often strayed, then returned to the horizontal.

The letter, from Subject A-65, Helen Delancey, said the following:

Dear Mr. Walller,

I'm writing you to let you know about your letter, dated July 15th. I've never been good with correspondence and my mind is cloudy today so bear with me. I'm writing in reply to your letter, but please excuse me if my words don't seem like much. I've never been much of a writer, and today, especially, feel a bit under the blue. But I'm sure you'll understand.

You asked me about my family. They are with me now, and a gift to me every day. Do you know Garrett? Of course you would. The best thing that ever happened to me. This is my proclamation to you. Find someone like Garrett. The rest takes care of itself. It might sound trite, but love is the most important fruit of all.

Please forgive me, I've never been good at drawing. But I'm trying to respond in the best way to your letter, dated July 15th. You ask about my family. They take care of me at the present. I have this terrible cold that I can't shake. There has to be medicine for it. Maybe I've forgotten to take it. I'm so sore from it that sometimes it's hard to stand. I'll stop singing. I know how you hate it. But I have this awful cold, and if it wasn't for my family, I don't know what I'd do. When I feel better, I'd be happy to drive with you. At the present, I'm in no condition to greet guests. I'm sorry if I seemed awkward on our last meeting, you are so dear to me, and I would never mean to offend.

I have your letter, dated July 15th. You tell me that you want to know about my family. Well, family is the most important thing in the world. The number one. I hope this advice will be of some use to you. I'm afraid I'm boring you. There are so many sounds already so I will have to end it here. I look forward to our meeting again, as soon as this awful cold is gone.

Sincerely yours,
Helen

It was already the end of July, and I hadn't gotten anywhere.

AFTER THAT, two more weekends passed and I hadn't seen my mom for two months. I hadn't done anything really, other than sit in my lairs, rereading *The Human Brain: A Portrait*. There were still names on my list to visit, but I knew that they wouldn't get me anywhere, that even the modest goal of my so-called empirical investigation would forever elude me. But I must have still had some fragment of hope, because the idea of visiting these last names, with the likelihood of the subsequent understanding that my pessimism was wholly accurate, rendered me immobile and nauseated. Carl Sagan said, "Absence of evidence is not evidence of absence," and I knew what he meant but also had trouble really believing it.

In the afternoon of the ninth Sunday in a row that I hadn't visited my mom, my dad finally noticed. The door to my room swung open, toppling the precarious tower of my empty Kleenex box collection.

"Hey— It's one o'clock. Feel like visiting your mom?"

"Not in the mood."

"Really?"

"Yeah," I said. "I'm sure you can understand."

"Excuse me?"

"Never mind."

Typically, if I were going to transcribe accurately my dad's re-action to such Too-Smartness, it would require heavy use of the exclamation point. But this time his voice only deflated. Through the tight O of his mouth, he produced a slow, long plume of sweet, sharp alcoholic breath that settled over me halfway through what he said next.

"It's just. You know. It's just that different people are sad in different ways."

"I know. I'm not five. Okay."

"It doesn't mean I'm not just as sad as you."

"Okay."

"Believe me."

"Okay."

"Jesus. It's not that I don't want— I mean, it's not that I don't feel— It's just that I was raised to think, well, stiff upper lip and all that. You didn't know your grandfather. But, believe me. Not say-ing a word, never letting him see a thing, that's all you had against a man like that."

"Okay."

"Okay exactly. It's not like you're exactly Mr. Heart on His Sleeve either, you know."

"Okay."

"What's wrong with you? Talk to me like a normal person."

"I am."

"Fine."

"Fine."

"Listen, all right? Why don't you want to go see her?"

"Not in the mood."

"But what's on your mind?"

If he were a different father and if I were a different son, I could have told him countless things. I could have told him about Marvin

Shellard's list of names, and about my empirical investigation, and begged him to finally tell me everything he knew about who my mom had been. I could have told him about Conrad Hamner and the Llywelyn sisters and asked whether he thought that my mom might also be able to find some kind of bliss in her own oblivion, or whether she was just suffering still, beyond all words. I could have told him about Mrs. and Mr. Bennington, then asked at what point we had agreed just to let my mom lose her mind all alone in that terrible place. At what point we had decided that being alone, apart from my mom and apart from each other, was the best way to manage. I could have told him that I was probably just as guilty as he, even if it would take a massive infusion of sodium pentothal to admit it. I could even have told him about Cara Crawford and my Mastery of Nothingness.

I said, "My mind is blank."

"Seth, please."

"Please what?"

"This is hard for me too."

"You already said that."

For a long while, neither of us said anything more. The clock that my mom gave me for my fifth birthday, in the shape of Felix the Cat, ticked away behind my stack of VHS cassettes. The vein in my dad's forehead expanded, as if filling with all the terrible things he'd like to say, his skin throbbing twice for every click of Felix's tail. Eventually, I half-rolled my eyes and the silence suddenly ruptured.

"Christ! Say something!" my dad yelled.

"Something."

"For God's sake—"

"Okay. Fine. I'll say something. It's just, when will you ever stop pretending like you didn't just put her away because you're too embarrassed to be seen with her?"

"You know that's not—"

"You'd be happier if you could just forget about both of us altogether."

For the minute that followed, we only sat there, silent again. Eventually, my dad stood and turned to the door in the calm, fatalistic way of action movie stars just dealt a coup de grâce, maybe a bullet in the abdomen. He tiptoed around the fallen pillar of Kleenex boxes, staggered out of the room, but his last words stayed behind.

"I think you should visit your mother."

Distantly, I thought the words *I'm sorry,* but they were quickly muffled by the noise of all the unanswerable questions, of all the unfairness, of all the dread of how much worse my mom must have already gotten. Every neuron screamed, neurotransmitters crashing into neurotransmitters, canceling one another out. It was enough to make even the human brain, the most complex structure in the history of the universe, slip into total chaos.

THREE DAYS LATER, the humidity was unbearable, and everything—my body, the houses, the trees, the rocks, the sky itself—was sweating. I decided to spend the day reading in my secondary lair, a hidden clearing in a dense cluster of park trees, access to which required passing by Cara Crawford's house.

As I walked, the straps of my backpack chafed my shoulders in two irritated, juicy strips, provoking the sting of my backne. My forehead seemed to be melting. My eyes filled with the thick, burning stuff of my face, blinding me. To keep the little puddles of sweat from gathering in my eye sockets and also to avoid looking directly at Cara Crawford's house, I practiced my Mastery of Nothingness, watching my feet smear the shriveled bodies of worms that had slithered their way onto the sidewalk, that Sahara Desert of the Worm World, dying before they could reach the other side.

When the high, perky voice called out my name, it caught me so off guard that the toe of my right shoe crashed into the heel of my left and I stumbled, nearly falling.

"Oh! Hey! Seth. Perfect," the voice said.

I lifted my head to find a sight I would later re-create in precise detail in the shower, after working up a good masturbatory lather: Cara Crawford, in full splendor, reclining on a pool chair in her front lawn, wearing nothing but a blue polka-dot bikini. She lifted herself to her elbows, the skin of her stomach pinching itself into a tight range of miniature folds, the topography of which I could still draw from memory. For a goofy, shameful time, I only stood still, as if I had come across an exotic animal; maybe a toucan or baby gorilla, and the slightest movement might scare it away.

"Are you going to come over here or what?" she asked and laughed.

I straightened my posture, as my mom used to constantly and emphatically remind me to do, as if slouching was the root cause of all human suffering. I crossed the street to her front lawn.

Of all the normal things that might be said in such situations, I—of course—chose the most unfortunate.

"What can I do you for?" An expression my dad often uses, but context is everything.

"Gaw," Cara said, lifting a thick textbook and shaking it in front of her face. "Biology. Ickville, right? I've got this test tomorrow, but there's no way I'll figure out all this crap before then. It's so stupid."

I glanced at the familiar cover of the introduction to biology textbook, with its cell caught in the anaphase of mitosis, the chromosomes cleaving apart like a fly being unzipped.

"Yeah, it's really tough."

"More like impossible. I'm totally freaking out. If I flunk it again, my mom will kill me. I mean it. Literally kill me."

"I didn't know you were in summer school," was all I could think to say.

"Yeah. Well. Not everyone can be like a total supergenius like Seth Waller."

The skin at my cheeks started to vasodilate; I hoped that the blush would be concealed by the already ridiculous red that extreme heat always paints my face.

"I just study hard," I said.

"Yeah, right. I've been looking at this shit for like four hours and I still couldn't tell you what, like, the—uh—Krebs cycle's all about." Cara let the book slip from her fingers, and it dropped into the grass. "Why on earth does it matter if I know about this junk anyway, right?"

I shrugged and did not have to try too hard not to say the Too-Smart thing.

"Annnyways." She lowered her eyes in a way that shot electricity into my own, blowing out my nervous system until it seemed like that fuse, my brain, might suddenly short-circuit. "I saw you over there, and I was thinking. I mean, if you're busy, you don't have to, of course. It's just I can't understand any of this and everything, and well, I know, I mean I *know* that you know this stuff, so I was thinking that maybe. I dunno."

"You want me to tutor you?" The shock in my voice probably sounded like hesitance in a way I would obviously have never, ever intended.

"If you have somewhere to go or something like that, it's fine. It's just, oh. Whatever."

"No, no, no, no." I tried to calm myself, looking at my watch, as if the time could possibly make any difference at all. "I mean, I guess I have a little time."

I plunked down my backpack next to where the biology textbook had landed and sat. With nothing for my hands to do, I flopped open the book and began flipping pages.

"What's the test on?"

"Metabolism. And photosynthetic and all that." Cara sighed, lowering herself from her chair to sit with me on the grass. I was now sitting Indian-style, laying the biology textbook (strategically!) over my lap.

"Great. It's interesting stuff. Really," I mumbled, not finding a way to force my mouth to stop. "I mean, I know it's totally boring. But of the boring stuff, this is probably the best. If you are into, I don't know, life processes and whatever."

Cara poked me in the ribs, shutting me up.

"Hey, maybe if you help me, I'll let you take me on a date," she said, half-meanly, half in the way of Cara Crawford in front of her cool friends. And yet, half not. I laughed nervously, hissing air.

At first, when I began to tell her about how glucose is chemically broken down, conjuring a metaphor of a bowl of mashed potatoes being passed around the dinner table, Cara sat with her legs out, crossing her ankles, her weight pressing into her wrists. But by the time I reached the end of the metabolic roundabout, having generated energy in the form of ATP, Cara, uncomfortable, had repositioned herself, sitting Indian-style like me, her breath a faint but cosmic force, like the aurora borealis, on my fingers as I pointed to different parts of the diagram. I tried, with great effort, not to look at the place where the skin on the uppermost part of her inner thigh indented, diving into the strip of bathing suit fabric. Is there any way that three inches of fabric could ever mean more?

Twenty minutes later, after a long lecture on ATP's myriad functions (a speech verging, I felt, on poetic), I had worked the skin of my ankle, the spot just above my sock, all the way to her knee. I made contact. She either didn't notice or—as I have chosen, a thousand times over, to believe—pretended not to.

Eventually, Cara looked up from the textbook, just as I was about to delve into the miracle of photosynthesis. She said, "Jeez.

How do you remember all this shit? You must have an encyclope-
dia up there or something."

She pushed the tip of her index finger against my temple,
lightly flicking it three times.

"I guess it's just how my brain works," I said, then instantly
wished I had not.

"I guess so."

For the kinds of seconds that can be described like hours, we
only looked at each other. But eventually I had to look away, had
to fiddle with something as nonchalantly as possible. I plucked a
blade of grass, ripped it in half, and analyzed the jagged right angles of the tear, preparing to show her how you could see the rectangular structure of plant cells without a microscope, when Cara
said, "I guess that's what makes you so weird, huh?"

"Weird?" I let the blade of grass, and my next lecture with it,
flutter away.

In the silent moment that followed, the rest of what she said fell
away except for the single word, which stood—as I then understood, fully and completely, for the first time—as it would always
stand, an insurmountable wall, a mountain range, the hopeless distance between the single touch of ankle to knee and the full, un-
stoppable touch of everything else. It was as simple as that. I never
would have a chance. I was too weird.

I plunged my fingers into a patch of the lawn just beyond my
knee and ripped away a great fistful of grass, as if from a green-
haired scalp. Cara, peeking over the word that lay between us,
maybe seeing—for a split second—what life must be like on the
other side, added, "Must be hard never to have a way to just let go
of all those thoughts."

Maybe there never would be a way to let go of them all. Maybe
my weirdness—like the bloom of zits between my eyebrows, or
like the devastating genetic neurological disorder of my mom, or

like the sadness of my family—was my albatross, the burden I would always have to wear in full, plain view of the world. But, later, as I walked home, abandoning another day of reading, snapping myself habitually with the rubber band, I had something like an epiphany:

Nothingness could never be mastered. For all my attempts to shrink away, all I had left behind for the world to see was the Weirdness. Weirdness with nothing to compensate for it, nothing learned from it, nothing greater or more profound than its zit-encrusted, slouching, skittish, Too-Smart surface.

At that moment, a strange feeling: all I really wanted to do was to continue my empirical investigation, to get on the bus, and then conduct my next deposition. I pulled out the list to see who was left and decided on Subject A-14, who lived in Cedar Park.

As I walked to the bus stop, I felt a stab of shame or of realization, felt how completely I'd deluded myself, letting my mom slip into total madness all alone in The Waiting Room, trying to convince myself that I was simply too busy or too tired or doing something more important, when that obviously wasn't the truth. After all, what difference could a single genetic history really make to the field of neuropathology?

Maybe the truth was that the work itself was the point, direction for direction's sake. Or maybe the truth was that all along what I had really hoped to discover wasn't entirely scientific but something even more desperate and more necessary.

Sometimes, I still like to imagine it: the bus to Cedar Park pulling up to the shelter, naïve and hopeless me climbing aboard, wanting only for the rattle and the velocity of the bus to bear away at least some small part of my sadness, having no idea I was mere hours away from the Breakthrough that would change everything.

Abel

The death of how to tune the radio. The death of how to open a can of beans. The death of Jamie as his daughter. The death of the value of money. The death of usefulness around the farm. The death of how to read a clock. The death of every year after 1960. The death of writing. The death of Gary, the mailman. The death of how to use a refrigerator. The death of Mae as his wife. By Jamie's eighteenth birthday, all of this had died, but the boy whose corpse he had seen, the boy who had died before him across the ocean, the boy for whose spirit my body had become vessel, came only more and more to life.

I turned in the outhouse from my urination to find Paul coming to join me, shutting the door with the two of us inside.

"I'm in here now," I said.

"So am I," Paul replied then laughed.

"Paul—" I began, but what could I say?

"Jamie," he said.

And then the unshaven whiskers of my brother's lip pushed as one thousand needles into my own. Because of Mama, I knew questioning or fighting delusions would only create more, but I couldn't help myself. Later, alone in my room, with Paul weeping in his, I would try to comfort myself. I would think, Such things must be illegal, after all!

With all the force in my good arm and even the little strength of that flapping outgrowth of my hump, I pushed at his chest. But he only grabbed the hair at the back of my head, opened his mouth, and I could feel my brother's breath rushing through the gap in his teeth. Eventually, I squirmed to freedom.

"What's wrong?" In my twin's face I saw all the fragility of my own, years before, just feet from where we stood then, when his wife had told me she had a plan.

Increasingly, there were many times I could not help screaming to his face that I was his brother, and this was one such occasion. Paul fled, clutching his temples.

For the weeks that followed, more and more died, and Jamie Whitman—in the form of me—came more and more to life. Concealment grew increasingly difficult. When we would sit down to dinner, because table manners had long since died, I would lean over Paul to cut his food into easily edible pieces, as I had once done for my daughter. Paul's hand would begin to brush against my thigh, and I would shoo it away with a quick spasm of my leg. At night, when Paul would sit near my chair, sometimes resting himself on its burly arm, and would smile at me in the fragile, loving way that I no doubt had once smiled at Mae, I would scowl until my face could no longer maintain the expression or until my brother's smile finally fell.

Two months passed with tenuous success. At first, perhaps, when he began to call me Jamie, my daughter did not long contemplate such confusion. She, as did I, knew of only one other Jamie that Paul had ever known, her namesake, that boy from the army who never made it home. Who could say why Paul could still mentally sum numbers but could hardly read a word? Who could say why he still responded when Jamie called him Daddy but introduced himself to her daily? Who could say why I was now Jamie?

For Mae, however, the issue was more serious.

"Jamie Whitman is dead," Mae would hiss at dinner, after the seventh or eighth time in just minutes Paul called me by that name.

"Don't you remember? The army. You saw him die. It was terrible."

Paul's face would dart back and forth, between the two of us, like that of a child who cannot comprehend a fight between his parents, who cannot understand how two people who know everything could possibly disagree about anything. Finally, his eyes welling with tears more simply than I would ever have believed they could, he would pause, his face to mine, expectant. With all the cruelty of an executioner lowering his sword on the command, I would nod.

THOUGH I KNEW THE PROGNOSIS as a simple fact of life, Mae and Jamie insisted on taking Paul to the doctor, and I capitulated. Dr. Haywood, the ancient, bearded medicine man who had overseen a great, devastating epoch of the disease, had died long ago of cirrhosis, the revelation of his alcoholism stirring a general air of neurosis around town, driving the people of High Plains to a great exodus of second opinions. Recently, a gargantuan hospital, Greater Methodist of High Plains, had been completed, a sprawling complex like an ancient castle, dulled and muted by the inexplicably popular new materials of crude cement and metallic blue glass. On a Saturday, the four of us made the drive.

At some point that now escapes my memory, we told our daughter of our family's curse. I cannot recall the specifics, whether she deplored our concealment or simply accepted the sad fact, or trembled with fear at the possibility that, long after it finished its degradations of my brother, it might someday come for her. What I can recall is that in recent months she had often set out for the library to find a name for the disease. Jamie was young, still of the age that takes great comfort in labeling the unknown, diminishing chaos by naming it. The name she discovered was "early-onset Alzheimer's," which she fearfully suggested to Dr. Appleton, Greater Methodist's young doctor of the brain, who—after a battery of tests involving flash cards, a written exam, and a great number of wires affixed to my brother's scalp—nodded his concurrence. So it had a name, fine, but that didn't change anything.

"It's a new diagnosis," Dr. Appleton explained. "There's some exciting research being done in the field. But I'm afraid, for now, the prognosis is quite grim."

In Dr. Appleton's little gray room, in a yellow vinyl chair, Jamie began to cry. I pressed her face into my chest. When she pulled it free, I discovered a deep, abiding horror had contorted its lines. Despite her research, despite every terrible description she had already read, Dr. Appleton's diagnosis now came as an irreversible verdict, a sentence of death. Death to be administered in its most painstaking, degrading form.

"So there isn't any hope," Jamie sobbed. She held her knees and stood, then fell onto my brother, who had spent the duration of the visit squinting dubiously out the window, as if trying to determine whether the sky was playing tricks on him. When Jamie clutched his hand, his face returned to Earth, surveying the room in panicked surprise.

"Is this a hospital?" he said.

No one said anything.

My brother asked, "But who's sick?"

SEPTEMBER CAME, thousands of words died, Paul now spoke in the simple sentences of a child, but Jamie Whitman was more alive than perhaps the actual Jamie Whitman had ever been. And in a single moment of an unremarkable afternoon, the silence of my brother's long-concealed truth died too.

Mae, Jamie, and I spent the day carrying bags of winterizer to the farthest reaches of our land. Paul, unable to understand how to help in such things, only trailed behind, his eyes following me diligently. We were near the end of it. Mae and Jamie fell for a rest on top of the pile of canvas sacks. Only for a moment, only to wipe the sweat that blurred my eyes, I placed my arm between my brother and myself. In that second of blindness, Paul wrapped his arms around my torso, his hands pressing the cotton of my shirt against the dampness of my back.

"Paul," I said sternly, but it was too late.

I reached my right arm around for his hand, but as soon as our fingers touched, he lurched forward, pressing his face against mine. In an aggressive jerk, I twisted my head free and watched Jamie's face fill with astonished comprehension.

That night, a rustling at the edge of my bed disrupted the blankness of my room and I awoke. I now expected to hear my brother's voice but instead heard Mae's. It had been so long since I had felt for Mae's hands in the dark that I thought that maybe I was losing it too, that maybe my mind had also begun to allow the impossible to become possible.

"We've got to do something," Mae said. "This can't go on."

A blister of thoughts swelled at the base of my skull. I thought, Did you know what Jamie Whitman was to Paul? Did you know what Paul was when you married him? Why didn't you ever tell me? Does this make what we did any less wrong? If you knew, why did you allow me to believe that our betrayal of my brother was something worse than it actually was? Did it ever occur to you just to let the truth be the truth?

"I won't let my daughter watch her daddy die like this," Mae said.

"Then what?"

"We've got to show him that he's wrong. That Jamie Whitman is dead."

"But Jamie Whitman is all that Paul has left."

For a long moment, it was as if the darkness of my room had sucked all possible words from our mouths.

"He still has us, don't he? I mean, for Chrissake, we aren't nothing. And, anyway, he'd want this too, if he could. We've got to do something, Abel. This is for our daughter's sake."

Perhaps it was only into the silence of my room in the dead of night that Mae could speak of our own silence. That she could say to me, for the first time, *Our daughter*. Our daughter. I would have agreed to anything.

"But what could we do?" I asked.

IT WAS NOW A LIFETIME LATER, and the monster had to be destroyed. For a time, he and the townspeople lived in peace, in their disparate worlds. But something changed, and now they marched on him, demanding his blood. If it had been a different time, they would likely have come with pitchforks and lanterns, would have held crosses at the gates, hissing Latin, waiting for the lightning to strike behind the windows, revealing the hunchback in monstrous silhouette. A man in a nightgown, the fuzzy tip of his sleeping cap dangling over one ear, would have taken aim with a shotgun and fired. The creature would then have crashed through the window, from five separate angles in slow motion, and would have fallen to the rusted finials of his gate, impaled. He would have lain there, sprawled and writhing, feet kicking pitiably for the ground. When he drew his final breath, convulsed a final time, the townspeople would have crowded around, at last given the chance to examine his hideousness with impunity. Maybe there would have been a lone, beautiful young woman who would have seen the sadness and beauty of the beast unrecognizable to the others. She would have wept.

But the year was now 1998, and the townspeople had traded in the flaming torches and crucifixes of antiquity for hand-painted poster board. The signs they held read, NO ROOM FOR BLIGHT! and ONE NEIGHBORHOOD! and EMINENT DOMAIN IS IMMINENT! Though only five or six may have agreed to take part in the demonstration, they had apparently phoned the local news; a white van, towering gadgetry sprouting from its roof, was now parked before my house. As they circumambulated a reporter and her cameraman, their chants of "Time for change! Eminent domain!" reached my ears.

I was nearly all that was left of the town High Plains had once been. I was the only one, and—as with a lifetime before—I was one too many.

After a time, I watched through the filth of my living room window as the reporter tapped the cameraman on his shoulder and pointed to my door. Once the man lowered the camera from its perch, my neighbors quickly retired from their efforts, falling suddenly silent. Without pausing, fearless of my tetanal moat, the reporter swung open the iron gate, its screech echoing against the windows. The two proceeded to my front door, the man's camera again at the ready. The woman knocked, and out of instinct, I pulled open the door.

THIS WASN'T THE FIRST TIME that it was in everyone's best interest for me to leave. A lifetime ago, in the last months of my brother's life, Mae had decided precisely the same. Perhaps she should have asked long before. Or perhaps I should have made myself leave when I had discerned the first pangs of love, all those years ago. I spent a lifetime as the one too many; perhaps what Mae asked was merely, finally, a realization of the natural order.

"Maybe he can never let this madness go," Mae explained. "But at least if you leave, he'll stop seeing Jamie Whitman every time he turns his head. At least our daughter won't have to suffer *that*. That on top of everything else. At least *that* we can do for her."

The truth is that I never fully agreed, that I knew no normal logic could comprehend or ease the final, desperate reversal of a life. But if it was what Jamie required, then I was prepared to travel to the opposite side of the earth.

Or, I should say, I believed I was prepared. The day before I left, I thought that, after forty-seven years' living on the planet, I might finally see some of it. Maybe the Grand Canyon, the Rocky Mountains, great cities, the sea. In the end, I made it as far as two miles, to the so-called studio apartment that Samuel Berg had cobbled together for the occasional ranch hand in a ramshackle old horse shed on the edge of his property. A yellowed box of a room with an ancient, chipped desk, a depilated armchair, an extended family of mice, and a bed stuffed with some unspeakable material, perhaps rocks. As my departure meant the total cessation of all of our agricultural endeavors, I rented our fields, for a modest fee, to a company called American Ag Consolidated, which shamed our primitive techniques with shining tractors, humming combines, and a small army of migrant workers. But I had some money in my pocket, a room that was less than a mile from Jamie's school, and I was prepared to wait as long as was necessary, until the second death of Jamie Whitman.

I considered never telling my family where I had gone. Perhaps I would send letters claiming to have visited fantastic places. I even considered simply ceasing contact. However. Beyond bearing witness to the terminal decline of my brother, Jamie was at a precipice of her own. A senior in high school, she had recently received letters of admission from a number of universities. Though she had not yet decided, many of the schools were in places as impossibly far as Boston and New York City and San Francisco. A parent's burden as he witnesses the end of his child's childhood? To find a way never to say: I don't know how I will live once you go. At any rate, time with Jamie was increasingly precious. I wasn't going anywhere.

Four days after I left home, I waited outside Jamie's school, leaning on the gate, my eyes fixed on the green front door, like a regular psychopath. When Jamie spotted me, she ran, threw her arms around my hump with such ferocity that her legs left the ground. I kissed her face.

This was 1977. Jamie was eighteen and already a woman. Her hair held light in a way that defied description. When she walked, she swayed a womanly sway. Her eyes beamed with the lofty air of that short, invincible time between the tempestuous frustrations of childhood and the dull discontent of adult life.

"Where have you been?" she asked, her smile unbroken.

I shrugged.

"I couldn't go. I got a little place. It's not much, but at least it's close by."

She kissed my forehead.

"Mama's wrong to make you go," she declared with the vehement certainty that is possible only at a certain age.

"Your mother didn't make me do anything," I said. "We agreed."

I kicked a stone.

"How is he?" I asked.

"Same as always, only panicking more since you've gone. Mama had to hide the keys to the door. He keeps looking for you. Or for him, or whatever. He grabs the doorknob and shakes it, trying to get out and come looking for you."

I kissed the crown of her head and held her hand as we began down the road.

"Let's stay hopeful," I said. "Give it time."

Jamie paused, clutched my shoulder, and spun me toward her.

"But don't you get it?" she said. "Time is exactly the problem."

"GLORIA STEWART," the woman informed me. "KTVY, Channel 6."

Each strand of her hair was carefully positioned; a chestnut sculpture perched atop her skull. Shamed, I pushed my palms into my disheveled mane, as if that could make any difference at all.

"Mr. Haggard," she said, as the lamp fixed to the top of the camera came to life, a portable spotlight that illuminated the beast in painful, lucid detail for the home audience.

"I was hoping to get your side of the story. Would you mind answering a few questions?"

I flinched, which Ms. Stewart seemed to mistake for a shrug.

"Great, great, great, okay," she stammered, straightening the tweed lapels of her blazer, grunting the phlegm from her throat. When she spoke again, each word was deliberately enunciated, simultaneously formal and accusatory and sympathetic.

"Mr. Haggard," she announced. "Your neighbors have described your property as blighted. They say this is grounds for eminent domain. Do you think this is fair?"

"Fair?"

"I guess the question is whether you think it's fair to call your house blighted."

"Blighted?" I murmured. "Of course."

"How long have you lived here?"

"Always."

"And how would you feel if your neighbors were successful, and you were forced to leave?"

I shrugged. I didn't mean to look uncaring, but what could I say?

"This is my home," I replied.

I WAS THE ONE TOO MANY. It is probably true that things would have been infinitely simpler if I had left when I was still a young man, before Mae and Paul had ever met. But we had lived how we had lived, and our family had taken the shape it had taken, our configuration fixed in the triangular, love and pity and indignation bending around the three corners, passing in both directions. What stability we had was forged by the longing and the impossibility and the reciprocity intrinsic to our shape: the incompleteness of Mae's love for Paul balanced by her love for me, the unrequited love between Mae and myself balanced by our devotion to my brother, Paul's impossible love for the boy whose shape I had taken balanced by Mae's insistent silence. We could only be as a triad. Into the endless oeuvre of the sacred number three, whose work spans from the Holy Trinity through Poseidon's trident to the three-bean salad, we added ourselves. I may have been the one too many, but perhaps, after all those years, there wasn't any alternative. Perhaps that is why, only weeks after I left, what remained of my family could no longer remain. Unbound, we collapsed and then shattered.

SQUINTING UNDER THE LIGHTS, I could just discern the protesters standing at my gates, observing me with careful scrutiny. My eyes met those of Mrs. Stanasel, from the red-brick monstrosity to my left. Ms. Stewart was speaking again, but I wasn't listening. I was looking only at Mrs. Stanasel, whose face fell with something resembling sympathy. She shrugged. Dangling from a string looped over her neck was a cardboard sign. On it, beneath the words ONE NEIGHBORHOOD! was a strange rendition of my house: chimney, windows, and door all in their proper places, but the whole thing upended, balancing on the roof's peak, the foundation exposed to the sky. From that distance, I could have convinced myself that, in one of the upstairs windows, Mrs. Stanasel had sketched a stick-figure hunchback clutching the top of the window frame for as long as he was capable, and that it was only a matter of time until he fell.

Once upon a time, during the War of Isidora, a small circle of Isidorans began to dream of a return to the time before the little girl had come, a dream that eventually led to the formation of the Amnesia Club. The club's sole aim was simple: to discover a way to forget. At first, many chemicals and formulas were tried, and though these early experiments led only to death in the trial subjects, new participants signed up all the time. There was even a waiting list.

Finally, the members of the Amnesia Club understood that they could only do for their children what they could not do for themselves. The only way to forget, it seemed, was never to remember in the first place. And so, for weeks, the Amnesia Club looked for the right place. They eventually found it in a massive cave, deep underground. They built a single tunnel to the cave and covered the door with dirt and leaves. They filled the cave with light and food and water, even plants and animals. Everything one needs to live. And when they had children, they placed them in the cave, wordlessly nurturing them as long as was necessary. Then the members of the Amnesia Club did the hardest thing they ever had to do: they left their children behind. And so, within a few years, Isidora had been restored, if in microcosm.

Only once in a generation would the cave be entered by an outsider, for the purpose of choosing the one for the Great Burden. The Great Burden was this: the chosen boy or girl would be thoroughly educated, would learn to remember as well as anyone in the now wretched land of Isidora. The chosen one would then be told by his or her predecessor of everything Isidora had lost, of the sadness of life as it had become, of the reasons the Amnesia Club had begun, and then finally of the burden of having been chosen—to be the only descendant of the Amnesia Club to remain with the memory of it all, to take sole responsibility for seeing that those hidden underground were protected and left alone.

And so, if you go to Isidora, looking for the land of your dreams, you can find it only in miniature, an ancient, hidden Isidora buried deep underground. A quiet, peaceful paradise, far from the reach of Isidora's war. And at the entrance to the underground lair, you will find the latest one to be chosen for the Great Burden. There he'll be, slouching under the weight of his weapons, slouching further still under the weight of his memories.

As far as we know, for the billions of years before our great ($\times 10^{10}$)-grandfather, the lone amino acid, was huffed out of hydrothermal vents in the cracks of the ocean floor, Chance alone ruled the universe. It was by Chance that the Big Bang spewed space and time in the ways it did, by Chance that certain dense clumps of the almost uniformly distributed aftermath drew particles toward them, eventually giving rise to the first stars and galaxies. It was by Chance that each nascent galaxy began to swirl this way or that, collecting stellar debris like dust bunnies, birthing planetoids and then, eventually, planets. Many even credit Chance for the Big Bang itself, many see Chance like a cosmic Thomas Edison, putting all the possible pieces onto its laboratory table, trying out this set of conditions and that, until, by Chance, the right elements were stumbled upon, and then there was light.

It wasn't until 10 billion years later, after Chance had held a long, unchallenged tenure, that Chance, being Chance, happened to create Memory. In a cradle of methane, ammonia, water, and hydrogen, in a self-forming lipid bilayer, a few monomers stood in line, broke in two, and then—remarkably—dutifully reassembled themselves into the same configuration once more. At first, that's all there was to Memory: a simple repetition of a few simple units, like a bar of a song stuck in one's head.

Even in its earliest stages, Memory existed for the same reason it continues to exist—because it could. Within the perfect, chance balance of severity and congeniality Memory could exist, and the more sophisticated it became, the better were its chances. Millions of years after its creation, Memory may have been only a process of replication, simple strands of genetic code repeated over time, but it had already begun to show some of its father's traits, Chance confounding, slightly but unpredictably, what was otherwise a predictable process. Sometimes, for example, Chance would interfere with the nucleic code of an incipient organism just enough to ensure it would be born with its face attached to its anus, quickly eating and shitting itself to death.

But Chance also created some astoundingly complex and resilient successes, and Memory didn't miss a chance to take these opportunities as far as it could. Eventually, with higher domains of complexity, Memory took on new responsibilities. Once Chance and Memory devised the nervous system, for example, Memory found work for itself beyond its endless, monotonous transcription. Chance interred Memory in their mutual creations, allowing, for example, a simple fish to remember not to eat a bluish alga, or swim too close to the coral. Chance encouraged Memory's new work, and in new organisms new forms of memory were invented all the time: instinctual memory, procedural memory, sensory memory, short-term memory. When, 3 billion years after it created Memory, Chance triggered the explosion of two nearby supernovae, producing the transformative shock wave that gave rise to the first humans, Memory rose to the occasion, maturing into work more sophisticated than anything it had attempted before, becoming introspective, inventing, in humans, the memory of memory.

And so life as we know it continued to develop, forged by the productive, if contentious, working relationship of father and son.

Life, in whatever its forms, being at its irreducible essence nothing more or less than the two.

For the majority of evolution, Chance may have been nepotistic, favoring Memory, but sometimes Chance would step in to remind Memory of who was really in charge. For example, in the late eighteenth century, as if to reassert itself, it was Chance, performing its routine shuffle, that invented the EOA-23 variant of familial early-onset Alzheimer's on the fourteenth chromosome of the future Duke of Iddylwahl. Memory, being Memory, had no choice but to replicate the new orders for the inevitable destruction of its most sophisticated creation.

Often, the highest levels recapitulate the lowest. A sheet of mica is formed of molecules of incredible flatness. The cells of a stalk of celery are vertical, rigid, and green. The rotation of the Milky Way, its particulate clouds swirling around a hot, bright nucleus, reflects the submicroscopic dynamics of an atom. The cells of our body are chaotic, watery sacks, bound together by the skin, and so are we. And since Life, at its base, is no more than Memory and Chance, then at the highest level of complexity yet known on the planet, the story of us is also the story of them. For example, the true narratives only hinted at in Dr. Shellard's report, the stories of the hundreds of lineages that spring from Lord Alban Mapplethorpe like the plastic strands of a pom-pom, are, from a certain perspective, nothing more than the stories of the engagement of Chance and Memory over time.

The dissemination of the EOA-23 variant that began that afternoon in London Harbor may have been sparked by Memory (the fearful ship's captain knowing all about Iddylwahl's supposed curse), but it was conducted largely by Chance. By Chance, Maximilian Barret, the tailor of Iddylwahl and the great ($\times$ 10)-grandfather of Sufferer A-50 (Conrad Hamner), climbed aboard a boat bound to Morocco. By Chance, Dr. Bennington, the great ($\times$ 9)-grandfather of A-24 (Dave Bennington), was able to hide for four days under the harbor's dock and then, by Chance, managed to slip into the cargo hold of a ship bound for the eastern coast of Canada. It was by Chance that Kenneth Marlboro, the great (× 11)-grandfather of A-67 (Claire Bennington), disappeared into London's crowds, ensuring the dispersion of the disease in the south of England, but it was by Memory that his great-great-granddaughter fled London for America, as the people of her neighborhood began to look upon the Marlboro clan as a group to be avoided as doggedly as one would avoid the lepers. It was by Chance that Maximilian Barret, living out his days in Casablanca, impregnated another British expat (the coquettish daughter of a prominent merchant in the East India Company), by Chance that he died in a feud over the price of figs when his son was only nine, but it was by Memory that his son took what little money his father left him and spent it on a boat ride to America, eventually resulting in North American EOA-23 familial early-onset Alzheimer's Sufferers A-70 through A-111.

The lineage of EOA-23 Sufferer A-39 (Jamie Waller) is similarly spun. It was the intertwining of Memory and Chance that passed the disease from Millicent Haggard to Charles Haggard, then to two of Charles's six children, then to five of Charles's children's children, then to fourteen of Charles's children's children's children, and so on, and so on.

It was, however, Memory alone, the memory of the family's curse, that scattered the great majority of Millicent Haggard's offspring. The fact that certain branches of the Haggard family tree were freed from the EOA-23 variant while others were doomed was almost entirely Chance, but it was almost entirely through Memory that other branches ceased altogether, sons and daughters swearing never to subject children of their own to their horror.

The endless project of Chance and Memory is both expansive and minute. In the mid-1970s, for example, at the subneural level of sufferer A-56 (Paul Haggard), it was Chance that made the simplest form of Memory, nucleic recapitulation, responsible minute by minute for stripping the most sophisticated. Though, as with all diseases, Memory was both perpetrator and victim, the way it conducted itself was often by Chance. It was largely by Chance, for example, that Paul Haggard, in his earliest stages, forgot that his daughter's favorite color was blue, that when she was a baby she used to hum herself to sleep, that his wife loved nothing more than the sensation of fingernails on her scalp, that her name was Mae. Was it also, then, by Chance that he quickly forgot his brother's name, then forgot his brother altogether?

Near the end of his life, Paul Haggard was left with a single salient memory. As Chance had worked its way into certainty, the memory of a man he loved filled the gaps. Was that also just Chance? Or had Memory, in Love, at last stood its ground, creating an offspring of its own, one strong enough to gird Memory, at least for a time, against Chance's inevitable progression?

But here one can only speculate. Just as one can only speculate which was responsible for the last moments of Mae and Paul Haggard's lives.

That night, Paul Haggard wandered away from his house, wandered down the gravel drive and the dirt road beyond it, wandered his way to the crumbling pavement of FM 39. This was Memory, Paul Haggard looking for a man he had once known, who had died years before. It was, however, mostly Chance that his wife found him, hours later, standing in the center of the empty road, weeping into his hands, glowing bright in the car's headlights.

On the way back home, at sixty-five miles an hour on FM 39, Memory and Chance were side by side once more. And in the moment when FM 39 veered to the left and Mae Haggard watched it slip away from her headlights, was it Chance that she did not respond in kind, veering with it? Had Chance, too, placed the massive oak tree at the exact location of the curve, underhandedly encouraging Memory all those years to make it grow sturdy enough to slice straight through the hood of an oncoming car? Or had it been Memory, the memory of her family's suffering, the memory of what was yet to come, the memory of her own guilt, that compelled Mae Haggard to, in fact, steer toward the tree? Or had it been something else entirely? Was it not exactly Memory or Chance that steered Mae and Paul Haggard to the end of their lives? Had it instead been a certain will, invented only recently, known to *Homo sapiens* alone: Mae Haggard's will to allow her husband to die before Chance plucked the last memory from his mind; her will to allow her husband to be at last with the boy whose death was impossible; her will to free the three of them—her husband, his brother, and herself—from their otherwise inextricable, interminable suffering; her will to allow the only peace she could imagine, that of her daughter and her husband's brother together, a life to be lived only in the present, freed from the constant intrusions and obstructions of the past? In a place ruled by Chance, 4.5 billion light-years in all directions, run by Memory, twenty-five thousand miles in all directions, had Love, adolescent and cloistered in its little room, devised a rebellion and taken what it could?

Seth

EOA-23 Sufferer A-14, Donald Shafer, was dead. He died at fifty-two, halfway through the course of the disease, the neurofibral tangles having snarled 1.5 pounds of his gray matter into a thick slice of dead meat. But long before the disease would have claimed every thought, long before Alzheimer's would have made its way to his brain stem's operational memory—the swallowing of food, the breathing of lungs, the beating of heart—he had died. The daughter of A-14, Taylor Shafer, explained this to me as I leaned against the door of her flat, boxlike, ranch-style house in the middle of a flat, boxlike neighborhood on the southern edge of Cedar Park. In the suburbs of Austin, they begin each subdivision with a blank slate, an empty, treeless prairie, and so you can glean a neighborhood's age by the height of its trees. Unlike in my neighborhood, where the top fifteen feet are nothing but tar shingles, in Taylor's neighborhood the trees formed a canopy high above the rooftops, which—in conjunction with the weed-strewn sidewalk cracks and the low, modest houses—meant that it had been built during a less flamboyant stage of suburban sprawl in the early 1980s.

As if in evidence of our shared genetic origin, Taylor, as I did, looked away when talking, bent her chin to her sternum, and spoke softly, almost to herself. She wore an oversize University of Texas T-shirt, and occasionally, as she shifted in the door, a part of it would catch against her skin, revealing her startling skinniness. Her hair was a loose, dull brown mess, with thick bangs matted over her forehead. Her face, however, was undeniably beautiful, vaguely reminiscent of my mom's: a nearly perfect heart shape with eyes as outlandishly over-size as E.T.'s. As she stood there in the open door, sweat began to form on her forehead, pasting her hair to her skin, and as she dabbed it with the back of her hand, the reason someone with a face as attractive as hers would choose to hide so much of it behind an opaque chunk of hair became clear. From the far corners of her eyebrows stretched a long, semicircular streak. A scar, bone white in the center, red along the edges. The scar had an odd neatness to it, as if it had been planned and executed, as if someone had de-cided to make a chalk etching of the sun dawning over her eye-brows. When Taylor noticed me noticing it, she quickly covered it with her hand, her embarrassment shooting through us both, mak-ing us both look again at the ground. She then shook her head quickly, as if in confusion, trying to tuck the gesture into an ex-pression other than shame.

"Oh, I'm so rude! Would you like to come in?"

I nodded, then followed the burnt orange sack of her T-shirt into the living room, where a dull, grimy light passed through the gingham curtains, which looked as if they hadn't been changed since the house had been built. Though she told me that her father had died three months earlier, the air still held a whiff of that un-healthy antiseptic scent that also fills The Waiting Room. At first, the dimness of the house blinded me, but second by second the room became legible. Dark, scrubby furniture lined the walls: a pair of dirtied powder blue sofas and a chipped walnut coffee table, identical to the kind that could have been found in any suburban living room in the year 1985, as if that was when her house had been sealed from the outside, given over to decay ever since.

"Do you want anything? Water? Coke?" Taylor asked.

"Water would be great."

Taylor smiled, nodded, and disappeared into the kitchen. She came back with two room-temperature Ozarkas. I chugged mine, the plastic buckling and snapping. Taylor chuckled quietly.

We sat on opposite ends of a sofa, the landings of our butts causing a visible cloud of dust to poof from the zipper of the single, warped cushion.

"So why again did you want to talk with my dad?"

"It's part of a study I'm conducting with Dr. Shellard. At UT?" I half-lied.

"Oh, right," she said. "Dr. Shellard. Marvin, right? He came here once. You're working with him? That's great. What year are you?"

"Sophomore."

"No offense, but I would have had you pegged as freshman."

"None taken."

"What dorm are you living in?"

"It's not really a dorm."

"Oh, an apartment?"

"Yes," I lied, completely.

"I think about going back, I really do. I used to go there, you know?" Taylor spoke to the dark bookcases lined with their dim, gray spines. "But at this point, I don't even know if they would let me. I never really even told my professors I was leaving. I just sort of left."

For a few minutes, in total violation of my modus operandi, I didn't talk about anything even remotely relating to my mom's genetic history. Instead, I talked like a normal member of planet Earth—complained about the weather, the public transportation system, the weather again—talked about the things that everyone has in common, maybe to avoid acknowledging that which we uniquely shared.

Though it wasn't exactly relevant to my investigation, after a time I decided to ask Taylor why she had left school. For a moment, she made an expression identical to the one I imagine my mom having made in the moment before her fall, standing at the edge of something, balanced between the dependable, muted sadness of what's behind you and the release to be found in the void before you, in the elegant simplicity of gravity, of falling. Taylor teetered there for a moment, but as soon as she started to speak, it was as if the story had been waiting, taut and coiled, within her for months. She immediately launched into a memory, skin-itchingly personal, breathless word after breathless word.

"It was like, one day nine, maybe ten weeks into my freshman year, my dad calls me at school," she began. "If I hadn't given him a cell phone with my number programmed in, who knows what might have happened? So he calls me and tells me he's bleeding. I ask him how bad, and he starts to cry into the phone. I ask him where my mom is, and he just cries louder. I tell him to yell her name, and he does, but she's not there. She's at the mall. Can you believe it? The goddamn shopping mall. I don't know of any person who has ever spent less time in their own house than my mom. Anyway, now she's gone for good. Moved in with her boyfriend. This guy Rod. It won't last. But anyway, I knew I couldn't depend on her. Not full-time, at least. So I just left school. Dropped out. I came home and took care of him. The doctors I talked to, they say a nursing home is usually needed for the last two or three years. But my dad never spent a day in a nursing home. I guess I can say at least that much for myself."

I had been watching Taylor closely, observing the way that as she spoke her scar disappeared, then reappeared into her expressions, like a tight string being plucked. When she mentioned the nursing home, heat rose into my face, which I wiped with my hands.

"I'm sorry," Taylor said. "Talking your ear off. God, I don't know why I always do this. It's— I guess it's nice to talk. Seems like every time I get the chance, I just go on and on. But you didn't come to listen to me gab, did you?"

She turned to me, her expression hanging awkwardly on mine, waiting for some nudge to tell me more.

"No, no, no. Please," I fumbled. "I mean, so what happened when you came home?"

"So my mom and I make this kind of schedule together. When we'll each take care of my dad, all the things we have to buy for him, stuff like that. But we're going broke, the insurance pays maybe half of what it costs, and my dad is just getting worse and worse. He starts seeing things. They say it's rare but not unheard of. Dr. Shellard said that, actually. That when the disease gets into a certain part of your brain, it sort of, well, it sort of makes you see things that aren't there. Have you heard of that?"

I nodded. Taylor then drew her fingers to her lips, which were trembling almost imperceptibly. Without thinking, I did the same.

"So one day, it's my mom's turn. I'm asleep in bed. He was up all night crying, screaming really, and when he finally went to sleep so did I. It's supposed to be my mom's turn, only she's sleeping too. So I guess my dad gets up and the house is empty. Maybe I woke up a little when I heard him fumbling around. I was half-awake when he came into my room. At first, I thought it was a dream. I used to dream about him every night. In my dreams, he died in a million awful ways. Only this time it wasn't a dream. He comes into the room, and his hands are bleeding, and he's holding a paring knife. You know the kind? One of these little curved knives, holding on to it by the blade. Squeezing it. He comes right to me and says in this low, calm voice, just like I was a little girl again and he was my dad and trying to protect me, he says, 'You have to stay perfectly still.' I tell him to drop the knife, that he's scaring me. But he says, 'Don't worry, sweetie, I'll get them.' I said, 'Get who?' He said, 'The bats.' I asked him what bats, but it was too late. He jumped onto my bed, held back my hair. And he, he thought they were on my face. He thought they were biting out my eyes. He said, 'Don't worry. I'll get them. Just don't move. I'll get them.' And he holds me down, puts his knees into my shoulders. I try to fight and push him away, but he's too strong. He just keeps saying, 'Don't worry. Don't worry.'

"There's so much blood that I can't even see. I call the hospital, and I can't see anything. But I can hear my dad in the corner. He's crying at first, and then he's just sort of moaning. I tried to wipe the blood from my eyes, but there was too much and I couldn't see a thing. But then I could see. He wasn't moving. In the end, it wasn't his brain. It was his heart," Taylor said, then sank her voice into a vaguely spiteful impersonation of the nameless doctor who must have offered his conclusion. "Myocardial infarction of the left ventricle."

Taylor looped the collar of her T-shirt over her mouth, pressing it to her philtrum with her thumb, as if to filter her words, or else to hold them back.

"I guess—I guess I'll never know why it happened then," she continued. "Maybe he was still seeing things. I don't know. Maybe he thought they were coming for him. Or maybe it's possible that he looked at me and for a split second understood what he'd done. Terrible as it sounds, sometimes I think that maybe, either way, it might have been the best way out. I mean, with a future like that, you know?

"Anyway. He wanted to be cremated, but he never told us what to do with the ashes. We decided to take them up to the place his family came from. A place near Dallas, called High Plains. I'd never been. He'd only been once or twice himself. Nowhere special, really. But at least he was home. We couldn't find his family's graves, so we spread the ashes into a lake. I don't know why we chose that, but that's what we did. Anyway, the day after his funeral, I went to get tested for the gene. I might not have had the courage normally, but then. Well, then, I only needed to know. If they had said it was positive, if I had known that was my future, who knows what I might have done?"

Something strange was that, when Taylor finished her story, folding her hands into her lap, all I wanted was for her not to stop telling it. I wanted to know more. I wanted to know how, exactly, her father had looked when she saw him. His blue, bloodless face. What her mother's expression had been when she finally arrived at the hospital. What her friends tried to say to her, what they didn't. How his absence filled the rooms of her house more fully than his presence ever had. What she would have done differently. Her guilt. Her sadness. Her relief.

But the story was over, breaking its delicate spell that had held us both in some other place, a place where the twitching of her eyes, the shaking of her fingers, the slumping of her spine had become my own. Now we were again only what we were: two awkward strangers, embarrassed and without words for the flash of intimacy we had shared.

As I stared at the skin of my knuckles, I started to think about the others I'd met in the course of my empirical investigation. I thought about Mr. Bennington grasping his wife's hand, and how, as he pressed into his wife's fingers, I pressed into my own. I thought about the Llywelyn sisters, how the three of them mapped one another's decline, and also my mom's, and also, maybe, my own. I thought about Mr. Hamner and his hope for his final years, a submergence into the meaningless beauty of things, not unlike my mom's stories of Isidora.

I had a thought I had never had before. Considering that I was a Master of Nothingness, the whole of my empirical investigation should have been next to impossible. The thought of going from door to door, interviewing complete strangers, should have stopped me in my tracks. But that was what I had chosen to do. And though at times I had itched with embarrassment, wanting to retreat into Nothingness, when all had told me their stories—for those few moments of complete transference, when their nerves became my own, when I disappeared into their words—I had felt myself, strangely, reappear. My imagination of their sadness and hope; it was as if there had been a hollow, unfathomable dark place and their stories had held light to its walls, mapping its depths. The thought was this: maybe what I really wanted wasn't to disappear, or to understand the disease, or even to find answers to who my mom had been. Maybe the point of my so-called empirical investigation had been as simple as that, to hear their stories and, by imagining the shapes of their burdens, to begin to understand the shape of my own. After all, albeit defined in the broadest of terms, these people were my family.

I lifted my face. Eventually, Taylor's eyes rose to meet mine.

"My mom has it too," I said.

"She does?"

I nodded.

"How bad?"

"I don't really know," I said. "My dad and I put her in this place. I haven't seen her for a while."

"So is that why you— I mean, so this isn't really just about research then, is it?"

"I guess not."

"So can I ask what it is then that you're hoping to find out?"

If it had been earlier in my empirical investigation, I might have told Taylor the rehearsed answer that I was trying to learn more about how the disease is inherited, to learn more about how it works, with the hope of someday finding a cure. Or I might have even said what was closer to the truth: to try to find out anything about who my mom had been. Recently, in a back issue of the *Journal of Personality and Social Psychology*, I read, "People tend to hold overly favorable views of their abilities in many social and intellectual domains. . . . This overestimation occurs, in part, because people who are unskilled in these domains suffer a dual burden: not only do these people reach erroneous conclusions and make unfortunate choices, but their incompetence robs them of the metacognitive ability to realize it" (Kruger and Dunning, 1999). It had been my own metacognitive incompetence that had kept me, over the course of my investigation, from understanding the ridiculously simple answer to this ridiculously simple question.

"Have you, by chance, ever heard of a town called Bethesda?" I asked.

"Bethesda? Like the place in Maryland?"

"No. This one's in Texas."

"Oh. I don't think so then."

"I lied." I smiled. "I have one more question. This one's going to sound weird."

"Shoot."

"How about a make-believe place called Isidora? Like in a story or something? It's this sort of fantasy world where— It's this kingdom. Gold, you know, like El Dorado or something. Except the thing is, the people of Isidora, they can't remember at all— What?"

Taylor didn't say anything.

"What?" I repeated.

"My dad."

"Your dad?"

"My dad."

"Your dad?"

"My dad— But how do you know about that?"

And that's when I had the Breakthrough.

WHEN I GOT HOME, I pulled the string that dangles from the door above the upstairs hall, and the hidden staircase unfurled. I climbed up, then made an all-out assault on the attic.

At first, I thought it was hopeless. The attic was like the opposite of Alzheimer's disease, was like the mind of the famous neurological case study S.: nothing disappeared, no matter how useless. Everything just went on existing, clutter piled on top of clutter. A senseless, incoherent mess. But after pushing boxes to their sides, spilling their memorabilia, which no one would remember, after digging and lifting and opening for almost half an hour, I found it. A box labeled SETH ART, in which, folded into a little translucent square, was the tracing I had made years ago of the Texas portion of Isidora.

Once back in the hallway, I pushed up on the door, and the attic's yawning mouth suddenly clenched shut, a deafening bite. I took the map into my bedroom, then had to dig through yet more piles of crap (these even more worthless than those found in the attic) in order to locate my old *Atlas of America*, the one from which I had once traced the map. Eventually I found it buried beneath my old corduroy armchair, buried further still beneath a scattering of Roald Dahl books. I grabbed a pencil, flipped on my Lava lamp, the ooze within quickly thawing to life. With the atlas in hand, I laid the tracing down on the stinking knots of my sheets and quickly flipped page after page until I found Texas. Without breathing, I aligned the tracing with the original.

The Breakthrough was this: it had been there all along.

The *X* my mom had drawn, the *X* that she had said marked the passageway from our world to Isidora, did, almost exactly, mark the spot. I wondered: could it possibly be a coincidence?

Through the wax paper, just north of Dallas, and partially obscured by the markings of the red felt pen, was the black speck of a town:

HIGH PLAINS

JUST AS I PASSED THROUGH the red enamel door of The Waiting Room for the first time in months, the hundred speakers hidden in its walls and ceilings began to ring: the Westminster Chimes, mealtime. Like the Eloi summoned by the Morlocks' siren in *The Time Machine*, the patients began a slow, kitchen-ward motion. Bald head after bald head ticked by, as haltingly persistent as a clock's second hand. I couldn't help but feel they were being called to some terrible fate, some chillingly systematized form of mass slaughter. I had to fight the urge to jump before them and shake them to consciousness.

I spotted my mom, a shock of pigment in a procession of geriatric albinism. I made a break for it, right past Nurse Jenny at the front desk; she yelled after me but did not bother to give chase, leaving that to the men who could easily be summoned through her intercom.

"Hey! You can't go in there!" she shouted.

Everywhere, old faces turned and sneered. The disturbance, me shouting my mom's name, dodging and pushing my way through the slow-motion parade, was enough for one astonishingly gaunt old woman to break into tears.

When I reached my mom, I rested my hands on her shoulders. At first, she didn't seem even to notice that anyone was in front of her. Her feet just kept treading the linoleum, her shoulders pressing into my palms, her face twisting with confusion. When at last she paused, she clenched her eyes shut, then pulled them slowly open, as if against a thick goo. The Haldol.

"I need to talk to you," I said.

"And it's a pleasure to meet you too."

"I have something I want to give you."

"How nice it is to see you. Can you stay for a while?"

"It's me," I said. "It's Seth."

"Seth . . . ," she trailed, then started to sing my name to the first bar of "Shave and a Haircut," which was distressing, of course, but since this was our family's secret knock, I wondered if it meant that some part of her was remembering.

"Seth, Seth, Seth, Seth, Seth," she sang. "Ha! And what a pleasure it is to meet you. Oh, what a beautiful boy you are. Just beautiful."

"Mom?"

"Yes, dear?"

"I have something I need you to see."

"Oh, good. Can't you stay for a while?"

"No. Now I need you to focus," I said. I pulled the square of wax paper from my pocket and handed it to her. To my surprise, she quickly unfolded it, then held it above her, softening the light across her face. The *X* she had drawn years ago cast a dark splotch over her left eye.

"How pretty," she said.

"High Plains, Mom. High Plains, Texas."

"High Plains . . . ,"

"Yes. High Plains. Do you know what I'm saying? High Plains, Texas," I said, then put the tip of my finger against the *X*, next to which I had written the name of the town. "That's it, isn't it? That's where you're from."

"High Plains . . . ," she whispered. "High Plains, Texas?"

"Yes. Mom. Can you try to think for me? I need you to focus and to think," I said. "Is this where you're from?"

My mom's face darkened: the ghost of a thought, bound and

desperate, its fingers clawing at a net of neurofibral tangles with no way out.

"Ahem!" barked a voice from behind me. It was Ish, the massive Puerto Rican orderly with the pencil mustache, whose thick, woolly arms were The Waiting Room's last and impregnable line of defense against the encroachment of the upsetting.

"You may visit your mom tomorrow," Ish decreed. "Now you must go."

"Please, I just need five minutes."

"I'll give you three hours," Ish replied. "Tomorrow."

He didn't budge. He only stood there, inches from me, arms folded, while Nurse Jenny stepped in from behind and nudged my mom by the elbow toward the dining room.

My mom, however, elbowed Jenny in the shoulder, slightly slapping the nurse's face with her palm.

"No!" my mom yelled. "I don't want to, goddamnit!"

"But, Mrs. Waller," Jenny cooed in the lilt some adults save for addressing those at either end of life, and also for dogs. "It's time for supper."

"No! No! I don't want to! I said no!"

I winced. I felt the pressure of oncoming tears, like churning, subdermal magma.

"Mom, it's okay," I called. "I'll see you soon. Don't worry."

With a flash of recognition, my mom began to cry. Not just to cry but to sob. As Nurse Jenny pulled her by her left hand, my mom turned to me, stumbling backward, her face as red and swollen as a fresh bruise.

"I'm sorry, I'm sorry, I'm sorry," she cried.

"It's okay," I said, my voice shaking. "Really. It's okay."

When she disappeared into the dulled fluorescence and the dulled murmur of the dining room, Ish said, "Now, just what part of 'come back later' don't you get?"

As the hushed scraping of plastic utensils to plastic plates commenced, I whispered that I was sorry.

THE DOOR TO MY PARENTS' ROOM (or, more accurately, now just my dad's room) was shut. Behind it was silence. More than anything, my dad hates to be bothered when trying to sleep, but I knocked anyway. Without thinking, I played "Shave and a Haircut." The strip of darkness at the base of the door flickered with light. Unfortunately for the importance of what I needed to ask him, my dad came to the door dressed as he slept, wearing only his tighty-whities, the hairy bulge of his stomach sagging over the elastic band.

He squinted at me as if I were an extraterrestrial.

"What is it?" he said, not in his typically disgruntled way but with a desperate murmur, as if I were just one more way the world had chosen to pick on him.

"There's something I want to ask you about."

My dad lifted his arm to lean against the door's frame, exposing the hairy snarl of his pit. He rubbed his eyes skeptically.

"Okay," he said. "So ask."

"How much do you really know about Mom?" I said, which sounded infinitely dumber coming out of my mouth than it had the hundred times I'd mentally rehearsed it.

"This again? Come on. *Please.*"

"How much?"

"What do you mean 'how much'?"

"Like, what do you actually know about her family?"

"Seth."

"What do you actually know about her family?" I repeated.

"You know what I know."

"So tell me what I know," I said.

"Well, now, what do you mean? Do you mean like the fact that she had terrible parents who are dead, just like mine? Or the fact that we agreed that some things are just too sad and too stupid to waste a lot of time and energy dwelling on? Listen. Please. Just go to bed. We'll talk in the morning."

"Did you know about the disease? I mean, obviously. Obviously, she had to at least *know*. I mean, it's called 'familial Alzheimer's' for a reason. Someone in her family had to have had it," I said, then added, "It's called '*genetics*.' So my question is: did you know too?"

"What are you trying to say?"

"I'm not trying to say anything. I'm asking if you knew."

"What difference could it possibly make?"

"Well, it's just that, if you both knew, then why did you ever bother to have me?" I said, as blood, heat, and a billion neurotransmitters rendered useless my prefrontal cortex, the part of the brain that holds back anger and keeps you rational. "I mean, really, what's the point of me existing at all when I'm just going to lose my mind?"

"Seth. Come on now. You don't even know if—"

"It's just—it's just, what are you trying to hide?" I interrupted. "Like why won't you ever just be clear and say what you mean? Say what's true? Just once."

"I don't. I mean," my dad said. "I mean—"

"You mean what?"

My dad didn't say anything else for a long while. The air conditioner huffed. I watched my feet shuffle because it seemed that if I looked directly at him right then, my face might explode.

Finally, to my feet, I half-said / half-whispered, "Things need to be different."

I raised my eyes to find my dad gripping his top lip with his lower teeth, his head falling back, his eyes to the ceiling.

"I know they do," he said.

"We need to find a way to be different," I said.

My dad's mouth shifted, spitting out the top lip, inhaling the bottom.

"I know," he said. Then he pushed the stubble of his jowls into the fur of his chest, giving the effect of what he said next being spoken not into the space before him but to a space within.

"But I don't even know where to start."

"Well," I said, the condescending snappiness in my voice vanishing for the first time from our conversation. "Maybe to start with you could help me."

"Help you how?" he asked, lifting his face to mine.

"Help me by telling me what you know."

"Such as what?" he said.

"Such as anything," I said. "Such as everything."

But even though I stared at him for a painfully long, painfully silent time, my dad didn't say a thing.

"Okay, okay." I turned back toward the dark emptiness of the living room, where the frozen, bitter air produced by the eternally exhaling vents collects at night.

Behind me, my dad drew a long breath, equal parts fear and hope, not unlike the breath Taylor drew before beginning her story. Finally he said, "Listen to me, all right?"

I turned.

"Okay," he said. "All right. It's like this. I mean, to start with, I guess, it's like this. It's like when we were first together, I don't know. There were so many things I didn't know. I think that the mystery of your mom might have been part of the reason I fell in love with her. I guess I always knew that there was more than I knew. Like, for the longest time, she didn't want to have kids. She wouldn't say why. So we never talked about having any, but after a while I think we both knew that we were trying. And then you came along, and it was like I suddenly knew that all the things I didn't know about her were the only things that could ruin how happy we all were. The life we had made. So the things that used to draw me to her became the things that I myself helped her hide. I didn't want to know. You learn to live with not knowing things. And after a while, it just becomes life. You sort of live with the silence and forget it's even there. But still, it's just that sometimes . . . Sometimes the hardest questions to ask are the ones that need to be asked the most."

My dad opened his hands, displaying his palms.

I faced him and nodded.

"I think there's a lot we don't know," I told him. And then I also told him about Dr. Shellard's database, about the people I'd visited, about how Taylor's dad had told his own stories of Isidora, and about High Plains, Texas.

It was like the introduction of a catalyst, or like the story of evolution, a thing that, once begun, continues all by itself. Once I started to tell my dad things I had never told him, I kept telling and telling: about the time I almost got tested for the gene, about what my mom said the last time I visited her, about the fascinating neurocognitive research I had read. I even told him about Cara Crawford and my Mastery of Nothingness. I told him everything. Everything except for the part about the Sloth.

My dad also offered revelations of his own. The most salient of which: the game of guessing my mom's maiden name was finally over. It might have taken the fifteen years of my life and all the weeks of my empirical investigation for me to extract such a simple fact from my dad, but I found I could quickly forgive him. Because now, at last, I knew. The answer?

Haggard.

Abel

Mae's left eye drooped. Unless you leaned in all the way, and perched your head at an unusual angle, you wouldn't notice it. But it was there. Maybe it was a mistake of the mortician. Other than the sliver in which one could discern the lower slope of her pupil, she was made up with horrendous perfection, in such a way as she had rarely been in life. Her cheeks glowed with rouge; her lips were as moist and red as they had been a million nights before, in the moments after we made love and before she turned off the light. She wore a dress purchased by the funeral home for her burial, as if she were attending one last ball, thrown for the occasion of death. Even her toes, famously, adorably grotesque, had undergone a delicate transformation. Behind the shining straps of new sandals, her toenails shimmered red. All that was left to remind one of the woman she had been in life was the slit through which her left eye peered: gazing wearily onward to the inevitable complications, never surrendering entirely to a single moment, not even to her last.

In the coffin next to her, my brother's body lay in more fitting preparations. He wore the military outfit in which he had returned from the army, a decision at which I arrived without hesitation. The color had returned to his cheeks, even if it was the simple trick of one skilled at painting the impression of life onto death.

Jamie had been the first to find out. The same police officers who would later arrive at my own door had knocked, hats in their fists, and had explained about the accident. Jamie knew they were mistaken, knew her mother and father were upstairs, asleep in their bed. But when she went to their room, it was empty, the sheets lying across the bed, blue in the moonlight, flat. She cried out then, the most fundamental of all human sounds, loud and terrible enough to fill the decades of silence that would follow with its echo. And I never even heard it.

Mae had left the door unlocked. If she had simply remembered to latch it, everything would have been different. But the door was unlocked, and as Jamie and Mae slept, my brother awoke with a single need, the single memory of Jamie Whitman. Maybe he looked for me in each room. But I wasn't there. And so, Paul opened the door and stepped into the night. At some point, Mae also awoke, now in an empty bed. Without even pausing to put on her robe, she got into the car to go searching for Paul as Paul had gone searching for Jamie Whitman.

That night, Jamie wept into her hands on the floor. The police had driven me home, and I moved about the house frantically, as if motion could keep the truth from settling. I crashed into books, chairs, dishes, doors. The noise was a comfort.

But eventually Jamie raised her face, her eyes swollen and narrowed, and asked the question that forced me to surrender to stillness.

"Why did you have to leave?"

"What?"

"Why didn't you stay with us? Why did you have to go?"

What to say? It was stupid? I thought it was the only thing to do? Your mother asked me to? But there wasn't an answer.

"It was wrong," I muttered.

"Maybe if you hadn't left, he wouldn't—" Jamie began, but stopped herself before that sentence's inevitable conclusion. Some thoughts, even shared, are too terrible to be spoken.

I crouched down to her, slung my arms around her neck, and pulled her face against my hump. For a long while, neither of us said anything, our tears mingling in the place where our necks locked. It could have been minutes or it could have been hours.

"What kind of a life can I have?" she whispered, the sadness in her breath dampening my ear.

I stroked the back of her head. I clutched her with both arms, covering her, but there was no longer anything from which I could protect her. An overpowering sensation of failure conquered me, and I thought I might crumple.

"Shh," I said, then whispered that useless cliché that springs to the lips in such instances. "It's okay."

"It's not okay," she sobbed. "How can I live when I know I'll just end up like that? Forgetting everything. Destroying everything. I mean, what's the point of doing anything? I mean anything at all."

"There's no reason you should believe that."

In an instant, she pulled away from me, made a fist, which she struck through the air. She screamed then, with such force that, for a moment, she had to brace the floorboards for oxygen. "There's every reason to believe it! Your great-grandfather, your grandfather, your mom, my dad," she wept. "And soon. Me."

God help me. I never planned to say it. Who wants to tell his daughter that the life he and her mother tried to make for her has been a falsity from the start? I never meant to. Perhaps it was wrong. Out of the possibility of my wrongness in that single moment, I would serve a lifetime of penitence, loneliness, and regret. Happiness would become impossible. But she was my daughter, and I believed that only the truth could protect her now. Could I have known that with a simple utterance, vague but true, I would lose my daughter to the years?

"You have nothing to worry about," I said. "Believe me."

"Don't lie to me. I'm not a child!" she raged. "I understand the goddamn truth!"

I shuffled toward her. Isidora may have never existed, but I hoped the gesture would still be understood. I opened my hand and placed it over her heart.

"No," I said. "I don't think you do."

"What are you—" she murmured.

Technically, I never said it. At least not in so many words.

"Your mother and I," I said. "It was a long time ago. Paul was in the army. It's—it's complicated, but we— I mean, you aren't. You don't. Have to worry."

Somehow, I knew that I did not need to say anything more. She stood, or rather jolted upright, the truth dilating her eyes.

If I had to say what has given me the most hope for life, it would have to be the ridiculous simplicity of opening what was opened in that moment. That love, even love as impossible as Paul's love for the boy who died, or as impossible as the love that Mae and I shared, or as impossible as my love of my daughter, is continuous, un-marred, in the place just behind all of our insistent foolishness. And that all it takes is the slightest loosening of memory, or a single touch in a willow tree, or a vague suggestion of the truth, and the fact of how we have loved, always present, overtakes us. For a brief instant, we faced each other as we were, father and daughter. The truth.

"I can't," Jamie mumbled, her lips trembling.

"Shh," I said.

"I can't."

"Shhh," I said. "What can't you do?"

Jamie's face rose then, locked in a state of— What? Con-fusion? Relief? Resolve? Anger so overwhelming it no longer ap-peared as anger? I would spend years trying to analyze her face in that moment, her unblinking eyes raised to the ceiling.

And then Jamie said, "I can't understand."

AT THE FRONT OF THAT SHABBY MAROON ROOM, heavy with perfume, the two coffins lay symmetrically, on display, their tenants careful facsimiles of a husband and wife alive but sleeping, like a wax museum's diorama of one of history's famous couples at rest. The only actual sign of a life lived, which is to say the only sign of actual death, was the glossy crescent of Mae's eye.

In that moment, into the space between Mae's eyelids, I wanted to talk forever. I wanted to explain, or to make an endless apology. I wanted never to leave it. I clutched the cold, stiff skin of her face between my palms. I brought my mouth next to her cheek, the closeness and my tears obliterating the possibility of focus. Words stuck in my throat, I choked on words. The words I coughed out were senseless: God! I! This! Didn't! Won't! Cannot! How! Love! Please! Someone placed a hand on my shoulder, but I didn't let go. The words weren't even words, they were simply the sounds that I barked. Like a dog. I could feel eyes on my back, but away I barked.

Eventually, I must have found a way to pry my hands from the face that had been Mae's. I straightened and turned.

Everywhere, eyes stared. Here was Phil Chapman, of Chapman's Pharmaceuticals, with his two sons. Here was Gregor Dempsey with his doughty wife. Here was Samuel Berg, the mesh of his Texas Rangers baseball cap crumpled in his fist. Here was Reverend Dawdkins, pastor of First Methodist, which I had not attended since I was nine. Here was Mark Aulier, of Mark Aulier's Funeral Home. Here were countless others I did not recognize, assembled for the unfathomable spectacle of death, their faces presently locked in the attempt to fathom me. And here too was my daughter. A dark smudge at the back of the room. There will never be more sadness or anger or confusion in the world than in Jamie's face in that moment. I stood silent and unmoving, and let their eyes sink into me. It would be more than twenty years until anyone would really look at me again.

I stayed at the funeral home for the duration of the wake. Until dawn. I don't know when Jamie left. Or maybe I knew she was leaving and could not bring myself to look. At any rate, it was my last chance to say anything, or to look one final time, and I squandered it. In the morning, I led a procession to the burial place in my family's plot behind the house. Before the pair of rectangular chasms stood two tombstones, fresh and shining in an unbearable way, as if Samuel Whistler, the grave cutter, had never come to grasp the basic concept of death. But I wasn't looking at the stones, just as I wasn't watching the coffins sink into the earth, just as I looked away from the first shovelful of dirt that Reverend Dawdkins insisted I pitch into the graves. I was looking for my daughter. My daughter who wasn't there.

When the gathering had faded in a flurry of pats and handshakes, I walked alone into the house, knowing I would find it empty. Still, I moved from room to room, calling out her name like on any other day. Routine is the easiest form of denial. Inevitably, I made my way to her bedroom, to find the closet as dark and empty as the graves had been an hour before. She had made her bed with careful, almost cruel consideration, as if she had been a polite guest who wanted to leave things exactly as she had found them. On the smoothed paisley of her bed, the inevitable letter. I didn't want to read it, but that was also inevitable:

> I've decided on New York. I know this is a terrible time to leave you, but please understand—it is even more terrible for me to stay. Please don't try to contact me. When I'm ready, I'll contact you. I need to live a life that I know is mine [the word *mine* underlined twice]. I hope you'll understand. I don't

know what to say other than the truth. That my life here is no longer possible.

Love,
Jamie

I read the letter again and again. When the blow comes, and you know its resonance will be measured in years, you want the moment of impact, immaculate and thoughtless, to never end. But that was inevitable too. The letter fell from my fingers, I fell after it. On the floor, I closed my eyes, which only made me see it more clearly: beneath the withering heads of tulips and roses, beneath a mound of loose soil, beneath the walnut gloss of her casket, I knew Mae's eye still hung open, like a final question unanswered. What was there to say for myself? What was there to tell her? I'm not what could be considered religious. But alone in the house in which I had been born, grown to become a man, had something like a family, and finally lost everything, I spoke to Mae as if she were in the room.

I said, *She's gone, what can I do?*

I said, *I'm sorry, is that what you want to hear?*

Mae's eye hung open.

I said, *What? What? Tell me what I can do now. Tell me what you want me to do.*

I said, *This is impossible.*

I said, *For her to leave? I know this is impossible. But for her to just. What? To just leave?*

I said, *I want to be with you.*

I said, *You are gone and Paul is gone and Jamie is gone.*

I said, *It wouldn't take much for me to follow.*

Mae's eye glistened.

I said, *Maybe I shouldn't have told her. Or maybe we should have told them both a long time ago.*

The darkness in Mae's eye neither waxed nor waned.

I said, *To say I miss you. No. I can't imagine you gone. I can't imagine life as it is.*

I said, *I need you.*

I said, *I don't know how to live.*

I said, *It wouldn't take much. Death is impossible. But dying is so simple: A rock tied to my ankles. A pistol in my mouth.*

The crescent of Mae's eye stared.

I said, *What? What?*

I said, *Tell me. Tell me what you want me to do.*

The darkness of Mae's eye thickened, swelled, filling the room dark.

I said, *I know.*

I said, *I know. I know.*

Mae's eye didn't flinch.

I said, *Forever.*

The sliver of Mae's eye shone through darkness, through dirt and flowers and walls and rooms, and then, also, through years and years.

I said, *Forever. I promise you I will wait for her forever.*

Tonight I'm going to tell you a story that very few people know. It's the story of the fate of the little girl who came from Earth and brought with her words and thoughts and memories. For most, her story ends where the War of Isidora begins, but it's not like the girl from Earth just disappeared once she brought unhappiness to Isidora. It is true, however, that, once the first fights broke out, as Isidorans discovered that words could be screamed for added effect, the girl knew she could do little to take back what she had done. Sometimes, she would stand between two arguing Isidorans, placing her hands on their chests at the same time, trying to remind them of what they were giving up. But it was useless.

Eventually, the girl decided she was better off leaving Isidora altogether. She bundled some food into a sling, found a sturdy walking stick, and began to hike. Isidora, however, was a massive place, as big as Earth, and worse than Earth for traveling. On Earth, at least, there were maps. And so the girl had no choice but to set out in a direction that felt right. Sometimes it seemed possible she was walking in circles. And everywhere she went, the words she had brought preceded her. "Hi!" people would greet her, and she would almost crumple.

The girl walked for years and years. Walking became her life, and as she walked she grew from a girl to a woman to an old lady. It's been said that she carried the same walking stick until the end, the stick growing a little shorter each year, as if her life would be over when the knob at the top was worn to nothing.

But years before the end of her life, the girl, who was now an old woman, did at last find the city of gold at the end of Isidora. But here's the twist. By the time she found her way, she had forgotten what she was looking for. As Isidorans remembered more and more, she remembered less and less. She was an old lady now, and, like many old ladies, she lost her memories. In the city of gold, Isidorans saw the strange, filthy woman approaching and asked her where she had come from. She couldn't remember: not only where she had come from but also how to reply to such a question. The Isidorans got angry. She reminded them of the ignorant people that they thought they too had once been. Isidora had become something else, they felt, and this old hag hadn't changed with it. Three brash Isidoran boys, deciding the old woman no longer had any place in their land, took her to a hole that connects Isidora to Earth and shoved her through.

And so, the only person ever to find Isidora and make it back couldn't remember a thing about where she'd been. But also, at last, she forgot the sadness that had made her want to leave Earth in the first place. You could say, then, that all that was left of what Isidora had once been was carried inside of her.

Seth

At 1:05 A.M., the phone rang. My dad and I, for a change of pace, were watching Alfred Hitchcock's *Vertigo*, the stairwell of the old church tower expanding and contracting simultaneously, when the phone emitted its electronic yelp. We both leapt. My dad snatched the handset from its white cradle.

"Hello?"

I stood next to him and could make out the voice on the other end, a distant, scratching crackle.

"Is this Mr. Waller?"

"Speaking," my dad said.

"Mr. Waller, this is Joe Klein from Willow Acres Assisted Care."

My dad squinted at me, as if for explanation. As in the game my mom and I would play when I was little, for a split second her bewildered desperation from earlier that day became my own. And, suddenly, I started to wonder if maybe there really was some wisdom behind The Waiting Room's strict visitation policies; I knew that whatever terrible news they were about to tell my dad was my fault alone.

"Anything wrong?"

"We don't want to alarm you. But we thought you should know that your wife. She has. Well. I guess the right way to say it is, uh, gotten away from us?"

"What do you mean, 'Gotten away'?"

"Apparently a window in her room had a broken latch.

She crawled out. One of the orderlies heard her and chased after. But he, well. He lost sight of her."

"What are you telling me?"

"I'm sure she's fine. We just thought you should know. A lot of the time they just wander home. Just so you are keeping a look-out."

"A lot of the time? How often does this happen?"

"I don't mean it like that. It's just, well. Just, please. Wait at home. Don't panic. I'm sure we'll find her soon. We've got cars all over the city. Even called the police."

"What kind of an operation are your running over there?"

"I'm sorry for this. I really am. But the best thing you can do is just wait it out. We'll call you when we know more."

My dad pulled the phone from his ear, striking it through the air in his fist, pummeling nothing.

"Fine. All right. Call me." My dad hit Talk, threw the phone onto the couch, fell into the La-Z-Boy, and grabbed his scalp with both hands, displaying the receding triangle of his hairline.

"Your mother," he finally said.

"I heard."

I can't say why, but what I did next I did without thinking twice. I stood, went to the front door, unlatched the lock, turned on all the lights, just in case she actually did find her way back to our house. But, of course, I knew she wouldn't. After all, there was only one explanation for why she had escaped.

I darted to the wet bar and lifted the clunky mass of my dad's key chain. The keys sang as I tossed them to the La-Z-Boy. My dad plucked them from the air into a tight, silencing fist. His eyes flashed and he nodded. Then we got in the car and drove into the night.

HOURS LATER, the sky lightened to the same shade as the pavement. Everywhere, Westrock's construction was frozen; even its tireless armies of Mexican workers were still at home, asleep. Because the construction of Westrock is endless, buildings sprouting with the logic of a bamboo forest, the city is never the same when you drive through it twice. But right then, in the weird, blue drabness just before the sun rose, everything exposed with the same grim dullness, everything completely still, it was like driving through a photograph, a frozen moment, everything not as it had been or as it would be but just as it was, a memory taking place in the present tense.

But, like an eyelash jumping across the glass of a slide projector, amid the vast, motionless image, motion: a speck, a body, a clumsy stumble through an enormous field dotted with the orange markers for future lines of electricity and gas. The field was fenced on all sides; at its front was a sign displaying a computer-generated model of the site's future, a building of metallic glass that sloped and bent in wild parabolas. And behind the sign, marching farther and farther in her awkward but insistent way, my mom.

"There! There!" I yelled. My dad screeched the car to a stop. I hurtled myself out the door, as if in an action movie. The fence was a low chain link, at the top was a row of sharp Xs. I was able to hop over with only a small tear to the crotch of my jeans.

"Mom! Mom!" I yelled, running.

The field's soil, which had been used for a massive crop of soybeans the spring before, was a muddy, clumpy mess. Three times I landed, palms and chin, in the muck.

"Mom!"

She still kept on but for a moment swung her head toward me and paused, as if trying to remember whether I were her rescuer or the person she had been fleeing from the start.

"Stop!"

Finally, no more than five hundred feet away, the wooden shaft of a fluorescent construction marker crunching under my foot, I yelled, "Jamie!" and she turned. Slowly, panting, I walked toward her.

"It's me," I said.

My mom nodded, hesitating. That was when I saw it, clutched in her right hand, her thumb rubbing against it as if it were a wishing stone: the map of Isidora.

Even though I thought my brain might implode, I knew how she heard tones more than words, and so I tried to sound nonchalant, almost whimsical.

"And where do you think you're going?" I said with a half laugh, showing my teeth in a wide grin. My mom analyzed my mouth closely and eventually peeled her lips from her own teeth in a happy, goofy expression.

"Just where are you going?" I said again.

My mom watched her toe mash a clump of grass, then lifted her eyes to mine, shy and helpless.

"I'm supposed to be home," she said.

I walked the three or four steps to her, took the map in one hand and my mom's hand in the other, my fingers pinching her wedding ring.

"Just your luck," I said, nudging her toward the car. "I'm here to take you."

When we reached the fence, my dad was on the other side, shifting his weight between his feet, his body swaying like the pendulum of a grandfather clock, overly wound. He was talking into his cell phone, explaining to The Waiting Room that we had found her, but he quickly snapped the phone shut. I pulled my black T-shirt over my head and laid it along the top of the fence to keep my mom from cutting herself as I hoisted her over. Once on the other side, she was met with my dad's crushing hug, her arms pressed against her ribs.

"Thank God," my dad said.

My mom laughed nervously, her neck straining away. But he only squished her body with a few muscular pumps, and eventually she turned to him, kissed his cheek, and exclaimed, "You're too much!"

When she was free from my dad's grasp and I had slipped back into my now badly torn shirt, my mom opened the door to the car's passenger side and asked, "Can we go home now?"

My dad nodded, madly.

In the car, my dad's shaking hands turned the ignition key and slipped the transmission into drive. At the intersection of I-35, he steered into the left, southbound lane. A red light hung before us: an angry, scrutinizing eye.

I was silent for a minute as I thought. On my lap, I smoothed out the map. At the top right corner of the intricate and occasionally muddled outline of Texas was the *X* my mom had drawn ten years before and, next to that, the two words I had added:

HIGH PLAINS

The light turned green. My dad lifted his foot from the brake, the car lurched, but I finally said something.

I said, "Wait."

"What?" my dad asked.

"She wants you to go the other way."

"What other way?"

"North."

"What do you mean 'north'?"

"Are we going home now?" my mom begged from the back-seat.

"Yes. Yes. Home. Now," my dad said, the car beginning to follow its blinker to the left.

"Take a right!" I half-shouted.

"Why?"

I pushed my fingers into the glove compartment's latch, its mouth falling open to reveal a stack of maps, dimly lit by an orange bulb. I pulled out the *Texas Road Atlas*, unfolded it in an instant, like a parachute filling with air, and the tip of my pointer finger quickly found the words "High Plains." The car lulled in the center of the empty intersection as my dad read the name printed just beyond the gross green crescent of my fingernail. He looked at me, paused, then nodded conspiratorially.

The car crossed four empty lanes, its tires squealing onto the opposite ramp. Soon we were speeding along the endless, wide streak of concrete, drawn north.

"Where are we going?" my mom asked.

The map crinkled in my lap as I turned and smiled.

My dad said, "High Plains, apparently."

My mom rested her head against the leather armrest in the backseat. She exhaled through her nose, long and slowly, like Coach Nelson, my old P.E. instructor, would after taking the last draw of a cigarette.

She said, "Home."

For minutes, the car was silent except for the drowsy *whoosh* of the tires. My dad turned to me, lifted his right hand from the steering wheel, spanked its rim a few times before extending his fingers toward mine and tapping my hand just once. It was the first time I could remember him touching me in years. I angled the map toward him and pointed again at High Plains, a black dot at the far end of the tangled highways of Dallas. My dad rapped his fingers three times on my knuckles, then finally rested his hand on top of mine.

Eventually, my mom sat up in the backseat, her manic eyes suddenly darting into the rearview.

"Where are we going?" she asked.

"Home," I said again.

"Home?"

I turned, smiled, and nodded.

Again she slumped into her seat, again she sighed. She closed her eyes. The mess of her hair jostled around her face.

"Home," she said. "It's about time!"

Abel

They had done it. One day, I stood again at the window, again giving form to the idle lulling of clouds: open book, one-winged pigeon, bust of Aristotle. Outside, the sound of Mae's footsteps approached. The mailman. A letter tumbled through the slot and drifted to the floor. It was as simple as that. A single piece of correspondence, signed by my congressman, who regretted to inform me it was in everyone's best interest to remove me from the land my family had owned longer than we could remember. "Never," the congressman assured me, "have I felt so confident that the laws of eminent domain so clearly apply."

I had until October 1 to vacate. I was being compensated, to the tune of 150 percent of the value of my property, and my congressman wanted to let me know that if I needed assistance with the move, he would be happy to provide it, free of charge.

This was August 1, 1998. In my head, I calculated what that meant. The answer was that I had waited for twenty-one years, thirteen days, and it wouldn't be enough.

Sad to report, I felt little. Perhaps it was only the numbness that accompanies such things. But still, days passed and little more came to me. I was a wealthy man now; if I wanted, I could have hired a lawyer. I could have battled with every last dollar and every remaining day to wait longer still. But more days passed, and I didn't do anything. Maybe, shameful to admit, there was relief to be found in the prospect of having no choice.

Still more days passed, and I didn't pack a thing. But what was there worth keeping, and where would I take it anyway? What would I do, head off to a condominium in Florida with boxes of rusted garden spades, mildewed books, and ancient farm equipment in tow?

Maybe when the bulldozers came, I would lie down in front of my house. Not in protest but in total capitulation. Maybe if I covered myself in leaves and branches and got lucky, they would not notice me and I would die efficiently, pressed right into my grave.

One evening, the neighborhood was as silent as it had been before the endless mansions had come. Minus the deafening croak of locusts that once rattled the windows, if I closed my eyes I could have convinced myself that all was still as it once had been.

I boarded *The Horseless Iona*. The engine came to life. In the dawning twilight, *The Horseless Iona*'s bright beams lit up the house unnaturally, as if Hollywood had constructed the set to tell the story of the most uneventful life of the dullest man in America.

I knew where I was going and yet never decided. I hadn't been to the place since it happened, not once. Why now?

The roads were different, but I found my way by instinct. The immaculate combed concrete stretched beyond the boundaries of the endless neighborhood, formed vast cement grids across cleared-away land, an outline of the future. Beyond that, with a left turn of *The Horseless Iona*, the featureless pavement finally gave way to the deteriorated asphalt of FM 39. But even FM 39 was being prepared for a new, strange fate. Alongside the road, bulldozers idled between orange cones, staking out FM 39's destiny as a four-lane highway, already renamed in places Pleasant Drive.

As I drove through all of this, these things registered only as distant facts, like the memory of a novel read years ago. The fateful curve of FM 39 approached like a dream, with an irrational logic, an image both strange and familiar that coaxed and reassured and threatened.

And finally, the tree. It was right in the path of the construction of the future Pleasant Drive, had as little time left on this earth as did I. The both of us being one thing, the world becoming another. I dismounted *The Horseless Iona* and walked to it.

There was a dent. A crook three feet from the tree's tangling feet. Beneath it, the tree stood with military uprightness, above it, the tree's rectitude continued. Only at the dent itself did the tree buckle, like a hip swaying slightly to one side.

I put my fingers into the hollow, even peeled away the bark scars that had grown over the spot. The leaves above me paled in the wind. The tree had taken the blow but had gone on anyway. I wished I could have said the same for myself.

There weren't words for it. It was like trying to photograph a dazzling sunset or telling the story of a dream dreamt, a private intensity, and attempts at its reproduction could only be met with a shrug.

I turned back to the road. Cars rushed past, trailing clouds of dust, souls that lingered for a moment then vanished. I stood there watching it all, then dreamt of watching myself from the opposite side, that I would be there one minute, then would be eclipsed by a passing big rig, then, when the dust cleared, I would be gone altogether.

And sure enough, within minutes, the imagined big rig. The truck's noise gathering in advance of it, its headlights flashing to remind me to stay at a safe distance, but I didn't. As the truck approached, I approached it, wanting only the comfort that could be found in the deafening thunder of a thousand mechanical parts functioning in unison. In the split second before the truck reached me, when it was too late for the driver to do a thing, too late for him even to see me, I stepped farther still.

The blood dripping down Iona's face. The tears of my daughter. The crescent of Mae's eye. My brother's face against me. Mae's face. Jamie.

The wind alone almost knocked me over. I stumbled but didn't fall. I had only to extend my arm and the rest would have happened in an instant: legs, organs, hump, every thought in my ancient skull instantly crushed, bearing the final zigzag impression of steel-reinforced rubber. It was like the opposite of Michelangelo's Sistine Chapel ceiling. Man with his arm outstretched not to the giver of life but to its taker. Nearly touching. But not touching.

Though I couldn't hear it, I whispered, "I'm sorry." Or maybe I whispered, "I waited." Or maybe it was something else entirely. Whatever it had been was sucked into the cacophony, into the invisible eddies spinning off the truck's flanks, vanishing behind the taillights.

For the War of Isidora to stop, it had to get much, much worse. Already, for hundreds of years, battles had been everyday events. The leaders of great armies would invent the stupidest reasons to march against one another. What would begin with a drunken dispute over which battalion had the better looking boots could easily end with the deaths of thousands. This had all been common for some time, but eventually something changed. Now war was being fought only for war's sake. Battles were fought over battles being fought. And then there was nothing at all, not a single thought in existence in the land of Isidora other than kill, kill, kill.

And so, unconditional war, like unconditional love, was a wordless thing. Battles raged endlessly; there was only fighting. No one had the time to think of anything else, let alone to speak. Or, even if they did, the deafening explosions would have muffled anything quieter than a hand grenade.

The last battle of Isidora went on for nearly a hundred years and ended gradually, as the soldiers ran out of ammo. If it had been an earlier time, the soldiers might have dropped their weapons and charged in for hand-to-hand combat. Maybe, at the end of the War of Isidora, they started to do just that. The armies threw their weapons aside, came out of the trenches, and met in the middle. But without their guns, Isidorans, wordless and thoughtless once more, had no idea what to do. Former enemies only stared blankly at one another, waiting around for anyone who looked like he might know what he was doing. But no one did. And so, Isidorans sat down where they were, placed their hands on the chests of those who had just been enemies, and resumed their ancient ways.

But there's one last thing I should mention. It's bad news for the Isidorans but good news for us. Though all war and memory and thought and language of Isidora can be traced through a little hole that separates Isidora from Earth, Isidorans, ending the war by forgetting everything, simply forgot to do what they should have done years before. They forgot to cover the hole.

Seth

To find my mom's old house, I deduced that the only leads we had were (1) to hope (dubiously) that if we got close enough, she might be able to guide us the rest of the way; (2) to find someone, maybe an old shopkeeper, who might know something, or at least be able to provide us with helpful clues. It may have been a long shot, like a physicist hoping that cold fusion would just suddenly invent itself, but I was still hopeful.

High Plains was a six-hour drive. For the first two, the car was nearly silent, my mom happily unconscious in the backseat, the road an endless asphalt stretch. But by hour three, at 9:00 A.M., the highway cluttered with traffic, and by the time the blue glass triangles and gray rectangular prisms of downtown Dallas came into view, the drive became an infuriating lurch, an endless mass of taillights blinking madly before us, like a collective episode of Tourette's syndrome. Even as my dad yelled, "C'mon!" and "Nice move, bozo," and "Just do what you need to do, asswipe," my mom's breath still huffed from the backseat in a contented, rhythmic sleep. Eventually, the vehicular blood of I-35 began to thin. At the first signs for High Plains, forty-five minutes to the north of downtown, we exited.

We passed a little white sign that read, WELCOME TO HIGH PLAINS, TX—AN ALL-AMERICAN CITY. Similar to the way the builders of Westrock's homes replicate a set of fifteen blueprints, ad infinitum, the city of High Plains was little more than a replica of Westrock, architectural elements reshuffled. The streets were lined with the same immaculate office buildings of reflective glass, the same neon-circumscribed movie theaters, the same brick houses with their massive arched windows, the same metal bones of future strip malls, the same wooden bones of future neighborhoods. From the construction, everywhere, dust clouds gathered and swept into the streets, temporarily blinding the view out the windshield.

I turned, slightly lifting myself from my seat, then placed my hand on my mom's knee, shaking it. She stirred, then startled upright.

"What? What is it?" she asked, her head darting left and right with the mechanized speed of a bird. "Where are we?"

"We're almost home," I said.

"Oh," she sighed. "Great."

"Do you recognize anything?"

My mom watched the steel ribs of a future church slide past her window. "Of course."

I steadied myself on the armrest and said, "Well, we're just a little bit lost. Think you could tell us which way your house is?"

My mom made a familiar gesture, rubbing her thumb and first two fingers before her, as if trying to feel the invisible idea she couldn't quite explain. Eventually, she dropped both arms and shrugged.

"Okay," I said.

"But where are we going?" my mom asked.

"Home."

My mom resumed her sleeping position, resting her head on her crossed arms.

My dad whispered, "So what do we do now?"

"I guess we keep driving."

But the more we drove, the more impossible it seemed. Nothing in High Plains looked more than a year or two old. It soon became abundantly clear that this would be the least fruitful place on Earth to go digging around for ancient history.

I looked at my dad, expecting him to ask when I would just give it up, but instead he stared at the road with the total, unbroken focus he typically reserves only for The History Channel.

"Let's be more methodical," he said. "We'll start at one end of the city and go up and down each street until we get to the other."

Beneath my sternum, I could feel exhaustion, or maybe it was dread, bubbling in a few nauseated burps that I had to suppress. Even though I had discovered that Taylor's father, whose family was from High Plains, had told Taylor the stories of Isidora, even though I had watched in aneurysm-provoking astonishment as the X my mom had placed on my old map aligned almost perfectly with the city of High Plains, it seemed entirely possible that I was drawing false conclusions from erroneously gathered data, that as an empirical investigator I was useless, that it would take a deductive mind far more advanced than mine simply to find out the truth about my mom, let alone construct her genetic history, let alone locate the one place she needed to go. If I could have done it in a way my dad couldn't see, I would have snapped myself with the rubber band until the pain became unbearable.

I was already giving up. Instead of watching out for anything that looked like it might have existed longer than the life span of a lemming, I closed my eyes and imagined my mom's old family. My imagination went everywhere. It went to the hands of my grandfather, whoever he had been, as they stroked my mom's hair. It went to the lips of my grandmother, whoever she had been, as they pressed against my mom's forehead. It went through my mom's eyes on the day my grandparents had died in their untold way, and gazed down at their bodies. It curled and bent and twisted into what she might have felt at that moment, looking at her parents for the last time. It became the single, lucid pain that she had spent the rest of her life burying. What had it been? Resentment? Confusion? Rage? A spectacularly simple, reckless grief?

"Yo," my dad said. "Hey. Earth to Seth. Aren't you even going to keep a lookout?"

I shrugged, then pressed my face against the sweaty glass of the window so that he wouldn't see me close my eyes.

After several minutes, silent except for the breeze of the air conditioner and the low hum of the engine, my dad finally said, "Holy shit."

I startled and opened my eyes.

Out the window, wedged in the middle of a neighborhood just like mine, a subdivision of a thousand variations on the same dull architecture, was something strange. My dad slowed for a better look. It was the shambles of an ancient house, two stories of slanting, splintering, peeling wooden decay. At the front were the remnants of what had once been an ornate fence, now grotesque in an oddly beautiful way, orange rust slowly disintegrating the twisting wrought iron, the gate door nearly fallen from its hinges to the thick, clumpy weeds beneath. It looked as if no one could possibly have lived there for years, as if it had only sat there for a decade or more, forgotten and rotting. I wondered how it had avoided getting plowed over, the way they'd plowed over the few old barns and sheds that still dotted Westrock at the start of its metastasis, when I was five or six. But, to tell the truth, these were the things I thought only after a long stunned moment, gaping up at the rust-eaten name sitting on its rust-eaten posts above the battered gate:

HAG ARD

"Haggard," I whispered.
My dad nodded. "Haggard."
And then I saw the house for what it was. A ramshackle, more

intricate version of how I had imagined it: a loose gravel driveway (but the stones now scattered into the grass), a slanting barn (but now slanting so far as seemingly to defy the laws of physics), an old white house (but the paneling now mostly exposed wood of weathered gray, only occasionally flecked with white). Once the shock of actually finding the place I had imagined for years and had searched out for months began to register, the sight of it stirred a giddy kind of disappointment. It was like watching a film version of a well-loved book, the excitement of seeing a thing that has existed only in your imagination suddenly materialized into reality, with the supplementary sadness that from that moment on you'll never be able to imagine it in any way other than how it appeared before you.

In the backseat, my mom perked up, then chimed, "We're there!"

My dad parked on the opposite side of the street, in front of a two-story house of immaculate stucco, then followed my mom and me as we got out of the car and tiptoed over the ruins of the gate.

The sun was already settling in the sky, the pebbles strewn over the path leading up to the ancient place casting inch-long shadows into the wild grass.

I don't know exactly what I expected to find, or what good I thought it would do my mom to see the house of her childhood, now as deteriorated as her mind. I only walked around its walls, my imagination leveling the surrounding rows of McMansions, restoring the emptiness of the fields, as my mom had once known them. I turned, faced the old place, and found that my imagination could remember it too, as it once must have been. My imagination straightened the bowing posts, uncracked the windows, healed the battered roof, returned the members of my mom's vanished family.

While my dad and I, dazed and mute, paced around, my mom snuck off. She walked to the place where two doors, stippled with bite marks of oxidation, rose from the grass. She pulled open one of the doors with an unhealthy yowl, revealing a short flight of concrete stairs that led to an underground storage cellar. She descended to the third step and curled herself into a tight ball beneath the still-closed door.

"What are you doing?" I said. "You shouldn't be in there."

My mom didn't say anything.

"You could hurt yourself," my dad said.

"Come on," I begged.

Finally, my mom emitted a long, belabored sigh, then whined, "I can't hear you. I'm invisible."

My dad shrugged, then suggested that, if we just walked away, she might follow.

And so we went to the opposite side of the house, eventually arriving at a scattering of graves. I looked down at the name Haggard, carved into stone again and again, and wondered which Haggards had been my grandparents, and also which Haggards had been killed by the EOA-23 variant.

Eventually, my dad sidled up to me, the gravestone of Mae Haggard at my feet. He rested his palm on the crown of my skull, like he used to do when I was younger.

Unexpectedly, I felt a rising wave of disappointment, flushing away any possibility of pride or satisfaction. I knew I had found my mom's old house, but what was there really to see? Only a name, the earth, an empty, rotting, forgotten house, all that was left of a family and a life my mom had fled, all that was left of people I could never know.

For a long moment we just stood there, my dad's thumb palpating my head.

Eventually, I turned. Heat rose into my face, radiating from my sinuses, stinging the corners of my eyes.

"What is it?" my dad said.

I must have started to cry, because before I knew it my dad's arms were around me and four wet circles were growing from my eyes and my nostrils on the gray cotton of his sleeve. His arms were heavier than I remembered.

"I need to know," I said.

"Know what?"

I thought.

I thought, That you still love her? I thought, That you will stop being ashamed of her? I thought, That you will stop trying to pretend she doesn't exist? I thought, That we still have each other? I thought, That once, we were a family and we were happy?

I said, "That we haven't lost everything."

If you start to feel like you'll never make it to Isidora, you have to find a way to hope. A way to believe. Your faith in Isidora and your distance from its lands are one and the same. To find Isidora is like so much else: faith and its realization are conjoined twins, one's heart pumping the other's blood. To find Isidora, you must only believe that you will find Isidora.

But if, when you're an old man, you stop believing; if you decide that you've looked long enough; if you start to number your burdens; if, defeated, you return home; if, at the end of your life, you should count yourself among the cynics, promise me that you'll keep your pessimism to yourself. Promise me that you won't be so selfish as to believe the idea of Isidora belongs to you alone.

Instead, you should tell others, tell your children, how close you came, that if only you had carried another canteen of water or another sack of food, maybe you could have made it all the way.

The truth is that the idea of Isidora has always been as important as Isidora itself. Isidora is the light coming through our window. Without it, the darkness of night would blacken all rooms, all corners, leaving us blind to fumble and crash about our things.

And so, in the last moments of your life, when your child presses his ear to your lips, both of you straining for a final word, promise me that you'll whisper Isidora's name. Promise me that you'll say, "Isidora," as if it's laid out before you.

Abel

Countless times over the years I had imagined it. Her feet shuffling up to the threshold, a knocking at my door. Unlatching its locks, I would pull it open, and Jamie's face would be revealed to me.

I would say: I am sorry. I would say: I am sorry for so much. I would say: There are so many things I should have told you earlier. I would say: Most of all, I am sorry that I did not have the courage to tell you the one thing that might have made a difference before it was too late. That I did not tell you the truth. We thought it was for the best. Your mother did. I was never certain, but I don't blame her. I blame only myself for the selfishness of my happiness aeons ago. That kind of happiness can only cause damage, and look what an example I have made of our lives. Happiness like that, I once thought it was the simplest thing in the world. But it was only suffering that turned out to be dependable. I don't know if I can take this. Maybe it's better to live with only the possibility of happiness than to abandon the old reliable and die of joy. Please, you don't have to say anything. I'll go. The house is yours.

And then, as a final gesture, I would give Jamie the only thing I still possessed that might be of some value to her, the journal in which her grandmother had written the stories of our family's imagination.

. . .

I HAD ONLY A FEW WEEKS LEFT IN MY HOUSE and still hadn't moved a thing. There were no plans, and the days were unraveling. Some days, I would do little more than sit on the balding, befouled sofa with Mama's book of Isidora stories balanced between my thighs, reading through them in the way of things memorized, a reading without the horizontal movement of my eyes. Other days, out of habit, I would spend useless hours plucking weeds from the garden, as if it weren't about to be plowed over with the rest of my home. On still other days, I would drive *The Horseless Iona* far to the north, an experience akin to watching the history of my farm in reverse: neighborhoods five or ten years old giving way to freshly minted houses, giving way to the frameworks of soon-to-be houses in their pinewood outlines, giving way to the concrete matrices where neighborhoods will one day rise, giving way—at last—to the landscape of my childhood, an endless study of the horizontal, punctuated only by the occasional farmhouse, its triangular summit rising ecclesiastically from the terrain.

That afternoon, returning from a two-hour journey to nowhere, I jostled in *The Horseless Iona* up the gravel drive.

In many ways, it seemed as if the end of the summer had begun to announce itself. The willow tree had already shed most of its leaves, exposing its tired, barren fingers. The tall grass out front, like the house behind it, stood in a stiff, colorless imitation of its former life, crumbling under the slightest step. But it was still far too early for fall; the seasons couldn't be blamed, just as they couldn't be counted on for eventual renewal. What was finally coming to the old place stood outside the dependable rounds of life.

This day, however, was a real beauty. The warmth of the sun massaged my face. I searched the sky's clouds for a time, naming their shapes: steamboat, Mickey Mouse, bear with open jaws, tattered pants, phallus. Suddenly, at the echo of voices from behind the house, my heart dislodged and sank to my stomach, beating it like bongos. The word *Trespassers!* leapt up my throat. I crept up, slid slowly along the wall. In case the trespassers were thieves, I searched the ground for a weapon. But there was nothing, not even a decent size rock. And so, instead, I only balled my hands into two tight fists, as if I believed my old body, now barely capable of knocking the fuzz from a dandelion, could still muster a good, old-fashioned clobbering, if the need for a clobbering should arise.

I peeked around the peeling paint of the corner, when I spotted them: two men sitting together on the earth of my family's plot. I loosened my hands.

At my age, each step is an undertaking, a small pain to any number of joints, muscles, and bones. But as I approached them, my perplexity extinguished the pain of walking.

"Excuse me," I said.

The two startled, quickly stood, and turned to me. Their faces were illegible against the afternoon sky.

"This land still belongs to me," I said.

The smaller of the two cocked his head and mumbled that he was sorry and that they would leave. But when he spoke, it was not the voice of a man but that of a boy. I walked to him for a closer look.

In the expression on the boy's face, pangs of embarrassment were overwhelmed by confusion. The man who was with the boy—it must have been his father—watched the boy carefully.

The boy searched me with his eyes, questioning with such intensity that the words seemed to slip, unintentionally, from his lips.

"Who are you?"

"This is my property," I said, the firmness in my voice fading.

Behind the dirt mottling his skin, behind the profusion of acne between his eyebrows (the mark of imminent manhood that I too had once borne), the boy's eyes narrowed.

It would be a lie to say I knew the truth instantly upon laying eyes on the boy. True to say, however, is that, though I had come to see my daughter's face in all of the world's faces, in the boy before me I thought I saw something else: not so much Jamie's face but rather the distance between her face and his, the way one looks into the face of a child and contemplates which elements, in the mixing of parents, have been kept and which have been abandoned.

"I'm sorry. We'll leave. But it's just that . . . Well, it's complicated, I guess. It's just that we think my mom is from somewhere around here, but we don't know for sure, but she used to tell me these stories, about this make-believe place called Isidora, and it's——" The boy stumbled on his words, then fell silent.

It took me minutes to believe. It would have seemed more plausible that Mama would suddenly leap up out of the earth than that this sad-faced boy would be standing at her grave nearly fifty years after her death, describing the stories she told me in my own boyhood. My bladder muscles, not what they once were, failed me for a fleeting moment, and I felt a short, warm rush on my thigh. Blood surged in my brain, and I prayed that if a stroke was coming, it would at least wait long enough for me to ask, "Your mother. Who is she?"

Our eyes, locked, were having a conversation of their own.

The boy turned to his father, gave him a desperate, perplexed look that sought explanation or maybe permission. His father only clenched his brow, a knot of confusion rising in his forehead.

The boy spoke again.

"Um. You mean her name?" he asked. "It's Jamie. Jamie Waller."

For a moment, I thought perhaps I had died already. Perhaps that big rig had taken me after all. Perhaps, for all the time since, I had been in limbo, the punishment for a life such as mine the simple knowledge that I would have to wait for my daughter for all eternity. But now, perhaps, I had already been punished enough, perhaps in the court of the heavens I was being set free.

I had to offer myself proof that I was, in fact, alive. I stomped my feet a bit to remind them of the hardness of the earth. I dug my fingernails into the flesh of my arm to feel earthly pain. The fingers themselves I ran over the wrinkled, worn flesh of my face to feel the effects of age that only mortality can bring. But it finally was the taste of salt, my nostril's tears on my lips, that did the trick and let me believe.

"Jamie is my daughter's name," I said.

The silence of all thoughts at once.

"My mom's parents are dead," the boy whispered, faltering.

I nodded.

I couldn't find a way to say anything else. All my old body would allow was for me to turn and gesture for the boy and the man to follow me.

In a collective daze, as if carried by an invisible breeze, the three of us drifted into the house.

Failing utterly to come up with whatever it is that should be said in such a situation, I offered the boy and the man some coffee. Though, truth be told, I hadn't had coffee in the house for over eighteen years.

"No thanks," the man replied.

The boy turned to his father, his face twisting with confusion, and asked, "Should I?" He then pointed, in a brief, shaking gesture, at the door.

"No, no," I said. "Don't leave. Don't leave. Please. Don't."

I lowered myself into my old, creaking chair at what was left of the dinner table. I gestured with an open palm for the boy and the man to sit as well. And so, for what could have been minutes, the three of us only sat there, each occasionally opening his mouth, but the words sticking, unspeakable, in our throats.

"Nice place," the man finally managed.

I shrugged and examined the delicate pattern of a crack in the wood.

When I heard her voice, I jolted, nearly toppling the old chair. Who can describe the actual sound of an actual voice that one has spent over twenty-one years imagining?

"Hellloooo?" she sang at the front door. "Anyone hoooome?"

I pressed my palms against the table. Somehow, at some point, I must have stood; when the song of Jamie's voice found its way to me, I found myself standing to meet it. When I saw her face, my brain thought a million thoughts, a cacophonous crush.

It was as if the great subterranean plates of my body shifted, not a joint was without tremor. Jamie, however, walked straight into the kitchen, breezing right past me.

"Oh, hey," she said. "God! I'm starrrr-ving!"

She opened a cabinet with a rusty whine and popped open a bag of Cool Ranch Doritos.

I perhaps said her name or perhaps did not say her name; either way, her name laid claim to all the oxygen of my lungs.

"Where is everyone?" she asked. "Mama around?"

I had seen her face everywhere. I had thought I was dying. I had thought that at the moment when the face of my daughter finally claimed all life, when the rocks and the water and the buildings and my own hands and the earth beneath my feet stared at me with her eyes, when there could be no life but her to see, I would vanish. But perhaps I was mistaken. Perhaps this entire time I had seen her everywhere so that I might finally find her somewhere. Here and now, before me. My daughter. I wanted to ask, in a million ways, how it was possible. I wanted to ask: Why? And why now? And how? I wanted to talk forever. I wanted to cry out. I wanted to clutch her and dance about. I wanted to lift her from the floor. I wanted to touch her face and ask, again, if it was possible.

So grateful and confused and impossible was the moment that it took me minutes to think: But.

But, if she had come back to me as my daughter again, if she had come back to me as if it were any other day from a lifetime before—then, what? Then either I had finally lost it, had dreamt of this moment with such necessity that my mind had made it reality, or else. Or else all the years in between—a husband, a son, the life she had cultivated—had died.

"Your mother," I said. "Your mother is. Not here."

She stepped toward me, pushed her fingers into my beard.

"God! You feeling all right?" she said. "You don't look so good."

"I know it."

"You look so old," she said.

I sighed.

I said, "Would you believe it's been more than twenty-one years?"

Jamie echoed, "Twenty-one years?"

I opened my arms, then filled them with her. My muscles may not be much, but with all my force, I squeezed. I squeezed and squeezed with all the strength I could muster, but it could never be enough. Never enough for her to be as close as I needed, never enough for our bodies to fuse, never enough for the two of us to become as one, never enough for me to know I would never lose her again. My tears took control of my breath with their own demands.

Eventually, dislocating her shoulder blades like Houdini in his chains, she wriggled free. She searched my face, that soggy mess, that pitiful smear of gratitude and remorse and, of course, plain, simple love.

"Lord! What's gotten into you?"

"I'm sorry," I said.

Jamie shrugged, pinched the corners of the Doritos bag, angling its bottom to the ceiling, a small avalanche of Doritos crumbs tumbling into her mouth.

Eventually, I knew what must be done. But first I stared at her face for sufficient time to convince myself that it would still be there when I turned, that it was something more than chimera, something more than a simple feat of mental prestidigitation.

In the living room, Mama's journal rested on its shelf at the top of the bookcase. Reaching, I lifted it.

When I returned to the kitchen, I found that the boy and the man had stood. The boy's fingers were fiddling with the arched back of Mae's old chair. The man's arm was clutching Jamie's shoulders. Jamie was methodically plucking the O of her mouth with her chemical-orange fingers.

I walked. Not to my daughter, but to my— What? Grandson? His eyes rose to meet mine. My arms trembled as I extended them, straining under the mass of the book. Our fingers interlocked on the spine.

"What is this?" the boy asked.

I shrugged. What to say? That this is all that is left of us? Better to say, simply, "I want you to have this."

Perhaps the boy understood. In his breath on my beard, I felt the breath of my mother and of Mae and of Paul and also of Jamie.

"Is she all right?" I whispered. But I knew the answer.

Slowly, the boy shook his head.

"Her memory?" I whispered. But I knew the answer.

Slowly, the boy nodded. His breath quickened, tears trickled from his nostrils down my neck.

I had spent every day of Jamie's life in fear of it. I had almost convinced myself it was impossible. When the doctor had said that only the child of one suffering with the disease could inherit it, something profound loosened within me. And still, for all these years, I carried the fear in the same way one carries one's own blood. Was it the fear that the doctor was wrong, that the disease has its own cruel logic that no one can predict? Or had the fear been something else? That perhaps Mae's delivery had not been delayed but had occurred precisely on schedule, nine months after my brother's return? Did that mean Mae had been wrong when she had come in from the outhouse a lifetime ago? Or had she lied? Or had she known our love was wrong with such profundity that it had rearranged the basic rhythms of her body, insisting upon what was right? I patted the boy's head. It didn't matter now. Little did. Little, but this. I was more tired and also more awake than ever.

Now that I knew the curse of our family had come for her too, I wanted only to comfort the boy, to say something that might explain anything. But what? To say that I was a person who had once fallen in love with everything, and what else could I have done? Or to say that all of my attempts to find a way to live had ended up becoming my life? Or to say that I had waited for so long that I had almost forgotten there was something I was waiting for, that waiting itself nearly became the point? Or to say that I would have kept on, that I would have waited forever, that I would have held on to the memory of us until the end of time because waiting was the only place left for my love? Or to say that it was only the impossible—my love for Mae, or Paul's love for Jamie Whitman, or my love of my daughter, or the belief that she would come back to me, or the world of my family's imagination—that could ever make life possible? That the impossible had made this possible too? Or to explain to the boy that now that he had arrived there was really nothing to say at all, that there was no wisdom, that there was only the meaningfully pointless fact that we existed? Or to scream, with all the breath that my lungs could still muster, that we will exist still?

But, instead, I only rocked my head in a long, slow nod. The boy drew the book to his chest. The weight left my hands.

For the great majority of its history, Alzheimer's disease, in its myriad forms and variants, has been considered little more than a part of the natural processes of aging, a collapse of mind as the mental component of an overall collapse of the body. As David Shenk notes in his book *The Forgetting: Alzheimer's: Portrait of an Epidemic,* long before the disease was scientifically categorized, it had often been described. The ancient Roman poet Juvenal, for example, opines, "Worse than any loss in body is the failing mind which forgets the names of slaves, and cannot recognize the face of the old friend who dined with him last night, nor those of the children whom he has begotten and brought up." Over the thousands of years before Alois Alzheimer peered into his microscope, allowing himself the world's first glimpse of the disease's subcellular snares and plaque, what we would come to call "Alzheimer's" had gone by many names: "*morosis* in Greek, *oblivio* and *dementia* in Latin, *dotage* in Middle English, *demence* in French, and *fatuity* in Eighteenth Century English." But even as many as fifty years after the prominent neurologist Emil Kraepelin named the syndrome *Morbus Alzheimer* in dubious honor of its discoverer, Alzheimer's disease was still considered nothing more than a neurological oddity of relevance similar to that of Huntington's chorea and Parkinson's disease to the world at large. Though, by the mid-twentieth century, the diagnosis had long existed, the middle-aged children of senescent parents still marched away from their family doctors satisfied with a vague verdict of "senility" or "dementia."

It wasn't until the late 1970s that things started to change. As modern medicine developed at an astounding pace, blood thinners and chemotherapy and robust antibiotics granting an extra decade or so of life, developed nations found themselves with a burgeoning new demographic. Largely retired from their jobs, often with little more to distract themselves than fretting over the weekly phone calls from their far-flung sons and daughters, the elderly began to congregate, compare notes, and make demands. Thus came the age of early-bird specials, senior citizen discount tickets, endless shelves of large-print fiction, and the most politically powerful lobbying group in the country, the American Association of Retired Persons. As massive numbers now survived years and years of their retirements, the elderly began to consider the collapse of their minds to be something other than normal. More and more, they demanded specific diagnoses and treatment, demanded that doctors begin to call the thing what it was. By the conflation of a cantankerous new generation and a slew of pharmaceutical companies eager for the market of a new, widespread chronic disease, Alzheimer's quickly rose in the public consciousness to the rank of true epidemic.

It was around this time, three years before the establishment of the Alzheimer's Association, that my mother, then Jamie Haggard (EOA-23 Sufferer A-39 in Shellard's report), left her childhood home for good.

What isn't known about my mom during this time is left for me to imagine. And yet, whatever the reasons, my image of her trip to New York couldn't be more lucid if I were remembering it myself:

After dawn on the third day of the bus ride from Texas, the monotonous, sprawling flatness of the Great Plains was suddenly punctured, in a single turn, by the Allegheny Mountains, standing like an epiphany before the interstate. It was at that moment, I choose to believe, that my mom made a vow. Later, she would sometimes laugh at the naïveté of it. An eighteen-year-old girl swearing away the past, swearing never to return, swearing herself to nothing less than rebirth. Even at the time, she forced herself to reason away pangs of doubt:

People take vows all the time, she thought. Vows of silence, of poverty, of abstinence, of fidelity. Even vows of rebirth. Maybe it's not so impossible.

And for her first years in New York, my mom kept her resolve. When the other kids from her classes cornered her at parties and asked in their hot, beery breath where she was from, she'd make something up. Even though the story would often change, three sisters in Florida becoming two sisters and a brother in Arkansas, the others rarely noticed the contradictions, and she took it as a lesson on how rarely people actually listened.

Even to my dad she told half-truths. She told him that she was from Texas, that her parents were dead, but when he asked the name of her town, she simply lied, simply said the first word that came to her lips. For a while, my dad pressed and pressed for more details, the repleteness of his newfound love like a torch that he was committed to carry into her depths, casting light on everything, searing away that which he had begun to sense held her from him at some unknowable distance.

But, still, she told him little more. And so, here I am again left only to imagine. Maybe it was that in all the years since she fled her home, one of the few comforts my mom found in her pain was its singularity, that such sadness and betrayal as hers were hers and hers alone. That she was beyond understanding. That her pain couldn't be reflected back, not even in the face of her husband, who carried his own tragedies. But maybe if she told him the truth, if she explained herself to him fully, then, reflected in his expression, she might at long last find a mirror to her grief. It would be like staring into a total eclipse of the sun: a pure and complete view of the local cosmos at the cost of one's eyesight.

According to my profusely blushing dad (an account offered to me only after I begged for more details, then pointed out how he too had once begged), after my parents made love for the first time, buoyant from wine, my mom held both sides of his face and repeated, more or less, the vow she had made years before.

"Let's be completely new people together," she said. "Just completely . . . new."

My dad, who had his own past to transcend, with a father who drank himself to death and a mother with whom he communicated as seldom and as cautiously as Kennedy had with Khrushchev, gratefully kissed her face and told her that he loved her.

They rarely spoke of the past.

Three years after they were married, my mom missed her period. After twenty days of anxious speculation, she finally went to the bodega in the first floor of her building, bought a pregnancy test kit, and verified the foregone conclusion. Though there is no way to know for certain, I choose to believe that it was at that moment, staring at the two red stripes, that my mom felt a sensation she had never quite felt before: a vertiginous, giddy dread.

And the next day, as she woke, the sensation was still with her. It would, in fact, stay with her, off and on, for years, would become nearly as tangible and dependable from day to day as the contours of my father's face. The sensation was something more insubstantial and more sickening than pure and simple guilt, but in the months and years that followed, as it often percolated somewhere within her, flittering up like bubbles trapped in her blood, filling her mind with a dread as light as helium, my mom called it guilt. That morning, however, she told herself it was only her first bout of morning sickness.

Whatever the sensation was, it stirred within her an irrepressible compulsion, a singular need to *do*. To do something, anything, claw at a chair, pound the air with her fists, run right out of her house. The gauzy dread, the lazy, crushing failure, life's inability to hold dependable shapes before her, its utter indifference to her most concerted and persistent efforts: in the years that followed, all that it took to summon it was a sudden irrepressible flickering of a childhood memory, or the noticing of how I held a pen just as her father had (clumsily, with the shaft between my middle and ring fingers), and my mom would suddenly jolt upright, or pace the neighborhood in a nightgown in the middle of the night, or clutch herself, arms wrapped tightly around her torso, as if to keep herself from disintegrating.

Though I can never know for certain, I believe that, as the symptoms became undeniable, as she silently admitted to them, as she knew what my dad and I would soon have to endure, as she understood that, despite all of her efforts, the story of our family had been written upon her most fundamental places, my mom understood the truth. That the feeling she had never been able to comprehend was, in fact, ridiculously simple. The feeling was guilt. Guilt over leaving her uncle, who was actually her father, who may actually have been her uncle. And, more than that, the guilt of possibly passing to me the one memory that no effort of will could suppress: the memory of our family, in miniature within each of our cells.

IN 2001, twenty-five years after the word *Alzheimer's* had entered common parlance; long after it had become the simple three syllables that a dutiful son could whisper, apologetically, to the waiter when his senile father launched into a rage at the table; long after it had become, in turn, the object of empirical scrutiny, intensive investigation, major government grants, and fund-raising walks, an innovative team of researchers from the Elan Corporation in San

Francisco appeared to have made a major leap forward in its eradication. They had invented a vaccine called "AN-1792," an injection of microbiotic instructions to the immune system, an order to dispatch armies of white blood cells on an interneural find-and-destroy mission to attack the nefarious amyloid plaque, one of Alzheimer's two means of degeneration. Researchers gathered hundreds of patients with mild to moderate Alzheimer's disease for a test run, and for a few rarefied months the news was good. The vaccinated showed dramatically improved immune response, without notable side effects. Already, experts began to estimate how long FDA approval might take, driving the families of sufferers, by the tens of thousands, to frenetic bouts of speculation ("Will Mom still really be Mom when it's 2005?"). Soon, however, came a major blow: in 15 of the 360 trial subjects, the vaccine rendered the immune system overreactive, and—like teenagers obsessively thumbing whiteheads and thus nurturing massive boils—the subjects' white blood cells had attacked and attacked, swelling their brains inside their skulls, almost fatally. The trial was called off.

After the failure of AN-1792, scientists continued at a feverish pitch, biopsying the disease's devastation from cadavers, probing its microscopic depths with electron-emitting microscopes, correlating its appearance with every imaginable environmental factor (intellectual stimulation, cigarette smoking, antioxidant dieting, red wine drinking, even gum chewing). In the absence of real hope, horror-struck family members, in between changing their parents' diapers and spooning them baby food, could go to the Alzheimer's Association website and read the latest findings: a new protein associated with neuronal failure; a new chromosome that carried genes linked to the disease; a new, vital enzyme discovered to be missing in Alzheimer's sufferers. And yet, behind each word they patiently read was invariably the same question, latent and desperate: Was science, in fact, advancing toward anything?

Or was it only giving more intricate form to a hopelessness as old as human history?

But maybe the research itself, the steady if stultifying march of findings, was a comfort. Maybe, in the absence of full understanding, each new discovery described at least the periphery of the dark, unknowable thing, offering the condemned a glimpse of their executioner, if hooded. If the new findings offered little more in tangible results, they offered vastly more to the imaginations of the sufferers and their families, allowing them to imagine a line of connectivity, an invisible rope that tied the smallest new facts to complete understanding. A rope that they might grasp at the last possible minute, and thus, dangling over oblivion action-movie style, be pulled to safety.

WHEN I WAS A CHILD in my bed at night, my mom's voice would hover in the darkness.

"Alongside this world there's another," she would say. "There are places where you can cross."

Maybe the point of transference doesn't have to be a place at all. Maybe it can be as simple as a single fact without context, a mystifying new finding, a story from the forgotten past, a name on a list of the dead, the point at which—like a wormhole in time-space—the knowable converges with that which can only be imagined. Each new detail of my mom's life that I have learned from my father and from Abel, like each of my nameless and forgotten ancestors in Dr. Shellard's final report on the EOA-23 variant of familial early-onset Alzheimer's, is exactly that: a slight presence that opens a bottomless absence, a portal to a parallel private universe that I can only pretend to describe.

Alongside this world there's another.

The mind, above all, wants to make sense. Almost everything it perceives it forgets. And most of what it perceives it does so only in the tiniest of fragments. Wholeness and continuity are false impressions, like a museum re-creation of a *Tyrannosaurus rex* skeleton fashioned from a few found bones, fragments of reality secured into a whole that seems real enough. Now a third-year graduate student in Marvin Shellard's Neurodegenerative Studies Lab, I spend my days taking measurements of what can be measured, gathering oral histories, entering data, correlating the findings. At night, however, I slip through the door of each datum, filling the vast emptiness that stretches around the tiniest pieces of my family's history, trying to fashion a whole in the way we always do, as my family has done before me, filling the dark, impossible places with my best guesses and also with outright lies, so that they might at least be filled with something.

There are places where you can cross.

One night, when I was fifteen, my mom awoke in a dark room in a dark house. It was cold, and she couldn't find the light switch. Maybe she wondered if she was dreaming, then wondered if it was possible to dream of nothing. Well, not nothing, she must have thought. The scratch of the carpet against her toes as she walked. A cold breeze. The old, familiar dread, restless and wandering. What was she looking for? Something above her clicked and breathed. Where was she going? A cold breeze. The friction of Berber carpet at her feet. Finally, she came to the edge of something. Maybe what she came there looking for lay beyond. She was at the edge, but there was something stopping her, a wooden railing in her hand. Behind her, there was a breeze and the carpet and the darkness. Beyond her, there could be anything. And so she pushed with her feet. She reached beyond, and then there was nothing. Nothing but a singular force, a falling, the heaviness of her own self, and finally the sound.

A spectacular pain suddenly split open at the base of her skull, like fault lines parting, and for a moment she was terrified. But when the pain ceased, it was followed by clarity: she knew then that she was asleep, dreaming she was just outside her house. Not her house as it is, but her house as it was. Or maybe, even, as it never was. Her old house, the home of her childhood, but set in another place. A place thoughtless and perfect. A place freed from the past and from the future. A place where nothing was remembered and so nothing could be lost. A place where whatever she needed she had only to imagine.

This book, like the disease it describes, began subtly, with a few stray thoughts that only after a long while became something classifiable. I owe most of these early ideas, as well as many of those that followed, to the work of other writers, filmmakers, and researchers.

To begin with, it was Jonathan Franzen's moving and sharply insightful essay "My Father's Brain" that forever changed the way I think of Alzheimer's, explicating its emotional complexities, bizarre paradoxes, and creative possibilities. Franzen's essay also pointed me to David Shenk's *The Forgetting: Alzheimer's: Portrait of an Epidemic*, the reading of which was for me an experience close to perpetual awe.

As I wrote, I often also thought of Alice Munro's short story "The Bear Came over the Mountain," John Bayley's memoir *Elegy for Iris*, and *Losing My Mind: An Intimate Look at Life with Alzheimer's*, Thomas DeBaggio's courageous and inventive account of his own descent into the disease.

When I needed to describe the bodily expressions of Alzheimer's, I inevitably returned to Deborah Hoffmann's humorous and humane documentary *Complaints of a Dutiful Daughter*.

To check my facts, and also to remind myself of the daily costs of life with the disease, I often read the useful and comprehensive *Alzheimer's: A Caregiver's Guide and Sourcebook* by Howard Guetzner.

Within the book are several references to scientific publications. The full citations for these articles are as follows: N. Benítez, J. Maíz-Apellániz, and M. Cañelles (2002), "Evidence for Nearby Supernova Explosions," *Physical Review* Letters 88, no. 8; M. Chivers, G. Reiger, E. Latty, and M. Bailey (2004), "A Sex Difference in the Specificity of Sexual Arousal," *Psychological Science* 15, no. 11:736–744; J. Kruger and D. Dunning (1999),

"Unskilled and Unaware of It: How Difficulties in Recognizing One's Own Incompetence Lead to Inflated Self-Assessments," *Journal of Personality and Social Psychology* 77, no. 6:1121–34; E. H. Rosch (1983), "Prototype Classification and Logical Classification: The Two Systems," in E. Scholnick, ed., *New Trends in Cognitive Representation: Challenges to Piaget's Theory* (Hillsdale, N.J.: Lawrence Erlbaum Associates), 73–86; D. M. Wegner, T. Giuliano, and P. Hertel (1985), "Cognitive Interdependence in Close Relationships," in W. J. Ickes, ed., *Compatible and Incompatible Relationships* (New York: Springer-Verlag), 253–276; C. Sagan (1980), *Cosmos* (New York: Random House); R. W. Tafarodi, J. Tam, and A. B. Milne (2001), "Selective Memory and the Persistence of Paradoxical Self-Esteem," *Personality and Social Psychology Bulletin* 27:1179–89. I am grateful for these authors' insight, diligence, and creativity.

At the neurological level, Alzheimer's generally follows a more or less predictable progression, but the symptoms and the meanings of the disease are as unique as each sufferer. For this reason, I am grateful, most of all, for all the personal accounts, offered by patients and family members, which I have come across in the abovementioned works and also in the online message boards of the Alzheimer's Association website.

While I have tried to remain faithful to the pathology of familial early-onset Alzheimer's disease, I have, in some places, somewhat bent it to meet my own narrative purposes. There are several very real variants of this disease, but the EOA-23 variant described in this book, like its chronicler, Marvin Shellard, is entirely fictitious.

For their faithful support, friendship, and advice, I am indebted to Ashley Selett, Lloyd A. Silverman, Rosadel Varela, Neil Davenport, Rebecca Stelter, Matthew Seimionko, Mariana Pickering, Kim Gardner, Brian Shier, Meera Damle, Stacy Brock, John Malloy, Brea Lubin, Michael Torres, William Davis, George Rhodes, and, of course, Erin Joy Haigh.

For all I have learned from them, it would be a karmic offense not to thank William Paul, Miriam Bailin, Jeff Smith, Pier Marton, Richard Chapman, Lynn Gafford, Caryl Gatlzaff, Marsha Cawthon, Barbara Pittenger, Scott Hanson, Steven Pijut, and, always, Karen Jane Shepherd.

For inviting me to work in their labs, I am beholden to Frank Keil and Marissa Greif of the Cognitive Development Lab at Yale University, Henry Roediger III and Michelle Meade of the Memory Lab at Washington University in St. Louis, and the entire staff of the Dr. Bessie F. Lawrence International Summer Science Institute at the Weizmann Institute of Science in Rehovot, Israel.

For faithfully guiding this work from manuscript to published book, I am grateful for the enthusiasm, wisdom, and labor of Matt Lewis, Matt Hudson, and everyone at Random House.

Through financial calamity, lengthy revisions, and a stunningly cold winter spent huddled beside a malfunctioning radiator, Joyce Lawrence inspired, encouraged, and generally improved me in more ways than I can know.

Colossal thanks to Anne Thibault for cleaning up my mess in all its forms.

Aaron Block encourages me daily and deserves my apologies for all the terrible things I have done (and probably will do) to brothers in my stories.

The two supernovae of this creation: David Ebershoff, who consistently saw the possibilities in things I had long assumed to be immutable, and Bill Clegg, a living avatar of that mythical being that one imagines while writing, the Ideal Reader.

For more on this novel, including a description of its personal origins, please visit www.stefanmerrillblock.com.

To learn more about Alzheimer's, to make a donation to Alzheimer's research, or to discuss your own experiences within a supportive and helpful community, please visit the Alzheimer's Association website at www.alz.org.

The Story of Forgetting

Stefan Merrill Block

A Reader's Guide

On the Origins of
The Story of Forgetting

STEFAN MERRILL BLOCK

When I was a small child, my grandmother was diagnosed with probable Alzheimer's disease. At that time, I hardly knew what the disease was (I thought the word was "old-timer's"). For the first year or two of her decline, her symptoms were subtle and I was too young to notice anything unusual. By the time my mom invited my grandmother to come stay with us, however, the disease was in its middle stages, and I was old enough to understand that something was deeply wrong. Just before my grandmother arrived, my mom explained to me what I should expect: Cognitively, I was now more advanced than she. Difficult as it was to comprehend, I would now have to think of myself as more mature than my grandmother. I would have to watch out for her, like a brother would for his little sister. During this conversation, my mom also made me aware, for the first time, of our genetic inheritance: When my mom made a list of her mother's ancestors, nearly everyone, on both her father's side and her mother's side, had developed Alzheimer's disease.

Years later, while struggling to begin my first book, I often thought about my grandmother and our family's disease. Days before I took a trip home to Texas for the holidays, I read David Shenk's *The Forgetting: Alzheimer's: Portrait of an Epidemic.* Reading Shenk's detailed account of the epic pathology of Alzheimer's disease, I continually compared his descriptions with my family's experiences. And my first night back in Texas, having dinner with my family, a sickening thought: In the disease's persistent march through the generations of our family, was it already starting to come for my mom? How could I know whether it was an early effect of the disease or simply my mom's lifelong touch of flightiness that gave her difficulty in instantly conjuring my name, or remembering stories I had told her over the phone just days before? I began to think about the terrible and inevitable role reversal that has taken place in every generation of my mom's family, the time when the child must become the parent's caretaker. I was terrified, of course, but I also felt something else: something overwhelming in the absolute power of history as expressed in our genetic material. It seemed to me that our inextinguishable, undeniable genetic inheritance touches upon something essential about what it means to be a part of a family.

In the months of writing that preceded this trip to Texas, I had experimented with a lot of narrative voices, but I hadn't yet been able to master a voice that I felt I could fully embody and enjoy. I had, in fact, written over fifteen hundred pages. Essentially nothing of what I wrote in the first nine or ten months now remains. In those early months, I often wrote myself into corners; desperate for ways out, I grasped at new plot lines that quickly disintegrated under the strain. It was often torturous. In hindsight it feels like that early work was dictated by some homunculus residing in my subconscious—some invisible foreman who knew better than I what I was doing, who knew what I really wanted to write, who directed me, through failure after failure, toward the writing of what became a very personal novel, steeped in my actual experiences.

Just days after my trip home to Dallas, through some confluence of my thoughts about Texas, my family, and Alzheimer's disease, I opened my word processor and the voice of Abel Haggard simply came. The remarkable difference from everything else I had written up to that point was that with Abel I didn't need to plan what I would write in advance; I just wrote and the details and stories materialized, until eventually the writing felt more like remembering than imagining.

After writing for a month or two in the shaggy voice of this old and regretful man, the voice of young Seth Waller also began to emerge. At first, I didn't understand the relationship between these two voices; the story just felt like it needed a young, precocious foil to aged, world-weary Abel. But as I kept writing, I started to feel that Abel's story required Seth's story (and vice versa) because the solace and understanding that both Abel and Seth sought required that they find each other. Their union began to feel inevitable.

Now looking back on *The Story of Forgetting*, I see the book as only the most recent manifestation of an unceasing need to comprehend and to make some kind of peace with my family's disease. When I was in college, I took a more scientific approach, working for a time in an aging and memory cognitive psychology lab. Around that time, I also started to think of the disease allegorically, producing the first draft of the Isidora fables that now appear in the book. More recently, I've written nonfiction, autobiographical accounts of my family's experience with Alzheimer's. Just as I have reached into science, fantasy, and personal history in the attempt to understand and transcend the pain at the center of my family's life, the characters I conjured in *The Story of Forgetting* seemed to want the same. Coming from me, they shared my compulsion to summon a range of voices and myriad forms of storytelling in the unending effort to find the best way to comprehend. And, at the end of the book, they also share the awareness I came closer to in writing it: that a disease of such ineffable loss may forever elude our attempts to contain it in language, but that we must keep trying.

A Conversation with Stefan Merrill Block and David Ebershoff

DAVID EBERSHOFF IS AN EDITOR-AT-LARGE
AT RANDOM HOUSE AND THE AUTHOR OF
THE 19TH WIFE.

David Ebershoff: You are a natural storyteller, gifted with an innate understanding of how to construct a good tale. How old were you when you first started writing stories? What were they about?

Stefan Merrill Block: There have been times when I haven't written much, but I can't remember a time when I wasn't arranging some story in my head. Before high school, almost everything I wrote featured a normal kid transformed in some fantastical way. These stories were almost always extensions of daydreams, and the hero, of course, was always a version of me. In one, I became highly magnetized. It was a problem because whenever I stepped too close to the road all traffic veered toward me, but it ended up saving the day when the engines of an airplane carrying my dad suddenly gave out and I was able to direct the plane safely to earth with my powers.

DE: I've always been fascinated by homeschooling. How old were you when you started studying with your mom? What was an average day like? How do you think this experience affected you as a writer?

322 A READER'S GUIDE

SMB: I left public school when I was nine, and homeschooled for five years. At first, my mom set a fairly regimented curriculum, but after a while our days naturally evolved into what we would later learn is called "unschooling," an education led by the student's interests. Usually, we would get up in the morning and chat about whatever subject interested me. It could have been anything, really, from French Impressionism to the creation of Walt Disney World. Then we would head to the library, where I would borrow whatever books I could find related to the topic. Then I'd write about the topic in whatever way I wanted. I would make a display board about the history of China, or I'd write a short story, imagining Vincent van Gogh as a child. I returned to public school in ninth grade, to a vastly different kind of education, one that felt much more like a job than like learning. But I finished high school and went to college. Since graduating, though, I sort of feel like I've created an adult version of homeschooling for myself. Essentially, how I spend my days now is nearly identical to how I spent them as a kid, reading and writing about whatever interests me. For good or bad, it seems like I'm a homeschooler for life.

DE: What did you like to read as a child? Because of the fablelike quality of the Isidora sections in *The Story of Forgetting*, I've always imagined that you read fantasy and science fiction as a boy. Is that correct?

SMB: Oh, David, if you only knew the breadth of my knowledge of Piers Anthony's land of Xanth, or the extensiveness of my Magic: The Gathering card collection you would know what a miracle it is that I'm not in some dark room right now, spending my twenties eating sugary cereal and playing World of WarCraft. Yes. I was particularly obsessed with Xanth, with Brian Jacques' Redwall books, and with the universes of Star Wars and Marvel

Comics. These obsessions provided, as they do for lonely, nerdy boys everywhere, a wonderful escape. But, really, the books that were my absolute favorites as a kid, and the only childhood books I return to as an adult, were not full departures into imagined lands, but half departures into magically altered realities, like the children's books of Roald Dahl, or Katherine Paterson's *Bridge to Terabithia*. My love of these books was an early expression of my ongoing predilection for stories that transform reality in some slightly elevated, slightly fantastic way. Actually, the name Isidora comes from an adult book I would consider to be of this spirit, Italo Calvino's *Invisible Cities*.

DE: Other than reading, what were your childhood obsessions?

SMB: I was an avid collector. Spelunking the closet of my childhood bedroom, you'd find a vast collection of collections: rocks, fossils, shells, comic books, baseball cards, Magic: The Gathering cards. Apparently, not long after I learned to crawl, my mom would find collections of objects, bearing no obvious similarities, in small piles around the house. I was also a great builder of forts.

DE: Place plays such an important role in the novel. Tell me about where you grew up.

SMB: I grew up mostly in Plano, Texas, a place nearly identical to the towns in which both Seth and Abel live in the novel. To me, Plano is an apotheosis of an ancient American dream, the dream of the Mayflower pilgrims really: to leave one's history behind and create a new society, unburdened by the past. When I was younger, our part of Plano was still mostly prairie, but around when I was ten, the subdivisions of McMansions colonized the area with astonishing speed. The few remaining old farmhouses, the kind in which

Abel lives in the novel, were razed to make way for this ultra-modern city. And so now there is this complete, spotless suburb, which looks just like a hundred other suburbs, with a transient population of families transferred there by big corporations. I often like to identify myself as a Texan, but the truth is saying I'm from Texas feels like like saying that I've been to Kuala Lumpur, because I once spent four hours in its airport, which looks just like any other airport. It sometimes feels the truth is that I didn't grow up in Texas at all. I grew up in an airport.

DE: I know you wrote the Isidora story first. Tell us about where you were in your life at that time.

SMB: I wrote the first draft of the Isidora stories when I was nineteen. At that time, I was working in an aging and memory cognitive psychology lab at Washington University in St. Louis. Studying related topics scientifically, I was thinking a lot about my family's history with the disease and the experience of watching it take my grandmother. Thinking of my grandmother also made me think about the storytelling traditions in my family, the stories my grandmother and my mom used to tell me. At the time, I was also reading a lot of Calvino, Singer, and Kafka. Through some confluence of all of that, the idea for the Isidora stories came, and writing them was a nice escape from the rest of my college life. I didn't plan ever to do anything with them. I put them away and didn't think about resurrecting them until years later, halfway through the writing of *The Story of Forgetting*.

DE: How did you construct the novel's structure? When did you know it was right?

SMB: Devising the book's structure was a dizzying, often torturous combination of obsessive scrutiny and blind faith. In ways, I think that the structure of the book as it now exists displays my process of creating it: my impulse always to look for different ways to describe a central dilemma, my recognition that there will always be truth to our experience that evades any kind of description, my hope that a final understanding of the story and its subjects will come through the parallels, contradictions, and fissures between different kinds of storytelling. For me, the great difficulty is to write as I'm compelled to write, shifting between time periods, characters, and genres while still producing a book that I feel transports me and propels me forward, a book in which every page feels necessary. Reconciling and satisfying these two needs was the hardest part of the writing of this book, as I'm sure it will be of many books to come.

DE: Who do you identify with more, Seth or Abel?

SMB: Abel. This was a real revelation to me, as I've almost always put a character nearly identical to myself at the center of everything I've written. And yet, in this book, the voice that felt truer to my own, more expressive of me, belongs to a character so different from me. I don't know why this is, exactly, but I think it's related to my impulse to write fiction instead of memoir in the first place, my understanding that my writing feels truer to me when I make things up. But, whatever the reason, I feel like my identification with Abel is a discovery that has opened up vast possibilities for me as a fiction writer.

DE: *The Story of Forgetting* has a lot of science in it. Yet of course it's a novel. What obligation did you feel to getting the science right?

SMB: Other than looking up a few facts, I never really did research for the book. Whatever science made it into the book was just the science I had, at some point, felt compelled to read and remember. I've read a lot about Alzheimer's because of my family's experiences with it, and because science is a very important part of how I try to make sense of things. But in writing this book I feel like I gave no special attention or priority to science over other ways of understanding my characters' predicaments. Whenever I stated something as fact in the book, I double-checked it to make sure my basic information wasn't incorrect, but I also sometimes let myself alter things just a bit to fit my needs as a storyteller.

DE: Some people have praised *The Story of Forgetting* as improbably upbeat. Is that a correct assessment? Do you see the novel that way?

SMB: It's nearly impossible for me to judge what the tone of the book might feel like to other people. I wrote the book for the same reason I write everything, for the same reason I read books and watch films obsessively: to escape for a while into a constructed space where things can make sense in a way they rarely can in reality. It always surprises me, when I look back on anything I've written and I think about how I generally felt in my life while writing it, how much of what I create is an effort to hold or transmit what I'm feeling at that time. I wrote this book at a hopeful time in my life, when I was just out of college and very much in love. I think that, in addressing one of the darkest aspects of my family's history, I wanted to transform it in order to allow, at least in this fictional world I created, some of the hope I was feeling at the time to enter.

DE: Since the book's publication, have people contacted you with their own stories about Alzheimer's? Are there any you can share?

SMB: Yeah, it's been a wonderful, unexpected part of the process. The early-onset form of the disease I describe in the book is inspired in part by the Noonan family, featured in the PBS documentary *The Forgetting*. I've heard from several of the Noonans, which has been an exciting and moving correspondence, almost as if my characters materialized into the real world to let me know that I haven't mangled their story too badly. One story that I remember and love was told to me by a woman at a reading. Years earlier, the woman's mother was in the late stages of Alzheimer's, almost beyond language, and she was dying of a secondary illness. The daughter was caring for her, even though the mother could no longer remember who her daughter was. On the night before the mother died, the daughter climbed into bed with her, to be close for the final hours. At some point, the mother awoke in a moment of clarity to find a body lying next to her in bed. When the daughter turned to her, the old woman's face fell. "Goddamnit," the mother said. "I thought you were a man!"

DE: Other than your family and friends, who is the one person in the world you hope you will read your book?

SMB: I don't know, but probably someone a lot like me! I try to write the stories that I most want and need. I'm my own ideal reader, but the sad truth is that I'll never be able to read my stories as anything but their writer. In *The Story of Forgetting*, Conrad Hamner tells the story of how the artist Willem de Kooning, as he descended into Alzheimer's, forgot he had painted the canvases that lined his walls. He could come to them completely fresh every day, and he was their ideal viewer. Sometimes I think it's too bad that I write instead of making more sensorial art, like painting or music. When I get Alzheimer's, I'll lose my memory of writing my stories but also the ability to experience them!

DE: What are you reading now?

SMB: Michael Chabon calls himself a promiscuous reader. I love that. I cheat on the books that I'm reading with other books all the time. I've been reading a lot of Paul Auster recently, currently *The Invention of Solitude*. I'd never gotten around to Nabokov's *Speak, Memory*, so now I'm correcting that. What else? I've been reading a lot of Herman Melville's short stories, and also some wonderful contemporary fiction, including an astonishing novel, *The 19th Wife*, by one David Ebershoff.

DE: When you're not writing or reading or doing anything related to books, what do you like to do?

SMB: For me, as I think it is for a lot of people, the great appeal of writing creatively is the feeling that essentially nothing is entirely distinct from writing. Joan Didion says that "we tell ourselves stories in order to live," that we need to create stories to seek arrangement for the shifting phantasmagoria of our actual experiences. Maybe writers are people for whom that need is particularly strong. So I jog a lot, see friends, travel, but some part of my mind never allows me entirely to separate any experience from the writing process. Whenever I'm not actively writing, I'm very often looking for potential fodder and insight, or I'm trying to work through whatever problems have come up in whatever I'm working on. That's a great blessing but also a great curse of writing as a job—that it has no boundaries.

DE: If you weren't a writer, what would you be?

SMB: I don't know. I used to think I could be a scientist, but my hands are too shaky for pipettes, my math isn't so strong, and my patience is far too thin. I tried to be a cameraman for a while, filmed some documentaries, weddings, and bar mitzvahs. Camera work is satisfying in a certain respect, the way you get to intimately enter people's lives as an observer rather than as an actor. But I found the lack of control over the creative process really frustrating. Life happens in front of the camera and you have to adjust. Really, other than jobs I've done simply for money, any work I've done other than writing has felt like a waste of time.

DE: What's next?

SMB: Of course it could and probably will change, but I'm working on a semifictional book about time that my grandfather spent in a mental hospital in the 1960s. To my surprise, it's turning out to be a love story.

Visit www.stefanmerrillblock.com for special extras that will enhance your book club discussion.

Questions and Topics for Discussion

1. The last words of *The Story of Forgetting* are "whatever she needed she had only to imagine." Why do you think the author chose to end the book this way? In what ways is imagination essential for the book's main characters?

2. What is the relationship between the fables of Isidora and the rest of the book? How are situations, characters, and feelings from the lives of the Haggard family transformed in these fables? What is the importance of this storytelling tradition to the Haggard family?

3. What traditions do you keep that help maintain your own family's identity? How do your traditions relate to your family's history?

4. In one of the Isidora fables, a group of elders wonders, "To remember nothing . . . what more could one possibly ask of eternity?" (p. 201) Despite the horrors of Alzheimer's disease, are there ways in which its most well-known symptom, memory loss, is liberating for some of the characters in this book? In certain instances, might it be better to forget?

5. By the end of *The Story of Forgetting*, Jamie appears desperate to return to her childhood home. Do you think she would have still felt this need if she hadn't developed Alzheimer's disease? Was it only after she had forgotten the reasons she had left, and her guilt over abandoning Abel, that she could return? Or do you think that

she would have tried to return eventually, even if her memory had not failed?

6. In the section titled "Genetic History, Part 4," the author, describing Paul's unceasing love for Jamie Whitman, asks if love is "strong enough to gird Memory, at least for a time, against Chance's inevitable progression" (p. 243). How is love stronger than memory loss in this book? How is it not?

7. Have you ever known anyone with Alzheimer's disease? If so, how does the characterization of the disease in this book relate to your own experiences? How does this characterization relate to depictions you've come across in other books or films?

8. Before Seth and Abel know of each other's existence, they are already linked by their family's two legacies: the stories of Isidora and the devastation that the EOA-23 gene has wrought upon their loved ones. What else do Seth and Abel have in common?

9. *The Story of Forgetting* is written in a number of voices, genres, and time periods. Why do you think that the author chose to tell the story this way? How does this style of writing relate to the themes of memory, storytelling, family, and the quest for understanding?

10. Reflecting upon his decision to tell his daughter the truth about his affair with Mae, Abel understands that "out of the possibility of my wrongness in that single moment, I would serve a lifetime of penitence, loneliness, and regret" (p. 264). Do you think that it is strictly guilt that compels Abel to spend twenty years as a recluse? Do you think he really believed, twenty years after the fact, that his daughter would ever come back to him?

11. If you were in Jamie's position, would you tell your child the truth of his family's genetic legacy, of the 50 percent chance that he has also inherited a devastating terminal disease? Might it be better for the child not to know the truth? If you were in Seth's position, aware of the possibility that you had inherited the gene, would you get tested for it?

12. How does the genetic history of the EOA-23 variant illuminate the story that takes place in the present tense? How do the scientific details in these genetic-history chapters change your understanding of the book's characters and their conditions?

13. Near the end of Seth's "empirical investigation," Taylor Shafer asks Seth what it is that he is "hoping to find out" (p. 252). Seth realizes then that his delusions have kept him from "understanding the ridiculously simple answer to this ridiculously simple question" (p. 253). What is the "ridiculously simple answer"? Does Seth find what he is looking for?

14. Describing his mother's death by Alzheimer's disease, Abel says, "Her old soul had not so much vanished as eroded, worn away by a million rubs. I stopped praying" (p. 182). How does Alzheimer's disease complicate or obscure the concepts of death and selfhood?

PHOTO: © CHRISTINA PABST

STEFAN MERRILL BLOCK was born in 1982 and grew up in Plano, Texas. He graduated from Washington University in St. Louis in 2004. This is his first novel. He lives in Brooklyn.